FIFTEEN BILLION YEARS III

TIME WARRIORS

"But as for the cowardly, the faithless, the polluted, as for murderers, fornicators, sorcerers, idolaters, and all liars, their lot shall be in the lake that burns with fire and brimstone, which is the second death."

Revelation 21: 8 (RSV)
Holy Bible

By Rand McLester

InfusedMedia Co. LLC
www.infusedmedia.co
1-888-251-6088

Because the Fifteen Billion Years Trilogy is an epic of Hope, based on the Book of Revelation in the Bible, apart from dedicating the first installment, Alpha and Omega, to my parents and the second, Secret of the Legends, to family and friends, with deference I dedicate Time Warriors, and the entire trilogy to those less fortunate than ourselves.

Perhaps occasionally we each should take a moment to give thanks for our blessings, even when misfortune and problems in life seem to overwhelm us.

This trilogy is dedicated to the sick and disabled, the oppressed and downtrodden, the bewildered and discouraged.

If you have Faith and Believe…
…There Are Always Possibilities.
May God Bless You, each and every one

ACKNOWLEDGEMENTS

I wish to thank Rozi and Amy for a fine job of editing and proofreading; and again my gratitude goes to Rozi for her assistance with cover design.

And of course, thanks to Infused Media and its competent production teams for putting the project together.

Thanks to all of you.

PART V

CHAPTER ONE

Beyond the Horizon Threshold of the Black Hole…

…Tian screamed.

"Focus. Look at me and breathe—breathe—just like we practiced." She lay flat on her back on the bamboo table covered with a black leather throw, heels propped in the makeshift stirrups, grimacing, gritting her teeth, a death grip on the edge of the bed squeezing her fingertips white. Naked, she was sticky with perspiration, her golden waist-length hair pulled to one side and draped over her breasts.

"Coming. Look at me," Ames told her. "Concentrate. Focus. Look at me," pausing then encouraging, "now take a deep breath." He was tall and lean inside the black leather vest, just into his forties with mahogany eyes and salt-and-pepper hair that curled at his neck and almost covered his ears. Three days growth suggested he shaved with his knife and trimmed his mustache with his teeth.

Her hazel eyes focused on him, standing between her legs, tense, like a quarterback waiting the snap. Grimacing she took a deep breath.

"Don't push, blow," —*puff, puff, puff*— "okay he's coming." Then squinting, digging deep, resisting the grating pain… but only for the moment.

The room was small; the hut was thatch, grass and bamboo with a door of goatskin leather folded back to let daylight in. There was no sepulcher or stone couch. There were no stone huts. Those all disappeared when the land of the Renoloi[1] vanished in apocalyptic destruction almost nine months ago.

This was a new world. Childbirth a new experience.

Wearing a worn, black leather Chiqua skirt and top, Tian's second, the fair-haired Nitana[2] stood at Ames' left side watching, learning things she could not have imagined before. Honed with wisdom and loyalty she was mature for her years; but being a midwife was entirely new to her. Tian[3] was crowning, and Nitana was paying attention. In this world there would be many new experiences, much to learn.

Seana,[4] eyes the color of sky and shoulder length hair the color of sand, stood beside Tian, hand on her arm squeezing with apprehension, pregnant herself thanks to Reed. Due any day now, her 'innie' bellybutton was unraveled to an 'outie' and her plump tummy rested against the edge of the makeshift delivery table. Seana was worried; this looked painful, and she knew she was next.

Peering over his shoulder Reed crowded Ames from the right, more curious than concerned or nervous; after all, this sort of thing had been natural for —well, billions of years now. Barefoot in his blue jeans and sleeveless, pullover black-leather shirt Reed was shorter than Ames, and younger; mid-twenties, and what he lacked in height he made up for in size with a weight lifter's build, sandy blonde hair and easygoing manner. Eyes darting with interest, he leaned in a bit more scrutinizing, not quite taking notes —but almost. Beneath the faded scar across his forehead his beaming smile was at the forefront and he wanted to help but felt inept, out of place; so he kibitzed with flair the way only he could.

"*Eewh,* that's nasty," his demented sense of humor.

A disapproving glance: "Reed, if you're not gonna help just shut up and get out of the way." Ames pushed him aside with a hip and he stepped back as Nitana slipped forward, chamois in hand, dabbing perspiration from Ames' forehead. Both were busy, too involved for his nonsense.

Tian screamed.

"Okay, try to relax," Ames instructed. Nitana chewed her lip, ready with the chamois. The Chiqua were gone now too.

Still watching, Reed moved alongside Tian gently taking her hand in his. "How you feeling, Babe?" Momentarily distracted her eyes met his, then saying nothing grimaced gritting her teeth. Compelled, his eyes traveled back to her hips for another look. "Gotta admit, you've got some nice muffins," he encouraged. Seana, standing next to him, smacked him causing him to jump. "Well, she does; 'cept... they're kinda stretched out'a shape right now."

Again, she screamed.

"Okay, push."

She did —and strained— squeezing Reed's hand so tightly it cut off the circulation to his fingers, and hurt.

"*Shii-it,* you really got a grip there," he admitted trying to seem casual. Tian gasped as Seana wiped perspiration from her face looking on nervously. In spite of everything, Tian turned her head to the man holding her hand, offering a pained smile. She knew him and he knew her; for all they had been through together, Reed was her friend.

Then she screamed.

"Almost, okay, easy now—push," Ames coached.

Reed was her focus and Tian concentrated on his face trying to think of something other than the pain of childbirth; but due to deliver very soon as well Seana was focused on the process itself, her eyes and expression detailing apprehension, betraying quiet disbelief. Knees wobbling, she went pale leaning against the delivery table to steady herself.

Reed noticed. "Seana, are you all right?" Her mouth moved, but nothing came out. "Seana?"

Finally, "Is this what is going to happen to me also?" she murmured.

"Well yeah," scruffing his hair, "what did you think?" Twinkling excitement, "Ain't it cool."

She seemed almost stricken. "Reed... you did this to me?"

Something in her voice sounded wrong and realization percolated with the settling ominous gray cloud of, *you're in trouble; better think fast.* "But, Seana..."

"This is going to happen to me too?" Her eyes locked on his. "I should kick—your—ass."

"—But, Seana."

Tian screamed distracting them.

"Okay, try to relax. Take a few breaths," Ames encouraged.

Seana clenched her fist. "The Renoloi sleep. We hibernate for three days and, and—I expected nothing like this."

"But—"

"You forgot to mention *this* part."

"But, Seana, bears and shit hibernate. Where did you guys ever come up with some stupid thing like that?"

Voice low, "Reed…" eyes narrowed, "are you calling me stupid?"

Serious mistake. He stuttered, then, "Heck no sweetie; how could you even think something like that?"

Now she was pissed. "Reed, I—should—kick—your—ass."

"Oh yeah, right; like it's all my fault. Blame it on me."

"I will. You, Uncle Remus —and that stupid Br'er Rabbit…"

"—Here he comes," Ames interrupted leaning forward with Nitana at his shoulder, both guiding the slippery neonate as it rotated in the birth canal. "Just a little more… you're doing it. Push, one more time." She gritted her teeth as Ames cradled his hands moving to one side like a quarterback for the snap.

There was silence… Reed and Seana waiting.

Quickly Ames said it. "We need a bulb syringe."

Reed, almost a reflex: "Don't have one."

Ames took the newborn in his cupped hands, leaning over and mouthing the infant's entire face —sucked— clearing the nasal and oral airways.

"Aww, Doc —*geeze*," Reed observed crooking his lip and squinting, "that's just gross."

Ames spit the mucus out, then did it again, and gently tapped the babe's heel with a finger.

—*Aaahhh*: a whining cry.

Life entered the world, and everyone breathed; and holding their son Ames looked at Tian, and she at him… and the smile then sweet laugh as tears came to her eyes. Nitana beamed as Reed wiped the gross look from his face and Seana's color returned as she too sputtered with happiness.

Smiling ear to ear Ames carefully handed the infant to Nitana and she tucked him in the black leather blanket and waited while he tied off the umbilical cord with two small strips of leather. A 'miracle' smile played about her lips as she tenderly cuddled the newcomer then offered a curious glance when Ames cut the cord and folded the blanket over his son.

Finally relaxing for a moment Tian's heels turned more easily in the stirrups and her tired legs spread wider apart to rest. A moment more and the placenta lethargically delivered, Ames gently guiding it with the attached umbilical cord like a novice leading in a rope. Nitana, Seana and Tian's eyes were on the baby, but Reed was watching his friend, wrinkling his nose.

Almost a whisper: "Good grief, Doc, that's just sick-n'-icky. Looks like some kind of tapeworm hooked onto a boiled-up-bubbly liver." Not quite annoyed but slowly shaking his head, Ames ignored him, waiting patiently while the placenta slid the rest of the way out. "For pity's sake, next you'll be draggin' out the sliced onions."

This time Ames looked up mischievously. "Got any Tabasco?"

Reed retreated a step, then, "Oh I get it; that was a 'blink' right? One of those involuntary subconscious thought processes that disrupts suppressed anxiety; spontaneous things you just can't quite control… like I have sometimes, like we all have sometimes."

Ames grinned. "Not all of us." Then a wry smile, "I'm just kinda hungry right now."

Not expecting that, then glancing at Seana and Tian, "And you guys think I'm warped." Back to Ames: "You're a sicko'; you really are, Doc. You're demented."

"More likely than not," his friend admitted, "probably 'cause of the company I keep." Then serious again, "But I hope you were paying attention, because you *are* teaching sex—ed you know."

For once Reed was speechless. Sex education had been assigned to him. Forgot about that; completely slipped his mind. "I need some fresh air." He went outside.

At length Tian removed her feet from the stirrups as the others covered her with a blanket. With a tender sigh she reached out and Nitana handed her her child. And for the very first time she held hers and John's son... and her eyes and her heart and her smile said it all.

* * *

Outside the hut...

...On the path that trailed through their village Reed took a deep breath then smiled, his green eyes absorbing the sights and sounds that filled his mind. He felt good inside, content; there was peace in their world... a New World.

Here craggy granite mountains, incredible rock columns and massive spires jutted from the landscape, climbing stately and towering loftily thousands of feet above, their summits touching an azure sky. The meandering valley basin, a landscape of dense meadows, lay emerald and pure, fingered with trickling brooks of clear water rushing in riffles filling pools and lagoons then continuing on, going to somewhere unknown, to regions never before seen by anyone's eyes.

Always moving, flowing easily. Perhaps just around the next bend or beyond the next rise a tributary might gather and pond creating backwater providing foothold and nourishment for rushes, cattail bogs, camass, pampas grass stands and others garbed in unusual ornamental colors, swaying gently, pushed by breezes of new design.

Violets, blues, reds and yellows, phenomenal fluorescent displays interspersed in casual array, this world was absorbed in drenching warmth of vivid color captured and revealed in flowering blooms. Tulips, hyacinth, four-o'clocks, azaleas, daffodils, morning glories, asters, roses, and a thousand others grew lush, oversized and gorgeous, bursting from a carpet of fringed phacelia.

The marshes were bordered with runs of emerald grasses: fescue, darnel, crested wheat, timothy and sorghum, anchored solidly upon nodes in mineral-rich loam as dark as anthracite. The understory and shrub layer were thick with plants of all shape and kind, and the herb layer and forest floor saturated with ferns, mosses, lichens and enormous woodland mushrooms. Glens and hollows rose to the rolling foothills adorned with forests of oak, walnut, hickory, weeping willow, sycamore, maple, aspen, and countless others; each proudly brandishing its cloak of verdant forest-green.

Sequestered within this world were small ones, microorganisms and single cells: amoebas, flagella and others. Insects scampered in limitless variety: ants, beetles and bugs—to butterflies. Fish, reptiles and amphibians filled water and fields, from perch and trout, snakes, chameleons and lizards, to turtles and frogs. An abundance of life; replenished supply. And scattered throughout the meadows bordering the wetland marshes grew flowering shrubs, fruit bearing bushes and trees: willows, dogwood, chokecherry, plum, elderberry and currant, along with a multitude of others.

Farther up the ragged slopes grew conifers: Douglas fir, Scotch, lodgepole, ponderosa, white and jack pine, Sitka and blue spruce, and larch. The evergreens stood proud and strong scaling the steep inclines of the mountains, columns and spires, and clung tenaciously to the irregular contour of the timberline where barren rock stood alone veiled in a cloak of snow, and silence, and sky.

And here there were mammals, small and large: chipmunk and fox, rabbits and bear, elk, deer, bobcat and lynx, wild dogs, various rodents and wild goats; and others, many others.

Yet even more beautiful and enchanting were the birds. From the meadows and marshes, from forest and mountains they rose in flight and incredible plumage. Resounding raucous caw and warbling song, flitting with butterfly motion or soaring and gliding on strong, feathered wings.

They were everywhere: birds of prey, waders, shorebirds, woodpeckers, swimmers, and perching birds. Coveys ran the grasslands and marshes, throngs skittered among thickets and shrubbery, innumerable flocks filled the skies and a new world. Untold varieties: warblers, finches, ducks, geese, hawks, falcons, quail, nuthatches, rails, cardinals, egrets, eagles, herons, condors, swifts, larks, swallows —and on and on— seemingly endless diversity and array.

But above all else, towering stately and awe-inspiring was the granitic monolith of Legend Mountain… a different kind of mountain.

* * *

Ames stepped out onto the path…

…Beside his friend, a quiet moment.

"Congratulations, Doc." The banter was gone.

Ames smiled with his nod, but didn't say anything. It was one of those times when there wasn't really anything to say, so he poked both hands in the back pockets of his Levis, looked around, and took a deep breath. The air tasted sweet. Life tasted sweet.

A low voice: "How do you feel?"

Ames blinked, drew a slow breath and sighed. "Good, I guess. Don't really know." A pause. "So many different emotions all at the same time… kind of confusing."

"Strange, huh?"

"Yeah."

Reed smiled. "Did you ever think someday you'd be a dad?"

Glancing sideways, then back to the mountains and spires beyond the valley, "Well, I guess I always hoped I would; but I never imagined it would be quite like this," he admitted.

Reed chuckled, "Well *shiiit*— I don't suppose either of us, or anyone else, would have ever figured on that —here." Then mulling it over he considered, "Here… where is here really? What day is it, what year, what galaxy, what —shoot I don't know what— and I guess most of all, what difference does it really make anyway?"

"Never imagined it would be quite like this," Ames said again.

"Me neither, Doc."

Ames smiled. "Curiouser and curiouser."

Reed smiled. "'To boldly go where no man has gone before'."

Quiet for a moment.

"Curiouser and curiouser," Ames finally said, softly.

"Congratulations, Doc," patting him gently on the back as he began to turn.

"Reed, Mr. Ames—" Kalo's soprano called from the distance. She, Lent and Tere[5] were trotting up the path, all three panting mildly as they joined the men in front of the hut. Kalo,[6] the silent one, never said much, and though slight in stature and only in her early teens she was endowed with a warrior's prowess. Excited, she bounced on the balls of her feet tossing blonde hair and the Tyrannosaur-tooth fetish she wore around her neck on a leather thong.

"Yo, kid—" Reed acknowledged playfully.

"Has Tian...?"

Grinning, "Yeah, you missed it big-time."

She turned curtly to her companions. "See there. It is your fault. I told you we should return sooner." Lent was rawbone-lean with a bushy mop of dark hair and mischievous sparkling brown eyes — and an indelible smile. Outgoing and effeminate, Tere, their friend and constant companion, beamed with enthusiasm and playfulness gleaned from the joy of just being alive. They were all young, but here, no one kept track.

"Where were you guys?" Reed asked. "I thought you wanted to be here for the delivery."

"We did," Tere and Lent chimed in laconic unison.

"They were goofing off and kept lollygaging inside the mountain, so now we missed it."

"Lollygaging," Reed echoed teasing with his frown. "You're startin' to worry me girl, starting to sound like Marvel Group Pilgrim there," referring to Lent and the fact that the boys, 'the Pilgrims' had all learned to read from comic books.

"I told them we should get back."

"True enough," Lent admitted peeking out from his Pekinese-hair. His lanky frame was filling out now with nine more months of growth, and his skin was a darker tan. Barefoot, he was in his mid-teens, all sinew and muscle, with a dingy old tee shirt full of holes and khaki shorts that were frazzled and torn up the sides along the seams of the legs. Almost as big as he was, Lent carried a twibil that glimmered in the sun and had a twelve-inch pike tip.

Playfully Dutch-rubbing his mop with his knuckles, "Christ kid," Reed chided, "you ever gonna get a haircut? Probably got a cootie cavalcade running around on the top of your skull."

"Keeps the sun out of my eyes," he threw back. "Sorry we missed the delivery."

"Well, there's always Seana," Ames offered, and Reed winced when he said it.

Disappointed, Kalo told them, "I am going in to see Tian."

"Me too," Tere piped up. Both entered the hut.

"Thanks, Doc," Reed groused once Kalo and Tere were gone.

Feigning innocence, "What?"

"You know bitch 'possum well that Seana's flat-out pissed, and you deliberately go and say something like that —just to remind me."

Ames grinned. "I'm shattered. How can you even think that I would do such a dastardly thing to my best friend?"

Facetiously, "Yeah, right— your *only* friend."

"I'm his friend too," Lent offered jumping in feetfirst.

Reed shook his head throwing a sideways glance, "Lent, just for once, would you just…" then he stopped.

Ames, under his breath: "Reminds me of you."

Reed sighed, "Forget it—what's the use," and he turned and walked down the path.

* * *

Inside Tian's hut…

…Kalo stood silently marveling at the boy child suckling at her breast, Seana and Tere quietly prattled on. From time-to-time Tian would add something to the conversation, but for the most part she just listened and let them talk. She was preoccupied with maternal stirrings that had been reawakened with the birth of her son.

This was new, just as the world was new, and this was the first time a boy child had ever been born to a Renoloi. Tian and her people were Renoloi, hermaphrodites; the Legends told that. The Inscriptions chiseled inside Legend Mountain told of all that had been and all that may be... would be, or could be.

When Ames and Reed first accompanied her inside the Sacred Temple, both were amazed. The Inscriptions: strange writings carved in the labyrinth of cavern walls and inlaid with gold. They had come when the Great Spirit poured out the stars and all the worlds to accompany them, through the black hole at the beginning of time. The Inscriptions were from a Milky Way galaxy in a far distant place; from an insignificant blue planet that ceased to exist long, long ago... a creation now gone, so this one might take its place. The Inscriptions were from a world that was once called Earth.

When Tian was just a small girl she had spent much time with her mother in the temple, and she had studied the Legends, very carefully... before the mountain peak was blown up. She read of many things and learned all that she could, committing some to memory when her mother told her she should. She did remember that the Legends spoke of twelve tribes, but she never saw what must have been written of Lent and his people—Pilgrims, John and Reed called them. Surely their origin must have been similar to that of the Renoloi; Tian could accept that explanation, plausible enough.

She was only a small girl then, and there were so many Inscriptions it would have taken many lifetimes and she only had a single childhood to learn as much as she could. Words chiseled in stone and inlaid with gold, she had read the Inscriptions, studied the Legends; but much of what she learned was now sequestered somewhere within the recesses of her memory. And the Legends were more, things the Renoloi did not understand.

The Legends were Magic.

Coming back from her thoughts and the memories, Seana and Tere were still talking softly and hovering as the babe cuddled and fed at her breast. Tian held and caressed him as she smiled with a mother's bond of love, while in the shadows, no more than arm's-reach away, unobtrusively, Kalo, the young Renoloi warrior observed, taking it all in. She would not often join in casual conversation. She was reticent. She was young.

But the silent Kalo always listened.

* * *

Early that evening…

…Almost eight hundred Renoloi and Pilgrims gathered at the meeting circle. A crackling cacophony of burning wood fed alizarin flames in the fire ring illuminating the area, then bled to shadows and the blend of darkness beyond the periphery where the shrub layer, understory and forest waited patiently and reclaimed the night world. In some ways the two people had merged and become a common village of sorts, but in others they were still altogether different.

As the Centurion Mystic had foretold months ago, Tian would be the first, and others would follow. Today was an unusual day, a special day; Tian had given birth to a boy child, the first to a Renoloi. But her son, and John's son, would not be the last; there would be more, many more the Mystic had told them.

This new world was only a small part, a snippet of a greater scheme, something more, much more; because with all things in the universe there is one constant which is undeniable and inevitable. This world, as with all worlds, was destined for change… beyond any imaginings.

A muted drone of hushed conversation hovering in the air, the throng waiting, anticipating, eating and sharing the day's experiences. The adults talked among themselves, children listening, learning things that those wiser and more experienced could teach them. It was a beautiful, peaceful evening at the gathering.

Seana, Reed, Nitana and Deet sat together near one side of the clearing. Deet, who looked much the same as every other Pilgrim, was an eager and enterprising individual with a shaggy head of dark hair trying to escape his worn-out New York Yankees baseball cap with the torn bill. The Renoloi were feminine individuals, fair haired and bronzed skinned, who clothed themselves with leftover black

Chiqua leather skirts and tops, and now, hair-on goatskins, also their new food staple. The Pilgrims were young, genetically masculine and dark haired, tanned by the sun and clothed with an odd menagerie of tee shirts, jeans, shorts, tennis shoes —or whatever else they had scavenged from the Accumulation, an unexplained, incredible junk pile that was somehow dragged through time then destroyed when the cataclysm occurred.

Briefly Reed glanced at Deet who sat with his hand jammed into the pocket of his bermuda shorts fondling his cache of corn kernels. "Wouldn't do that if I were you, Deet," Reed advised, a casual warning, eyes drifting back to the fire, "it'll make you go blind."

Reflex, the Pilgrim jerked his hand from his pocket scattering corn on the ground; then summarily disgusted he quickly began gathering his precious seeds as he glared at Reed and frowned. "That's not funny. Mr. Ames already did that to me."

Reed grinned. "Twice, huh? Slow learner."

Deet defended, "Lucky for you I saved the seed stock, or we'd never have any more shine." His assertion set lightly with Reed because he didn't really care all that much, but Seana and Nitana both felt suddenly queasy. The word 'shine' dredged recollections of overindulgence and a retching aftermath of penitence. Both squinted, and inside, both squirmed then watched as Tere and Lent approached weaving through the crowd.

"How's she goin'?" Lent greeted them in a western drawl he'd fabricated more from his imagination than from the comic books the Pilgrims had scrounged in the Accumulation.

"Jest fine," Reed drawled back, joshing politely. Lent even smiled when Reed added, "Buckaroo— now that's a *real* cowboy word, Lent." Seana jabbed him with an elbow for making fun of the boy.

Lent considered, "Buckaroo—yeah, I like 'at one, Reed. Thanks a powr'ful lot."

"Betcha' fer sure. Yer fine as frog hair, kid." Seana elbowed him again, harder. He chuckled rubbing the twinge from his ribs as

Lent sat down, Tere next to him, while from a nearby tree limb Kalo quietly observed.

Walking together they entered the meeting circle from the path, Ames with his arm around Tian, she carrying the babe wrapped in the black leather blanket held closely to her bosom. All eyes turned and conversation hushed, the sudden absence of noise drawing their attention like a warning note, the couple almost hesitating, looking around as they joined those at the circle.

A Renoloi and Pilgrim rose from their places and approached, just for a peek. Tian folded the blanket back. "He is so beautiful."

"Thank you, Nema." Others did the same. This was something new, and this was what they had all been waiting for. As a throng formed around Tian and Ames, Kalo dropped smoothly from the tree limb lighting on the forest floor without making a sound. Deliberately ignoring Lent and Tere, Kalo asked, "Reed, Seana... are you going to see the baby?"

Seana looked at Reed who answered for the both of them. "Nah, you go ahead, we saw the tyke earlier remember... when he was still all blue and slimy." Seana frowned when he said that. "And besides," he explained, "it's too much work for Seana to get up off the ground once she's down here. She's too fat." Seana playfully bopped him on the head for saying that. He laughed lightly and winked as Kalo evaporated within the crowd.

"Hey, Doc— I'll be sitting here with the little fat woman when you guys are done over there."

From somewhere within the huddle Ames' voice trailed back, "Soon as we can."

Reed turned to Seana, leaned affectionately against her and shook his head with mock sincerity, "Kids— should just sell 'em all on the Black Market to South African slavers while they're still precious, cuddly little munchkins."

"Really?" she replied mischievously. "Perhaps you should just tie a knot in it and you would not have to worry about kids." He blinked surprise but couldn't think of a comeback —right offhand like that— as Seana grinned.

Eventually—

Tian and Ames joined them and sat down as Deet, with his hand in his pocket, scooted over to see the baby.

Casually Reed asked, "You ever gonna plant that corn, or just let 'em sprout in your pocket when you collect enough lint?"

"Soon as I find just the right spot."

"Soon as you find just the right spot? For cryin' out loud you've got a gazillion acres of pristine world out there," motioning with a hand, "how much more 'right spot' can you get?"

Intently Deet asked, "Is that more than a hundred?"

Ames smiled. "Sex—ed seems to be going well; guess it's time for Math—101." Reed just stared.

Deet decided, "I will keep looking for just the right spot."

Reed: "Yeah kid, you do that; but in the meantime, don't rub the yellow off 'em or they'll never sprout."

Nervous, Deet turned to Nitana. "That true?" She shrugged.

Reed to Ames, disgusted: "Math—101 my ass... *reeeal* funny."

* * *

The evening was captivating...

...A pleasant time for all. The night was cool, the fire warm, the stars enchanting. Motherhood agreed with Tian, she was beaming. Ames was content and proud, and in love. This was the way he had always imagined fatherhood would be. Life was good.

Crossing his legs and leaning back against a fallen log, from the corner of an eye he saw them scooting closer, bright with expectation, inching their way toward him. Lounging idly he faked a yawn and stretched out full, then slurred his words over the yawn, "Boy-o-boy, sure am tired tonight. Must be 'bout time for bed," and with that, unspoken despair swept over them —but not one made a peep. Jade, one of the very smallest children and Reed's favorite, crouched anxiously behind him, silent and persistent as a shadow. The children looked at one another hoping against hope 'Uncle Reed' was not too tired tonight. The grownups smiled.

"That is…" Reed managed to finally say flushing the stretch and the yawn, "unless somebody wants to hear a story tonight."

"—*Yes!*" they all shouted in unison swarming him in earnest. In spite of the fact they were from completely different worlds and milieu, Reed had a place here, and in their hearts. He was their storyteller of harrowing escapades and romance and myths, of life and death drama and legends. And although somewhat unorthodox and usually distorted, each tale was always delicious, because Reed was truly a gifted storyteller.

"You guys wanna hear about Pee Willey and the leeching bloodsuckers under the bed?"

"Yes!"

Eyes wide, scanning, *the mood* settling in, "'Course you know," he explained, his hands mimicking claws, "covers are magic, and monsters can't get you under the covers —and suck out your brains!" with the lurch.

When they screamed Ames looked, and Tian frowned.

Reed got the message, and reconsidered. "Well, second thought, maybe we should do something else okay, something a little less nail-biter, you know, something more mellow."

That was fine with the children. Anything was good for them.

Within a minute the kids had converged as an aggregate mob of small bodies with arms and legs, and he gladly arranged them *just so.* Then, as always, Jade climbed onto his lap and he gave her a loving peck on the nose, and she kissed him back. He was irreplaceable, her 'Uncle Reed'.

"Well let's see then; what'll it be tonight?"

"We do not care, just tell us a story," one of them said.

Reed thought briefly then smiled, deciding on another story for the evening's fare. "Okay then, tell you what, I'll tell you about Snow White the Blizzard Babe and the busy midgets who mined diamonds —and their after-hours promiscuous escapades."

"Yes!" the children rejoiced. Reed's grin evaporated when he looked at Ames a second time, his expression asking, *what after-hours promiscuous escapades?* And Tian gave him 'the look'.

"Okay, okay— second thought, maybe we should do the Three Little Pigs and the Billy Goats Gruff or something." Looking around, checking discretely—no disparaging glances. "Yeah, we'll save Snow Babe and Grouchy till you guys are just a tad-bit older."

"Years older," Ames encouraged, his voice tinged with warning that drew Tian's agreement.

Reed caved. "Yeah, Blizzard Babe might be just a trifle to risqué for you guys right now —informative years and all." Ames nodded, and Tian grinned.

"Okay now let's get this puppy on the road—" and, "Long, long ago in the enchanted forest lived three…"

"—Uncle Reed," a child asked popping a hand in the air, "is this the same enchanted forest where Batman lives?"

He looked at her, serious, sadly. "No, that one got burned up in the forest fire when Bambi got torched. Remember?" She shook her head, frowning intently, recalling poor Bambi. "New forest, new story; so, where was I? —Oh yeah. In this enchanted forest there lived three little pigs: Wiggley, Squiggly, and Ralph —and a'course their mutual girlfriend Rapunzel who lived next door in this great, high castle made out of Oreo cookies and gingersnaps."

"Now back then, in the olden days, the three little pigs were constantly harried by these three bully billy goats that lived under this rickety old wooden bridge. The bridge was rickety 'cause the Billy Goats Gruff disassembled a large part of it to make themselves some fancy-ass beds. The daddy goat's bed was real hard, and mama goat's bed was real soft, but the little goat's bed was ju—st right." He stopped, reconsidered. "No, I'm getting ahead of myself now; so I digress."

Digression or no, he had their undivided attention. "Now as I mentioned previously the Billy Goats Gruff were always after the three little pigs and trying to do them in by vile means. So one gloomy Wednesday the Billy Gruff clan accosted Wiggley pig, the first poor soul, at his house made of dominoes. Big Billy said 'Wiggley, let me in or I'll huff and I'll puff and I'll blow your house down'. And by golly the little pig ran to the kitchen and got under the sink just as Billy Gruff did just that."

The kids were shocked. "'Course now, you also need to know that while this was transpiring there was this Big Bad Wolf hiding nearby in the woods. He was the Billy Goats Gruffs' understudy; but at this particular time he was also intimately involved with some promiscuous cutie wearing a scarlet jezebel's outfit. Personally, I think they had a thing going, but I can't prove that —so back to the story."

Grinning, "Yeah," he went on, "Bully Billy blew the whole house down, and the dominoes caved in violently and much a-clatter. There were black-dot sixes and threes and fours everywhere; but miraculously Wiggley Pig escaped certain peril through the emergency tunnel he had the foresight to dig under the kitchen sink. Hustlin' an'-a-humpin' he scurried underground and popped up at Rapunzel's place." Reed stopped.

"What happened next?" a child asked.

He frowned and scratched his chin pretending to have forgotten. "Don't quite recall."

"Yes you do," another insisted. "What happened next?"

"—Oh yeah, after Wiggley escaped their clutches the Billy Gruff crew went to Squiggly's crib and set upon him. Now Squiggly, the second little pig, lived in a house made out of Bicycle playing cards; so needless to say, when they huffed and puffed his place crashed like a house of cards. Squiggly hotfooted it out'a there with the three tromping Billy Goat Gruffs right behind him."

"He was scooting an'-a-bumpin' through the woods at a pretty good clip for a fat little pig, and the Billy Gruffs were gaining on him and were about to stampede him to pork sausage when —*squizzz*— from out of the trees shot a sticky blast of web. Spiderman laced 'em good; stuck all three Billys to a honking gnarly hickory tree. And with Spiderman's assist Squiggly made good his escape and went straight to Rapunzel's. She was this hair-laden chick who had a castilic-domicile where his chubby brother was already hiding out."

"Castilic-domicile—hair-laden chick?" Ames teased.

Quick side-glance: "Yeah, castilic-domicile, as in like a castle—you know—so don't bug me." And he went on. "Now in the meantime the Big Bad Wolf—being the understudy and all with not much to do really 'cause he'd already memorized all his lines— was just hanging out with Lil' Red," gesturing with his hands, "and one thing led to another, and so forth. So, first thing you know, they're both necked—but naturally, we all 'spected that"

Ames started paying closer attention.

"What happened next, Uncle Reed?"

Bumping his eyebrows mischievously, he continued. "Well, both being necked and whatnot, and wolfie with no condom or other such protection —so— he just ate Little Red Riding Hood," he blurted out quickly.

"Reed—" Ames warned.

Wiping off the smile as he scanned his audience of tots, "Okay, forget that part you guys. That's going off on a tangent anyway."

A child asked, "What happened at the castle?"

Playfully focusing upon her, "I was getting to that. Just give me a minute, okay?" He took a breath.

"Soon as you get off your tangent," Ames interjected wryly.

Reed ignored him.

"Back at the castle Wiggley and Squiggly are in a dither because the Gruff clan are finally peeling their way out of the spiderweb. So they yell, 'Rapunzel, Rapunzel, let down your hair' and she unfurls sixty feet of beautiful and meticulously braided locks and they start climbing up her hair to the safety of her castle turret. Now you gotta understand, this is quite an accomplishment because little pigs don't have fingers like we do, they're hoof—ed."

"Hoof—ed?" Ames asked. Tian just shook her head.

"Yeah, hoof—ed," Reed threw back, "as in cloven. Now leave me alone so I can finish the story or we'll be here all night."

"Do not mind us," Tian quipped. "Heaven forbid we should interfere."

Turning to the kids again, Reed, pretending to ignore her, muttered under his breath, "What-*ever*. Now where was I?"

"Okay, so the two little pigs are climbing up Rapunzel's hair, but alas, the two porkers weighed so much they jerked said bitch right out of the castle window and the three of them land in a heap all mixed up with a shit-load of braided hair."

"'Great, now what do we do?' Rapunzel asks. 'I've got an idea,' Squiggly professes, and he makes a slip knot and loop with the end of her hair. Then both pigs fling her over a big old branch, so now they've got a snare to capture up the Billy Gruffs. Sure enough, the snare works too. Only when they snagged the Gruffs —all three of them running full speed and all— they damn-near break poor Rapunzel's neck and 'bout jerk her prissy-ass out'a the tree. Brain-damaged her for sure."

"So Wiggley and Squiggly leave Rapunzel to her own devices and race frantically for Ralph's place. Now Ralph, unlike his dipshit siblings, built his house out of titanium alloy; but the three of them are trapped inside now with the billy goats stampeding around and 'round it. The Billy Gang couldn't blow the place down so they decided to smoke 'em out by raising a nasty-ass big cloud of dust."

"Now, unbeknownst to our piglets, in the county adjacent to the enchanted forest other pivotal events are simultaneously transpiring —that means at this same time. And down this quaint little New England carriage trail, from out of the trees comes this gomer named Paul galloping full-tilt on his dashing black steed. He's accompanied by his trusty sidekick, a chubby little bear named Winnie-the-Pooh, who's riding Eeyore an old gray donkey. Eeyore isn't nearly so fleet as Paul's horse though because he has two lanterns tied to his tail and they're bouncin' and bangin' along on the road behind him."

"Old Paul's yelling, 'The British are coming, the British are coming,' and doesn't even see the Billy Goats Gruff in the dust cloud, and tramples right over the top of 'em inadvertently saving the Three Little Pigs. Now offhand this might seem to be a stroke of luck, but actually it wasn't 'cause without intentions of being an alarmist, Paul's serendipitously embroiled the boys in some Middlesex village and farm controversy —that means he didn't do it on purpose. And that dissension ended up getting blown *wa-ay* out of proportion—you know—civil disobedience, revolutionary stuff, ship-loads of Red Coats; such like that. I think that had something to do with Alice and the white rabbit having a tea party, but I'm not 'xactly clear on that historical connection."

"Anyway, Old Paul Revere and the patriots are holding their own —in the bushes and behind the rocks and trees— against all the king's horses and all the king's men, but that's about it. They don't really make any headway until Long John Silver shows up with his swashbuckling crew of corsairs and they surround the British vessels in the harbor and confiscate their tea on December sixteen, of seventeen and seventy-three —just to piss off old King George the Third." And the story went on…

Listening quietly, leaning against Ames and holding their son, Tian looked at him and asked, "John, do you suppose Reed will ever change?"

"Lord, I hope not," he answered casually, "then we'd have to get used to him all over again."

Tian smiled. "Yes. After all, he is, *just* Reed," and she sighed, weary.

"Tired? Want to call it a night?" She nodded and without speaking he helped her up. Quietly they left the circle heading up the path in the direction of their hut.

"Leaving, Doc? Gonna miss the spine-tingling climax, the part where Captain Nemo and the Nautilus surface with this giant octopus stuck on her hull and it scarfs up all the limey blokes."

Not looking back: "We'll catch it on cable."

"Okay," and he resumed for the children.

Night's presence and sounds closing in, Reed's voice fading in the distance, they walked together, the campfire light and crackle of wood dwindling, gradually blending to the gentle background music of their own enchanted forest. A peaceful night, they walked quietly, Tian holding their son, Ames with his arm around them.

Theirs was a promising future in a new world, filled with new hope and beautiful flowers, and trees that rustled gently in the breezes whispering unheard murmuring of…

...Something yet Unfinished.

* * *

In the hut…

…They lay together, speaking softly, making plans for their future. Propped on an elbow Ames rested on his side watching as Tian sat kitten-like, curled against an overstuffed pillow fashioned with leather filled with dry grass. A small enclosure of stones in the far corner of the room formed a campfire ring that burned easily nibbling dead wood as it cast dancing shadow-fairies upon the bundled-thatch ceiling and walls.

John gently brushed his son's cheek with a finger that seemed almost as large as the infant's face; but the babe only paused for a breath then resumed feeding at Tian's breast. He was a beautiful small thing, and he even had hair, not bald and homely like so many were when they first embarked on the journey of life.

"What shall we name him?" she asked.

"That's up to you. Whatever you decide will be fine with me."

She looked at him, eyes twinkling playfully, "I like the name Reed."

He chuckled. "Yeah, well *almost* anything will be fine with me. One Reed is enough, don't you think?"

"Definitely. One is enough," she agreed, then told him, "I must think about it for a while."

"Take your time." He played his index finger back and forth as his son held it lightly with a tiny hand. "Sure is small."

"That would depend on your perspective," she said gently. "I did not think he was so small this morning when he was being born."

"Yeah, and I forgot to put in an extra stitch too."

Puzzled, "I do not understand what you mean."

Grinning, "Just a bit of passe' humor." The smile faded; sincerity stole its place. "Do you feel any differently?" he asked.

"My back does not hurt when I stand now, and I do not waddle when I walk."

"No, I mean, inside; do you feel any *different*?"

She understood, his question rekindling the image of the angelic warrior and mighty horse at Legend Mountain; the Mystic and the 'Prophecy of the Strangers'—*men who are different, but not enemies... and they would change our world. The Renoloi possess a gift... you are human.*

"Human," she whispered; then, "I do not know. I feel so many things, so many emotions that are difficult to describe."

Ames, considering the depth of it, in a low voice, "The Mystic said, 'Now you are human; the Renoloi is gone'."

"Yes, I know." Then seriously, and tantalizingly, she lifted the leather blanket with her free hand and toyed, "Feel me. Would you like to examine my organs?" mocking the first time the subject of their anatomical differences arose. Dumbstruck he just looked at her and she quickly let go of the blanket and slid her hand to his crotch. "But I did not know the male organ could be so rigid."

Smiling, he pulled her hand from his penis and playfully chastised, "Cripes, you're as bad as Reed; you know it."

"Reed... that *is* a good name," she feigned coyly glancing at the baby.

"Gimmie a break, will ya?" But in spite of himself he laughed quietly as they snuggled together, their son tucked safely between them.

His mahogany eyes, her hazel eyes, their faces barely inches apart, each radiating body warmth, "I love you, John," she whispered.

"I love you too. I always will."

Soon, they were sound asleep.

* * *

Hours later...

...The small fire had dwindled to embers. It was very dark in the hut. Very quiet. Ames was sleeping peacefully beside her, the babe cradled in her arms on her chest. Tian's eyes darted back and forth beneath closed lids, searching, gathering images, then suddenly opened. It all seemed very real; then again, perhaps, it was only…

…Her Dream.

It was a cold October morning as she walked a stone path that led to a place where she had never been. A dead wind whistled over the barren landscape and she approached an imposing cave with shining entrances and the fire of death deep within its bowels. In bare feet she tread softly upon the stone and viewed the strange and mysterious thing… and voices in the distance murmured,

"…Something yet Unfinished."

All the entrances were sealed with the silence of reflection and darkness, and Tian did not know how to enter the great cavern, so she stood still and alone on the footpath and listened for something she could not comprehend. There was sadness in the eyes of the pure white statue high up on the mountain, and all around her were the echoes of time, and a frigid, desolate… *Relentless Wind.*

A voice said:

"And a great portent appeared in heaven, a woman clothed with the sun, with the moon under her feet, and on her head a crown of twelve stars; she was with child and she cried out in her pangs of birth, in anguish for delivery." (Rev. 12: 1-2 RSV)

Tian heard the words and sat up in bed. Her son was gone. John was gone. She was alone with the dancing shadow-fairies that frolicked upon the walls and ceiling. But she knew the fire must have burned out and quickly looked at the fire ring. Glimmering embers shimmering like amber dust, her gaze drawn to the soft light of the coals… and the embers reignited returning to life.

No more than flittering sparks at first, they twinkled and glowed then stirred more brightly and wound like a delicate sparkling vortex of light that rose from the ashes revolving on spiritual wings. Upward, the winding spiral climbed becoming brighter still as the amber changed to a glittering whirlwind of clear scintillating light;

quasars, pulsars and minutiae of glimmering starfire explosions blended within its texture.

Eyes wide Tian silently watched as from within the mysterious spiraling flame the Centurion Mystic appeared: magnificent, garbed in gleaming armor of lorica segmentata and tasseled helmet with visor, wearing a cloak of pure white sackcloth, tussets and sandals, and a waistband of wide harness leather holding a scabbard and broadsword, true as the limits of creativity. The Mystic remained still.

A voice said:

"And another portent appeared in heaven; behold, a great red dragon, with seven heads and ten horns, and seven diadems upon his heads. His tail swept down a third of the stars of heaven, and cast them to the earth." [in part] (Rev. 12: 3-4 RSV)

"What does it mean?" Tian asked.

The shimmering vision did not speak, but in her mind she heard, *"That answer is forbidden."*

The interior of the humble dwelling glowed shimmering in the reflected light of the vision before her… and enigmatically spiritual shadow-fairies danced upon the thatch. Tian watched with wonder. The Mystic opened a hand.

A voice said:

"And the dragon stood before the woman who was about to bear a child, that he might devour her child when she brought it forth; she brought forth a male child, one who is to rule all the nations with a rod of iron, but her child was caught up to God and to his throne, and the woman fled into the wilderness, where she has a place prepared by God." [in part] (Rev. 12: 4-6 RSV)

"I do not understand," she whispered.

Inside the helmet green eyes smiled, and without speaking the Mystic said, *"What is to come, will be... and has been. Reality is possessed of many dimensions."*

Softly Tian asked, "Who are you?"

"That answer is forbidden. A long journey still lies ahead woven with the fabric of hardship and loss."

"A journey, for whom?"

"For those you love."

"Will they return?"

For a moment she heard no words; then almost sadly the voice came to her. *"Some will return... but not all will return."*

Nervously Tian glanced down to her empty arms, then next to her on the bed. "Where is John... and my son?" and even as she thought the words, the reply came back.

"They are with you."

She looked again —a flash of light— her son was cradled peacefully within her arms and Ames lay quietly beside her, and the vision, the Centurion was gone.

The small fire had dwindled to embers. It was very dark in the hut. And very soon it would be a cold October morning as she followed a path to a place where she had never been, because there was...

...Something yet Unfinished.

CHAPTER TWO

Several days later…

…He sat on Legend Mountain plateau, an overlook from where he could survey the New World, all the way to the convergence of horizon and sky. Ames was alone with his thoughts and he digressed, back to the beginning.

How long ago, he wondered; *when did it all really begin?*

Time is like a book; the pages of our lives' neatly tucked within the binding of each of our beginnings and end. Where we are, determined by which page; but the pages are always there.

'Reality is possessed of many dimensions,' the Mystic had told him. What is real; what is imagined? What is time, no more than a page, an event somewhere between the beginning and end? And before the beginning, or after the end… there lies the realm of Beyond.

He and Reed constructed a geodesic sphere, a time machine if you will, and arrived in a primitive world of Renoloi and Troglodyte, a land of hermaphrodites. A strange new world, it was a place he never had time to appreciate, a world somewhere between now and then.

The Inscriptions within the temple of Legend Range prophesied two strangers would change this world, would be a catalyst precipitating cataclysmic evolution amidst a preordained conflict. And as surely as it was predicted all that happened, prophesied with words chiseled in stone inside a mysterious mountain. Inscriptions from a planet called Earth, a world that ceased to exist long ago.

He had never seen the Legends, nor could he explain the origin of the mysterious mountain range that collapsed into this world many generations before he and Reed arrived. The Inscriptions were writings chiseled on the walls of seemingly endless tunnels and caverns. But Tian said the Legends were more. The Legends were things the Renoloi did not understand...

...The Legends were Magic.

Neither was Ames sure how he and Reed had arrived here. Tian told them through a black hole, when the Great Spirit poured out all the stars and worlds and moons to accompany them. That was when this universe was born, this creation began...

...After fifteen billion years.

That alone was more than he could comprehend. But he thought on. He knew he should certainly have died when he blew up the temple to kill the last of the Trogs hiding in the labyrinth of passageways inside the mountain's peak. But he did not die. Somehow, he was catapulted back through time, back to the Complex where Smith had taken over the world.

General Smith, not what he seemed, not what he appeared to be... more than an evil person; he *was* Evil. Smith was the demagogue of mankind's worst aspects, most disappointing characteristics, the boiling lurid stench in the broth of all humanity's wickedness and failings. Smith was the ultimate opportunist and the epitome of baseness, spit-polish black, and brass and green...

...He was Satan.

Then he considered the geodesic sphere. The Federation duplicated and constructed it with information gleaned with their mind probes. And that, paradoxically, was the means of his return to the future where he was reunited with Tian and Reed whom he thought he had lost to the shaded back alleyways of death.

After that there was peace in the land of the Renoloi, but only for a little while...

...A bottle floating in the river changed all that.

A lot of things changed the day they went to the lowland and Reed found a bottle floating down the river with a message inside it, a scribbled note in a Coke bottle, from a far distant past. That was the day Tian intimated...

...*'Something yet Unfinished'*.

Their journey to help another village exposed them to the horrific, adroit killers, the Night Hunters... and the quaint and personable gray dwarf twins Phineas Taylor Barnum and 'Just Plain' Wilson. Then the ocean where they embarked upon an odyssey in a perilous green sea wound with mystery and enigma...

...And an inexplicable circular storm.

Reed speculated the storm might be a connective corridor of unknown origin that linked the past, present and future somehow —where they encountered the 'Marine Sulphur Queen', a freighter that vanished without a trace in the Bermuda Triangle, a long time ago. That was Reed's theory. But then again, after all...

...He is, *just* Reed.

When their party's survivors met Lent and his unnamed people on the Island Ames nicknamed them Pilgrims, like those intrepid souls at Plymouth Rock so long ago. They were neophytes; the analogy seemed to fit, appropriate enough, and the name stuck. After coexisting for generations with each unaware of the other, the Renoloi and Pilgrim finally met. Was it chance...

...Or design?

But that was not nearly as unusual as the Accumulation —things, countless things— junk, entire buildings, and even cities dredged from the past. He could not explain that; nor could he explain how an entire ocean vanished overnight. It happened once before; a strong East wind caused it...

...So the Bible said.

The wind, another consideration... especially a cold, *Relentless Wind*. Something we all take for granted; though perhaps none of us should. In every world there are forces like wind and rain and fire... and light. Perhaps they are only natural forces...

...Then again, perhaps they are not.

It was a long journey home from the Island, crossing an unstable world destined for cataclysmic change. And Smith. He came after them from the past rousing the Hunters from the darkness of their burrows to do his bidding on a volcanic battleground, sacred ground, where Night Hunters swarmed as a Tyrannosaur roared. Where Legend Mountain rose while a planet rattled and quaked…

…And a world was reborn.

Legs pulled to his chest, chin resting on his knees, he scratched his forehead. So much had happened, so many things he didn't understand. He sat quietly a bit longer, thinking, trying to sort it all out, until at length he sighed with resignation; he may never know the answers to the questions that still haunted him.

Gazing down from the plateau on Legend Mountain he could at least console himself in knowing this was a new world, and here things were as they should be. Things were right here. So, with that in mind he drew a deep breath, slowly rose to his feet brushing dirt from the seat of his jeans, and began walking the trail to the village below.

There would be a gathering tonight, the evening meal. And there would be contentment and celebration. Tian, the woman he loved more than life itself, had born him a son; and Seana was due any time now, another milestone in the journey and story of their lives.

Ames ambled leisurely; and as he did, he considered and reconsidered so many things, all that he could remember. But so like the faint tracks his bare feet left in the soft loam of the winding path… everything that had happened so far was only footprints in the sand, on a beach of endless realities that stretched beyond any imaginings. All of it, everything, still only pieces of, *the Puzzle*…

…*Something yet Unfinished.*

* * *

Late afternoon, sun above the horizon…

…In a beautiful world filled with bounty and adorned in unusual fluorescent colors, he was nearing the village when she called out, "Mr. Ames—"

Turning, he stopped and waited as Kalo caught up with him. "Hi —and just call me John. Out for a walk?"

"No, I was looking for you." Then lowering her voice, she inquired, "May I ask you something… just between us?"

"Of course," his nod assuring, *just between us*. Kalo fidgeted rising on the balls of her feet as she wrung her small hands together, hesitant, darting a sideways glance, then down at the ground. "What is it? Is something bothering you?"

"It is nothing really."

"Kalo." The tone of the word spoke more than her name.

She looked at him. "Why does Lent like Tere more than me?" She blurted it out then looked away, and momentarily her question puzzled him; then somewhere inside, understanding configured a grin —but it didn't get out.

"I don't know that he does," he answered seriously. "Why do you think that?" Still reluctant, she hesitated so he gently took her chin and turned her head. "Kalo, why do you think that?"

"It is clear to me that it is true," she told him. "They laugh and play and tease one another all the time; and they deliberately exclude me." She was frustrated. "We are supposed to be friends. Is that the way friends treat one another?"

His reply was the question, "Does it bother you?"

"No." She rocked back and forth on her heels, pretending and denying, then bunched her shoulders with exacerbation and admitted, "Yes, yes it does. It hurts my feelings when they do it."

Slipping an arm around her shoulder he pulled her close and hugged her, and they began walking together. "I hadn't noticed that they're mean to you. Maybe it just seems that way to you."

"No. Lent says things that hurt my feelings, and I believe Tere enjoys it when he does."

"Give me an example."

"He said I do not have bumps," she reminded, referring to their first encounter on the island.

"That was months ago," Ames defended, then reassured, "and he was only making an innocent observation." Then empathizing he agreed as he went on, "I can understand that your feelings were hurt, but I'm sure he didn't mean anything by it. It was only…"

"—Yes he did," she interrupted, "I am certain of that."

"Why?"

"Because, in sex—ed class, when Reed speaks of penises or vaginas —or breasts— Lent always sits next to Tere and smiles like 'more than just friends'. And when he examines her breasts," she added plainly, "I believe he even enjoys touching them."

Ames mumbled almost involuntarily, "Well shoot, I hope so."

"What?"

"Oh nothing," quickly dismissing the remark. Warmly he 'one-arm-squeezed' her with a quick hug as they walked. "I think you're making too much of something that you needn't worry about." He was lightly distracted until she stopped and looked up at him. There were tears in her eyes.

"Why will my breasts not grow? What is wrong with me?"

Amusement vanished, sincerity stepped in and he knelt, eye to eye with her, a precious, dear friend. "Sweetheart, there is nothing in the world wrong with you. You are more than you can imagine, more than anyone could ever wish for. Mother Nature isn't on the clock. Every woman matures in her own time; simple as that. Don't be in a hurry. Be patient. It will happen."

"But Tere is so pretty and I…"

"—Don't *even*—don't *ever*—think something like that." His words almost scolded as he counseled. Then tenderly brushing golden strands of hair from her face tucking them behind her ear with his finger, softly he said, "You told me once, 'Because I believe'. You remember saying that?" She nodded. Next question: "And do you also remember when we were all together on the island?" Acknowledging again, and his final question, "Of all of us, who was the person Lent most wanted to talk to?"

She knew the answer, but needing reassurance still asked, "Then why does he treat me the way he does?"

Ames smiled. "That's something only time will tell. But I would venture…" he paused as he considered how best to explain, then said, "many times, for most of us it's easy to talk to others simply because they are just that—others. Then, once in a while someone comes along who is not, *just others*. So be patient, and wait... until the moon is full."

Innocently, "I do not know what that means."

He confessed, "I didn't think you would, not just yet anyway. Now wipe your eyes," pursing his lips, "a Renoloi warrior does not cry." Bashfully she wiped the wet smudges from her cheeks as he kissed her on the forehead and began to stand.

She put a hand on his shoulder and stopped him, still eye to eye. "I love you," she told him earnestly.

With the smile, "I love you too. I will until the day I die."

"No," she revealed almost reverently, "much longer than that." But he did not understand what she meant.

They were friends; and without saying anything more, each with an arm around the other they continued down *the path*.

* * *

Later, the meeting circle...

...Rows of fallen logs were arranged for seating, a robust fire converting wood to illumination of yellow flame and ash. The people were gathered and conversation was as animated as it was diverse, the mood light, anticipating the evening gathering.

"Kalo, Mr. Ames," Tere hailed as they approached. She was sitting with Lent, Deet and Ronto and about six others, all laughing over some unheard remark. Ames spied Tian seated with Nitana, Reed and Seana just beyond them, so he and Kalo headed that way. Jade, as always, was sitting on 'Uncle Reed's' lap.

When they arrived, "Kalo, where were you earlier?" Tere asked. "We could not find you."

"There was something I had to do," she answered modestly.

Almost disregarding her reply Tere eagerly informed, "We went to the falls and went swimming in the pool." Without speaking to them Ames smiled a, *hello,* as he stepped over their log and sat down with Tian.

"That must have been fun," Kalo replied politely as she sat down with Lent and Tere.

"Yes, very," Tere assured. Lent offered a fleeting smile but seemed almost reluctant to agree with her. Fondling the corn in his pocket Deet only grinned from beneath his frazzled Yankees ball cap. "And Kalo—" Tere volunteered, "you will never guess what I discovered today, a curious thing."

With half-hearted enthusiasm, but being careful, "What did you discover?"

Beaming, "The penis shrinks in cold water," she said loudly enough for anyone nearby to hear. Mortified, Lent flushed with embarrassment.

Spontaneously, "They always do that," both he and Deet defended in unison not sure why it should be such a big deal. It had never seemed so important before.

"Really?" Kalo feigned disinterest, hurt feelings telling in the word.

Seated with his back to her and not turning around, Reed confirmed in a stodgy monotone, "They sure do."

Distracted, they looked over their shoulders at Reed until Tere recaptured their attention again assuring, "Yes, and they get hard like short little leeches."

"Let's change the subject," Lent suggested.

Mischievously Tere darted him a patronizing glance. "No, I want to talk about penises."

"Sure as shootin', let's change the subject," Deet seconded. Kalo remained quiet so Deet followed up, "Tere, what's the big deal, and why is that so fascinating? Your nipples get hard when they get cold, don't they? Reed explained all that in sex—ed, so why are you so enthralled with our penises?"

She: "You should not know words like that."

"What—enthralled?"

Pouty: "Yes."

"Oh yeah; well for your information, I'm learn'ed." For once Lent didn't say anything; Deet was doing just fine.

"—And stupid," she threw back.

"And you're obsessed with penises. Let's talk about boobs —or perky round nipples— how 'bout them?"

"Fine, but nipples do not shrink so much…" and their conversation continued.

Behind them, looking past Seana, Ames turned and asked, "How's sex—ed going, Reed?"

Edged with frustration, "Doc, I just can't do it anymore."

"Why not?" Tian asked from Ames' right side as she cradled the baby between them.

"Because these guys don't have one morsel of shame; they're absolutely uninhibited."

"Well, it's all new to them," Ames allowed.

"No Doc, you *reeeally* don't understand." Almost squeamishly, "I mean— they're examining each other —and doing things. Shit it's just too embarrassing, even for me. And it's getting *waaay* out of hand —literally."

Deadpan, Ames replied, "Well you know what they say about adolescents exploring their sexuality…"

"What?"

Stoic Ames confided, "A bird in the bush is better than one in the hand."

Not thinking it all that humorous, "That right? Well you're— you're as bad as they are—all of 'em put together." Ames chuckled and Tian grinned; the week before she sat in on a couple of Reed's classes.

Within the large clearing varied conversations fashioned a rhythmic composition of a hundred different subjects that persisted during those waning hours of daylight, while 'almost-done' roasting wild goat disseminated its warm succulent flavor in the barbecue smoke that wafted with the breeze. The late afternoon-early evening was beautiful, joyful; a warm setting sun… and a full moon just rising.

A young Pilgrim, with all of ten years tucked into his clothes, zigzagged through the crowd, a knotted piece of frayed rope and one hand holding up his pants. He was focused on Reed —and Reed saw him coming. "'Scuse me, Mr. Reed."

Unenthusiastically, "Yeah what, Cargill?"

Stepping forward more boldly now that the teacher had acknowledged him, "I want to come to class."

Plainly, "I told you before, absolutely not; no little kids. You're too young to be hearing that kind of stuff."

Peering defiantly from under a scruffy mop of hair at least as bushy as Lent's, the boy looked like a pocket-sized version of him. "I am not too little. I'm just short."

Impatiently, "I told you no. Now beat it."

"I have been, just like Deet showed me —but nothing happens."

"Twaddle me duck-walking." Reed picked up a stick and threw it as Cargill darted off melting back into the crowd. "If you don't quit talking like that, I'll wash your mouth out with soap you fuzzy pygmy."

"Ivory. It makes lots of bubbles," Jade quickly offered, innocent as she was enthusiastic.

Reed glanced down at her, then back, "Yeah, Cargill—Ivory."

Hiding behind several others, from a safe distance, "I'm going to sneak in."

Reed yelled back, "Get a haircut," and quickly looking around, checking some of the others in the vicinity, "—all of you, get haircuts. Bunch of frickin' cootie communes. You guys are making me crazy." Ames was grinning when Reed's eyes skipped over him and found Deet: lock and load. "Deet, I ought to choke the living shit out'a you." Deet offered his palms and shrugged innocence and mock surrender, then grinned. Reed started to get up but Seana stopped him with a hand on his thigh, so he simply looked at Ames, frustrated and rankled. "Truthfully Doc, I think this sex—ed stuff might'a been a bad idea."

Ames toyed, "That's understandable; we all know it's a tough business. Sex has always been a dirty job," and the sigh "—but somebody's gotta do it."

"You too; great. My friends."

Tian joined in, "But Reed, who could be better suited, or more capable than you?"

"Well, that's true..." then he stopped and glared; then back to Ames, "no really, they're crazy as bedbugs, running around with their weenies hard as milk-bone dog biscuits and..."

"—Childbirth seems very painful," Seana interrupted out of the blue. She snatched his train of thought.

"What?"

Looking at him she said it a second time. "Childbirth seems very painful."

"Christ, where did that come from?"

"Well it does."

He scowled. "Does a bear shit in the woods?"

A puzzled expression, she asked, "What?"

"Does a bear shit in the woods? Makes about as much sense as what you just said. Talk about left-frickin'-field, we were talking about..."

"—I do not know what field bear shit in the woods is in," she interrupted, "but do not raise your voice with me."

"Good going," Ames taunted, "now you're picking on a poor little pregnant lady."

"Cheap shot," Reed barked jostling Jade on his knee in sync with his agitation.

"I believe it hurts," Seana decided. She looked around Ames, to Tian. "Does it hurt?"

"Very much so," Tian assured. Sympathizing Seana nodded, then slapped Reed on the thigh, his eyes skipping from one to the other following the banter, just trying to keep up, Jade bouncing back and forth each time someone spoke.

"No it doesn't," Reed argued, "not that bad."

Tian snapped, "—And how would you know?"

"I should kick your ass," Seana muttered.

"Picking on a poor little pregnant lady."

"Think you guys could lay it on any thicker?" Reed asked snidely.

Nitana joined in, "You hurt Seana and you feel no remorse at all, do you?"

Reed: "It's getting deep."

"Do you?"

Defiantly, "Not one iota whatsoever; she certainly wasn't complaining before —bumpin-uglies, in doin' mode— and besides, Tian's exaggerating."

Tian, crooking an eyebrow: "Exaggerating?"

Nitana: "Perhaps if it were you, how would that feel? Would you like that?"

Reed stared her down. "Gimmie' a break —and furthermore, you certainly don't know what it's like. You don't have a clue, so just get off my donkey." She had no idea what that meant.

"I do not exaggerate," Tian reminded, "you said so yourself."

"Attitude," Ames squeaked. Tian smacked him.

Reed recalled her describing the Trogs, and had to concede, "Okay Tian, you're right. You got me there."

"Then do not say I exaggerate."

Again: "Picking on a poor little pregnant lady."

"You should be ashamed," Nitana scolded. Reed was having difficulty keeping up and Jade was getting dizzy, being jostled as she was.

"Reed, I should kick your ass."

"Got a better idea," he said. The ribbing stopped and Seana eyed him, waiting. "Well, don't you want to hear it?"

Ames, under his breath, "This better be good."

"All right, what?"

"Well…" he grinned, "you know how I've always wanted to come and go at the same time —so after you have the baby why don't you just *do* me till you kill me off." Seana smacked him on the back of the head so hard it interrupted his laugh and he had to huddle over Jade to make sure she didn't get hit.

Behind them Tere was still prattling on when Kalo decided she'd listened long enough, rose, and began to leave causing Lent to ask, "Where are you going?"

Without looking back: "To the mountain."

"But we haven't eaten yet."

Kalo, stopping and turning, "I am not very hungry," and she was on her way.

"I'll go with you," he volunteered, and he was up and moving as well.

"If you wish," Kalo said affecting disinterest, "but we will need more rope this time."

"No problem," Lent assured, "we have plenty. I'll get it and meet you."

Not wanting to be excluded Tere decided, "I am not hungry either," Following, she got up then called back over a shoulder, "Deet, are you coming?"

"Not a chance, I'm starved and I'm staying right here." That said, he sheepishly looked at Ronto who was eyeing him and wondering why he would turn down an opportunity to explore Legend Mountain. She didn't say it though. "Well," he finally mumbled, "I am. We gotta eat sometime."

* * *

Each with a long coil of rope over a shoulder...

...The trio hiked the steep trail from the valley up the mountain. Etched into the rock walls and cliff faces the path crisscrossed back and forth ascending the mountainside until it ended at the high plateau of Legend Mountain.

Finally on the plateau, they stood catching their breath. Quietly and invisible as water droplets within fog, it stole in surreptitiously, enfolding, moving all around them and within them. Silently the mood came.

It captured them.

They looked on reverently, instilled with the wonder and mystery of this gray-tan granite monolith. Almost glowing with minerals and secrets the cave entrance resembled a natural amphitheater as it towered in a stately arch before them. Each knew that within the mountain and passageways, somewhere the great legendary cavern waited silently and dark; dark not with the foreboding of evil and malice, but cloistered within the shadowy realm of not knowing, with the most precious of secrets that must be kept hidden from them all. Standing there, gazing upon the mysterious mountain, each knew the story of Legend Mountain, what happened there.

Tian had told them:

Many years ago, when she was just a young girl, she had spent countless hours in Legend Mountain, its passageways and caverns lined with gleaming metal that John and Reed called magnesium oxide ore. She said the Inscriptions were there, and many other wonders, things the Renoloi could not understand; but the Legends were more… the Legends were Magic.

Then one night a great storm and sudden quake left only the Sacred Temple remaining above the landscape; perhaps an explosion or implosion caused by the shiny magnesium metal that burned with white fire. No one would ever know for certain.

Since then, the great mountain remained below the surface waiting patiently with its secrets, until the day of ReCreation and the birth of this world. That day Legend Mountain rose from the depths to again touch the sky. That day was like no other. More than a new world was born.

And when the sun rose on that day the aureate glow of its radiant warmth somehow transformed Legend Mountain washing away the gray-black glitter of quartz, feldspar and mica embedded within the granitic monolith's face. The Sacred Temple ruins and the Inscriptions were gone… and the mountain changed from shimmering black to gray-tan. That, and so many other things, the Renoloi could not understand.

Granite and mystery—

Now, before them the great cavern waited silently as the trio gathered torches from their cache, lit them, then quietly, venerably entered Legend Mountain. A honeycomb of tunnels. Stepping softly, they moved into one of the many passageways.

Inside—

The other world, the outside world... fading behind them. Six more steps, going into the dark. Without warning —sudden commotion of fluttering wings— a bustle of zigzagging shadows teeming with high-pitch click-echoes and sonar ricochet-barks burst from the ceiling and walls in an abrupt rolling swarm, causing all three to duck. Above and around their heads a colony of little brown bats sprang to their wings. Frightened from slumber and their upside-down roosts of inverted domain the harmless insect eaters exploded to life on pulsating, membranous, delicate little brown wings. Erratic aeronauts, they were suddenly everywhere flitting about.

Flustered, quickly swatting at one, Tere whispered, "I hate when they do that; it always startles me, even though I know they are there."

"They are harmless," Kalo dismissed without looking back.

A bit nervous, Lent added, "Not uncommon for a colony to live inside caves, near the entrances."

"I know; but they still make me jump every time they do that."

Eyes still trained on the ceiling, he seemed to agree, and quietly proceeding again they stepped lightly following the corridor, its walls and floor glistening with a sheen more lustrous than polished stone.

Shortly they entered a chamber boasting beautiful stalagmites that rose from the floor and stalactites descending from the torchlit darkness overhead. There was twisted flowery helictite, and great watercolor pillars and spires that shimmered beyond richness with a plethora of color and minerals composing their solid strength. Amid flowstone and dripstone mist swept over the floor, wisps of phantom that would flow, evaporate and disappear, then swirl and pool in amorphous eddies as it formed again.

This was no ordinary mountain, these no ordinary caverns. Water dripped from above and trickled down the walls as constantly as ocean waves washed ashore upon the beaches. But unlike other caves with cold subterranean water and cool mist, these caverns and this water were warm.

All around them tepid veins seeped, percolated and burbled as the water followed minute cracks in the ceiling, walls and floor forming small streamlets that settled and pooled with the shimmering clarity of pure crystal. And above the pools swirled gossamer winds of fine mist and extraordinary mystery... that magically caused the water to flow back up the walls. Over and over the small streamlets trickled, easing along, defying gravity, never stopping; unceasing motion. Things the Renoloi did not understand.

Their torchlight pushed back darkness fashioning dancing fairy shadows on the ceiling and walls of incredible rock formations that surrounded them. They flickered and frolicked like lacewing sprites of silence and light, cavorting incessantly, but never uttering a sound. And within those stalagmites, spires, stalactites and pillars was another phenomenon they could not explain.

The first few times they explored Legend Mountain they hadn't noticed that the colors constantly changed within the formations. What was cerulean, cobalt blue, or gold one minute, might be emerald green or deep violet the next; color exuded and flowed with pellucid evanescence. When they first discovered this anomaly they supposed it might be an illusion caused by the unending flow of water, but that idea was dismissed once they sat down and watched more closely.

The formations slowly and constantly changed colors before their eyes, perhaps because of the mineral content or some other unknown but logical reason. But then again, maybe not. Because not only did the formations continuously change color... they also changed in shape and size; never the same, always transforming, evolving. Things the Renoloi did not understand.

Inside Legend Mountain the water was warm, the air was warm, and the breeze unbroken, a gentle stir, a hush of breathing zephyr that carried peace within its embrace as it flowed constant as shimmering starlight from the vast and eternal heavens. It pushed around them and through them from somewhere distant, somewhere far too distant to imagine... and carried the softest of mellifluous music, as though sung by a choir. It was beautiful music, enchanting music, but distorted, like the underwater sounds of rushing bubbles and flowing waves washing ever so gently through their heads. Things the Renoloi did not understand. Magic.

Legend Mountain was more than beautiful... much More. Even now, after so much had happened, Legend Mountain was a safe place, a warm place, with the most precious of secrets that must be kept hidden from them all.

Torch above his head, looking around, almost reverently, "Which way?" Lent whispered.

Kalo pushed hers in front of her, motioning, "This way."

Her torch off to the side, Tere reached out taking Lent's free hand. "I will stay with you," she told him. He nodded and the three of them slowly moved on.

* * *

At the meeting circle...

...The sun was low in the sky, crowding the horizon, a full moon breaking from the distant peaks, rising directly below it. The barbecued goat complimented with wild yams, carrots and grapes had been delicious, and now the Pilgrims and Renoloi talked and laughed anticipating another enjoyable evening. And the children, as always, began to sidle in Reed's direction hoping for another tantalizing episode of his twisted, fabled folklore.

Sitting beside Reed, wrapping both arms around her over-plump belly Seana suddenly moaned and looked at the ground. Liquid was trickling down her legs, puddling beneath her in the dirt. Both men saw it and knew—*it was time.*

"Water broke," Reed announced, "time to go." Nitana and Ames were onto their feet, Ames offering his hand helping Tian with their child.

Uncertain, Seana's eyes swept from the ground to Reed. "What shall I do?"

"Whatever comes naturally, we'll take care of the rest." Levity evaporated; now he was serious. He and Nitana helped Seana to her feet and waited while Ames made sure Tian and the baby were all right; then each man took a side and they started toward Tian's hut. Seana stepped carefully. This was a new experience.

From the expectant throng of children Jade's voice piped up, "No story tonight, Uncle Reed?"

Looking back over a shoulder, "No, Sweetheart, not tonight. We're gonna be busy for a little while —but we will tomorrow. We'll do Goldilocks and the Rough Riders, okay?"

"Okay, Uncle Reed."

Turning again he, Seana and Ames were moving as he added, "Just remind me tomorrow so I don't forget, Sweetie."

"I will," she assured as the grownups headed up the path.

CHAPTER THREE

Inside the hut…

…Seana was on the makeshift delivery table as Nitana volunteered, "I will boil some water—the blankets are under the bed." Reed learned that from the movies —and of course he passed it on.

Tian asked, "What do you want me to do?"

"Uhh… you take care of the baby," Ames said, "we'll take care of Seana. Hopefully you can just watch."

Stooping for a blanket and pillow, "Unless something goes wrong," Reed interjected extemporaneously.

"—Something goes wrong," Seana blurted out between puffs of breath and stabs of pain. Now more worried, "What can go wrong?"

Without thinking, "'Bout a million things," he joked offhand; then quickly realizing his mistake and considering the consequences, "—nothing babe, nothing's gonna go wrong. Just a slip of the tongue —you know, a 'blink'."

Distracting her Ames smiled encouragingly. "You know how he's always having those dumb blinks."

"Yes," she agreed; then back to Reed, "but if something does go wrong more than his tongue will slip…" and she screamed with a contraction.

"My fault again," Reed fretted.

"Here we go," Ames coached. Nitana stepped closer. Reed hovered. Gritting her teeth, she held the scream. "Here we go."

Seana looked at Reed; bit her lip, pain and irascibility in her eyes. "Reed, I should kick your ass." Already perspiring profusely she threw her head back mussing her hair, locking a death-grip on the side rail; this hurt. She breathed hard and panted —and screamed.

Lovingly he brushed her hair from her face, leaned closer, and softly, into her ear as they focused on Ames between her thighs, "Yeah, I know, but you'll have to do it later, okay? We're gonna be busy for a while," and her delivery continued.

Holding her son Tian moved to a corner of the room where she could watch without being in the way. She whispered, "I will be over here... should you need me."

Focused on what he was doing, Ames shook his head but didn't look back. "I think he's coming." Writhing, Seana screamed and gripped the edge of the bed.

Reed, to his friend: "What do you want me to do?"

Legs bent, wobbly-kneed, feet braced in the stirrups Seana arched her back. "She is trembling so," Nitana observed as she took hold of her right thigh.

"Yeah," Ames agreed, "hold her other leg; she's shaking pretty bad." Lovingly Reed squeezed Seana's hand then scooted a step to her waist to help hold her still.

* * *

The passageway ended...

...A mammoth cathedral cavern opening before them, one they had explored before. It spanned two hundred feet across, was almost as high, and was divided in half by a wide vertical crevasse that was deeper than they could guess. Kalo dropped a torch over the edge once and the flame disappeared before it hit bottom so they knew trying to descend was out of the question.

To cross this seemingly bottomless chasm the first time they crawled around it along the sheer rock ledges, then ran ropes across the expansive drop-off. With the span ropes tightly stretched they constructed a makeshift three-rope bridge that resembled a long swinging 'V' consisting of two handrails and one rope to walk on. The span ropes were tied together with smaller zigzag lengths, like in the Tarzan movies, and although it was unstable, it served the purpose allowing them to continue on into the mountain.

Without talking, one at a time, each crossed the swinging bridge. Bow strung across her back, torch in hand as she stepped lightly but confidently, Kalo led, climbing across the span of empty darkness and distance below. Tucking the twibil handle in the waistband of his cutoffs and down the leg, Lent went second, followed by Tere.

After the crossing they took one of several tunnels and went deeper within until it branched again and they stopped. It was quiet; heat on their faces, torch smoke in their hair, Kalo looked to her companions so they all would agree.

"Doesn't matter," Lent murmured, "either way is fine with me." It seemed wrong somehow to raise their voice inside this mountain. They never did. Kalo pointed to the passage that led to the right and Tere nodded; so they went that way.

Secrets kept in the darkness in an unusual mountain's core, their torches illuminating the way.

Shortly the passageway opened revealing another large cavern adorned with stalagmites and stalactites that resembled a jumble of mirror-image soldiers standing in formation on the floor and hanging from the ceiling. Throughout the cavern shallow pools of water rippled with ever-expanding riffles of distorted motion caused by water droplets seeping through the mineral formations overhead, then falling, *kerplink*. Bleached almost pale in their perpetual-night world, scurrying along the cavern ledges and irregular shelves small spotted blind salamanders darted like wraiths when fingers of torchlight found them stealing their darkness and security.

Blip—expanding ribbons of water. Disturbed, minnow-sized cavefish flitted erratically in the pools, their oversized eyes and fins lacking pigment caused them to resemble delicate skeletons of fish with translucent skin.

At the far side of this cavern was a rope ladder that ascended allowing access to a high shelf on the wall, and the trio quietly made their way through the maze of stalagmites, climbed the ladder to the ledge, then spread out on the spacious alcove beyond. A cluster of seven honeycomb-tunnels led from this shelf.

"Which one?" Tere almost breathed. Undecided, Lent turned to Kalo with the same question in his eye. So far, they had explored five of the seven following each until some bottleneck or impassable crevasse had stopped them. Now only two remained, the largest, nearly ten feet high, and the smallest, barely large enough for an emaciated Ethiopian waif to squeeze through.

Pausing, Kalo closed her eyes, took a deep breath, then opened her eyes and whispered, "The small one."

"Really?" Lent asked dubiously, almost expecting she would have chosen the other. She nodded. "Why the small one?"

"It feels right."

"Okay," with just a tinge of reservation, "you lead."

Pushing the torch in front of her, Kalo crawled into the narrow passage that would have given a claustrophobic pause. Shimmying on elbows and knees Tere followed as Lent brought up the rear.

Crawling, they continued on.

In the expansive cavern behind them, on the floor below the high shelf, as the flicker of torchlight faded within the cramped passageway, blending again to black obscurity colorful mirror-image mineral sentinels stood quietly and vigilant… in the dark.

* * *

Inside the hut…

…The others were busy, while from the corner of the room, silently, nervously, Tian watched. Outside, in the sky, the sun slipped down and the moon crawled up, rising to meet it. They seemed to touch.

Seana wrenched, gripped the bed and screamed.

"Here he comes." Ames leaned forward a bit more as the baby's head began to emerge. "Okay, stay focused now," he encouraged darting glances between her determined eyes and the delivery. "Don't push. Breathe now —take a breath— okay, now push."

Seana took a deep breath, held it, and pushed.

Reed's eyes danced back and forth parroting Ames, from the baby's just-emerging head, to Seana's face fixed with pain and the focus of concentration. "You're doing it," he reassured. Delivery blanket folded neatly beside her, Nitana held on, ready for the new arrival.

Seana screamed. She puffed twice and drew in a third, much deeper, filling her chest. She gritted her teeth and pushed.

A fleeting glimpse as he gently began to support the head with his fingertips, "Doing fine," Ames told her.

Reed was wired as a two-forty outlet, his eyes sparking, bouncing back and forth between her straining countenance and her pubic mound, his son squeezing into the world, Seana enduring the pain of her love for him. "Doin' good." Then he blushed with his smile. "Good hell, you're doing great." She tried to return the smile, but pain shot through contorting it to a grimace —and she screamed.

* * *

Inside Legend Mountain…

…Tight. Wedging their hips, almost oozing along, the three continued crawling. Torch smoke and residue tinged the crawlspace with filigree soot and flaking smudges on the tunnel ceiling inches above them. Were it not for the usually unnoticed sound of rolling ocher flames, squirming bodies, and breathing, this horizontal vent would be remarkably quiet —and dark.

"See anything yet, Kalo?" Lent asked from behind them.

"No."

They crawled a moment more, until, "No. That's it —just no?"

"No, Lent. I cannot see anything yet."

From behind, "Quite a talker, you are," he remarked

Tere: "Are you lonely back there?" crawling between their conversation.

"Cute," he carped.

Kalo, from the front: "I only speak if I have something to say."

There was hardly room enough to shake his head but Lent managed and commented, "So I've noticed." They kept moving. Quiet again for the moment, until, "See anything yet?"

Without looking back: "No."

"No. That's it —just no?" Elbowing along in the middle, Tere smiled.

"No, Lent. I cannot see anything yet."

From the rear: "Well we've come too far to crawl out of here backward —so keep looking, okay?"

Tere asked, "Where would you have her look?"

Puzzled that she need ask, "Well, straight ahead of course."

Tere, facetiously: "Really?"

"Sure. We're in a tunnel; where else is she gonna look?" Tere didn't bother to respond.

Then, from ahead: "I see something."

"What?" from the end of the line.

"Darkness."

"Darkness?" Lent echoed, almost irritated with what he assumed was a false alarm.

"Yes, darkness. The tunnel ends just ahead."

A moment more and all three squeezed from their cramped quarters into another cavern. In the center of the chamber at the fringe of illumination was an irregular black space in the floor indicating an abyss or vertical shaft. Holding her torch in front of her Kalo picked up a stone, stepped to the edge and dropped it into the abyss counting as the small rock fell. Several seconds, the interlude of silence; there was a faint but distinctive echo of, *plink,* when it struck bottom.

Peering over the edge, "It is a long way down," she observed.

Lent considered, "Could tie our ropes together and see if they reach, then climb down."

"But will we be able to climb back up?" Tere asked.

Lent, pragmatically, "Guess that depends on how far you can climb."

Tossing sarcasm over a shoulder Kalo extolled, "You are the clever one."

Lent heard her, and to the back of her head, "What happened to—just no?" Kalo didn't respond, and didn't let him see the smile, so he dismissed the jab deciding, "Didn't wear out my knees crawling in here for nothing; let's see what's down there."

Tying the three ropes together, with a torch at the end, he slowly lowered it into the chasm. While Lent, hand-over-hand, was letting out rope, Kalo tied the tail off to a sizable pillar, being careful not to damage the mineralized structure. That felt like it would be wrong, a desecration somehow. They knew they'd reached bottom when the dangling torch quit swaying and rolled to one side, still. Curiously, they had just enough rope.

Stuffing the handle of the twibil inside his khaki cutoffs so it stuck out the leg of his shorts, "Long way," Lent said, "but we can make it."

* * *

From the corner of the room…

…Silently, nervously, Tian watched, while outside in the sky the moon began blotting out the sun. Many years ago, when she was just a small girl her mother had taken her to the Sacred Temple, and she had seen many wonders. She had been there, looked upon words chiseled in stone and inlaid with gold, committing some to memory when her mother told her she should. The Inscriptions told so much, disclosed many mysteries; but there were some, no matter how she tried, she could not remember. And the Legends were more than a young girl, a Renoloi, could understand. The Legends were Magic.

Holding her son, from the corner of the room, Tian intimated, very softly, "I will be over here… should you need me."

Not looking back Ames assured, "We're doing fine. Shoulder's coming, beginning to rotate. We're doing fine." He looked up at Seana. "Focus. Take another deep breath then push as hard as you can."

* * *

Inside Legend Mountain…

…Legs wrapped securely around the rope and locked with a foot, hand-over-hand they descended. While they climbed down no one spoke, the torch light below growing brighter as they got closer. Their lifestyle kept them fit and although it was a long way, almost one hundred yards, all three were capable of the descent.

Several moments and a couple of minor rope burns later Kalo let go and dropped smoothly to the bottom alongside the still-flickering torch lying on the stone floor. Lent was next, then Tere, each hoping the same thing; that they had not gone to all this effort only to find themselves at a dead end, nothing more than the bottom of an exceptionally deep pit. Brandishing their torches to illuminate the area, at first it appeared that might be exactly what they had done; but more careful scrutiny revealed another moderately sized tunnel on a steep downgrade.

The tunnel was about seven feet high and half as wide and trailed like an English garden hedge maze or labyrinth with countless crosscuts and switchbacks. All the walls were engraved with letters and numbers and symbols resembling a mixture of ancient Hebrew or Aramaic and computer binary code. The three explorers and sometimes-speleologists tried, but could make no sense of the writings as they moved slowly from one script to the next; and they became so engrossed in the tangle of passageways none of them noticed three very obvious peculiarities.

Here there was no water, the air was cool, the stone surface was cool, and the mineral-rich texture of warmth and subterranean formations were gone. Here the irregular floors, ceilings and walls were all the same; shimmering of feldspar, mica and quartz, a glittering monolith of gray-black granitic stone. Almost bewildered by the passages and puzzle-piece writings, the three stopped and looked around.

Frustrated, shaking his head Lent whispered to Kalo, "This is strange. Got any idea which way we should go?"

"No."

Looking at her, "No. That's it —just no?" She smiled but did not reply so he turned to Tere for her opinion... and that was when he noticed, torchlight reflecting from her face. "Tere, are you okay? You look kinda pale."

* * *

Drenched with perspiration...

...Seana clenched her jaws and pushed. Her hair was wet strings of effort stuck to her forehead, but her blue eyes twinkled with anticipation and she quit shaking, so Nitana and Reed eased up on her thighs expecting the rest of the delivery would proceed more easily. Scooting nearer to her head again Reed took Seana's hand in his; and getting ready, Nitana picked up the blanket and took a step back.

"Focus, Seana," Ames said, ready to receive the newborn in his quarterback stance and waiting hands.

Seana took a deep breath as Reed looked into her eyes and noticed and said, "You feeling okay?"

She shook her head indicating so. "Yes, I feel wonderful. Can you see him?"

Eyes skipping down then back, "Yeah. Sure, I can see him."

"Is he beautiful?"

Reed kind of winced and admitted, "Well, right now he's sorta blue and slimy..."

"—But is he beautiful?" she insisted.

And again, from the birth to her face, Reed assured, "Sure, I guess so." He squeezed her hand lovingly. "Yes, he is beautiful — most beautiful kid ever was."

Seana beamed and inhaled getting ready for her final push. "One more and we will have a son." She smiled with excitement and happiness, almost managed to laugh.

Then...

"You look kinda pale," Reed observed.

From the corner of the room Tian intimated, very softly, "I will be over here... should you need me."

Outside, in the sky,

The sun and moon converged.

The dark shadow of eclipse flowed over the land.

…And somehow, within her Seana felt it; a strange, unworldly sensation, a tingling that made everything look blurry —and panic swept through her.

"Reed… what is happening?" she entreated. Her skin color turned ashen as the tingling flowed within her, growing stronger, more powerful.

Reed's eyes flashed back and forth, from her head to her feet. He knew something was wrong, but he didn't know what.

Amazed, Ames stopped. He wasn't sure he could even touch Seana and the baby anymore. Couldn't feel them. His hands seemed to pass right through the neonate's partially exposed body. Astounded he brought his hands up and away. They did. His hands actually did penetrate Seana's thighs as though both she and the baby were an illusion… a fading illusion.

This isn't real, flashed through Reed's brain. Then he realized, *but— it is real.* Seana and the baby were in fact leaching color and evanescing texture and substance.

Ames stammered, "What the…"

"*—Fuck!*" Reed gasped.

Both stood immobilized with disbelief. This —whatever it was— was simply impossible. But it *was* happening, right in front of them —and reaching out desperately— Ames realized there was nothing they could do. Seana's hand melted from within Reed's. It just drained away like trickling flakes of uncatchable, untouchable wind.

They couldn't stop it —whatever it was— it was happening and they couldn't stop it. Reed watched helplessly as Seana's pleading eyes ebbed from sky blue to gray, then duller, and fading…

"Reed, what is happening to me?" The sound of her words was carried away as she dissolved, fading, evaporating, vanishing, turned to dust… and was gone.

Staring at the empty table, Reed couldn't move. He didn't understand. He couldn't believe it. Only a moment ago she was there. Now she was gone.

Ames turned, his stare sweeping past Nitana to the corner of the room. Tian was gone. His son was gone. His eyes flashed back to Nitana as Reed managed to look up from the table —and she was gone. They were all gone. It was too unbelievable, too incredible—*impossible.*

But it happened. They were there. They saw it.

Then Ames noticed one more thing, minute swirling particles within wisps of filigree wind, precious minutiae dust that drifted ever so slowly... settling. Where each was only a moment before, there now were meager, vapid accumulations of shimmering dust... and the silence of absence.

Another endless minute crawled away before he carefully reached out to the delivery table and touched it with his fingertip, to be certain. Then he looked beside him where Nitana had been, then to the corner where Tian had been. They were gone, and in their place, very small piles, no more than innocuous splotches.

Dust remained... the dust was real.

Staring at empty space, "What happened..." Reed asked, him and Ames looking at each other, his voice wavering, "what just happened?"

"I don't know."

"Well..." uncertainty filling the void, "where did they go?" Ames, still standing where he was, only shook his head. "Where'd they go, Doc?"

Himself disbelieving, "I don't know."

"Hell," Reed stammered, "people don't just disappear —*they don't!*"

Looking around the room again Ames didn't answer; Reed's eyes following his, perhaps expecting to find them —the answer— both perhaps expecting Seana, Tian and Nitana would reappear. But they did not. Except for them and three diminutive piles of glittering dust, the room was empty.

"Well —*fuck!*" Reed slammed a fist on the vacant delivery table. "People—don't—just—disappear! *They don't!*" his confusion turning to anger then winding to a twisted knot. Worried.

"—Don't!" Ames cautioned throwing out an arm with his fingers spread wide. "Don't touch anything." Then more moderately, "We've gotta figure this out." Still studying the room as he surveyed, "Don't touch anything. Just leave everything exactly the way it is and we'll try to figure it out."

Calming down Reed carefully raised and withdrew his hand taking a moment to consider. He knew their must be a logical explanation, some reason, a rational explanation, because, *people do not just disappear.* "Any ideas?"

Still blinking disbelief Ames answered softly, "Just one." He looked at his friend. "Leave everything exactly like it is—and let's go outside—until we figure this out." Slowly, with measured steps both men eased away from the delivery table and silently moved to the door.

But outside,

Things got worse.

It was strangely dark.

Each took a deep breath to unravel frayed nerves, and when they did they noticed immediately, almost a subconscious awareness, but nonetheless singular in its peculiarity. Stagnation. The air tasted different, musty, almost dry, and shriveled or worn-out somehow, like it wasn't clean and refreshing anymore. It tasted like the pause of bad breath between inhale and exhale.

Everything was still. The grass didn't move, the trees didn't sway, and the wind didn't blow. There were no sounds; no birds, no animals, no activity, no life… just a pause. It seemed, felt restless. And it was quiet… too quiet.

They looked around. No one moving about, none of the usual activity, no one on the path, no one doing any of the usual sorts of things that Pilgrims and Renoloi were usually doing. No one standing outside their huts or crouched playing with the children —and no children.

The problem was,

There was no one. No people.

All of them were gone.

Somehow, not only had Seana, Tian and Nitana disappeared; but every single Renoloi and Pilgrim in the entire village had vanished as well. Scattered throughout the huts, near bushes, next to nodes of flowering shrubs, on the path and countless other places, were small, telltale piles of glittering powdery dust.

On the path were traces of dust side by side, where people had apparently been walking together. Along the front edge of a tilted homemade stool was more that bled to the ground. In the doorway of a hut was a pile and another off to one side in the grass. The people were gone, but the dust remained… the dust was real.

And in the shade of a shrouded sun both men finally looked to the sky.

There, near the horizon a blood-red moon casting long deep blue-black shadows of mystery and foreboding looked back at them. In sadness and despair… the eclipse remained.

"This shit isn't real," Reed muttered.

Both just stood for a while, looking around, trying to figure out what had happened, how it happened. Why? But no matter what either hypothesized it still made no sense. There was no logic or rationale that could explain this. This was not just some unusual phenomenon; it was more than that, much more… something beyond their imaginings.

Ames pushed the hair from his face with his fingers then scratched the back of his neck, eyes scanning, voice subdued. "I've gotta think this through."

"Yeah—okay. While you do that, I'm gonna take a look around." Visibly, he was disconcerted, frustrated. Things here were problematic, and that bothered Reed. "Meet you later." And as he started down the path, under his breath, "Curiouser and curiouser my ass, they couldn't all have disappeared."

"Reed—"

"Yeah, Doc," turning around and slowly walking backward.

More moderately, "Don't touch anything."

Offering a jerk for a nod, and a 'thumbs-up' he replied, "We already decided that, remember." Still moving, he turned again, and over a shoulder, "Be back in a while."

"Be careful."

Without looking back: "Later."

Pieces: *the Puzzle*.

CHAPTER FOUR

He sat alone…

…On the high plateau of Legend Mountain. Oftentimes he would come here when he wanted to be alone, needed to think. It was a long way to the valley and village below, so he wasn't often bothered here. But today, being bothered shouldn't be a problem.

Before him the eclipsed sun hid in the clouds, low on the horizon, now no more than a smeared globe of blood-red rimmed with a violet corona that faded within the gloom. Scouring the eerie blend of congealing atmosphere were bizarre streaks of yellow-green light resembling ribbons of fire that rippled and skittered like vapor lightning waves. And the sky was changing, not really sky anymore; something similar to an artistic rendition of an alien world: unworldly primordial soup. It was thickening and pooling like lethargic backwater murk that stirred and descended as undulating fog of dismal obscurity and gray.

Sitting alone on the ground he could discern the bland taste of stale in the air, like musty cardboard decay crawling insidiously into his lungs each time he took a breath. The sensation reminded him of undisturbed damp attic mold that filled his head and stuck in his throat.

All around him anemic florets were withered or wilting. Not only were the rich colors of the valley's plantlife shrouded and tainted within the long blue-black shadows of the eclipse, but they also seemed to be fading away. The grass, trees and plants all drooped, pale and sickly, almost as though their life and beauty were being siphoned from them, drained by a sickness and festering misery. Granted, this transition was occurring more slowly than the people disappeared; but it was happening.

Gorgeous blues and yellows, florid golds and shimmering fluorescents evanescing, the flowers were flagging and withering. One by one their colors were evaporating, their vibrant caricatures and personalities bleeding out, dissolving into the thickening soup-mist that crawled over the valley like creeping pestilence in a fog of plague. Four o'clocks, azaleas, fringed panacea, and others turned pathetic shades of gray as the layers of murk wound finger-holds around them, the exude of seeping smog coercing the passion, vigor and life from them. One by one they were fading and withering to shriveled ravel-flakes like butterfly wings burnt in a fire.

Listless and abandoned, the thatch huts were not the color of golden grass anymore, now bleached to pallid shades of sallow gray. And the ropes that bound them together seemed to be decaying too somehow, because as he watched, on the far edge of the village a roof collapsed causing the hut's walls to cave in. Yesterday what was someone's home was now nothing more than decomposing stalks of moldering, mildew-withered thatch that lay in a heap of squalid crumbling decay.

Darkness was growing stronger; creeping in from somewhere beyond the horizon as it smothered the world with extending tentacles of despondency, dismal gloom and long blue-black shadow. Death and decay were pervasive; around everything, percolating into then through everything, moving with the sickening touch of insidious infection crawling into and festering open wounds.

He sat alone on the high plateau of Legend Mountain trying to figure it out. Before him a world was dying. It was irritating, illogical. In the lackluster murk of mixture-shadows and semidarkness Ames blinked slowly. He was tired. None of it made any sense. Frustration nagged, just behind his ear. Sitting there, all alone on the high plateau of Legend Mountain, his eyes closed, and consciousness slipped away...

...His Dream.

He was alone in the sky, floating lissome and free, cerulean winds and golden flames flowing over him. Cascading, diving and gliding, he soared with the rush of peace in his eyes and a gale through his hair. Below the landscape spiraled with rolling hills decked in emerald and black of bold oaks, hickories and softwoods scattered upon hillsides of fertile dark ground. Above was the shimmer and sparkle of Light, clear as crystal and more powerful than the sun, yet it did not blind him.

And within the Light were the noise and pandemonium of war, the confusion of screams and the cry of battle. Lightning seared like shooting stars with fireball bursts and explosions of red... and the heavens poured rain in drenching whirlwinds of blood.

A voice said:

"Now war arose in heaven, Michael and his angels fighting against the dragon; and the dragon and his angels fought, but they were defeated and there was no longer any place for them in heaven. And the great dragon was thrown down, that ancient serpent, who is called the Devil and Satan, the deceiver of the whole world." [in part] (Rev. 12: 7-9 RSV)

Three great wooden crosses of sacrifice and pain stood on a hill shaded within the eternal eclipse of a fading, dying sun and blood-red moon. And there was a great coliseum and tall throne with a war ax embedded in its backrest. It dripped crimson and tyranny between two silent pillars of stone... where a future was conferred hope.

A voice said:

"And when the dragon saw that he had been thrown down to the earth, he pursued the woman who had borne the male child. But the woman was given the two wings of the great eagle that she might fly from the serpent into the wilderness, to the place where she is to be nourished for a time, and times, and half a time." (Rev. 12: 13-14 RSV)

In a time and place with no name, a great city was lost in hailstorms of fire and brimstone and quake. It lay in the ruin of collapse and smoke drift that trailed away with a cold incessant wind. By the fury of heaven and the breath of the cosmos it was shaken and torn like Babylon. And a statue of bronze stood alone, with a book in his hand... such is man's struggle to persevere, determination that would endure to the very end.

A voice said:

"The serpent poured water like a river out of his mouth after the woman, to sweep her away with the flood. But the earth came to the help of the woman, and the earth opened its mouth and swallowed the river which the dragon had poured from his mouth." (Rev. 12: 15-16 RSV)

On a vast ocean of mystery and green a lost freighter emerged from the past, where the ends of time give birth to the continuum of eternity. There a circular storm spawned in the realm of unknown and the gateway to forever, waited to bind coincidence and design within the pattern of destiny. Then to another place where time and space collide in the jaws of oblivion with the lost fragments that accumulated... and the garbled, distorted underwater sounds of the Green Sea were gone.

Holding her son in her arms, from the corner of the small room Tian intimated, very softly, "I will be over here... should you need me."

A voice said:

"Then the dragon was very angry with the woman, and went off to make war on the rest of her offspring, on those who keep the commandments of God and bear testimony to Jesus. And he stood on the sand of the sea." (Rev. 12: 17 RSV)

Words were getting mixed together, garbled, unintelligible...
"Doc, you okay?"

"...Okay."

"You sure?"

"Yes," Ames mumbled, wondering why he would ask.

Reed eyed him curiously. "You're sure?"

Awareness had recaptured him. "Sure. Why?"

"Well, we've been sitting here talking for ten minutes, at least," Reed explained, "and about half that time you've been going on about some war or something—and the wilderness."

"Just a little preoccupied." No response. "What? I was paying attention."

"Okay, don't get all in a dither; it's just that..." Reed paused considering how best to explain it."

"Just what?"

"Well, I'm not exactly sure what the 'just what' is —or whatever."

"I'm listening."

"Well, it's like you were having two conversations simultaneously; or you were in two different places at the same time," his friend admitted carefully, "and believe me, Doc, we are the only two still here."

"No one?"

Reed shook his head. "No one, anywhere. They're all gone, every bless'ed one of 'em." He picked up a stick, rolling it over his knuckles like a gambler turning a coin. He went on, "After we split up I went to the meeting circle, and what do you 'spose I found there?" rhetorically.

"Little piles of dust."

Sitting, heels together, legs drawn almost to his butt, knees spread apart, "Yeah, no shit."

"Everyone?" Ames asked, uncertainty laced in his voice and threaded with the word.

"Everyone. All of them." A look sideways at his friend, "This bullshit's impossible; we both know that." Serious, he added, "But it sure as hell happened. We both know that too."

"Reality is possessed of many dimensions," Ames murmured.

"What's that supposed to mean?"

Ames blinked twice, admitting, "I don't know, just a thought that came to me."

Reed snorted and *humphed*, a futile grin. Then serious again, "Pretty much when people die, they just die —get sick or tip over dead and shit like that." He looked down and began drawing circles in the dirt with the stick as he grumbled, "Shoot they don't evaporate into teeny little piles of dust."

Ames didn't respond.

Doing circles with one hand Reed's eyes trailed to his friend then out over the shadowed gloom and blue-gray shaded landscape beyond their perch on the rim of the high plateau. "Yeah, this is some weird shit."

"As Alice would say, 'Curiouser and curiouser'," Ames observed.

Clinging to his sense of humor Reed appended, "I assume you're referring to Acid Bitch and Puff Bunny."

Ames managed a grin. "Yeah, whatever."

Mimicking, "Yeah, whatever..." his smile evanesced, fading words that went with the mood; then serious again. "This is strange, Doc."

"I know," a deep breath, "but we'll figure it out. Always do." His words betrayed uncertainty, telling concern. More subdued, "Somehow... we will figure it out." They were friends, more than friends, each willing to lay down his life for the other if need be. And soon... that would happen again.

They quit talking after that, sitting side by side, gazing over a world that seemed little by little to be growing darker and more layered with gloom. This was an unusual problem and neither could fathom how it happened, much less what they could do to make things right. They needed to think this through, so quietly they sat together on the high plateau of Legend Mountain...

...All the while, Reed drew circles in the dirt with the stick.

* * *

An hour later, from behind them...

...A pebble skipped then clattered across the plateau shelf. Not expecting, both spun and were instantly onto their feet as Kalo and Lent approached in the near-darkness. Lent had stubbed his toe spinning a pebble their way.

"You're alive!" Ames spit stepping forward to the young cavers.

"Yes," Lent answered; then snipping his reply short he glanced at Kalo.

She told them. "Something happened to Tere, inside the mountain."

An impromptu guess, "She vanished," Reed said.

Surprised he already knew, "Yes, but how could you know such a thing?"

"We kinda have a situation."

"Situation?" Lent asked.

"Happened here too," Ames told them. "They all disappeared."

Both blinking amazement, "All?"

"Yeah," Reed filled in, "as in all of 'em, everybody, the entire village, the whole kit 'n caboodle. They're all gone. Hell, we thought you guys disappeared too."

Lent remarked, "Well nothing happened to us—that is—Kalo and me."

"Our good fortune," Reed assured facetiously.

Missing the barb, "We are still here, same as you," and as he said it, the question came up.

"Why?" Ames asked.

Reed and Lent together: "Why, what?"

"Why are we still here? What makes us different —more to the point— why didn't we disappear with the others?" Somewhere to begin.

"We're special," Reed suggested, a half-hearted joke.

Ames, 'the frown': "Stick it."

"Granted, not the time. So why are we still here?" Reed wondered. "Why didn't it —the phenomenon— affect us too?"

"We were on Holy Ground," Kalo offered.

Ames looked at her, "So was Tere," then away, "that can't be the reason; and Reed and I were in the village, nowhere near the mountain."

Reed: "In the middle of Seana's delivery. So that's not it."

"Perhaps then because you are different," Kalo proposed.

"Different in what way," Ames asked, "because we are men, human?"

Lent spoke. "The Pilgrims are more like you and Reed than the Renoloi."

Reed: "Agreed; but you are physiologically still hermaphrodites like they are. And Tian and Seana—well Tian at least—should have been more like us than any of you. She's human, has metamorphosed. Maybe Seana hadn't completely changed, but Tian had."

Ames: "So that's probably not the reason either."

Reed looked at Kalo. "The ceremony, the 'White Warrior and Serpent'," referring to the unusual holographic ritual they were present at several months ago, "could this phenomenon in any way be connected to that?"

"I do not know;" shaking her head deliberating, "no one ever understood the ceremony, but certainly no one was ever harmed by it either."

"We don't know that anyone has been harmed," Ames offered, "—not yet anyway."

A crooked eyebrow fixed with a stare, "Okay, we'll all agree with that for now; but whatever's going on may not be doing them a whole lot of good either, Doc."

"Reed…"

"Yeah?"

"However—or whatever—the fact is, the ceremony was some kind of holographic projection that we don't understand, maybe just an illusion," Ames said.

"Maybe," the other granted, "so what's your point?"

"Tian, Seana —all of them— they're real." Reed didn't know what to say; he turned to Kalo and Lent. Kalo was silent.

"Well, I don't know," Lent admitted. "Don't look at me."

Again to Ames: "It's gotta have something to do with the ceremony. The dust is the only connection, even though it doesn't make any sense."

"That's a stretch, so thin it's almost transparent."

Pursing his lips to respond then reconsidering, Reed acquiesced, "Okay, so what do you think? Any ideas?"

"Only one; but first we need to get a few things from the village."

Reed: "The pulse laser?"

"Yes." Then to Lent and Kalo: "Can you show us where Tere disappeared? Can you find that passageway again?"

More than willing, both nodded. "Sure." "Certainly."

Ames took a deep breath. "I have no idea what has happened or what's going on, but somehow we will figure it out... and Legend Mountain is where we begin."

Pieces: *the Puzzle.*

* * *

The muffle of rolling torch-flame...

...And the odor of smoke. Once again they would explore the depths of the enigmatic mountain, searching to discover the secrets that it kept so well concealed within its bosom of darkness and silence.

This time, as before, their torchlight roused the little brown bats from their inverted security of nesting nooks on the cavern ceiling with their peculiar up-side-down view of the world. They rustled to flight with high-pitch click-echoes and sonar ricochet-barks, a whirlwind confusion of small dark faces, pink mouths, puffball bodies and translucent wings cluttering the upper reaches of the caverns, filling the dark empty spaces with their uncanny ability and unparalleled flight. It was peculiar that beneath their roosts there was no accumulated guano, not one single dropping. But focused on other matters, once again, no one noticed that.

Darkness and secrets just beyond the periphery of their torches, the four moved quietly through the passageway of Legend Mountain, retracing earlier steps. Each carried an extra torch and coil of rope over a shoulder. And their weapons.

In the lead, Kalo had her bow and quiver strung across her back. Following, Lent brandished his twibil with its ponderous gleaming twin blades and twelve-inch pike tip. Behind them Ames carried the scimitar in the scabbard sheath diagonally across his back, and Reed pulled up the rear with his right hand gently resting on the pulse laser slung over his shoulder.

Walking softly, nervous, Lent watched overhead. Following four steps behind him Reed whispered past Ames, "They're harmless. Only eat insects."

Lent: "I know that."

Then his lips curled in a grin when Reed added, "Unless… they decide to make a nest in your hair." Lent looked back uneasily and Reed bumped his eyebrows. "If that happens, they usually get all tangled up and can't fly away so they eat through your skull and suck out your brains."

Frowning disapproval Kalo shot Reed 'the look', then turned casually to the front again —but only so he wouldn't see her smile. There were times when even she could appreciate his sense of humor. Scanning the bustling scatter of brown-flutter wind they slowly kept moving.

Shortly—

The four arrived at the mammoth cathedral cavern with the rope bridge spanning the expansive abyss. Kalo's one hundred pounds, even soaking wet, hardly strained the taut ropes enough to notice, and Lent being lean as he was, didn't do much more than bow them a little. More solidly built, and older, Reed and Ames however, were another matter. Being less agile they strained the ropes with a noticeable tension-bow, shimmying and swaying as they crossed the span with unsure, bouncing steps.

With the others waiting for him, Reed, the last to cross, hopped down from the bridge and joined them. "Decent job," he commended. "Pretty good bridge."

"It usually does not sag and sway so much," Kalo observed candidly.

"Too many Twinkies," Ames whispered.

Reed dismissed the remark. "Yeah, yeah," then realizing, "haven't had a Twinkie in a coon's age."

Lent: "What's a Twinkie?"

Reed looked at him. "Oh for pity's sake, nevermind."

Ames to Kalo: "Which way?" She pointed and they continued on.

Arriving at the cavern with the mirror-image stalagmites and stalactites the four silently made their way through the jumble of mineral formations that resembled miniature sentinels standing on the floor and hanging from the ceiling. Respectfully and carefully they avoided the drip-water pools that time and erosion had carved on the floor and kept full to the brim so they overflowed following small depressions creating a patchwork-web of tiny streamlets that knitted them together. In addition to clear mineral-rich water many of the shallow pools were home to blind salamanders and darting cavefish. They were all very small, and very fast. In the flickering light—now you see them, now you don't.

Stepping around a stalagmite and over a small pool Reed remarked in passing, "Wonder how the fish got here?"

In a low voice, "I was wondering about that too," Lent admitted.

"Carnival Cruise Lines," Ames murmured, but only to himself.

They crossed the spacious room to the rope ladder and climbed to the high shelf where Kalo and Lent waited until the men caught up. From the ledge the four took a moment to gaze down upon the beautiful cavern below. Built with the patience of time and a resplendence of fluid color, Nature's handiwork lay before them; turquoise to gold, cerulean to violet, and scarlet to umber, it was an incredible cathedral caressed with beauty, secreted in solitude, and drenched in vivid mineral-watercolor.

Noticing the seven honeycomb passageways leading from the alcove Ames asked, "Which one?" Kalo pointed —the smallest.

Reed, being the stockiest of the group, eyed it deciding, "Well this looks like fun," and as Kalo stooped and began to crawl in he mumbled, "could be interesting."

She stopped, her eyes smiling along with her grin. "Too many Twinkies?" Then turning and scooting into the narrow channel, "Just keep your arms out in front of you. You *should* fit."

"Should?" Reed looked at Lent.

Deadpan, peering from beneath his hair Lent told him, "It's a long way too, impossible to crawl back out," then mischievous, 'the smile' "—and I'm going next, before you, just in case." He scurried in.

Expecting more from Ames, Reed turned but didn't say anything as the other man knelt and peered into the horizontal vent. "What, no wisecrack this time, no zinger?"

Ames looked back and forth between the passageway and his friend, then said, "Nope, not this time." He gently patted Reed on the tummy and grinned. "But I think I'll follow Lent."

As Ames crawled into the crevice Reed muttered, "My friends," and squeezing and wedging followed them in. Tight. It was a rabbit hole of long tunnel, and the shuffling noises of the cavers gradually diminished then faded within the claustrophobically narrow passageway.

Back there, in the mineral cavern behind them, unassumingly melting once more within total blackness, on the floor below the high shelf, colorful sentinels stood quietly and vigilant… in the dark.

Dissolving as ocher and orange—

Flames pushed billows of soot-smoke along the fissure ceiling inches above the hard-breathing sound of scraping feet and wedging arms and elbows; people squirming and weaseling, until, "I can see darkness ahead," Kalo finally announced in a low voice.

Eventually they began squeezing from the rabbit hole into the cavern with the irregular black space in the floor, the vertical vent. Close by, off to one side, a rope tied to a large pillar descended into the chasm, being absorbed by the darkness below.

"The rope is just long enough to reach the bottom," Lent whispered, "three lengths tied together."

Peering over the edge, "Three hundred feet," Ames whistled, "that's a long way down. You made that climb?"

"Had to," Lent said matter-of-fact. "Nothing to eat down there, and I was getting hungry."

"How clever," Reed extolled squeezing from the vent.

Their torches were low, soon would burn out. Without fanfare Ames pulled up the rope, hand-over-hand coiling as he did, then tied his torch to the free end and lowered it again following the flicker as it descended. It touched bottom and gently rolled to one side. Reed joined him.

Looking over the edge they dropped their spare torches down the shaft and again Ames looked at Lent. "And the two of you climbed back up?"

"Yup."

Reed, dry as rye toast, "No elevator," and when Ames snapped a glance he grinned. "You deserved that —and just in case you can't climb back out, I think *I'll* follow Lent."

Down—

Into the dark and unknown, nerves wound tight as the rope and taking half the time that it seemed to, they were at the bottom. After lighting fresh torches before the old one burned out, they were ready again. Lent pulled the twibil from the leg of his khaki cutoffs and Reed shifted the pulse laser from behind his back, to his side by his hip, nearer his right hand.

Kalo and Lent had retraced their path to the moderately sized tunnel, and the maze. The air was cool, there was no water, and the rock was all the same, shimmering with feldspar, mica and quartz; gray-black granitic stone.

Watching ahead, Kalo tread slowly, easing forward as she quietly told them without looking back, "We are close now."

Stepping into the ravel of stone wall passageways that composed the maze, to both men Lent admitted, "The markings are very strange and I don't recognize any of the words. They don't make sense to me, but maybe they will to you."

Ames asked, "What makes you think we'll know what they are?"

Looking back, "I learned to read from comic books, remember." The youth was aware of his meager literacy, only functional at best, and willingly admitted, "I don't understand words and things like these." Like a wisp floating through shadows Kalo listened as they spoke. And they kept walking, slowly.

As the four threaded their way through the stone corridors, very lightly the young warrior drew her fingertips along the walls, tracing, into and over the perfectly chiseled symbols, letters and numbers carved in the stone. She touched the markings, listening, and inside she felt it... very close now, just up ahead.

Following, carefully scrutinizing the walls by torchlight with each step, Reed observed, "Doc, this isn't a single dialect, it's an amalgam. Several languages."

"Yeah, more than fifteen so far."

"'Bout twenty: ancient Hebrew, French, English, Aramaic, Latin, Prussian, and some that I can't even venture a guess."

Ames stopped. "But the interposed numerics and symbols are inconsistent."

"Binary codes —the numbers anyway. The ones and zeroes look like binary configurations, some sort of computer binary code."

Glancing from the wall, "And the symbols and other markings?"

Confused, Reed shook his head admitting, "Never seen anything like them before. They could be hieroglyphics or mathematical links tied to the code... very complex mathematical links. No, this is something new, or *really* old. I've never seen any configuration like this before."

Ames turned, forward again, to Kalo, "How much farther?"

Near where the maze ended ahead, she stopped and looked at the floor. "Here." Lent moved alongside her and together they waited quietly for the men who were half-a-dozen steps behind. As Ames caught up, she told him, "It was here." She pointed, then gestured, *empty hands*. "Tere vanished here."

At their feet was a very small pile of glittering dust. Looking up again she explained, "We were standing here... and she just disappeared." She looked as though she might cry.

Reed lay a gentle hand on her shoulder. "We know," and wrinkling his nose he assured, "we're gonna figure all this out." Lowering his torch he knelt beside Ames, both studying the dust on the floor.

From the dust Ames looked around for a minute or more; then back to his friend. "Any ideas?"

"Just one, let's see where that tunnel leads." With a tip of his head and pushing his torch closer Reed cast more light on it. A narrow passage in the shadows not far from them.

"What tunnel?" then Ames saw it, surprised. "That wasn't there a minute..."

"—Probably just didn't see it in the dark."

All four, being careful, mindfully stepped over the meager mound of dust, Ames leading the way, walking the downward slope of the narrow corridor until it made a sharp right turn and came to an end at a solid stone wall. An oubliette.

"Dead end," Reed said.

From behind him, "No," Kalo intimated.

Turning, Reed looked at her. "It's solid rock."

She stepped forward.

Inside, she felt it... and gingerly running her fingers over the wall the young warrior moved closer as the others stepped back. Caressing it, her forehead and breasts almost touching it, she searched fastidiously probing with fingers and palms and an inner sense of awareness... until she found it.

They watched silently as Kalo knelt and repeatedly traced curious hidden markings with her fingers, delicately wiping dust and granules away, revealing them, gradually clearing tightly packed particles that had completely filled and perfectly concealed the symbol in the stone wall...

$$A/\Omega$$

"Spoo-ky," Lent whispered.

Not looking back Kalo placed a hand on either side of the symbol, and in deference, introspectively closed her eyes... being drawn away.

Almost imperceptibly at first the granite began to lighten then radiate and shimmer, then glow more brightly until before them words became visible... words chiseled in stone and inlaid with gold.

Fascinated they watched, and waited. Eyes closed, Kalo went deeper within, and captured, they listened as she began murmuring softly reciting words; and as Kalo spoke...

...From far away, Tian's voice said:

> *Three Wise Men watch when the flock returns,*
> *Where a vortex myth... and dark fires burn.*
> *When two warriors stand with a cloistered sun,*
> *In a war without end, never lost, never won.*
>
> *There the hourglass stops with an endless wind,*
> *Where yesterday waits... and tomorrow's been.*
> *And the power of light crosses darkened skies,*
> *Before it enters a bridge infused with sin and lies.*
>
> *For destiny lies on the sand and plain,*
> *In a place that was... should it be again.*
> *There a turbid sea will flow in red,*
> *Until the final song harvests lost and dead.*
>
> *In the fabric of time laced within the eye,*
> *Heralds of prophecy... they forever ride.*
> *To save a world that is flawed in a place that is sorrow,*
> *Wielding the winds of eternity on the wings of tomorrow...*
>
> *...Time Warriors.*

Lent whispered, "Whoa, *re-eal* spooky."

Reed: "How did you do that—Tian's voice? What... does it mean?"

Without looking back, still on her knees, Kalo didn't answer; her eyes still closed... then drawn farther and deeper.

Kneeling reverently, placing her palms together, she raised her arms above her head, then apart to either side in wide sweeping arcs, then down to her sides. Then together again, as if to pray. Before her the words of the 'Time Warrior Prophecy' glowed brighter, intensifying to alabaster light —then burst into flames— a scintillating scattering fire glimmering with pinpoint quasars and pulsars and whirling white winds.

Kalo was deeply absorbed, entranced, arms before her, trembling.

Reaching out, Reed whispered, "Kalo..."

Grabbing his arm Ames stopped him. "—Don't touch her!"

Withdrawing Reed watched as the mysterious fire spread quickly over the wall of the oubliette, the granite luminescing with the expanding ring of shimmering flames, until the stone seemed to dissolve revealing another passageway that led deeper into the mountain. Then quickly, like a splendid vanishing zephyr the ring of sparkling fire swept the outer rim of the entryway one final time as it diminished with glimmering fading embers that whirled and evaporated as evanescent delicate sparkling light, then completely burned out.

Darkness and shadows returned. Kalo remained on her knees, the others behind her. Silence.

Finally, "Well I'll be, I've never seen anything like that before," Lent confessed in a whisper.

Reed, under his breath: "It's not a dead end."

Opening her eyes Kalo turned and revealed, "It is a beginning."

* * *

They entered the mysterious passageway...

...A narrow vein of tunnel that meandered for miles; and as they proceeded, not far behind, in the darkness something followed, not a shape really, just a slinking flow of movement, a black, amorphous slithering motion. Appearing then vanishing, it slipped from one place to another, stopping frequently, being absorbed in the dark,

keeping the interval, laying back. For some time they kept moving…
and it kept following.

It was quiet in the passageway. Too quiet.

At length, with dwindling torches, far ahead they detected soft
light; very faint, a sea-blue glow, and finally opening the fissure
splayed at the entrance of a mammoth luminous cave of blue-green
light. Around them the cavern walls rippled with undulating flows
of liquid motion that teemed with life. Within the blue-green texture
of sinuous liquid movement floated wave after wave of small aquatic
creatures: shrimp, minnows, jellyfish, squid, anemones, starfish, an
unending medley of sea creatures. Above them, underfoot and to
all sides within the glimmering walls, iridescent, luminescent life
leisurely flowed as an endless slow-moving blend.

Stepping quietly, filled with wonder they moved into the incredible
cavern gazing upon the spectacle of motion and life gliding gently
about them. It was a kaleidoscope of watery primordial and marine
life that flowed and glimmered, translucent sea creatures whirling
and blending to clouds of synchronous cascade, an illusory realm of
myriad sea life of the deep scattering layer. Unhurried, swimming
all around them.

"Unbelievable," Ames whispered.

Reed: "Yeah, that's putting it mildly."

"Ouch—" almost spent, Lent's torch burned his hand and he
dropped it. The floor's surface resembled water but was not, and
when the torch landed there was no sound—no thud, no splash.
Stooping to pick his torch up, the strange surface glowed intensely,
and curious, Lent put his hand, fingers-spread-wide, on the surface. It
radiated vivid light and he quickly withdrew; but the glow remained
defining perfectly where he had touched it.

Looking around, "Heat-sensitive?" Reed speculated, wondering.
Puzzled, Kalo looked at him, so he explained, "Our body heat may
be causing the cavern to luminesce, phosphoresce, whatever."

"I do not understand," she told him.

"We're warm-blooded, we give off energy; or it could be some
chemical or magnetic phenomenon we emanate generating the

light. Could also be neuro-magnetic electrical impulses, sorta like energizing the ballast of a fluorescent light tube." She still didn't understand.

"Unbelievable," Ames whispered.

"Yeah," Reed agreed, his green eyes twinkling, reflecting the misty light.

As the four marveled at the cavern surrounding them —peripheral vision, Lent saw it— a flash of black to his left that swept around and behind them in a contrast of dark shadow-wind against the sea-green backdrop. It moved so quickly he wasn't even sure but believed he'd seen it, enough so he reeled trying to find it.

"What was that?"

"What was what?" Ames asked as he and Reed turned.

From Lent's right, "I saw it also," Kalo told them.

Searching, "It was like a shadow, but had a shape."

Reed asked, "What did it look like?"

Shaking his head he admitted, "I don't know… a cape or hooded cloak. We were all sorta looking that way and it went across over there," indicating with a hand, "then disappeared behind us," completing his turn, still watching. For a minute all of them looked; but it had vanished.

Nothing there. Whatever it was, now it was gone.

Captivating—

The dazzling beauty of the cavern quickly preoccupied them again pushing thoughts of the unidentified movement aside, and they soon forgot about it. To the matter at hand, trying to learn what they could of this unexplainable cavern the cavers separated, fascinated with its beauty, investigating, taking in this unusual mimicry of waterworld phenomenon.

Stalagmites and stalactites grew and expanded as they rose from the floor or descended from the ceiling, then withdrew and contracted with sinuous liquid-like motion resembling living blue-green whirlpools taking a breath. Flowing pillars swelled three or four times in size then shrank to wound shafts of spiraling strands and enigma. Finger-like spires ascended in tethered twisting veins then opened like grasping, blossoming anemones offering swaying fingerling strands. They seemed to float placidly momentarily, then like startled sea creatures would suddenly shrink again, curling as tightly as butterfly proboscises, withdrawing and disappearing within the design of the floor.

All around them was unusual motion and iridescent living creatures; a sea that was not a sea imbued in beautiful phosphorescence of blue and green waves and surreal texture that constantly moved… and always changed.

Walking alone near the far end of the main cathedral Kalo found an opening that led from the cavern, so she called to the others. Once together again they headed into the corridor that gradually funneled to a narrow passageway, and after a time ended abruptly at a stairhead atop a spiraling staircase that descended, leading farther into the mountain.

Slowly and quietly the four began going down: Ames, Reed, Kalo, then Lent. At first the walls of the cramped stairway were vivid blue-green like the cavern; but with each descending ellipse their luminescence paled and the light gradually dimmed, waning as the explorers went down.

Descending—

The walls were now no more than faint silhouettes, barely outlines alongside them. Fading, almost entirely gone. At length only the steps themselves remained visible, the encompassing walls providing a sense of security now ostensibly having melted away.

Still going down—

Peering around Ames, Reed could see the seemingly endless oblong spiral of steps, shimmering blue-green and unfurling below; almost beckoning, leading them. The winding staircase appeared to go on to a vanishing point somewhere beyond the limit of vision.

"Long way down," he whispered over his friend's shoulder.

Nervous, concentrating, not looking back: "I noticed."

Although they could feel the walls on either side they could no longer see them. Now around them there was only darkness, with a luminescent trail of stairs spiraling steeply before them; still going down, leading to somewhere unknown. Their descent created the sensation of walking down a tightrope with nothing to hold on to, nothing to keep them from falling off on either side. Ames kept telling himself, *the walls are there, I can feel them;* but he couldn't see them. It all seemed like nothing more than empty darkness.

Behind them—

On the stairway above, concealed within the enfolding darkness the shape moved then stopped, just a fleeting image of motion that was there then wasn't, maintaining the interval... watching.

Forty steps above and behind them narrow, bloodshot liver-red eyes observed... and from within the hooded cloak dingy-gray rotted teeth drooled saliva laced with loathing and crimson. Staring from the darkness it glowered; and lecherously the shadow of malevolence followed.

Below—

Uncertainty kept them alert. The explorers moved cautiously as they descended. Unsteady, each footstep treading lightly and carefully, not knowing where the spiraling staircase would lead. The sensation of, *height,* was almost overwhelming, like standing on the edge at the top of a skyscraper and looking over. One step at a time.

Back there—

Not so difficult, vulnerable, easy prey. It moved downward again —quickly— then gone.

On the glowing staircase—

Following Reed, with Lent behind her, Kalo sensed it; something was wrong. She felt an inner stirring of awareness, that sixth sense of premonition; and quietly the young warrior closed her eyes, searching for whatever it was. The Mountain was not safe anymore. Something was there... and *it* was coming.

Shaky, Ames tried to keep his balance, each step like descending a very steep staircase with no handrail. It was unnerving. Now all that was visible was the glimmering trail of stairsteps, a footpath taking them down into the unknown of Legend Mountain. Their last torch burned out some time ago and now all they could see was a telltale winding stairway coiling above and beneath them with empty darkness around them. Very cautiously he took another step, and from somewhere in that darkness the walls whispered, *no farther... Beware.*

Hair on the back of his neck stood on end as he turned looking at Reed whose wide eyes revealed he heard the voice too.

Inside, Kalo felt it —and reeling— grabbing Lent by the arm with extraordinary strength she screamed, "Look out!"

From above —*the rush*— black as darkness itself and cloaked with malicious intent it swept toward them as a frigid wind of shadow-phantom. No more than a fleeting image of speed with the force of cause and effect the phantasm rushed upon them focused on Lent.

Glaring from narrow, bloodshot liver-red eyes it flew like a gust of whirling evil and menace with dingy, rotted teeth as an arm emerged from the loose-fitting sleeve of the cloak. Coming, the withered extended arm rose above the hood and a black timeworn hand with fingernail claws clutching a scythe appeared, ready to strike, to slice off his head...

—Behind him, the dark shadow drawing back,

—Below him, Kalo pulling him forward and down,

Instinctively, during that split second of awareness Lent sensed danger and ducked shielding both himself and Kalo with the twibil's ponderous blade. Turning, both Reed and Ames spun, Reed's hand on the pulse laser, on its way up. In the confusion Kalo and Lent fell onto the men, all of them staggering...

—Beginning to tumble, then falling,

—Hard, onto the staircase, going down,

Kalo still hanging onto Lent's arm and being lost in the crush as Lent, still brandishing the twibil, using it as a shield, toppled over her...

—When he saw it,

—A wave of pitch-black,

Motion rushing over him, only inches above him, narrow liver-red eyes and a wretched, crooked black mouth; then darkness and wind. From around the shadow-phantom there was a glimmer of steel —*a blade*— his ax already there when he heard the resonant, sharp

—*brring*— then blinding shatter-bright sparks of metallic collision, the razor edges slamming and careening ringing out through the dark. He felt the steel edge slicing his flesh, the sudden sparkflash startling and blinding him; then falling with Kalo beneath him, black wind above him...

—Sweeping, moving incredibly fast,

—A shrill whine and white flash,

Reed squeezed the trigger, but the ebony apparition vanished as the pulse laser screamed with streaking power and stunning white light —instantly blinded— white-splash and scattering little dots that snatched his vision away. It was night blindness and pitch-dark wrapped in the commotion of sliding and falling with echoing noise in his head...

—All of them going down,

—Another whine, and distant blast,

Then from somewhere in the darkness and confusion came ricochets of shattering stone scattered in an explosion, instantly followed by a tearing then cracking and crumbling sound as the four people toppled over one another going down the spiraling stairway— bumping, hitting, sliding and slamming into each other. All mixed up, one on top of the other—shoulders, arms and legs hitting hard and soft things as they went...

—Pitch black, night-blind,

—Scattering white spots,

There was a deep rumble and more breaking noise, and the wrenching, grating sound of tearing then fracturing stone...

—A glimpse up,

—The top of the stairs,

Far above, the shattered luminous staircase was coming apart and crumbling, steps toppling away, plummeting into the surrounding abyss. It was all falling, coming down at them; their skidding menagerie of bodies still tumbling over one another...

—Darkness and vertigo,

—Nothing below,

Beneath them the security and structure of the walkway vanished as it too collapsed and they felt the rush of wrecking force speeding downward from above, then past and beyond them. Rattling vibrations rising from below, quaking, all of it coming apart...

—All of it crumbling then dropping,

—They were tumbling and falling,

Suddenly there were beautiful colors around them, wave upon wave of yellow and gold, then orange and red. They were plummeting, free-falling through spiraling nebulous auroras and clusters of stars...

—Over and over,

—All the beautiful colors,

Magnificent winds of starlight wrapping around them, enfolding them, absorbing hues: reds spiraling to azure and cobalt and violet, then darker and deeper...

—Still falling, going down,

—Falling,

Another glimpse: the spiral chain of interconnected stairs disintegrating above and below, all around them, everything cascading then disappearing down there in the dark...

—They were falling,

—All of them. All of it.

And in a tumble of —*rush*— the blue-green was slipping away, the staircase disappearing far, far below, one stone at a time, then vanishing completely as the four went down, tangled and confused...

—Still tumbling,

—Darkness and nothing. A void.

Turning over, still falling, rolling and bumping into one another, falling; whirling winds, not able to see...

—Going down. Confusion everywhere,

—And still falling to somewhere far, far below,

　　　　　...Into the darkness.

CHAPTER FIVE

Brown water and muck…

…The fetid taste of decay; all around them was quagmire sludge and a putrid, rank swamp. Congealed waves of floating duckweed petals and pond scum pushed aside when, one at a time they sat up in the knee-deep water, taking a breath after the splash. Skin slimy, hair slick with viscous globs, the four wiped their faces and looked around, butts in the mud and mired to their chests.

Near-darkness.

Overhead the sky was lackluster soup of thickened atmosphere that resembled pan-burnt crusted leftovers in a sink of day-old-dirty, cold, dead suds. Not really sky anymore, it seemed more like something else; but in the dusky shadows it was hard to say what. The layered stratum moved in listless waves that mingled blending charcoal and dun with tawny and deep mahogany brown; but not like clouds, it sifted back and forth undulating as it flowed and wound like vapor snakes crossing a pond. Petulant, not seeming to go anywhere it lethargically stirred and percolated, spanning horizon to horizon as near as they could tell; but in the dim light they couldn't be sure.

The only light came from just above the horizon, a smeared globe of murky violet with an eerie flaming corona that oozed out and drained over the landscape creating long blue-black shadows of gloom, decay, and despair. Companions, both were still there in the sky, a hidden, diminished sun almost absorbed within the eclipse of the blood-red moon cascading a fire-lace aurora that fanned out wine-colored to violet, bleeding dark red in a despondent atmosphere.

Unworldly and ominous the eclipse appeared to fashion circular wings burning a hole through the sky, as though drawing in and draining a world through its core.

Tainted, the water they sat in smelled of decay, the offensive damp of a rotten-carcass lake covered with broken mats of pallid green or dead-black duckweed clusters. Lifeless weeds and rancid bent-over grass floated flat like tangled slimy tresses; and here and there were scattered flotsam clumps of green and black decomposed thatch resembling thick strands of horsehair or unraveled rope that swayed indolently when waves quietly pushed past.

Protruding randomly throughout this endless spoiled lake were shallow rises of landfall resembling small scattered mud islands where twisted bare trees stood askew in aberrant groves like wretched cadavers with bent arms and broken hands dangling crooked tortured fingers that silently scratched fog goblins in the mist. Mold and lichen nourished by the swamp partially concealed the trees, creeping up their trunks beneath pendents of still, hanging matted strings like Spanish moss dripping brown water back to the swamp. All of it was shrouded in a dismal gray flow of fog that stole over the surface crawling in wisps of incessant exuding motion as it stirred, rose and wound, then congealed and sank ever so slowly again.

Looking around Reed found Kalo sitting in water up to her neck, combing out her hair with her fingers and Lent was plopped down just beyond her, his face and head covered with mud. Spitting duckweed petals, "What happened," he wondered, "where are we?"

Taking stock of their surroundings, Ames quietly answered, "Don't know," not looking back. Not too far apart, they were in an awful smelling swamp, drenched with dirty water and speckled with petals of dying duckweed; all covered with mud.

From behind them Lent almost hollered, "Where are we?"

Volume-startled Ames and Reed looked at one another, and squirming to turn, Reed said, "You deaf? Didn't you hear what he just said?" Then, very plainly, "We—don't—know."

To Reed, "What?" trying to read his lips as he dug in his ear with a finger. "Got mud in my ears." When he said it and opened his mouth his teeth almost shined compared to the mottled color of his face, skin and shirt. Not bothering to repeat himself, Reed shrugged waiting until Lent leaned over and bopped himself alongside the head, looked up smiling, and then more moderately said, "There, now I can hear you."

"I wonder about you sometimes, I really do," as he turned mumbling, "...twit." When he looked back Ames was smiling. "What's the smirk for?"

"Just sounds sorta familiar."

Rather than respond Reed looked back at Lent. "Next time you get mud in your ears..." then he noticed, "—shit kid, you're bleeding."

Lent gave the wound on his upper right arm a cursory once-over as Kalo sloshed forward. "It's not that bad; just a scratch. It'll stop bleeding pretty soon with the mud packed in it."

"Save the John Wayne routine," Reed chewed warning, "ever heard of sepsis?"

"No."

"Figures—not in comics."

Examining his right arm and shoulder and visibly worried, Kalo scolded mildly, "It is bad. Can you not smell the infection around us?"

"Smell the infection. How can you smell...?"

But he didn't have time to finish before she interrupted, pulling her leather top over her head, talking through her shirt, "I will bandage it." And the top came off exposing her chest. Lent hadn't really noticed before; but now, sitting so close, he couldn't help it. She had full, smooth, beautifully rounded breasts with perfect small nipples; and even covered with mud she was an eyeful, definitely blossoming —and Lent's jaw dropped when he saw them.

Reed immediately caught what Kalo's innocence missed and he snatched his own shirt over his head. "No—here Kalo—use mine." Still holding hers and gathering it to her chest, she accepted his offer as more softly and slower he said, "Put yours back on." Smiling with the excuse, he explained, "Mine's a lot bigger. I'll just cut some off the bottom; that'll be plenty." Amenably she slipped her top back on and waited while Reed sliced several inches from the bottom of his shirt with his knife, cut it through once to make a long strip and tossed it to her. Pleasantly, her gracious, *thank you*, was her smile.

Lent never said a word, and didn't close his mouth.

Unassumingly Kalo pushed dead weeds and crud aside with her hands, then cupped them and washed the mud and blood from his wound. She was so methodical and careful bandaging his arm that she didn't notice Reed and Ames exchange suggestive glances while she wasn't looking. Reed's expression detailed surprise, almost flabbergasted; but Ames' was more of a grin, because he knew in spite of his crass exterior, Reed was her friend.

Kalo was still wrapping the wound when Lent's stare finally weaseled loose from 'those bumps' and drifted to Ames as he finally managed to ask, "Where are we?"

"Don't know."

Reed: "Well, we're not in Kansas anymore, Toto," —but Lent didn't get it.

"Who's Toto?"

Swishing the laser muzzle through the murky water Reed just ignored him, washing off some crud.

Mildly Ames considered, suggesting, "It would appear we're not inside the mountain anymore either," then, "so, what's the last thing anyone remembers?"

Reed, offhand: "Kalo getting squashed and all of us falling." Ames nodded. Then to Kalo, but she avoided suggesting anything, instead looking back at the dressing and pretending to be busy. By now though it was securely tied, so she sort of fluffed it, evading.

Ames looked at Lent who seemed uncertain, thinking it over. He answered slowly. "Something dark, like a cloud —but with a shape, like a person. I felt it coming just as Kalo grabbed my arm and jerked me down."

Almost a whisper, "You felt it?" her eyes meeting his when his head turned.

"Yeah," surprised she should ask, "like when you feel there is someone behind you —*and someone is.*" Studying his eyes Kalo offered an almost imperceptible nod, but said nothing more.

Not noticing, Ames asked, "What else?"

Again to Ames: "The blade —some kind of weapon— but I'm not sure exactly what it was."

"Can you describe it?" Reed asked.

Concentrating, Lent answered, "A long handle —wood— and a long thin blade —curved— yeah, curved on the end."

Ames didn't say anything, but Reed muttered, "Crap, I knew it."

"What?" Lent asked spontaneously.

Ames: "Nothing."

Reed fixed him with a stare. Their eyes locked. "You know frickin'-a-well he's describing a scythe —and I saw it too."

"Yeah, yeah," putting up a hand, gesturing dismissal, "and the Bermuda Triangle is real," he countered facetiously, mocking him.

"It was a scythe, and I saw it too."

"You think?"

"I know what I saw."

"Really," an invective.

Reed, disgusted: "Yes, really—and just maybe if you'd quit being so—so condescending and stubborn about it. And *maybe*, if you'd be just a little more open-minded..." he was almost angry, "then maybe we might be able to figure out what *the—fuck* is going on."

"That stuff's make-believe," Ames argued.

"Well, you got any better ideas?"

Frustrated, the other admitted, "No I don't," then taking a breath, more moderately, "no, I don't," and thinking, "I just don't know." With that Ames looked at Kalo, who'd been listening, passively looking back at him. "You saved Lent's life," he told her. "You knew it was there, it was coming, and you saved his life."

"I suspected."

Unconvinced, "Really?"

Blinking surprise, "That true?" Lent asked. "I thought you saw it behind..."

"It was pitch dark, Lent," Reed interrupted, also just realizing the implication, "not even a bat can actually see in the dark. Whatever it was, how could she see it?"

"I never thought of that," he admitted; and to Kalo, "you couldn't have seen it." But he didn't know what else to say, so after a pause beneath a mop-full of mud he simply settled for, "Thank you."

Silent, Kalo just nodded.

Planting both feet Reed said, "Well I don't know, but unless somebody's got a better idea, let's get going."

All of them getting up, "Where to?" Ames asked.

"Beats the shit out'a me, but I can't see sitting here all day." In no particular hurry they began wallowing in the most convenient direction, and after sloshing a few soggy steps a thought occurred to Reed. "Shoot, if this is the day, I sure ain't looking forward to nightfall. That should be a real treat."

With that thought in mind they headed out across an endless, unimaginable swamp.

*　*　*

Some time later...

...The four vagrants had no idea how long they'd been wandering when they heard noise in the distance, an unwelcome noise, one that stirred recollections of danger and dread. In the gloom and fog the broken sounds of murky water and mudsplash seemed to come from a long way off, but they couldn't be sure. They all hoped so.

Down, Ames signaled with a hand—an opened palm, *stay still.* Stock-still, stopping and listening they waited as the buoyant push of ever-expanding swamp water riffles eased past slipping into the fog.

—Then a roar.

Closer now, cumbersome wave-crashing steps punching holes in the bottom from somewhere out there in the almost-dark and slime, and cracking noises of dying twisted trees being knocked down and crushed. Underwater vibrations buffeted as opaque waves caused by enormous mud-sloshing steps buoyed them.

—Another roar. Strange howls.

Much louder now, too close, a bellow less than thirty yards away. Something huge was out there... and something else. There were creatures roaming the blended gloom of gray-brown smog and duckweed-muck, danger they couldn't see.

Submerged to their chins within the camouflage of dismal, long blue-black shadows and coalescence of grays, the four crouched silently listening to the unseen creatures' roars as they sliced poignantly through the dense shroud of fog. It sounded like something was being heckled and harried, presumably being attacked by something else; perhaps more than one animal. Guttural then savage growls slicing through the fog were interrupted, then piercing roars, all of them distorted within splashes of rushing footfalls and sloshes of ruthless attack. Shrieking yowls of untamed viciousness were choked and cut short, overpowered by boiling sloshes and burbling snarls like something going under, until sudden explosive spray betrayed continuing violent conflict soaked with splatter and mud.

Listening they could almost tell when an animal was bitten and wounded. There was the aggressive, agitated sound of frothing water thickened with the blend of mud. Next, the rush of foam and floundering momentum of unseen animals maneuvering and charging one another through the mire. Then, the briefest pause when fangs sank in flesh with the wave catching up and sloshing over the beasts. And last, the painfilled sudden-scream and thrashing furor of biting back in counterattack.

Laying a hand on Ames' shoulder Lent whispered, "Too close," garnering Reed and Kalo's attention as well. Stirred water pushing past, with a tip of his head he indicated, *this way.*

Not a sound, four bobbing heads, they eased through the quagmire away from the struggle being careful not to disturb the surface; little more than muted, *glucks,* or a, *gurgle,* almost oozing along with them. One after another they silently slipped away, putting more distance between themselves and whatever was fighting in the swamp, somewhere in the dim gray shroud where they could not see.

More than an hour—

They continued, half-floating, half-crawling, until finally the noise sounded like it was a mile or more behind them. Peering into the gloom and placing her hand into the water as she crawled, Kalo abruptly stopped. Statuesque and quiet as dust she looked down at the water.

"Snake." A quiet alarm, so the others would know. She stared at the water's surface only inches below her chin as the submerged creature slithered beneath her, then headed in Reed's direction.

Near her he went ignition dead-stall, holding his breath as the murky ripple traveled between them. "Yeah, no shit," he whispered nervously, eyes following as the v-wave tracked like a drunken crow flies, weaving back and forth, then directly under him. As the snake swam between his arms and legs, he breathed—*big honkin' snake.*

He froze. Ignition off.

Eyes locked on —and *not* moving— "Sucker's sliding against my thigh," very slowly turning his head watching the wave as it finally moved behind planing to his left, then beyond him. Oozing relief and sweat he managed a sideways glance as the snake swam along the back of Ames' butt. Ames stopped and held his breath, then watched as it kept going in Lent's direction. Lent was a bit farther back and to Ames' left.

When Lent saw it coming he tweaked the feeble complaint, "Piffles, I hate snakes."

Amused, Reed started snickering then spit-sputtered a trifling snort as they all followed the wake with their eyes, floating duckweed clutter and dead grass pushing aside as it swam.

"'Spose it's poisonous?" Lent worried, hoping it wasn't.

Reed: "Heck yeah, probably is; more likely than not it's prehistoric poisonous."

"Ah crap, you're a big help."

"Good thing they don't strike underwater," Ames commented rallying false optimism.

"Bad news, Doc," watching as the snake approached Lent, Reed went on, "well actually, I guess it's worse news for him than you; but that's just an old wives' tale—proven to be completely false. They do strike underwater."

Lent: "Ah shit."

Ames: "By whom?"

"A whole bunch of dead people. Quite a few snakebites were documented while they were submerged." Reed grinned mischievously, the rascal grin.

"Oh…" slowly turning so as not to disturb the water, Ames said, "that's nice to know; 'specially now."

Lent: "Double shit."

Again, Ames encouraged, "But I'm sure those were only rare exceptions."

Pants-wetting nervous Lent was already tracking the snake's backwash, his eyes moving slowly, and absolutely nothing else. It came directly for him, swam under him weaving between his arms and leisurely slipped between his legs rubbing against them; then it eased on out from under his butt. He shuddered and managed an edgy grin and, "*Whew,* that was close," relieved as he looked up again.

Ames: "Just be still, Lent," looking on as the unwelcome caller began doubling back.

Reed was watching too, but was less worried than Lent, because the snake was by him. Whispering, "Actually Doc, underwater strikes were a lot more common than most people realized." A meandering torpedo, the v-wave approached Lent from the side, went under again, then around to the front. "In Southeast Asia, for example, people got bitten by banded kraits all the time. I think they called them 'Two-steps' —'cause if one bit you, you only made it a couple of steps— then, dead meat."

"You're being *re-eal* helpful, Reed," Ames assured blandly.

Buoying gently duckweed and dead grass plied aside as the snake swam between Lent's arms again, then out from under him. After that it turned casually circling off to the side. "And in southern Africa," Reed went on, "several hundred people were killed every year by black mambas…"

"—Shut up!" Lent snapped not moving a muscle, the mud on his face melting and running with his sweat.

The situation was tantalizing. "What —I was just trying to be helpful— was it something I said?" Reed teased as the snake went under him again. Nervous as a treed 'coon with the quivering wobbles, on his hands and knees Lent could only glare.

Grinning egregiously and taunting some more, Reed asked, "Don't know if you should shit or go blind, huh?" Lent didn't say a word so he started in again. "'Course in the South American rain forests you had your Anacondas. Well, I guess they weren't really deadly poisonous or anything," slowly rising up on his knees and lacing his fingers, wringing his hands, "They'd just coil around you and choke the livin' shit out'a you and crush you till your bones were pulverized and your eyes popped out." Then pretending to think about it, "And there was the Inland Taipan or Fierce Snake, from central Australia —number one most poisonous— they'd sure kill you dead as a mackerel all right. But truth is," he interjected reassuringly, "we don't actually know if your snake there is even poisonous," willingly delegating ownership to him. "Shucks, Lent, that one of yours might just be medium-poisonous; no way to be sure 'less it bites you. So, all things considered, I guess this isn't really such a big deal." The snake was circling around him.

"My snake—since when is it my snake?"

"Well it seems sorta fond of you so…"

"Reed…" Kalo whispered without moving; but he didn't hear her because he was still tormenting Lent and generally making him a completely nervous wreck. "Ree—ed."

He heard her that time, and casually, almost playfully glanced at her. "Yeah, kid?"

She tipped her head, indicating, "You may want to watch this other one —your snake— and stop pestering Lent."

Following her eyes he saw it, a second snake swimming on the surface as it pushed through the mire heading straight for him. "Aww—*shit*," shooting a glance to Ames, "this just really sucks. Let's get out of here," looking around, "that rise—that 'sort-of' island over there. Let's make a run for it." The second snake was almost to him, closing fast. The first was surface-swimming, planing now, still circling Lent.

Looking back and forth to make sure they all agreed Ames asked, "Everybody ready?"

"Ready, you kidding? If we don't do something pretty soon..." Lent began.

"Let's all get up *re-eal* slow," Ames suggested.

And as they did, "...I'm gonna pee my pants," Lent finished.

Serious now, "Oh man, don't do that," Reed said, "they're attracted to heat. It'll be all over you."

"Shut—up!"

A forced whisper, "Go for it—" Ames sounded.

Heaving water, he and Kalo high-stepped and ran as Lent and Reed both jumped —Olympic broad jump contender wannabes— over the snakes. And in less time than it would take to say it, and with more flailing arms, hopping feet and kicked-up mud than could possibly describe it, all of them were out of the water on the shallow rise dripping like tadpoles.

Catching their breath after the sprint all four immediately crouched, silent again except for dripping puddles and their heavy breathing. Scanning, they knew noise attracted predators, worried that the commotion may have drawn the attention of something.

They watched. Nothing moving. As sloshing water settled and sounds evaporated in the mist with the rest of the empty silence and gloom, everything seemed all right. It was quiet again in this transcendental netherworld... for the time being.

"*Whew,* made it," Lent murmured with a nervous shudder.

Kalo readjusted her bow across her back while Reed wiped a daub of mud from the pulse laser muzzle as he surveyed. Noticing it, blasé he reached over and took hold of a churlish, strapping-big leech that had attached to her shoulder. It was a chunker all right; black and squat as it was stubborn, and leather-tough, a portly sucker. With dogged pressure he twisted firmly pulling it off; a nonchalant toss and, *kerplunk,* back into the swamp.

Casually, "Leeches; better check each other."

"Are they poisonous?" Lent asked.

"No," Ames assured setting his mind at ease.

"You're just no fun, Doc," Reed groused. They all got up giving each other the once-over, and as they did Reed commented, "Wonder if they're edible."

Ames: "Don't mention food," checking Lent and tugging at one.

Lent: "They're nasty," checking Ames.

And Reed: "Ah, they're not so bad," plucking another from the back of Kalo's neck, "a lot of cultures used them for medicinal purposes —but I 'spose if you cooked 'em they'd pop."

They traded partners.

As Reed finished checking him, Lent admitted, "I really don't know much about leeches."

"Really?" With that tidbit Reed grinned, and knowingly, almost bragging like an 'old salt' said, "Well leeches aren't that bad. Now microbes on the other hand, that's what'cha gotta worry about. Watch out for them."

"Microbes?"

"Yep. They're teeny microscopic little bugs and shit that you can't even see, and they'll crawl up your parts —your weenie and such, you know— and they set up shop. Then you've really got problems."

"No kidding?"

Ames: "Let's go."

Regrouping Reed picked up the pulse laser. "Terrible shit," he said with an emphatic sigh, then went on nonchalantly, "but leeches aren't really a problem. Nothing much for a guy to worry about..." and as he got ready to move out, nudging Lent with an elbow he confided just above a whisper, "unless a'course, one gets up your butt." He had his attention.

Worried, "What happens if one gets up your butt?"

"It'll suck out your brains." Lent was dumbstruck, and without further ado, straight-faced Reed casually changed the subject. "Come-on, let's go figure out where we are and what's going on." Easing into the swamp he was on his way.

Lent looked at Ames, but the man never flinched, and deadpan, bumping his eyebrows he followed Reed mumbling, "Tough luck then."

Lent, two steps behind them, never said a word and would never know if it were true, while behind him, Kalo smiled.

* * *

Following a sodden, decomposing path…

…They entered a clearing of sorts, an area of bent-over dead grass. Mired in muck to their ankles the four looked around for a minute before noticing that the black rotted piles seemed to have some semblance of order. They were thatch huts and they were standing amid the decaying, collapsing remnants of their village, only now it wasn't much more than an untidy collective of slimy heaps of weeds and caved-in rotten thatch. Everything that was once their home was gone, drained to vapid gray.

The vibrant flowers and plantlife were now wet rot and slime that lay pathetically in the mud or floated sluggishly resembling stringy long-since-dead worms in an uninteresting mixture of bland scum. It all reeked like raw sewage coated with a tasteless surface-film of methane residue that traced lacewings on the surface harboring wisps of invisible fumes just above the flat gray sheen.

"Well at least we know where we are," Reed remarked.

Lent: "What has happened?"

Ames: "Don't know."

Trying to figure out what to do next, they talked things over— remain here, return to Legend Mountain, assuming it was even still there, or go farther into the swamp to see what they might discover?

While the others explored their options, Kalo, who was only listening anyway, withdrew and stepped quietly away. With their voices fading into the background she stood alone, her senses focused… and she closed her eyes. Images flashed as her gift transcended, her inner awareness capturing her consciousness. Inside, she felt it.

Summarily entranced she ducked her head taking the bow from her back, drew an arrow from the quiver and nocked it; then opening her eyes glanced over a shoulder to her companions and evenly said, "They are coming."

All three looked up.

Lent: "Who's coming?"

Wondering, Reed looked around; but unquestioning, Ames unsheathed the scimitar, already mindful of Kalo's unique ability. Her sixth sense of cognizance and skill saved them on the rimrock and willingly he would stand alongside her again.

"Get ready," he told them.

"For what?" Lent asked. "I don't hear anything—can't see a thing," trying to stare through the fog.

Ames, now wary, "I don't know; just get ready." Lent pulled the twibil from his khakis as Reed wiped the laser muzzle with the palm of his hand. Together, standing quietly, eventually they could hear the noise...

Rushing feet—padded paws loping synchronously scattering waterlace and mud, running a shadowworld of mist and gloom.

...The pack was coming.

Huge as a rhinoceros and hideous as iguanas, black and mangy in front with zebra-striped hindquarters, the Hyenadons loped through the mire splattering dark whorls of mud, duckweed flakes and slimy, black rotted grass. They were mammal-like reptiles resembling enormous dogs with long snouts dressed with vicious incisors and trimmed with bloodletting canines. Their death-dark eyes were deep-set in the socket and sat far back on their skulls with a coarse, overrun brow.

At the very least they were natural born killers that feared nothing in their range; at worst they were voracious savages, cold-blooded machines that ate meat, hair and bone, and even the teeth. As solitary predators they were beyond ferocious and more than most prey could manage; but in a pack they were devastating and virtually unstoppable.

Panting and slobbering in rhythm with their stride, they roamed the mire in a free ranging pack. Cloaked with long bristling hair crusted with green-black mud that made their hides tough as leather they were well adapted to the most hostile regions, and with eyes like the cat they could see when other animals couldn't. Sounding their advance, they bayed long strident howls forewarning their savor of slaughter and propensity for savagery. Two hundred pounds of voracious prowess and eleven strong they ran the miles of bog with tyrannizing desperado killing anything unfortunate enough to cross their path. The Hyenadons were honed for survival and very close now, out there in the dim light and smog…

Rushing feet—padded paws loping synchronously scattering water-lace and mud, running a shadowworld of mist and gloom.

…As Kalo reeled and let fly with a resonant —*snap, ssst*— the fletched messenger planing into the darkness of mist, undeviating, unerring, and lethal. Unseen, sixty yards out, a yowl and terminal scream as the pack leader went down nostrils furrowing mud.

Lent was astonished.

In half a heartbeat the young Renoloi had nocked another arrow and fired into the surrounding gray world of lingering waves suspended in the wind. Another caterwauling bay sent a chill up his spine.

Reed watched, amazed.

Warrior instinct aroused, Kalo moved like a wraith and faster than sight —as she did it again, and again— taking a third, and fourth…

Disbelieving, "But…" Lent stammered looking at Ames, "she can't even see them."

"I know," his focus swinging back to the haze.

…The fifth, and sixth.

Eyes bartering disbelief Lent then looked at Reed who was just shaking his head as he leveled the laser over the plane of the swamp and lay a rapid-fire fusillade of tearing torpedo-light and pulse-pounding blasts that slashed furrows in the mud and splattered opaque explosions of black-violent waterstorm spray.

—Ripping pulse-power and shatter-destruction!

Trailing fire-whines of laserflame his weapon shredded unseen things for fifty yards. He killed the seventh…

…Kalo, the eighth, and ninth.

—Then from the dismal semidarkness they pounced.

Kalo was reaching for an arrow when the first Hyenadon splashed down beyond Reed, between Lent and Ames, briefly blocking her line of fire. Reacting, the man and youth reeled taking on the bloodthirsty carnivore as another lunged from the bog in a flush of dark speed and deadly fangs.

Flinging muck and spray it spun and came at Reed —a bristle of teeth and demonic eyes— locked on. Leaping at him, legs braced with ripping claws, its momentum dragging a train of splattering black slop, happening so suddenly he didn't have time to move, couldn't get out of the way; finger squeezing, muzzle on its way up, the cold-blooded killer upon him. In that instant of reaction he saw its eyes, black and focused as the depths of a hole, mouth and fangs glistening with saliva, its curved claws like talons peering from mud…

—He ducked, then a solid-wet splash,

…The teeth and claws missed but the muscled chest slammed into him, the impact hurtling him back—and a whine and a blast. His finger was pulling the trigger.

—Laserflash boiled blowing light past his face,

As the muzzle sank into the huge dog's throat splattering its head, the blowback stung his face with bloodspray and shattering scraps, the carnivore's skull and flesh a whorl of scattered bits and scarlet windstorm of brains. The flashburn impact stabbed like an ice-pellet burst that battered him aside dumping him on his chest. Muck in his face, cold on his chest —the mud felt good— now in wet sudden-darkness.

Stunned, he was momentarily blinded —get up— and scrambling, he tried to regain his feet but tripped on something huge. Down again. Mud burning his eyes and trying to blink his vision back on, he stumbled a second time over the decapitated Hyenadon. Clumsily sideslipping but still trying to get up, he felt Kalo's heel and weight in the small of his back. She knew he was helpless, couldn't see, and for the moment was out of the line of fire, safe in the mud.

Dodging, Lent and Ames avoided then attacked, twibil and scimitar foiling grisly fangs and claws of the last of the pack. The

Hyenadon rushed and leaped like a dog —but they both stood their ground— Ames carving a gash in its shoulder. Bowled over it yowled, whirled and snarled as Lent quartered from the side.

—And the lunge,

Viciously the Hyenadon jumped at him —his timing perfect, full-weight with the blow— his blade hacking as deep as the cracking sounded thick, the twibil centered between its glaring black eyes. That same instant the scimitar swept through again severing its spine and brainstem slamming its head onto its chest. Down. Gurgling, it quivered retching blood that oozed into the mud, then let out an agonal gasp and was still.

Settling water and disturbed wisps of gray fog. The world seemed absolutely quiet again… until one of them expelled an audible sigh.

Stepping back Kalo offered her small hand as Reed, still floundering, finally marshaled his wits and got to his knees. When their fingertips touched he managed to blink enough to find her, then rising slowly made it to his feet slipping an arm around her waist and gave her a slippery hug. Smiling lovingly, she tenderly reached up helping him wipe some of the mud from his face.

Unwinding from the rush and looking around Lent decided, "We'd better see if there are any more out there."

Still tending to Reed, "They are gone," Kalo murmured.

Glancing back, "But don't you think…"

"They are gone."

Sullenly he acquiesced, "Okay, if you say so."

Calmly she turned again to Reed, his eyes shining through smudged cheeks. "Thanks," he said, she smiling graciously as Ames and Lent knelt looking over the dead Hyenadon.

"Boy-o-boy, that thing's powr'ful nasty, ugly enough to make a freight train take a dirt road," Lent observed. Ames chuckled.

Reed, peeling a wad of mud from his neck with his fingertips, "Yeah, kid; what do you know about freight trains?"

Lent grinned, his inimitable grin. "I'm learn'ed. I read books."

"Oh that's right," Reed chided, "Marvel Group Britannica." Glancing at Kalo and bumping his eyebrows, still overdone in muck,

"Learn'ed," he snuffed, "crimadently, he sounds more like me all the time." Back to business. Checking the muzzle for mud he readjusted the laser sling on his shoulder then trudged off; and as the others followed, behind them, the silent Kalo nodded.

* * *

All around them, decay…

…A world was dying incrementally, retrogressing to a primordial bog as its texture and life decomposed. None of them knew how it happened, nor did they know how to reverse the process as it crawled inexorably toward a seemingly inevitable end. All they knew was that the longer it continued the worse things were becoming, and that somehow they must figure out what was going on and find some way to fix it.

A piece of… *the Puzzle.*

CHAPTER SIX

No more than spoil…

… Behind them somewhere in the gray darkness was their village. It was now part of this place, had been assimilated and absorbed within the deterioration that floated and crawled around them. Increasingly the sense of being alone in a foreign place lurked in the back of their minds; but they would not say it. In spite of their circumstances they clung tenaciously to the fragile fabric of hope. Each knew somehow they must figure out what had happened; only then could they change it. And if that were beyond their reach, to the last, they would die trying.

In all directions were filigree fingers of fog and mire, and dead slimy grass mixed with scatterings of floating duckweed and pond scum melange that stirred and percolated sewer gas stew. The slurry of dead vegetation pushed aside as they pushed forward, but always slipped back after they passed, almost as though they were sealed in a trap, a conundrum. They were tired and the unending quagmire wove ennui threads that crept from chilled aching leg muscles, up along their spines seeping into their shoulders, then colonized as bland tedium and aggravation in their heads.

It was all dead or dying, tainted with gray, laced with long blue-black shadows, and they didn't know where they were going or what they were even searching for. But they pressed on.

"Let's talk about something," Lent suggested.

"Like what?" Reed asked, a vapid tone.

"Anything, I don't care."

"Getting tired?" Ames asked without looking back.

Eyes traveling from Reed to the other, "No, not really; just bored."

"Pick a subject," Reed said mildly.

Carrying the twibil mid-handle Lent raised it rotating it with his hand, admiring the gleam of pirouetting steel as he suggested, "Kalo. Let's talk about Kalo."

Shyly she looked at Ames as he looked back at her, then to the front again before asking, "Why?"

To Ames, with a side-glance in her direction, "Why not?" And not really expecting a reply he went on, "She's the most unloquacious person I have ever known.

"Unloquacious," Reed spit back, "there's no such word."

"Oh yeah," Lent defended, "—is so. I read it once."

Turning, walking backward he challenged, "Where? Where did you ever see that? —And don't tell me some retread comic book either; ain't no way you're packin' that in a sack lunch."

"Don't remember," Lent lied, "but it will come to me eventually and..."

Somewhat irritated, "Why do you wish to talk about me?" Kalo interrupted mildly. "I told you before, I only speak when I have something to say."

Lent was impressed; his eyes showed it. He deferred, "You know what loquacious means?"

Not quite hostile, but certainly not pleased, "I know more than you think," she told him curtly, "and prattling gibberish is pointless."

"Well, *excu—use* me."

She stared him down as they waded, then, "Considering the source, you are excused."

Now he was pissed, and when Reed and Ames chuckled, it only got worse. The 'intellect' wouldn't work, nor would the 'dolt'. So he came right out and asked her. "Where did you learn to fight like that?"

Circumspect, Ames said nothing but Reed was curious because he'd been wondering the same thing; now that the roundabout nonessentials had zeroed in on the question Lent wanted to ask from the beginning, he was all ears.

"Interesting question," Reed admitted.

Lent accepted Reed's remark as encouragement enough, and when she didn't answer he asked her again, more softly, and earnestly. "Where did you learn to fight like that, Kalo?"

Almost a whisper, "All Renoloi warriors can fight. My ability is nothing unusual."

"Ability is one thing," Lent conceded, "but your skill is far beyond that." She did not respond, so he prodded, "What Nitana told me when we first met," recalling word for word, "'Kalo may be small, but do not underestimate her. For as invisible as she is within the jungle, Lent, she is more deadly with a bow'. She wasn't exaggerating; she meant that literally, didn't she?" Kalo did not answer. "Well, didn't she?"

"Don't badger her," Ames cautioned.

"I want to know."

"Why? Why is it so important?"

"Because what she did is—it's not..."

"Probable?" Reed finished for him. "Nor is shooting marbles through honkin'-big trees," he added plunking down his two-cents worth, "but I saw that too; so I agree with the doc."

"But don't you want to know how she..."

"—No," Reed snapped, "if she doesn't want to talk about it, leave it alone."

"But..."

"—But what, kid? What frickin' part of 'no' is giving you so much trouble?" Defending her, his eyes narrowed and grudgingly Lent backed down. With the gauntlet passed, the 'mean' and authority of his voice dissipated, and peeling the stare his grin reappeared. "Besides, something else just came up, literally," tipping his head indicating.

They all looked, and there, just barely visible through the fog... was a city.

As they approached the outskirts from the bog, its most striking features glared starkly. The buildings were all square and without doors, windows, or roofs; four sandstone-type walls about twenty feet high rising from the swamp. There were no streets or sidewalks; instead, an elevated span of worn expanded-metal screen floor was set in place approximately halfway to the top of the structures. Roughly half the buildings were covered by red transparent domes anchored at each of the four corners and arched so the wall length was open. Around the perimeter of the city stairs led from the swamp to the platform, however, nowhere within the city was there access down to the bottoms.

It was like a scene with a client waiting for Holmes on the cobblestone street in front of 221B Baker Street, London; or something even more sinister, the moors of the Baskervilles with lethargic waves of night fog crawling in from the bog, drifting into the shadows and dark places.

Wary, alert, the four scaled the stairs to the platform, their bare feet making no sound as they proceeded. The city was quiet, seemed completely deserted. Looking around, they entered through what must have been a main artery, wider than most of the other walkways, perhaps one hundred feet across and stretching several miles before them to the opposite end of the city. Side by side they proceeded cautiously, observing, and not speaking for some time. No one was around.

Finally, "What do you think?" Reed asked, almost a whisper. "Look familiar?"

"De'ja vu."

"Yeah; what do you 'spose it's doing here?"

"On vacation maybe."

"Will you be serious," not a question.

At first Ames didn't reply, Kalo and Lent following their dialogue quietly, until at length he murmured, "Curious."

"What does that mean?"

"Means I don't know. What do you think?"

Reed: "Real curious."

They continued on.

* * *

Farther into the city...

...Bare feet padding silently on the platform, and the lingering quiet of fluid gray fog, "Brings back memories, huh?" Reed intimated.

"You've been here before?" Lent asked, puzzled.

Still moving, looking around, "Yeah kid, a while back."

"How? That doesn't make any sense."

"Not much of this does."

"No, I mean how could you have been here before?"

"Oh that. Long story," dismissing his question, "not actually boring or anything mind you, just a long story."

Darting 'perturbed' with his glance, "So you're not going to tell me."

Watching as he went, not returning the look, "Nah, rated R, mature audiences only." Solemn, Reed didn't crack a smile. "Doc, you want to go see Old Moses?" Ames shrugged.

"Who's Old Moses?" Lent asked. Reed ignored him. After the pause, long enough to be irritating, "You know Reed, you just really piss me off sometimes."

"Think so?"

"Yes, I do"

Still scanning, offering the 'cold shoulder' of disinterest, "Yeah," Reed finally said casually taking a breath, "I 'spose." Ames suppressed a grin.

Quietly the four walked to the coliseum, an amphitheater with stairstep tiers. With a capacity of several thousand it was spacious but not opulent, the entire structure made of the same tan stone as the other buildings in the city. Stepping softly, as though perhaps expecting ghosts, they walked through the archway into the arena, an expanse of screen floor similar to the streets and walkways.

This time it was abandoned.

At the opposite side of the arena was the raised circular platform where the bearded old man once stood.

This time he wasn't there.

The ornate wooden throne was still between the two stone pillars with the Viking war-ax embedded in its high backrest, and the gaping hole was still in the screen floor; only this time it was quiet. Looking around both men sensed they could hear them, faint echoes… from a time long ago.

Not really knowing why, almost involuntarily both men looked over the top of the amphitheater to where a hill and three giant crosses had once been. There was no hill, were no crosses.

This time there was an amalgam of rancid sky.

Now it was damp and dark and the images were only shadows and phantoms of slate-brown fog… and memories.

In deference they left the arena, and after passing several of the buildings with no domes, single-file they turned and approached one of the nondescript structures that rather resembled a stone box without a top. Circling it they found an incline of protruding spikes and one after the other the four climbed up and peered inside. In the center of the room was a dull red spiral coil mounted on a raised, square, stone base —nothing else.

This time it was empty.

"Well shoot, no bodies," Ames teased lightening the mood, "'spose Bloody Bones got 'em?"

"What?" disbelief edged in his voice. "You're doing imaginary childhood monsters that snatch up little kids when they take the garbage out at night again."

"Bloody Bones isn't imaginary." Ames paused, a crucial effect, then concluded ghostly, "Bloody Bones is *real.*"

"Get away from me —and don't *even* mention Flying Piggy." Reed didn't know if he should laugh or jump down from the wall as Kalo and Lent looked at each other like—*are we missing something?* But neither of them said anything, so they all just sat there for a minute until at length Reed pondered, "Wonder if they're still over there at the far end of the city?"

Ames nodded. "Let's go."

* * *

A short time later...

...They turned from the central street toward one of the structures with a dome bubble, and circling behind it found the ramp built into the rear wall, ascending to the top. They walked up, looked inside beneath the dome, and everything was still there, a massive array of glass tubing and hollow rods, each perhaps three inches in diameter. Inside the building the ramp descended ending at a platform near the bottom which was partially concealed by ground fog.

Followed by the others Ames eased inside and down, carefully avoiding the glass menagerie. Half-crawling, he made his way to the center of the floor and brushing the mist aside with a hand uncovered a small circular pond of clear liquid. He cupped a handful, smelled it, then tasted it.

"Still water... thirsty? It's good water, distilled."

Reed smiled. "Perhaps, Doctor, just a sip," and he knelt and drank as Kalo and Lent joined them.

Ames considered, "Good-a place as any to make camp. Let's get some shuteye."

"Sounds good," Reed seconded.

"Camp?"

Reed looked at him. "Yes, Lent, camp."

"But..."

"We're calling it that —even without the campfire."

"But..."

"But what?"

"Camp... in here?"

"Yes, in here." And emphasizing, "What's wrong with *in here*? Or would you rather sleep *out there* where the lizard-dogs can put the sneak on you and eat you up?"

Logic won him over. "Oh, sure; I see what you mean;" then nodding and agreeing, "in here would be good."

"Thought you'd see it our way," Reed said; then under his breath, "thick-headed dipshit."

Pragmatically, "Just find a nice damp spot and make yourselves comfortable," Ames told them as he crawled to a corner. Being careful not to break the hollow tubes each found a spot and satisfactory contorted position, and without having to get back up and turn off the lights, they all got some sleep.

* * *

Something touched Reed's leg...

...And waking, his eyes opened. It was Kalo snuggled next to him, her calf on his thigh. Moving carefully, not wanting to wake her, he eased his leg free; then rubbing sleep from his eyes, still groggy and needing to stretch, crawled through the glass maze and yawned on his way up the ramp. At the top, expanding his chest and diaphragm with outstretched arms and fisted hands—*that felt good*—the yawn delicious. Refreshed and relaxed he limbered then bowed his back popping his spine, and stretched again. Glancing down into the labyrinth he saw that the others were stirring. Then he looked around.

"Doc, you gotta see this."

From below, "What?" as he headed that way.

"Better come take a look, because, *you are not going to believe it.*"

Still half-asleep Lent sauntered up the ramp arriving alongside Reed, and with a half-turn urinated off the top of the wall. After that, now more awake, he also looked around. "This must be some kind of magic city."

From behind him, "More than that," Kalo whispered. They only half-heard what she said, and missed it.

"You're right, I don't believe it," Ames murmured.

Towering like titans of things that had been, surrounding them as far as they could see through the fog, was another city, the *other* city. Dwarfed by its magnitude they were mere specks on a seemingly endless concrete floor. All around them were battle-scarred and broken skyscrapers looming gaunt or lying in ruin: New York and Chicago combined and seeming to go on forever the way Los Angeles did, a sprawling megalopolis... and more.

This city could have accommodated thirty, perhaps fifty million people, and still had, 'For Rent' signs in some windows. It was immense. The summits of the taller buildings that survived the meteor shower long ago were lost in the overcast of smog, indistinguishable from the ground; they were that tall.

The four stood amazed.

Across the expanse of dead metropolis gray wings of fog wafted in rivers of mist like gossamer waves flowing over and around crumpled behemoths, and through gaping tears with naked, exposed I-beams that resembled bone-like fingers protruding from great listing slabs and stark concrete walls. Going nowhere in particular, dimly illuminated smog stole through blown-out windows and disfigured doorways of larger buildings that lay toppled like fallen giants that crushed and obliterated smaller ones to a melange of gray-powder sodden mush. The destruction and waste were extraordinary; but above all else, it was quiet.

First impressions of the city, its magnitude, detracted nothing from its complexity after more scrutiny. Intermingled among the broken and collapsed skyscrapers were myriad lesser buildings, the entire aggregate of structures at one time having excluded the outside environment by means of interconnected glass transport tubes. Scattered like shatter-debris, broken tubes that once linked buildings hundreds or thousands of feet overhead now lay in the water and mud.

Once upon a time most intersected with perpendicular tubes resembling some futuristic byway, but others were express, nonstop to unknown destinations, enabling people to move from place to place like impulses zipping along neuro-pathways in the brain. But that was a long time ago.

When there was life here this city was surely magnificent. Now it was dead, an empty shell of what it once had been. All of that was gone, lost in the ruins of a civilization vanished.

During the meteor shower the remaining transport tubes were almost all destroyed, now lying in disarray like enormous shattered hamster tunnels. And the surviving buildings, those still standing, were now missing enormous sections of concrete, several with huge holes that went completely through as if shot by missiles —in one side, out the other— a city charred and deserted. The fractured concrete floor lay gray and cold, littered with incredible piles of debris and scarred by craters, the aftermath of impacts and shockwaves.

One by one—

They eased down from the wall and wandered into the megalopolis. Quiet, resembling four diminutive creatures crossing an endless landscape of incredible debris and mud-dust concrete that was once a skyscraper forest and was now destroyed colossuses of gray stone and steel.

At one point as they walked silently past two towering buildings Ames peered down the darkened dead end alleyway between them. In the dim light, at the far end he saw a small leafless tree enclosed in a circular garden of dead grass that was protected by a short ornamental wrought iron fence. It stood all alone, withered and barren, branches mostly drifting to the left, quivering without the wind. Because this place was lonely… and empty.

For the third time, he said nothing.

Eventually the four arrived at a five-story granite building fronted by Roman era pillars and concrete stairs a hundred feet wide, that a long time ago ushered people through the two-story arched glass doors. But now the glass was gray with dust and mud, and the inside was dark. Lettering ten feet tall along its facade indicated it was a museum. Somehow, amid the unbelievable destruction, the museum had survived.

A fascination with him, Reed grinned. "Shall we?"

Ames: "Let's make some torches." They did, and went inside, again.

As with most museums, inside it seemed larger than it did from the outside. Immense ornately engraved marble pillars rose stately and solid from a floor of similar stone and supported the domed ceiling fifty feet above. Towering silent and dark it boast unseen frescoes and art from a civilization long since past, a Sistine Chapel from a different time. The sensation of emptiness was omnipresent; silent beyond sound, still beyond motion, even the air did not stir. The slightest whisper seemed to intrude, interrupting the mood, as their padding feet squish-echoed through distant halls in the blackness: the feeling, *perhaps the night watchman will hear.*

All around them were millions of relics, a civilization lost, and sadly now, what might have been was a void. Remaining in the quiet was a treasure trove of knowledge and artifacts, ample exhibits and informational memorabilia to occupy an ardent individual for days, or weeks. Although there were countless objects deteriorated beyond recognition there was a like amount unaffected by the ravages of time.

The four moved from one exhibit to the next reading by torchlight. They moved leisurely. As before, there weren't any clusters of foreign tourists crowding them from behind, speaking gibberish they couldn't understand, making them feel uncomfortable for looking at a particular display for too long, rushing them when they might prefer to read a bit more.

There was no hurry. They were completely alone.

For several hours they meandered: fashions, household, music, agriculture, leisure, machinery, medical, architecture... on and on. To Kalo and Lent this was all new, and even better than comic books.

In one hall a chronicle of avionics history: replicas of every aircraft ever built, from the Wright Brothers' Kitty Hawk, to biplanes, 747's, space shuttles, to interstellar or exo-atmosphere space fighter jets... all hanging from the ceiling.

In the literature corridor Reed again located the archives section: journals, books and scripts on many subjects, all hermetically sealed in glass display cases with two spring-loaded levers. Pull the right lever, the pages turned forward, the left, the pages turned back enabling one to read the entire text: pinball literature. He picked one he had seen before, a journal from early in the twenty-first century, and he quickly thumbed to the name... Samuel something. He still couldn't make out the last name, but this time he and Ames knew who Samuel was.

The journal told how they'd merged the Common Market into a Federation of Nations, and again, the more Reed concentrated trying to make out the words, the more difficult it became, the words fading away; and in the back of his mind the thought occurred—*something he should not read.* Like an invisible companion a zephyr of warmth enveloped him, and as before, he felt a peculiar sensation; subliminal, almost hypnotic, as though touched somewhere deeply within. This time, he blinked twice... and smiled.

Next was Medical.

They left medical, ambled into science. "Nothing works here," Reed reminded, "no power."

Finally, they arrived at the weapons corridor. It was larger than the others, but knowing man's nature that wasn't surprising. The displays began with Neanderthals' slings and arrows representing virtually every killing tool ever devised.

There were thousands of weapons, every kind from sticks and stones to fusion and laser plasma. The aisles were crammed full, from the lowly South American blowpipe to the fastest seventh-generation jet fighter, an F-121B with low-level stealth capabilities, to scale model battleships, carriers and submarines. Mankind's destructive creativity had not stopped with terrestrial weapons. Space had become a second battleground, equally equipped and better financed. This corridor was truly amazing.

Ames shook his head.

"Still can't believe it," Reed whispered, "All this ingenuity wasted on destruction. It's just sad, really sad." They separated moving along opposite sides of the great hall, viewing various sections leading from it individually. For a while each explored separately until Reed called from a section of antipersonnel devices. "You'd better take a look at this."

"What?"

A second time, "You'd better take a look." As the others approached Ames immediately saw that the pulse laser wasn't there, nor were any of the similar-looking weapons.

His reaction was, "Shit, where did it go?"

"Shouldn't it be here?" Reed asked wondering, "What the hell, what next?"

His answer came from the darkness; a crescendo of deep-throated guttural growl, then another, then a third. Hunter-tense, padding cautiously, the Hyenadons moved closer, one by one stepping into view. Spooky eyes focused, shoulders hunched, hair bristling they approached drooling saliva and hunger, beginning to circle the four intended victims.

Reed carefully brought the pulse laser up, Ames slowly reaching to the scabbard for the scimitar, Lent rotating the twibil with his hand, and Kalo notching an arrow. Then...

—A roar and thunderous crack —then slam— the entire museum trembled!

...Reflex reaction, the four dropped to the floor as the noise and movement exploded around them—and the mud-dogs ran disappearing in the dark. Startled wouldn't describe the flush of adrenaline, momentarily too surprised to think none of them moved.

—Then onto their feet; tense, rigid, coiled,

"Holy shit, what was that?"

Ames shouted, "Outside—"

Four cats on an asphalt roof in August, they ran, sprinting to the nearest exit and the presumed safety outside the trembling museum, but the expansive concrete floor offered just the opposite. In the open now, unprotected, the ground rumbling and violently quaking, everything was in upheaval. Shuddering and shaking, titans were breaking apart, concrete and glass jitterbugging on the ground and raining down from above, bouncing at their feet, thundering, crashing and splattering everywhere...

—It stopped,

…Sudden calm, leftover pieces clattering, then still. Not a whisper of noise.

Watching them Kalo and Lent wondered why the men acted so strangely. Both seemed so nervous as they watched the sky; after all, it was nothing but a convoluted blend of brown and gray smog that winnowed and stirred.

"Just a minor quake," Lent decided.

Taking a breath, both men seemed relieved… still quiet.

Soon after—

Without talking the people crossed a great expanse of quake-fractured concrete and rubble that was rimmed on all sides with tremendous mounds of skyscraper debris, collapsed titans from a time only two of them could appreciate. They walked to the center of this iceflow of cold dead cement where a tilted fountain rested akimbo on top of a rise of debris. It resembled a lifeboat in rough seas.

When they arrived at the fountain all four stopped and looked up at it. He was still there; the bronze who looked like a Quaker or Pilgrim. His arms were extended, apart, as though welcoming someone, and clutched in one hand was a book. The men didn't know whom the bronze personified, but he seemed familiar.

Once again Reed looked at the sky, almost expectantly but not disappointed with only a smear of soup and smog sifting above them. This time, the atmosphere, the sky, whatever it was, was empty. Shouldering the pulse laser he glanced back at the bronze mumbling, "Wonder what it all means?" No one said anything, so scratching his head he started out again and one by one they followed crossing the fractured concrete landscape.

Constantly moving—

They did not know what was going on, nor were they even sure where they were going. Still and quiet… and padding footfalls.

They made their way around monstrous piles of collapsed skyscraper rubble and crossed vast expanses of scattered debris littering the muddy concrete floor. It seemed to take forever; broken chunks of stone and shards of sliver-glass everywhere, cold and ashen as brittle corpses in the gloom.

Walking—

Slowly but doggedly, always within the womb of perennial smog, they kept going, watching as they went, searching but not knowing what they were looking for. It seemed that with each step they moved farther into a maze they couldn't unravel, with no way out, deeper into a problem they couldn't solve, an enigma that was sewn in layers with the fog. This incredible devastated metropolis was reduced to clutter and stone shrouded in gray-dark and dun-colored smog... all of it still and quiet.

After several hours—

They reached the outskirts of the city and climbed down from a mountain of rubble. That was when this strange place and its secret conferred one more clue for them to decipher.

Looking out over the landscape Lent peered through the smog as far as he could see. "It can't be; it was destroyed," he said under his breath.

Ames muttered, "That's..."

Reed: "...Impossible."

The entire city was sitting within a vast basin, a gigantic basin. The city was on top of a colossal mountain... but not of stone.

There were:

Stoves and refrigerators, all rusted and old. A Harley Davidson frame without wheels or a seat, and televisions with broken screens that were piled on top of crushed computers. Vehicles spanning more than two hundred years of automotive progress created enormous heaps of scrap metal, literally millions of them... and more.

Scattered haphazardly stagecoaches, buggies and Viking ships with wood rotted away, were mixed in with countless missiles and tanks. Guns, personnel transports, artillery and aircraft were crammed among schools, churches, and ribbons of concrete interstate highway that lay inert and silent circling the blown-out aircraft carrier USS Enterprise... and more.

Clothes from the Goodwill were stacked in great rotting mounds near water-soaked boxes of Barbie dolls without arms, or with broken-off heads. Carousels and roller coasters with horses and benches thrown askew, were buried under billboards and a Buddha statue. Charred Roman chariots with broken tongues and spokes lay abandoned in huge shredded piles of books, magazines and newspapers alongside an Egyptian pyramid tipped onto its side. Dead lawnmowers were amassed as red, green and rust, and a single Lone Ranger action figure lay twisted and dead without his mask. Amidst all this were Legos, comic books, ten billion cell phones... and more.

There was:

The Chernobyl nuclear reactor, its half-life radiated away. Entire trains with locomotives, steam engines, Pullman, and boxcars and ribbons of rail lay like string in a pile. Seeming ready to launch, a space shuttle protruded from a city-sized jumble of houses with broken windows and shingled roofs torn apart. Built in the 1470's by Ivan the Great, the Kremlin's Cathedral of Assumption was now lost in the aggregate. Nuclear missiles mounted on overturned mobile launch racks leaned against Saint Peter's Basilica... and more.

Radio Flyer wagons and tricycles and bicycles with bent or missing wheels, a Daisy Red Ryder Western Carbine air rifle, and untold numbers of toys were crushed beneath the Eiffel Tower. Tarnished and twisted, entire skyscrapers listed gutted and burned with blown out window glass; and dwarfed by them, a solitary clapboard steeple and belfry from the mountain jutted out... and much more.

It was a junkyard surpassing their wildest imagination, enormous beyond comprehension. Surrounded by endless swamp the conglomeration fanned out for miles and miles, complete cities encapsulated within the incredible mass, the entirety cloaked with algae, seaweed and kelp. It was the Lost World of Atlantis one hundred-fold, from an insignificant liquid-blue planet and universe of long ago, now lost somewhere in the dark void of space.

It was from Earth... the Accumulation,

A piece of... *the Puzzle.*

CHAPTER SEVEN

Everything imaginable…

…Was in the Accumulation, somewhere; and Reed had never seen the Accumulation. "Where did all this come from?"

"Through the 'Hole in the Sky'," Lent answered soberly.

"Possibly temporal residue,"[7] Ames told him.

Skeptical: "Temporal residue? Yeah, okay."

"Pieces of the past dragged along through time."

"Doc…"

"It was never considered to be much more than a postulate notion, but apparently under just the right conditions or a coalescence of unique circumstances, the phenomenon is possible. My guess is, it must somehow be associated with the magnetic-gravitational horizon of certain black holes…"

"Doc…"

"Yeah?"

"I've heard the theoretical possibility of temporal residue."

"I figured you had."

"But this—this doesn't make sense. This, I don't understand."

"No one does," Lent told him. Reed rolled his eyes, but Lent ignored that and went on, "I'll explain what I can," and as they stood there looking around, he did…

…And after Lent related his theory Ames inquired, "Well?"

"Okay."

"Okay; that's it?"

Reed sighed, "Nothing else makes any sense, so why should this?"

Bobbing his head, Lent agreed, "That makes sense to me."

Ames: "You're both idiots."

More than looking for a needle in a haystack, trying to find any one item within so much would be a challenge beyond reason and common sense. It was incredible, huge, and seemingly boundless, an unexplainable treasure trove of 'what might have beens'. But regarding more than the width and breadth of its presence, they knew it should not be here.

Kalo walked quietly among oxidized skeletons of automobile corpses perched on rotted black tires or half-buried in the mishmash of rusting, jumbled car frames. Scrounging, Lent squatted not too far away sorting through catty-wampus stacks of dog-eared comic books. Perhaps she pondered the greater meaning of the Accumulation's presence while he tended to focus on more commonplace matters.

"Plenty. Peer' stroke of luck," he decided, "more than enough to last quite a while." Then rummaging deeper into the heaping piles of soggy literary treasures, the afterthought, "Never realized just how much I missed quality reading material I guess."

Ignoring him the young Renoloi found a rusty Mercury Monterey hubcap lying flat and half-full of sort-of-clean water. He was pretty much only talking to himself anyway, so she quietly knelt cupping her hands and began washing her face. It felt cool and refreshing, and in spite of their dismal circumstances, even felt passably clean. Crouching modestly, she delicately combed through her hair with her fingers.

Spying another unfamiliar issue Lent scooted nearer to her on his haunches. The comic book was soaked with an upside-down coffee filter-spill and a pile of soggy old grounds —but that wouldn't matter all that much as long as it wasn't mushy all the way through. Briskly he snatched the grungy paper filter and tossed it away flinging coffee ground splatter when he did. Then he tenderly laid the comic across his thigh and painstakingly squeegee'd the juice from the pages with the side of his hand. Liquid coffee drippings and grounds dribbled down his leg as he wiped his hand on his khaki shorts and peeled the issue from his thigh examining it with satisfaction.

Still combing her hair Kalo watched the production disfavorably and remarked, "Lent, you are such a scrounge."

Put off by her unexpected criticism he looked up. "What?" He considered it creativity. Mildly disgusted she eyed the wet spot on his shorts. "Oh, that— what difference does it make? They're almost the same color anyway. Won't even be able to tell after it dries."

The frown. "You are so uncouth."

"*Pshaw—*" waving her off with a hand as he carefully laid the comic aside and went back to rummaging. Concentrating on what he was doing and not looking at her, he observed, "What do you know; you talk funny anyway."

"What do you mean by that?" she snapped defensively. "How do I talk funny?" Decidedly, in her opinion that remark was uncalled-for. But wedging both hands between stacks of soaked magazines and newsprint he ignored her, carefully prying them apart with his fingers. "How do I talk funny?"

She quit combing her hair —maybe that was a bad sign— it might not be safe to ignore her again; so from under his shag rug of muddy hair his eyes rolled up lackadaisically and he dismissed the barb. "Nothing. Don't worry 'bout it." But it wasn't going to be that easy.

"No, tell me. You brought it up and I want to know." She definitely wasn't smiling.

Being cautious, "Well," and still trying to maintain control, "you never combine words."

"Combine words. Why would I do such a thing?"

"Because everybody does, and when you do conversation flows more smoothly and euphoniously." Then almost defiantly, verging on arrogance, "It's more harmonious, if you can grasp my meaning."

She defended, "The Renoloi never combine words. We were taught the proper way to speak and use words; and we do so accordingly."

"That right?" Now he was getting a bit ruffled too.

"Yes, *that*, is right," and the jab, "and please tell me, where *did* you learn a word such as euphoniously, Marvel Group Britannica?"

she huffed flipping her hair, referring to the old joke. Eye contact, Lent didn't respond; then frustrated he snatched up the comic book he had set aside, rose, carefully rolled it up and stuck it in his back pocket and began to leave as he mumbled something. "What did you say?" she challenged.

He stopped, glared back, then answered, "I said, you're sorta persnickety, dont'cha think?" and with that he turned and stomped off passing Reed as he went.

Reed's attention moving from one to the other as he approached, to Lent: "Contractions; when you combine words you're using contractions." To her, he calmly inquired, "What was that all about?"

"Nothing," looking away, but not before he noticed her eyes were misty, and not from the water.

"Nothing?"

"My face is dirty," she denied cupping her hands and focusing on the hubcap water basin.

"Sure, Sweetie," he went along, "I can see where you missed a spot there on the side of your cheek." Water dribbling from her hands, without looking up she listened as he confided, "Well, I'll be around," a pause, "just in case." Not to embarrass her and having said enough, he looked away, poked both hands in his pockets and ambled off calling, "Hey, Doc, find something useful over there? Something dry."

Head down, still looking into her cupped hands, momentarily she considered what he said, and slowly tears welled in her eyes —so she splashed water in her face.

* * *

Makeshift camp...

...Charred walls laced with soot and smudge-freckled plasterboard around her, dancing fireglow keeping her company; she blinked placidly, pensive. Listlessly gazing through the blown-out window from inside what was once an executive suite of a high-rise office building that now lay on its side in the Accumulation, Kalo stood alone. Across the room the others were huddled around a campfire kindled with broken furniture, pieces of scrap wood, and Reed's GI waterproof matchbox. There were times, like now, when his foresight came in handy. He only had four or five farmer matches left, each a precious commodity now because the warmth and glow of something as simple as a campfire could ward off the infection of despair in such a dismal, depressing world.

Warming his hands and pushing his bare feet toward the flames Lent grumbled, "I'm hungry."

"We're all hungry; don't think about it," Reed said.

"Don't think about it? It makes my stomach hurt."

Ames tried to relax on the sloping wall that was now the floor. "He's right; if you dwell on it, you'll only make it worse." Lent began to complain again, so Ames suggested, "Read a comic book or something."

Eyes brightening, he reached to his back pocket and pulled out the flattened, sodden roll. "Yeah, good idea," and a minute later he was satiated with fantasy from a time long ago.

Watching him, *simple pleasures*, eking out a smile; then Ames' gaze was drawn back to the magnetic fairy-dance of alizarin-orange, and slowly the smile waned as contemplation slipped in taking its place. The longer he watched the flames the deeper his thoughts took him until the clear focus of flickering firewings faded to a blur of sinuous yellow-orange frolic. The fire felt good, warm… security in a strange, wet, savage place.

"What're you thinking?"

The voice brought him back; he blinked. "Nothing really, a million things; I don't know." He looked up in time to see compassion in his friend's fleeting grin; then Reed's attention also drifted to the fire again.

"Yeah, me too. Nothing and everything." Then back at his friend, "A million things, and none of it makes any sense." Reed took in a breath, let out a sigh, "But we'll figure it out, always do." Captured, the mood was taking them both. "They're okay."

"I know," Ames went along, each mindful they were not as sure as they pretended to be. Reed leaned in and stirred the coals with a stick, and as they spoke, from the blown-out window Kalo overheard, gently stroking the fetish she wore. She didn't say anything and did not look back, only gazed out the window over the incredible junkyard of the Accumulation. She seldom spoke; but the silent Kalo always listened.

"I miss them," Ames finally confessed. "I can't tell you, can't even put into words how frustrating it is not knowing if they're all right or not —you know, alive or dead."

"The 'White Warrior and Serpent'," Reed muttered. "The ceremony. Same thing."

"Except..."

Reed looked at him. "...That was a hologram Tian said, some kind of hologram anyway. People are flesh and blood, and that makes it different."

"I miss them," Ames said again.

"Yeah, I know, Doc. Reminds me of something that happened to me a long time ago..." he let out a breath, remembering, "the time I accidentally ran over this cat." Thinking back, Reed shook his head, "Boy that was a long time ago." Surprised by the analogy Ames quietly listened as his friend went on, "Well, actually it was just a kitten; ran right out in front of my car. Sucker was so little, when the tires smunched it, it didn't even go, *bump, bump*." Incredulously, Ames just kept listening.

Peering over the top of his comic book Lent interrupted, "What is a kitten?"

Looking at him as he answered Reed said, "Oh, they were these fuzzy little animals—baby cats—that little girls played with, mostly anyway. Boys usually had dogs," as if he would even know the difference.

"Dogs?"

"Yeah, pets," gesturing with his hands as he explained, "cold noses, floppy ears, waggity tails —well sometimes the ears were floppy, sometimes pointed and whatnot." Not having a clue, Lent nodded appreciably indicating that somehow he might, then returned to his literature.

Unable to grasp the meaning of his analogy, "Reed, what in the world does running over a cat have to do with us, with what's going on now?" Ames asked.

Turning his head and attention, "Well, it made me feel terrible." Then considering, "I don't know, maybe it doesn't have anything to do with anything —probably not— just made me feel awful... bad, like now."

Frowning, "Friend or no," Ames mused, "you re-eeally need help."

"Yeah, I know" the other admitted. "Shoot, I still think about that kitty sometimes, even now." Serious: "Doc, it's too bad you weren't a psychiatrist or something —you know— a *real* doctor."

"Thank God for small favors."

"Well it would help to have someone to listen sometimes and..."

"—I'll listen," Lent volunteered, lowering his 'Marvel' again.

With an unenthusiastic side-glance Reed decided, "Wouldn't that be classic, the blind leading the blind."

"I don't know what that means," the youth said; and Reed didn't explain so he went back into his comic book.

Slipping onto his side, scooting around and trying to get comfortable as he lay down, Ames muttered, "Good grief." There was a moment of silence as he stretched out and sighed, and at length said, "I'm tired. It all just makes me tired."

Reed: "Get some sleep."

Peeking over the top of the pages, "I'm still awake," Lent volunteered, "want to talk to me?"

A wry grin: "No, not really."

Feelings bruised, "Fine; then I'm going to sleep too." With that he rolled up the book and curled on the floor, butt to the fire.

Across from them Reed sat feet to the flames, watching as they both drifted off. He was tired, but remembering that first night on the trimaran, he kept an eye on Kalo. For just shy of an hour, she stood quietly at the window looking at nothing in particular, staring into the surrounding gray-twilight. He knew there was something on her mind, and when she was sure the others were asleep she turned, crossed the room and sat down with her friend.

Gently, "How you doin'?" nudging her with a shoulder.

She looked up at him. "There is something I wish to speak with you about, to ask you."

"Figured as much." He was Reed; that easy smile of encouragement and confidence only he could project. "What is it?"

Sitting quietly, she thought how to ask what she wanted to know, considering what she had rehearsed while she stood at the window. Looking at the fetish as she slowly turned it, she finally whispered, "Reed, I want to know what love is." Her revelation made him smile and he tenderly reached out and lay his hand upon hers.

"Stop fiddling with the tooth."

Sincere, eyes focused on his, "Can you tell me?"

"Sure, your anterior singular cortex lights up," he joked; then time to be real, the smile evanesced. "I don't honestly know if I can answer your question, but I'll do the best I can."

"Please."

Slipping an arm around her he coaxed a bit and she willingly snuggled closer as he began. "Love isn't a single emotion; it's more like a blend, an amalgam. It's happiness and sorrow, hope and despair, security and doubt, hardship and reward, good and bad all mixed together and nourished with a flame that needs no fuel yet never burns out. Dreams and aspirations are born of love, but we can't explain how or why. Love is the faith within each and every one of us that binds us together, yet makes each of us different." Still considering, he paused until she looked up sheepishly.

"Is there more to love?"

"You mean a different kind of love, don't you? The feeling... that glow." Almost embarrassed she nodded and he hugged her fondly, understanding. "Yes, I suppose there is. Somewhere inside, within us, is the small corner where we possess an inherent desire to 'belong', a yearning that make us want to be more than we are in and of ourselves 'alone'. It's intrinsic, a part of us that can't be taken away:

to want someone, and to be wanted by someone, the predisposition for sharing our lives and ourselves. God gave us that longing, that glow, and wound it intricately within our souls so it would endure... so it would be an inseparable part of us."

"God?" she inquired softly.

"The Spirit who opened space with a hole and poured out all that you see, everywhere. Stars scattered forever, and worlds and moons to accompany them, all throughout the emptiness that was before," recalling Tian's explanation.

She nodded.

He sighed. "So many people spend their entire lives looking for love, seeking it from others around them; and that's sad really, because they're looking in the wrong place. That's not love, that's usually co-dependence or wanting approval, but not love; neither is even important."

Intently, "Where shall I look?"

"You don't need to look; it's already there."

"I do not understand."

"Inside, Kalo—inside you," almost whispering, "all the love in the world is already there. Like a butterfly waiting to emerge from the chrysalis... when you believe in yourself, and love yourself, you will feel what I can't explain. You will know love and be ready to share it... and from someone it will be given in return."

She listened.

He asked, "Have you ever been near someone and felt like a 'piece' was missing, or been in a crowd of people and felt like you were still all alone?"

"Yes," she murmured.

"When it's right, when it *is* love, it won't feel that way. The piece will be there and you will feel fulfilled... complete."

She listened.

"Be patient. Love is more than something physical, so much more. Love is the nexus, the link that binds the pieces—the parts—to an inseparable union and gives us strength and faith that no one can tear apart." Affectionately he kissed her on the forehead and told her, "There's an old saying, 'Wait until the moon is full'."

"What does that mean?" she asked intently.

"It means be patient. When the moon is full, when it's time and you are ready, you will know."

"Then I will be patient."

He looked at her, and softly, "Why are you asking me about love?"

She answered, honestly, "I wish to know what I feel inside so I can understand what you and John feel; your pain for Seana, his for Tian. I cannot understand what I do not know."

Prying, "'What you feel inside', for whom? Is there another reason?"

She looked up to her friend, and whispered, "Wait until the moon is full."

Two smiles.

"You tired?"

"Yes I am."

"Yeah, me too," he admitted as she curled within his arm. Imprisoned within a gray and unexplained world, holding one another they snuggled together and soon fell asleep... because they were friends.

* * *

While they slept...

...Gray and gloom remained, constant, infectious, digressing. Limbo: a time of in-between and never-been.

Opening his eyes, eventually Lent stirred. He woke with one hand in his khakis, the other scratching his head. He rose quietly, ambled to the blown-out window, yawned, and then crawled out to have a look around. His scavenging nature, as much a part of him as his curiosity with the world around him, soon instigated the impulse and he gave in to the urge and began scrounging. What useful things might he find in the Accumulation; old habits die hard.

Wandering off into the 'Never-Land' of junkyard, with all it had to offer; first one thing, then another, it was all interesting. He was gone for a while.

* * *

One-by-one the others woke...

...Rested, prepared for whatever; to continue their journey to wherever they were bound. In no particular hurry, they idly stretched and yawned moving about leisurely.

Suddenly the building rattled and shifted, then the overhead wall that was the ceiling traced wormtrail cracks —splitting apart— and broke loose dumping concrete and plaster. Noise cried with the splinters of fracturing wood and swirling dust clouds as the wall-section that was their floor shattered in the center and heaved up, the wall where Kalo had looked out the window splitting up the middle then breaking in pieces as it crumbled and collapsed. Plasterboard, metal and wood framework and molding spun as it flew then tumbled and crashed.

—More dust, debris, and rising confusion.

From under their feet the awesome head, glaring yellow-green eyes and monstrous jaws and shoulders of Tyrannosaurus Rex emerged. A dust-wind volcano erupted, the floor rising up, breaking apart then shattering like a stone-blizzard waterspout hurling pinging fragments that splattered around them as its hulking shoulders and a mighty foot broke through heaving sheetrock and debris with its three crunching claws. The dinosaur roared as it climbed from beneath the floor, pushing its bulk from crumbling stone and debris.

Twenty feet from them it clawed out from its burrow; then with a single crunching step, rose as its powerful flank and tail shoved and swung crashing through sheetrock. Now free within the close quarters of the room it turned, and with one mighty heave tore the rest of the outside wall away sending pieces of campfire wood and debris flying. Splattered fragments spun and concrete dust whorled as a gagging-gray rush saturated the office suite in a blanket of confusion and swirling eclipse of chalk dust.

Hand traveling the sling down his side, Reed reached for the pulse laser but lost his balance as the floor vaulted pitching himself and Kalo down into a corner. Sliding and scrambling with the floor rising above them, he landed on top of her, the slope so steep they couldn't get out —they were trapped, stuck— unable to help.

Heaved up just as quickly and alone on the high side of the room, face to face with the intimidating reptile as it turned on him baring its interlocking six-inch incisors, Ames drew the scimitar. Megalosaur head rearing back, gargling noise, six feet between them, eyes fixed, saliva-sheen jaws open.

With a powerful sideswipe head-butt the dinosaur slammed broken furniture aside then lunged as he ducked behind a filing cabinet, ripping chisel teeth barely missing as the bite-crushed metal cabinet fell dead. With sweat and muscle and a glimmer of steel he struck back peeling a separation-gash in its leathery hide. Enraged and gushing blood T-Rex reeled crashing its head through another section of wall, then amid the scattering debris its tail swept dust trails and destruction as it slammed it again, the wall buckling and giving way.

The Tyrannosaur attacked a second time shoving the dead cabinet with its head, slamming Ames back, pinning him against the rear wall. It came again and he tried to move but was held fast —no where to go, no way out— fighting back, slicing furiously through the side of its face. Lodged solidly, penetrating the upper jawbone between two teeth the scimitar cut so deeply that when the dinosaur flinched it jerked him from behind the cabinet —up off the floor— like meal in a sack. Dangling now, he could not let go.

Suddenly Lent leaped into the room through the hole in the wall, twibil already in motion —the noise, the sound— an ax blade crunch and blood-splattering hack to the side of its skull just below its eye, the force and fury of his blow shattering the jawbone. His twibil sank in the side of its head.

On their hands and knees Kalo and Reed were still trying to climb the sloping wall, but kept sliding back down. They couldn't get out, and unable to do much else Reed was firing blindly, explosions blasting holes through the ceiling, trying to scare the predator.

Ames was finally able to jerk the scimitar free and fell back hitting the wall before again scrambling to his feet, his arms in motion whirling a glistening shield of blade —faster and faster— *swishing*, figure-eights. Muscles flexed to violin strings Lent yanked for all he was worth wrenching the twibil out, then spinning away he drew back to fight. After Ames, the Tyrannosaur reeled and lunged again, the man's blade no more than a blur of momentum with his overhand strike, the razor edge flashing between the yellow-green eyes as the twibil whacked from the side boring into the skull, the pike disappearing behind the brow —and the dinosaur blinked— then tottered momentarily...

Wavering, its eyes rolling back and to the side, T-Rex retched blood streaked with pink mucus froth. Its tongue went slack over glistening incisors; then a gasp of blood-bubble burst in its face.

...And done.

Dead on its feet the huge head slammed to the floor dragging the hulking torso with it. Floor-trembling loud the dinosaur collapsed as shuddering muscle and a cloud of dust and crushed stone with a deflated exhale that sprayed bloodstained vomit-breath. Convulsing, its toes curled and it kicked once knocking down another section of wall before they relaxed then splayed; then with a drawn agonal gasp it finally lay still. Lent and Ames looked at one another, both with the wobbly trembles.

Crawling and helping each other, "Messed-up way to start the morning," Reed grumbled as he and Kalo finally managed to reach the upper edge of the upended floor and pull themselves out onto the debris field. But the skirmish was over; T-Rex was dead.

Examining the fallen predator Lent wondered, "Where did that come from?"

Kalo: "From under the floor."

Rolling his eyes, "What I meant was, how did one of your dinosaurs get here?"

"I do not know."

"Our dinosaurs?" Reed spouted.

"Well, if the snakes are mine the dinosaurs are yours."

"Yeah, right, what—ever." Then taking-in the fallen reptile, "Well what the heck, one thing's for certain," waiting until...

Lent asked, "What?"

"...They taste like chicken," bumping his eyebrows. And 'the grin'.

It would only be a matter of gathering the scattered pieces of firewood that were still burning, and then adding some more kindling graciously provided by the Tyrannosaur. With the campfire reassembled and a veritable banquet at their disposal, soon it would be time to eat.

* * *

Three standing together...

...And Kalo approaching them from behind, time to decide what they would do next. No one really had any idea.

Reed asked, "What do you think?" looking over the Accumulation.

"Don't know," doing the same.

Lent glanced back, saw Kalo coming, then returned to their conversation. "Wasn't luck," he decided omitting the precursor information.

"What wasn't luck?" Reed asked, one of those 'fill in the blanks' sort of questions that got Ames' attention as well.

To both of them, "At first I thought the Accumulation being here was just a stroke of luck; but the thought occurred to me..."

"Do tell, a thought," Reed quipped.

Ignoring him, "If it was destroyed during the cataclysm, that means there's only one way it could be here now." He stopped, waiting.

Longer than a pause, both considering, "Okay, I'll bite," Reed finally said, "and that is?"

"The 'Hole in the Sky'."

"Jesus Christ on a crutch in Vicksburg," Ames blurted out, exasperated.

"What—" Lent defended, "you got a better idea?" Reed listened, thinking.

"No, but I'm really not up for time warps or the Devil's Triangle right now."

"The circular storm," Reed suggested, "that could be it. That could be the key to this whole bizarre mess somehow."

"For Pete's sake, you're as bad as him."

Reed looked at his friend. "Doc, we met two little gray midgets..."

"—Dwarfs."

"Yeah okay, dwarfs —whatever— who deliberately set us out on an ocean where we got eaten by sharks and chased by the Loch Ness monster —and— thirteen waterspouts, not to mention getting swallowed by a giant-ass whirlpool. Then you're marooned on an island while Tian and myself are somehow sucked under a world —and believe me, I still haven't got a clue how that happened." This time he didn't even grin. "Getting a little freaky, huh? Then, according to you, an entire ocean disappears..."

"—It did," Lent assured.

"Okay," waving acceptance with a hand, "an entire ocean disappears —and still— still Doc, you can't accept something as simple —simple hell, mundane— as a circular storm, or the Bermuda Triangle? Come on, gimmie a break."

"Mariner folklore, nothing more."

"So what—so what if it is?" Reed challenged. "We've got nothing else to go on, and I am convinced that somehow, someway, that phenomenon is connected to this," offering a wide sweep with an arm, "to all of this."

"I agree," Lent jumped in.

Ames acquiesced. "Okay. Okay then, if you two are so bound and determined, then that's what we'll do." He rubbed his nose with the side of his hand, scratched his head and admitted, "Guess it can't hurt. Sure don't have anything to lose."

Lent beamed as he looked at Reed. "Oh this is gonna be great, a real supernatural adventure."

But Reed wasn't so sure. "Yeah, well I don't know just how 'great' of an idea this may actually turn out to be. Last time, that was an accident and we didn't know any better, and it damn near got us all killed. But this time, to deliberately go looking for this phenomenon, whatever it is, when we all should certainly know better..." massaging the back of his neck, "well, we gotta be crazy as cooties."

Lent beamed. "So, we're going to find the 'Hole in the Sky'?"

Reed grinned, a reluctant grin. "Well, yeah, if we can; that's what we're going to do."

"Cooties," Ames mumbled. "The more things change... the more they stay the same."

CHAPTER EIGHT

It was a dismal place...

...Dark and rank, the stench of raw sewage and decay pervasive in the smog. Pushing duckweed and slime aside their footfalls stirred black soup from the mire that turned over as it floated in mahogany waves, then slipped into the melange as undulating gray. The air was bitter now, gray-brown fog burning their throats, tasting as sour as the greasy sensation oozing inside their pant legs, or under her skirt. No one spoke.

Step after step they kept moving, into the dusky swamp and unknown. It was very quiet except for the, *blurp, squisssh, blurp,* suction of bubbles choked from mud beneath a stirred landscape of filthy quagmire and floating dead slimy weeds. This was a dying place... very quiet.

Following, pulling up the rear, easily Lent's finger pushed the switch —Buffalo gals won't you come out tonight, come out tonight, come out tonight— music blared.

Reeling, *"Jesus h— what—the..."* Reed spit out, the pulse laser sweeping up. Also unnerved by the bellow of sudden noise, Kalo and Ames spun as Lent's eyes shined with puppy dog surprise from a few steps behind.

Startled himself, "It works," he yelled as 'Buffalo Gals' was going into the encore, still blasting from the two-finger-sized gadget.

Stepping forward Reed shouted, "What is that?" Lent shrugged. "Well for crying out loud, turn it down."

He shrugged a, *how?*

Reed pointed. "That button, the one on the left." Lent poked it with a finger but the volume remained at, *make you completely nuts and stone deaf.*

No good.

"Oh, for pity's sake, give it to me." Lent didn't even have time for another shrug before Reed snatched it from him, fiddling with it, and after five more deafening seconds and the fourth rousing chorus, frustrated looked up. "Volume control's broke." The song was okay but the noise was overpowering, and with danger lurking everywhere it was nerve-racking.

—*Click.*

Overwhelming silence again except for the, *blurp, squisssh, blurp,* suction of bubbles choked from mud beneath a stirred landscape of filthy quagmire and floating dead slimy weeds. The song seemed to be reverberating through the fog, until finally fading like the residual echo after the toll of a bell; but then again, maybe that was just in their heads. Settling, the surface flattened and the swamp finally stilled as the four exchanged looks of surprise or disgust.

"What in the world," Reed whispered toning his voice to recapture the mood of the swamp. He handed the compact player back to Lent. "Where did you get that?"

Straightforward: "The Accumulation."

Ames: "Of course." Speechless, Kalo was still unnerved.

Lent explained, "I woke up early and went out to have a look around; you know, to see what I could find. I didn't know what it was, but it was interesting so I decided to keep it."

"'Spose it would be expecting too much to hope you could stick with comic books," Reed decided.

Reaching to his back pocket, "Oh not at all. I got several new issues," as he produced a wad of soggy rolled-up books.

Waving him off with a hand, "Why am I not surprised," not a question.

"No volume control?" Ames asked.

"Nope; broke as a fishing bobber with a hole in it," Reed answered.

"Earbuds, headphones?"

"Nope."

Ames, to Lent: "Well, if you're going to listen to it, you're going to have to follow us, a—long—way—back."

"Okay," and he added, "it has a lot of songs in this little blue place…"

"Window," Ames told him.

"…In the little blue window; but I think it only plays the one."

"Imagine that," Reed observed dryly, "might explain why it was in the Accumulation."

Lent defended, "But I like the song."

"Right. Tell me that again in a few hours."

Worried, Kalo whispered, "Noise attracts predators."

"Well if he gets eaten," Reed assured, "he'll be *wa—ay* back there all by himself, and it'll be his own fault."

Even that didn't put her mind at ease and she told them so. "I do not think it wise to let the little box make noise at all."

They all looked at Lent, and Ames agreed, "She's right, could get all of us killed."

"I can fill the little holes with mud," Lent bartered. "That will make it quieter." Scooping a handful, he quickly packed the speaker holes and pushed the 'play' button. "Buffalo Gals' bubbled-and-blurbed, but the base notes vibrated so much it made his hand tingle —and it was still way too loud.

"Nope, no good; still too loud," Reed said; and Kalo and Ames made the decision three against one, majority rule. Lent acquiesced and turned it off, swished it around a few times in the water to clean off the mud, then tucked it in his pocket.

Distracted, "What is that?" Kalo asked pointing to something floating in a tangle of weeds not too far from them. Pushing raveled knots and trailing strands of dead grass aside they waded to it, an unfamiliar creature floating face down in the mire. Grabbing what appeared to be a hand or foot or paw, Lent turned the creature over. Sodden and covered with mud and slime, half-submerged the dead animal rolled languidly onto its back and slowly began to sink so Lent tugged at it bringing it to the surface again.

"Boy I don't know if I'd be handling that thing," Reed cautioned.
All of them looking it over, "Why not?"

"Bacteria, germs—shit like that, kid."

Studying the animal, "Go figure," Ames quietly said without looking at either of them, "we're wading in a veritable cesspool and you're worried about germs."

"Cleanliness is next to Godliness, Doc; or haven't you ever heard of that?"

"True enough," Ames agreed, then smiled, "but in your case I don't think even lye soap will help."

"Oh, that's rich; I'll take a dollar's worth." Then changing the subject, "What do you think it is?"

"Don't know."

The creature was covered with slimy black muck and looked like it had a feline body without the tail. It appeared to have a distended abdomen, but they attributed that to water-bloat. It had four legs, or feet and hands, but not fingers and the digits looked like toes almost, with claws. The head was rounded with what looked like a wide beak and deep-set rotted eyes, where beetles and worms or maggots had worked over the mouth cavity and orbits, eating the decaying flesh on the face. It may at one time have had wings and the face resembled something simian, a primate perhaps, but in its present state of decomposition they couldn't be sure. It was about the size of an orangutan or small ape, but didn't look like one, or for that matter, any animal they had ever seen before.

"Any ideas?" Ames asked the others this time.

"Nope."

"Nope," Lent seconded, then pointed. "There's another one."

About twenty feet away was a second floater; but it wasn't bloated with water-soak. It was shriveled and brittle like wet-oiled parchment stretched tightly around a dehydrated skeleton, and was wizened as a sun-dried coconut-husk mummy so it floated more easily than its companion. Dragging it through the water he retrieved the second carcass and let them float side by side for comparison; but they still couldn't tell what the creatures were.

At length Ames commented, "I've never seen anything like them before."

"Almost look like gargoyles or something, don't they?" Reed decided.

"Gargoyles?" Ames half-teased.

Kalo's eyes passed from one to the other of the creatures as she thought, *mirror-image mineral sentinels rising from the floor and hanging from the ceiling, standing quietly and vigilant... in the dark.* Then she began to sense something more.

"Well one thing's for sure," Reed said, his voice snatching her back.

Lent asked, "What?"

"This proves it, beyond any shadow of a doubt."

"Proves what?"

Beguiling, Reed had him, eye to eye and ghostly, with the deep-breath effect, "Bloody Bones is *real.*" Gullibly Lent stared at him, eyes bright and wide, mouth open —but nothing came out.

That quickly Reed's nonsense swept away the images and sensation Kalo felt, and playfully she slapped him on the arm. "Reed, you are so weird."

Turning from Lent to her, "No I'm not —well— not when I'm asleep."

"Not when you are asleep?"

"Heck no. Why?" Then considering it, "Is this some kind of trick question?"

"Let's get going," Ames cut him off as he and Lent assumed the lead.

Following, Reed told her, "But I did have this really weird dream once."

She, "Really," feigning innocence, "only once?"

"Yeah; in fact, it seemed so real I'm not sure that it was a dream."

"And now you are going to tell me about it," she led, as she grinned.

"Well, seein' as you brought it up," disregarding her banter, "I suppose I could. See, I was in this long tunnel filled with giant aquariums, but there wasn't any water in them, the aquariums —or fish. There were people, a whole bunch of us, mostly derelicts and malcontents —'cept for me of course."

"Of course."

"And I kept picking my nose and eating the boogers and…"

"—That is disgusting."

"Heck that's nothing; wait 'til I get to the good part." And as they waded through the brown water and mud, Reed related the seemingly disjointed fragments linked to fuzzy images that he could still recall. It had been some time ago now since that night —and after all— it was only a dream.

Up ahead Lent wondered, "What do you think killed those animals, creatures, whatever they were?"

"Lizard dogs maybe; I've no idea," Ames replied candidly.

They kept going, farther and deeper into the swamp. Ahead lay the unknown and unexplained; danger and darkness that stirred below and within the gloom of a soup-fog realm, a blend of something-else-night, not really sky anymore, not really atmosphere either. Everything was digressing, decomposing… dying.

Reed's conjecture was closer than he knew, but his untimely interruption prevented Kalo from deciphering her subconscious intuition. So the four continued on, and as they did, in this primordial quagmire of putrid broth and swamp water filth; one bloated, one shriveled and wizened, floating in the bog and gray-brown mist behind them… two griffins[8] were dead.

* * *

Many hours, and miles later…

…Up ahead, in the transient images composed of fog, a massive form began to take shape. Huge, more than huge, it was immense and dead, and empty as the ghosts of their dreams, listing gray and dark, moored in the mud.

The rusted steel-hull freighter waited quietly, thick with mud, encrusted barnacles and accumulated marine growth that evidenced the centuries since its demise. Adorn in tangled seaweed clinging to the deck and tentacle fingers of kelp that hung from the rails then draped to the water, she wore a green bridal train that flowed in the mire. Lost for eons, she lay still and silent on the bottom immersed in mystery below, now appearing again to transport cargo in an inexplicable, eerie afterlife. A ghost ship.

She was a leper with gaping dark holes infecting her skin. Rotted and torn with the ravages of time, her superstructure and hull were pitted, oxidized and eaten away. A widowed bride in her gown of gloom and despair, again the strange apparition had risen from the depths and a time in the past. Gray and rusted she rested silently in the dark, waiting in an unexplained and unfathomable place of fog and interlude.

There was no one aboard the entire vessel. Even from below, looking up to the deck they all knew the ship carried no crew or passengers; the feeling of it, empty, dead, completely alone... a journey to nowhere.

—A foghorn blare,

Startling them, the sudden plaintive blast cut through the encompassing shroud as a vacant bawl of lament, a solitary, painful wail —long, drawn and distant, removed from reality, the painful sound of a soup-fog night, hollow and empty as the ship itself.

—Then silence.

It ceased creating the impression it may have been their imagination; and with spooky-quiet still ringing in their ears they exchanged glances, not wanting to ask, wondering if it had been real. Each believed they had heard it, but couldn't be sure.

Focusing on the bow, "Oh, hell no—" Reed brooded, "the 'Marine Sulphur Queen'."

Almost disbelieving, again Ames regarded it, and wondered. In places the rusted holes in her hull appeared dark and blackened concealing the interior within; but with others dim light was visible ferreting through from the opposite side. There was no logical way, no possible way it could be here; yet there it was, rusted and hollow, dripping water and mystery, gray as death itself, wearing a bridal train of seaweed and silt dredged from the depths of an unexplained mire.

Ames' lips scarcely moved, "How can it —that— be here?"

Kalo said nothing; two things felt wrong.

"The legendary ghost ship," Lent offered, cryptic.

Sliding him a glance, "The what?" Ames asked.

"Ghost ship. Folklore recounts strange appearances of a transport vessel that conveys lost souls from place to place, from times in the past."

"Conveys them… to where?" Reed asked.

Lent, eyes wide, taking it all in: "No one knows, the passengers are all dead."

Reed swallowed hard. "All dead?"

"Yup." From one to the other they traded unsettled expressions; by now disposed to believing almost anything was possible.

She loomed before them—

Dark and dreary, tattered by the ravages of time and demise, ashen as the fingers of mist that slithered through the holes in her hull, the 'Queen' intimated purulent malevolence imprisoned within the blend of duckweed and muck that floated around and throughout her. Superstructure towering high overhead the freighter rested aground in mud that gurgled as it oozed through her bowels with the blebby flow of cold liquid decay filling dark empty places with the texture of quicksand and agouti silt.

It was an eerie scene of shadow and mystery and creeping gray fog. She was vacant and despondent, from the deck high above them laden with tangled seaweed and layered blue mud, to the slime-stained hull that groaned with the contagion of leprosy, to her bones of exposed I-beams creaking moans of despair. The sullen mood of darkness lingered inside her hollow, lifeless carcass, almost whispering… ushering recollections of prose and poetry that stirred reviving dark and layered images of Edgar Allan Poe.

Beneath them, *blurp, squisssh, blurp*, quagmire telling footsteps, leaving a trail behind that they could not see, the four cautiously approached the ghost ship; nervous, perhaps watching for her crew: a deck hand, cabin boy or steward. But on deck nothing moved. In the companionways nothing moved. The pilothouse was empty. There was no wheelman to steer the ship. No one was there. The freighter was lifeless and empty... or so it seemed.

Very close now, they stood at the keel looking up, surveying the length of hull. It was rotted, rusted, and rivet-hole steel. Anticipation was crowding from behind, breathing, pervasive, thick in the drafts and infused in the odor and sensation of this 'Titanic' that was somehow dredged from the Bermuda Triangle so long ago; and then had sailed the realm of a mysterious green sea within the boundary of an unfathomable circular storm, embarked on a voyage that brought it to here and now... to this place, with them.

As the four viewed the gigantic freighter, inside, Kalo felt it. "They are coming," she whispered.

Ames: "They—who?"

Closing her eyes, drawn by the inner voice, inside, Kalo felt it, felt them. Hand to the quiver —and an arrow came out— eyes decisive, "Behind us!" —as she reeled.

—The foghorn blared!

Leaping from the shadows, they were enormous —Night Hunters!

Six feet tall and jet-black with twenty-foot leg-spans, their cephalothorax-heads had four pair of glowing, white night-vision eyes and pedipalps, front leg-like appendages possessing an incredible crushing grip, with chelicerae, mandible jaws that drove their venomous fangs with lethal precision. Sleek and blue-black as ravens with coarse-bristle hair, they ran on ragged-barb legs fixed with bale-hook claws —and driven by external stimuli and instinct they were just as deadly as before. Like gigantic wolf spiders they caterwauled white noise of savagery and mindless insanity —resurrected from Hell— they had returned!

Punching holes in the mud and flinging whorish scabs of slop —trilling chattering, cackling animalistic screams— the dark killers rushed from the fog. Twenty-inch fangs weeping venom, they attacked in shatter-splashes of violence and waterwind mud ripped up by their feet —hideous, macabre— and deadly.

Snap—sss—thwack!

The first Hunter caved in a wash as more attacked from the bog —suddenly everywhere— pouncing from all directions; streaking black villains emerged from the shadows and gray. Coming up, the twibil swung viciously as the scimitar whirled, their weapons tearing and slicing chitin with gray-splatter blood. The laser spit flares and flametrails of lightning torpedoes —blinding and shrill— havoc screamed as chitin spun through the fog.

Strafing fast and furiously Reed shattered them like rockets blowing holes through fine porcelainware. Bullets of light searing around them, splashing glutinous-thick waves —Hunters being ripped apart, exploding— then flames! Crazed fireballs scrambling through the bog with tailflames tracking then catching them —then collapsing in mud— it was confusion of ragged running legs, torn water and ravaging fire splattering duckweed-petal muck.

Gray and speed and chattering flames, they dashed as black dervish velocity and fire-swept hulls —rackets of sloshing claws on scuttling legs— they were burning everywhere, violently colliding then ricocheting and collapsing in the swamp. Impossible to track, within the bedlam of speeding afterburn animalistic screeches were cut short by shrill teakettle sizzles of overboiled-chitin and sudden-vapor clouds of explosive flame —gone— flittering pieces splashing into the bog.

But charging from all directions the rush was unending and the four intrepid nomads were being pushed back. Attacking raven and night-vision eyes —an arrow, explosion, or glimmer of steel— and, *sploosh,* in the mire as another went down. Time after time they repelled the arachnids, their weapons nearly invisible with force in the confusion and commotion, lost in the haze. Maneuvering back and forth the determined band defiantly covered one another; they were inseparable, unrelenting, unflinching and indivisible, standing together as a cohesive fighting team.

"Gotta do something fast," Reed yelled, "can't hold 'em off much longer." He fired, the blast creasing another shattering half of its legs, the impact-flash ripping through its abdomen then splashing out its back launching it sideways in a bloody whirling-gray spray. Plashing down it spun shoveling in circles heaving mud-bubble froth, shrieking and snapping at anything within reach. As the head came around Lent waded out quickly and hacked dead center in its eyes, just jerking the twibil out as another leaped —reflex reaction— his weapon flashing up as the Hunter came down, legs splayed, claws ready, fangs wide...

—A shrill whine, the bright flash and overhead a scattering-blast!

...Laserflame splattered the head slamming through its hull, ripping it completely in half. Instantly soaked with bloody gruel as ghastly chunks scattered and plashed, he stood drenched in sticky slop but was still alive, and hastily scrambled back alongside his allies.

Striking and evading Ames wielded the scimitar with deft precision and ecliptic speed, parceling Hunters then twirling the weapon, switching hands and following through with finishing blows, plying the blade so skillfully it seemed almost a part of him, now an extension of his will. Enjoined by determination and shielded by whirling razor edge he blueprinted strikes as attackers rushed in. In less than an eyeblink another slice through the jaws, the next paring through its eyes dropping it in the boil of rancid water and mud.

Kalo was a shadow of speed springing onto fallen carcasses and drawing each arrow, instinctively searching the gloom for what she could not see...

—Split second awareness of raven motion,

...Two Hunters leaping from the camouflage of gray-black shadowland, their night-vision eyes locked on —both airborne— fangs ready. The first was thirty yards out, the other ten yards back. Like black h.a.l.o. parachute commandos they jumped in majestic arcs turning their bale-hook claws forward to take her.

More quickly than one's eyes could follow, her senses guided her aim, the arrow slicing through the first's open jaws then out the back of its head. Dead in midair it plummeted as its glowing white eyes went dark —then again, *thwack*— the same arrow taking the other in the throat. With its fall the second rogue's legs folded —off-balanced, a side-roll— then it crumpled as a splatter of mud.

Even before the second arachnid was down, she had another arrow on her bow. Her ability was uncanny, her speed extraordinary, and her aim was unerring, as straight and true as the perfection of sunbeams.

"Too many of them," Ames yelled slicing through another, "get inside the ship."

Disbelieving Lent turned —and hacked, "Inside what ship?" Laser flares illuminating the fog, a Hunter reared; Ames spun as it lunged —and slashed. Crunching through fangs and chitin Lent's twibil sank in its head. "But that's a death ship."

Spraying pulse laser blasts, Reed reeled. "Let's go!"

Wading to a rotted-through hole in the hull, "Kalo!" Ames called out.

She let fly and darted into another opening as Lent, deciding it was better than being left outside alone, quickly followed ducking inside. Covering their backs Reed was at their heels; into the dark, and all out of sight.

Hunters pounced on the hull—then skittering.

Outside there were grating sounds of claws scraping and their jaws chewing metal, scouring the hull; that quickly they were all over it. Within seconds, through rusted-out places they could see the Hunters swarming the ship like dark scavenging roaches crawling on a dog food bowl; and as the four vagabonds swiftly backed away from the ship's hull easing deeper into the gloom of her hold, they left them behind. The spiders continued clawing, scraping and biting, but were unable to find any opening they could breach.

Expeditiously and silently all four slipped into the darkness feeling their way around machinery, piled or scattered wooden crates, sodden coils of heavy rope, stacked metal drums that most long ago had leaked their contents, and other obstacles and garbage. All of it coated with greasy agouti-dark mud.

As they went farther within the abrasive sound of scraping claws finally diminished and they stopped to catch their breath. Darkness.

Hard breathing indicated to each where the others were; but that was about all. It was pitch black.

Ames whispered, "How many matches d'you have left?" For a moment he could hear fumbling and the familiar rattle of the little metal GI matchbox as Reed shook them gently coaxing one out.

From the dark: "A few, but not many. Three, maybe four."

"Anything in here dry enough to burn?"

"Don't know, but I doubt it. Give me a minute."

There were rummaging sounds and a metallic clatter thump of someone kicking something and knocking it over, then a heavy splat like a drum tipping over and rolling a half-turn in the mud. Next was soggy thumping noises followed by the distinctive, *rrrip*, of a knife blade through canvas; sloshing footsteps and something unscrewing followed by, *gluck, gluck, gluck*, and the piquant odor of old diesel fuel permeating the darkness. Then —*skriitch, pfssst*— a match burst into flame illuminating Reed's face and hand.

He lit a torch made from a vintage billet wrapped with damp canvas and doused with diesel fuel—and grinned. "Smells old," he said. "Can't be more than twelve octane. Wonder it still burns."

Unaccustomed to the ostensibly bright light Lent squinted, offering, "I'll make some more." He and Kalo set to rummaging, gathering more stuff: a broom handle, a short length of rusty galvanized pipe, a wooden bedstead and some rat-eaten gunny sacks, while Reed wedged his torch between two parallel pipes running the bulkhead and cut more strips of canvas.

After the pair wrapped the handles Reed doused them with fuel oil from one of the drums. It smelled old and musty and broken down, but it still burned. A minute later they had four makeshift torches —and two, maybe three matches left.

Flickering illumination—

Looking around they all felt the ambience, sensed the profligate emptiness and hollow of loss that resided within the 'Queen'. Her pitted walls were rusted and, in some places, rotted through. Steel companionway staircases were twisted, broken, or missing entirely. White enamel that once presented high-gloss sheen now ran the gamut: stained russet-brown, seaweed green and a dozen pallid shades of gray.

Moving slowly, exploring—

Numerous companionways, bulkheads and cabins, and what used to be storage decks, galleys, an infirmary and officers' quarters or crew's berths, no longer bore much semblance to the judicious structure and order required on a sailing vessel. Now the ship's interior resembled an insipid multilayered, multilevel, perforated labyrinth-maze, a random patchwork of oxidized metal Swiss cheese. The interior was rotted through just as badly as the hull, everything covered with slimy green-black algae and draped with putrefying runs of matted seaweed or clinging ropes of collapsed sargasso kelp.[9]

In a time and a place somewhere else, she was once a proud and seaworthy vessel; but now her crew was lost and she was no more than an empty shell, a tarnished vestige of halcyon days and a time long since gone. Dearly departed… the 'Marine Sulphur Queen'.

They presumed the pilothouse, or wheelhouse as it was sometimes called, must be somewhere above, in the superstructure above the main deck; and the engine room somewhere astern beyond the cargo hold, in the darkness where they could not see. Here, amidship, all around them was algae, seaweed and kelp, and primordial ooze of decay, a flowing suspension of semiliquid green-black silt that slithered in viscous layers creeping into every possible crack and miniscule cranny. And here, there was something else.

Watching the overhead, "We are not alone," Kalo warned softly.

Lent: "Night Hunters?" as they all began searching.

"No," she whispered, "a different kind of hunter."

"Different," Ames asked, "how?"

Kalo closed her eyes, drew within, and inside she felt it, "Something…" then she felt *it*. "Death is here."

In the blackness of catacomb I-beams above, cloaked in obscurity, superstition and the suggestion of 'things that go bump in the night', it was wound with the pith of acrimony and moved in the still of a dark, dead breeze. Unseen, nocturnal and featureless, a black shadow slithered along the overhead as it circled then perched on some large steam-transfer lines high above them.

After crouching a moment, making no sound, the phantom moved again. Its face was without definition, shadowed and concealed as it glared down with narrow bloodshot liver-red eyes from beneath the hooded cloak. Saliva drooling from its dingy-gray rotted teeth, it crept slowly along the large transport pipes clutching a scythe in its hand. Dispatched by his overseer, eyes following, observing those below, the shadowy form watched them.

Nervous, "What do you mean, death?" Lent asked.

"One and the same as Legend Mountain," she replied.

Recalling the attack and touching his bandaged arm, "Where?"

Scanning the high ceiling Kalo searched the dark recesses above them, an abyss and a thousand places to hide; unseen corners and behind obstacles where their torchlight could not reach. "Up there," she intimated.

Tense, all eyes followed hers with the strain of expectation and that sense of dread; fine hairs tingling and cold on the back of their necks, that feeling that something was about to happen, anticipating, afraid to look away... and being vulnerable. It crept up from their feet and into their chests making it hard to breathe; not a pause of held breath, but that knot that sticks in the chest and squeezes it tight.

Below—

Back and forth, their eyes moving slowly, looking for it, the men side by side, Kalo and Lent a short distance away. It was very dark up there; and it seemed even darker.

Above them—

Bloodshot liver-red eyes, wizened shadowy hunchback shoulders, and ragged dingy-gray rotted teeth dripped saliva laced with loathing.

Below—

Sensations of spine tingling cold crawled through them, but there wasn't a wind, only an occasional dead breeze; the still of disquiet and a shiver of silence. All around them the chill moved invisibly and crept in, inside, where each could feel it and couldn't shake it off.

It was an odd feeling, an eerie sensation, the foreboding of danger lurking nearby...

—A foghorn blare,

...And the, *rus—ssh!*

Black as malevolence and saturated with darkness it flew at them in a frigid wind of shadow-phantom. Within the hood narrow bloodshot eyes, ugly teeth—and the sleeve and weathered hand with the scythe. The specter swooped down appearing as a liquid-boil of sinuous motion wearing a trailing robe of whirling raven flames.

Startled by the foghorn and diving for cover the vagabonds bolted and ducked just as the dark assassin swept upon them, Lent swinging his torch at the form overhead as Kalo shoved him aside...

—*Whoosh!*

...Missing the target the shimmering scythe hacked savagely through a crate just above Lent's head spilling and scattering its rusted contents of junk with splatters of mud. Reed, torch in hand, brought his weapon up.

The phantom whirled and ascended so quickly it seemed to evaporate above as laserfire streaked through it exploding on the overhead beyond, sending rusted metal scattering. Then echoes— bits of shrapnel splattering and dimpling unseen bulkheads and companionways before they fell in the darkness and mud.

Stop-silence again. The quiet of absence... followed by a whiffing twirl of flaked seaweed and shredded kelp spiraling down around them, sloughing as it rained like helicopter chaff.

In an instant Kalo was onto her feet and leaning over Lent as Reed and Ames searched the overhead. "Stay down," she warned, "it is after you." Eyes rifling the imaginary shapes in the shadows above them, he did as she said.

"Yeah, it sure is," Reed agreed. "That's twice—and that's not coincidence."

Crouching beside her, "Why me?"

Still scanning the overhead, "I do not know..." then, "it is coming again." The others couldn't see it as her bow spit an arrow through the dark, *tanging,* when it struck the ceiling somewhere snapping in two, Kalo leaping aside as the shadow flashed past swooping over their heads.

Strafing fiery blasts shred the ancient steel: another crate detonating dumping rotten mulch of decomposed foodstuff, pipes and staircases splintering, bulkheads and hatches flying apart, chunks of spinning, whirling metal being struck again and again, all of it torn to pieces of ripped-up confetti and a tangled flashburn of seaweed and cinder-glob mud. The laser ripped through everything solid, shredding it to slivers of debris. Spinning twice he blew gaping holes through the overhead —then suddenly stopped...

Everything was quiet. Too quiet. Deathly quiet.

...Until unexpectedly the 'Marine Sulphur Queen' moaned — long, drawn and hollow, an eerie lament of the pain in her guts; then an intensifying groan as the engines growled churning her enormous pistons, powerfully bringing her screws to life. Shuddering and grinding the mammoth freighter forcefully lurched and the bow rose as it heaved, and she began to move. Disbelieving, incredibly they could hear and feel the vibrations of the screws sloshing immense whorls under the stern, her monstrous teardrop blades sucking up mud. Underfoot the deck trembled and shifted as the ghost ship pried loose furrowing through the unending quagmire.

Unnerved by the ship's sudden movement, their voices nearly drowned out by the engines' metallic-clang pounding and head-rattling noise, Reed yelled, "Did you get it?"

"No—"

Almost stunned, "You missed?"

"No!" Kalo yelled back.

"Then what happened?" But suddenly the floor shuddered violently and, "Nevermind, we gotta get out'a here."

Scanning as they ran, constantly searching the overhead and watching their backs, weaving and scrambling around spoiled goods and rotted cargo they fled for the ship's outer hull. Bumping into things, they kept moving. Almost knocked down by rolling cargo drums, they kept going. Leaping from here to there and avoiding obstacles, they kept sloshing and running. Panic and darkness, and sweat in their eyes.

Breathing hard, when they got to the starboard hold, they found a river of mud pouring in through the holes in the hull, overrunning anything in its way. Flowing like a lava cascade it was a liquid-black bulldozer of greasy waves that picked up and carried the junk and debris along with it—then with turbid strength churned it all under.

Lent jumped onto a companionway staircase, the others following his lead; then to an overhead pipe and hand-over-hand crossing above the ominous moving avalanche of black slime that flowed relentlessly below them. Noise was everywhere, out of place: groans skreighing over the deafening sledgehammer of pistons and metal's stretched-to-the-limit moans.

Hurrying, one after the other they crossed from the quarterdeck stairwell, over the cargo hold, to the outer hull. But just as Ames was about to jump from the metal staircase to the overhead line the mudflow tore the anchor bolts and stairs from the lower deck dragging the entire structure down—him along with it.

Fighting the mudslide, he tried to withstand the torrent but went under; then abruptly surfaced struggling to get to his feet, then went down again in the suffocating chest-deep flush. Covered with slime and dragged by the churlish flow he fought but went under again, then flailing reappeared and finally got his footing just as an ugly surge of sludge sent a linebacker crate that took him down again. Momentarily just flowing mud —then he popped back up— black as a tar baby fighting for all he was worth, and another fall before he managed to get to the bulkhead and a vertical pipe —grabbed it—and slowly pulled himself up.

Wiping some of the goop from his hands and then using the pipe's anchor straps to climb, he made it above the deluge to the overhead lines. Dripping sludge, hugging a large steam line with his arms and legs, he was finally able to crawl and cross the span of the cargo hold where he caught up with the others.

Noise was everywhere, out of place: groans skreighing over the deafening sledgehammer of pistons and metal's stretched-to-the-limit moans.

Outside, riding the keel and washing along the freighter's hull sideswells of mudflush poured in enormous black waves, building up and surging as they rolled, then sliding and congealing as they turned over filling the trench dug out as the wake. The mire's power was incredible and as suffocating as the backwater-roll of a dam's spillway, turning over and churning like quicksand that would never let go, with no way to get free. And although no one said it, in the back of their minds perhaps they believed it wanted to smother and kill them.

Studying the churning backflow of liquefied silt Lent decided, "If we jump, we'll be dragged under for sure."

"Probably," Ames agreed, trying to think of something.

"So we dive," Reed said slinging the pulse laser across his back —and he did— an awful sounding bellyflop-splat with outstretched arms and as flat as he could. Planing facefirst and spread-eagle he mud-surfed sliding up and over the rise and crest of the swell, then skimming the surface scooted into the swamp beyond the immense wave of muck turned up by the freighter.

Disbelieving his insanity but inspired by his success, Lent did the same, sloshing angel wings with his arms as he followed; then Kalo, then Ames. Gliding quickly and smoothly as greased little pigs, they splattered beyond the vessel's tremendous suction and finally stood up sloshing in waist-deep swamp boil; then washed themselves off as...

...She whined in her bowels, then clanged and groaned skreighing over the deafening sledgehammer of pistons and metal's stretched-to-the-limit moans. And as the freighter pushed on and away, into the fog... together they watched.

No law of physics or logic could explain the empty vessel, less than supernatural or surreal, it should not be here. Yet it was. Navigating an undeviating course like a ponderous gray hulk bound with metal-dead skin the freighter plied through the green-black mire and fog arousing sideswells of floating duckweed and swirling whirlpools of muck.

The dead ship slowly sailed away from the vagabonds. Pushing onward with the churning propulsion of engines secreted within the darkness of her bowels, eventually the ghost ship was absorbed by distance. Then silence again.

And as they watched the behemoth vessel, gray and dark as it was... faded. It was as though the curtain of fog had taken it away, or swallowed it up. Hollow, empty and dead, the ship disappeared leaving upon the surface a floating legacy of duckweed and slime, lifeless and tangled as the mysteries of this place... on a voyage to nowhere.

CHAPTER NINE

Long blue-black shadows…

…Etched images of slippery banshees and lecherous lacewing ghouls that slithered over clumps of moldy floating duckweed and decomposing tentacles of green-black grass, as algae and slime buoyed indolently in the brackish mire. Stagnant, the air carried a dank, dead-earthworm and sewage taste in its palm that permeated their lungs… a swampworld hidden in fog.

Circumspect and watchful they pushed on through the endless gray bog stepping in muck-slime that, *queezed*, between their toes as they went. On the bottom, where they could not see, the silt harbored microbes, black leeches and other such alien creatures that dwelt in dark places.

Following the others she waded through a copse of drifting dead grass, leaned over a bit and squeezed as she pulled coaxing another six-inch leather-tough bloodsucker from her thigh, then tossed it away, *kerplunk*. And they pressed on.

Alongside Lent, Reed mumbled something. "What did you say?"

Tired, "Nothing; just talking to myself," Reed answered abstractly without looking his way.

"You can talk to me if you want," Lent offered, "this place is spooky."

Reed glanced over and grinned; then eyes drifting back to the shadows, "What I said was, I don't know how she missed."

"Missed—who missed?"

From behind them, "Me," Kalo answered. Lent turned and looked back as she added, "I did not miss."

Reed, still easing through the swamp, looking around: "You sure?"

"Yes."

"That's what I was afraid of; I was hoping you did."

"Why?" Lent asked rejoining the conversation.

"Nothing, kid; don't worry about it."

But Lent persisted, "What was that thing inside the ship?"

Allowing a glimpse, then back to the fog, Reed answered evasively, "Not sure."

"But you do suspect… something."

Still moving, "Yeah, I always suspect… something."

"Mind telling me?"

Now the other stopped and turned, looked at him, studied him. "You don't really want to know." Ames knew what was coming, but didn't look back.

"Yes, I do."

They started moving again and amenably Reed nodded then explained, "Kalo already told you; not necessarily what, and not necessarily who."

Exasperated, he urged, "Just tell me what you think, Reed."

"Death," Kalo said from behind them, turning Lent's attention with a start.

"Death?"

"Yeah, the Grim Reaper, Devil's advocate, envoy, henchman, harbinger —whatever— the garbage man of wasted souls," Reed agreed.

Ames finally spoke. "That's just a figment of someone's imagination."

"Call it what you want, Doc." Then back to Lent, "And it gets worse."

Swallowing a lump, "Worse, how?"

Blasé: "He seems to be after you."

"After me?" The lump stuck.

Looking back, "That's enough, Reed," Ames warned, "you're scaring him." And he was.

"Tell me I'm wrong then," the other contended. "Once was random —inside the mountain. But twice is premeditated."

"Maybe so, but it missed; whatever it was."

"Well we gotta do something before it shows up again, Doc. Seven lives only works on cats."

"So let's kill it," Lent suggested, more than willing.

"Small problem there, kid."

"Problem —what? What's the problem?"

"Kalo put an arrow through it and I hit it at least once I know. Nothing —absolutely no effect." He paused and wiped a smudge of mud from his cheek with the back of his hand. "It's the Grim Reaper, kid—Death."

"So?"

"How do you propose we kill something or someone — whatfrickin'ever— that's already dead?" They all stopped; quiet enough to hear the muck ripples moving away.

Lent, momentarily speechless, then nervously, "Well, where did it come from?"

Reed looked at Ames and Ames at Kalo; then Ames looked back at Lent and quietly said, "I think I know."

"Regardless of where it came from, Doc, we have to figure out a way to get rid of it."

"How are we gonna do that?" Lent asked turning to Ames.

"That," Ames said, "I don't know."

"Nor do I," Reed concurred, "but we'd better come up with something pretty soon… or else."

Worried, "Or else what?"

Eye to eye: "We lose you, buckaroo."

"That isn't funny."

"And I ain't laughing."

Lent, again to Ames: "Why is he—it—after me, and not you guys too; you know, all of us?"

"Don't know," he admitted. "And at this point it's only conjecture, a presumption on our part —so far anyway— but that's sure how it looks."

"Well that just really sucks," Lent griped. "I don't like this, not one particle of it."

Reed sympathized, "Yeah, poop occurs, but don't let it get you down. We're all in this together."

"That's real comforting; so we all get hacked into tiny little pieces together."

Grinning, Reed bumped his eyebrows. "That would make quite a piquant stew wouldn't it; be like goulash."

Both agitated and frustrated, "Doesn't anything spook you, Reed —and don't say Bloody Bones, 'cause I *am not* in the mood." Then an abrupt transition in thought, "And where did the ship go?"

"Talk about mind-skip to an arcane subject," Reed remarked pragmatically, "why don't we start with how it even got here in the first place."

"And the Hunters," Lent suggested.

"Curious," Ames remarked. They both looked at him with stupid, *what's that supposed to mean,* expressions. "I should think they would have all been wiped out when we were inside Legend Mountain and the surface was blown away."

"Most of 'em probably were, but some were below with Tian and me," Reed reminded, "at least one that I know of anyway," referring to the one that had envenomed him.

Lent: "You said you killed that one."

"I did, but there could have been others, you know, brothers, sisters, cousins. Shoot, for all we know there could have been a whole litter of 'em."

"Litter spiders," Ames piped, deadpan monotone.

Reed, blasé: "Was that a blink, Doc? Because if not, you know you actually do have a skewered sense of humor at times."

"Pin cushion skewered?"

"Yeah, pointed like that." And back to their problem. "So, we know we've got dinosaurs, Hunters, a ghost ship, the Grim Reaper, leeches crawling up our asses, and this endless 'Never-Land' dismal frickin' swamp." He sighed. "Damn, this just keeps getting better and better, doesn't it," not a question.

"Could be worse," Ames offered.

Shaking his head in the face of adversity Reed almost grinned, "Okay, go ahead—how?"

"Could be completely dark."

"Don't *ee-even* say that," Lent barked, "just the thought of that gives me the willies."

"Hopeless," Reed sighed shaking his head and the banter away as he turned to Kalo; then calmly, moderately, "you realize of course they're making me stark raving crazy." She smiled, but didn't respond.

"Curiouser and curiouser," Ames whispered.

Lent looked at him. "Mr. Ames, what exactly does 'curiouser and curiouser' mean?"

Straight faced, the man tousled his scraggly mud-caked mop. "It means get a haircut. Come on. Let's go."

* * *

Eventually...

...They came to a shallow rise of muddy ground, not really so much an island as a mud slick covered with duckweed scum and matted dead weeds that wasn't completely submerged like almost everything else. On this 'sort-of' island there was a small leafless tree. It stood all alone, withered and barren, branches mostly drifting to the left; still, with no wind. And at the far end of this peculiar islet was a sizable mud mound that looked like a boulder covered with muck.

Climbing from the water Ames suggested, "Let's make camp here."

"Make camp?" Lent mocked.

A tired glance: "Take a break then... s'that better?"

Two steps onto the flattened soggy grass Reed stopped mid-stride, backstepped carefully, then slowly stooped and snatched a coiled water moccasin behind its head from a hollowed-out niche. Without fanfare he threw it back into the swamp. Noticing that Lent had seen him do it, he laid the pulse laser on the grass and plopped down; then nonchalantly said, "Too tired to screw with it. Snake had my spot." The muted, *splish,* that followed suggested the moccasin landed quite some distance away.

"We could have eaten that," Lent told him.

Casually looking around for more snakes, "Do tell, probably could; but I don't see anything dry enough to make a campfire and I'm not hungry enough to eat one raw."

Without saying so Lent conceded he did have a point and they all sprawled out to rest. Deciding he couldn't get much dirtier than he already was, Lent lay on his back and stared into the fog as he asked, "Does anyone have any idea how all this happened?"

"Nope," Reed said abruptly. He was already considering something else when Lent glanced over at Kalo. She merely shook her head.

"First we need to figure out what has happened," Ames decided. "Maybe then we can figure out how it happened."

Still looking up, "Then what has happened?"

Ames scooped a small wad of mud with three fingers, and rolling onto his side flipped it and hit Lent's chest. "Haven't figured that out yet."

Eyes traveling from the man to the new mud-splot on his tee shirt Lent inquired lackadaisically, "What was that for?"

Pragmatic: "You missed a spot."

Smiling, the youth rubbed it in and they continued talking. "It had to be caused by 'The Hole in the Sky'."

"Don't think so, kid; this is too widespread. Your 'Hole in the Sky' might create some sort of anomaly, but it would be more localized."

Lent, puzzled, "Uuh… in simpler words."

Ames nodded. "Your 'Hole in the Sky' might do something like this, but it would likely only be in one place, or at least in a smaller area. This swamp seems to be everywhere."

"That's true."

"And the others, they vanished from different places."

"Except for us."

"Exactly," the man said. "—And why not us?"

"Do you have any ideas?"

"Nope, not really."

His attention drawn away from their conversation, Reed studied the large mound of mud not too far from them. He tried to listen in on what they were saying but couldn't seem to concentrate. Kalo sat quietly. Reed kept thinking, *mud pile*. Something about it just didn't seem right, and in the back of his mind the thought occurred—*it doesn't fit in*. He was enveloped with a peculiar sensation; subliminal, almost hypnotic. He blinked twice. *It doesn't fit in*. They weren't actually talking to him anyway, so without saying anything he got up and ambled over to the mound, just to have a look.

Kalo listened, and watched.

As Reed got closer he kept eyeing it, sizing it up, and walked around it a time or two before scooping some of the mud with his hand. Examining it; it was mud all right —so he did it again.

He moved farther back, to another spot, more to the rear. He could still hear them talking behind him, around the other side, back there; but they were speaking so softly he couldn't understand them anymore, didn't even know what they were saying anymore. And they weren't talking to him, they were talking to each other; and he wasn't paying attention anyway.

Sizing it up, he moved to the far side of the large mound and scooped more mud away; it was mud all right —so he did it again. Curious, he scooted over a little bit more, and did it again. Kalo blinked twice—and Reed blinked twice.

Just then Ames called out, "Reed, what's your fascination with that pile of mud?"

"Nothing, just goofing off." That's when he noticed, eyes brightening when he saw it... an inconspicuous, glowing red sensor.

Intrigued —then excited— he swiped with both arms removing a giant scoop, his hands sliding on a smooth surface —*mud all right*. It was covered with mud and filthy-dirty —*but it wasn't just mud*. He took two steps back, whispering, "Spank me special." Then louder, "You gotta be shitin' me." And he sang, "I knew it!"

CHAPTER TEN

"Doc, you'd better take a look..."

..."Now what?" but he got up anyway.

Reed took another step back and stated clearly, "Initiate embedded source code, file override, voice recognition, Reed... encryption signature Philadelphia I-B-6-U-B-9."

The inconspicuous red sensor embedded in the polycarbonate panel flickered between ruby and emerald, then steadily glowed green —and peeling mud away as they opened, the sliding panels whisked apart and the lights turned on inside. The interior was a 'USS Starship Enterprise' console boasting two upholstered captain's chairs on sliding floor tracks with an expanded-metal platform floor and another below it chock-full of neatly packed fuel cells sealed in black and yellow HazMat wrapping-plastic.

On the walls, from below the platform to the top of the domed ceiling, were horizontal rows of magnetic coils overlaying the interior, each row evenly spaced a couple of inches from the next, all of them perfectly aligned.

The exterior skin was made of polyhedral lattice framework with metallic-flake bullet-resistant polycarbonate panel sections composing the walls, a mud-covered ball from mire to fog. The geodesic time sphere.

As he approached Ames immediately recognized the portal and saw the illuminated interior, "Holy crap, it's..."

"Yeah, it sure is."

Following Ames, Lent asked, "Sure is what?"

Months before the Pilgrims and Renoloi met it had been hidden in the jungle: cold storage. Lent had never seen the geodesic sphere.

Beaming, Reed told him, "Our time machine."

"Unbelievable," Ames whispered, "how did you know?"

Reed shrugged, "Had a strange feeling; it just didn't seem right." Wondering himself and shaking his head, "Everything else has been pretty much flat, except this, this wasn't; and mud wouldn't form a mound like that, it would have settled unless there was a big rock or something under it. It was just too symmetrical to be random; didn't seem to fit in"

"And it still works?" Ames asked, hoping.

"Well, the portal does, and according to what you told me, the Federation must have been so intent on duplicating our operational files that they somehow missed the encryption signature for the underlying override and hidden source code. Can't really say for sure until we fire her up and find out."

Poking fun Ames inquired, "But, 'I-B-6-U-B-9'?"

Grinning, "Just picked something I wouldn't forget, and I knew I wouldn't forget that." Reed quickly stepped up into the machine, the sensor going green to red.

"Figures. Voice recognition, Ames," he stated clearly. The light flashed again, ruby to emerald, then stopped flickering and glowed steady and green, and Ames stepped through the portal.

Never having seen the geodesic sphere, curiously Lent leaned forward to peek inside, "Can I…"

Ames: "—Don't touch it!"

…Too late.

The instant his hand made contact with the portal opening — *zzzap!*— sharp voltage and azure-hot sparks blew his hair straight out with a scatter of mud launching him from the ground and twenty feet back. He landed as a limp splash of frizzed mud-crumble hair with pissed pants, scary-wide eyes and surprise. Kalo and Ames hustled over to help as he sat up stunned and quivering water and the jolt of electricity away. His hand burned like a bitch and the residuals tweaked out up the crack of his butt in flatulent little bubbles.

"Sorry," Ames apologized, "didn't have time to warn you; should have said something sooner."

Shaking the bite and stinging burn from his hand, "That hurt," he grumbled, "—a lot!"

"But it won't kill you," the man assured. "It's only been rebooted. Reed still has to codify operational codes and reconfigure the config-sys-ini embedded source code override. Don't touch the sphere's exterior until he does."

"Don't worry, I won't. That dog bites."

Reed popped his head out from the portal. "Hopalong Cassidy flies again. Packs quite a jolt, huh?" Then disappearing inside, his voice trailing, "Be back in a minute."

Wobbly, "Boy howdy, shot me right out of the saddle," Lent admitted as they got him back on his feet.

Shortly, from inside: "Okay, it's safe now, reinitiated. We're reset; good to go." Approaching the sphere again, not quite convinced, Lent stabbed at it lightly with his index finger. Nothing. More at ease now, he smiled.

They climbed inside.

Seated at the console, Reed's fingers were going like busy-wizard-woodpeckers feeding the systems data and instructions. Having eased inside, marveling at the technology within the cramped quarters, and afraid to touch anything, Kalo and Lent stepped aside and let Ames get to the console where he sat down.

Reed darted him a glance, then back to the keypad and overhead monitors. "Didn't reinstall the voice recognition files, but I did leave it in the embedded source code and encryption signature; so that way we can all get in and out and you or I can still lock this puppy down." Checking instrumentation Ames nodded as the other went on, "Star sixty-nine initiates lockdown and will activate on our voice recognition patterns."

"Good enough. Any particular reason why you picked star sixty-nine, if you don't mind my asking?"

"It's been obsolete in the phone system for so long I don't 'spose anyone would ever think of that." And the, *clever of me,* grin.

Ames: "Star sixty-nine, obsolete."

"Yeah, so, what's wrong with that?"

"Nothing really. But there are only four of us, and I don't think two of us even know what a telephone is."

Point taken Reed conceded, "Well fuckit, old habits die hard."

Ames: "Creatures of habit to the end; don't suppose we'll ever change."

Shyly Kalo and Lent stood off to one side looking the cabin interior over, unsure what they should do. "It is so beautiful," she complimented.

Circumspect, "Don't touch anything," Lent warned.

Overhearing, Ames grinned and over a shoulder, "Kalo, in that compartment —to your left, bottom row— there's a first aid kit with peroxide, dressings, triangle bandages and some other stuff in it. Clean his wound with the peroxide and patch him up, okay?"

"Certainly," she obliged scooting to the cabinet and poking around until she called back, "The white box with the red cross on it?"

Over his shoulder, "That's the one."

She and Lent huddled, opened it, and began rummaging through the contents: ointments, antibiotics, syrup of ipecac an emetic, dressings, splints, 4x4 and 4x8 squares, sutures, halazone, hydrogen peroxide, various medications and equipment. All the essentials.

As they occupied themselves on the floor and the men reprogrammed the computer's systems Ames instructed, "The hydrogen peroxide should be in a brown plastic bottle."

Searching the contents, "—Found it."

"Sulfadiazine, a disinfectant white powder, is in shiny flat envelopes with black lettering."

"—Got it."

"And the triangle bandages look like little folded cloths wrapped in clear plastic; brittle, clear paper that crinkles when you touch it."

"—Found them." As Kalo got the paraphernalia together Lent unwrapped the leather bandage on his arm.

"Wash the wound first," Reed said. "There should be a few gallon jugs of distilled water in the cabinet too, in the back. Go easy on it though; we need it."

She reached in, "—Found them."

"Okay. Got everything you need then. Fix the urchin up."

"I shall," and back to her assignment as Lent removed the last wrap of his makeshift dressing. The injury was bad, severing muscle and coagulated with blood. "That is deep," she observed adopting a medical-maternal tone.

"Nah, just a flesh wound," straight from his comic books. "Just wipe it off some and throw another bandage on it and it'll be just fine," trying to conceal a smidgen of reservation.

Shaking her head —and back to the first aid kit. "No, we have what we need in here," as she dug around a moment retrieving a #4 suture, a sterile needle and thread. Methodically she peeled the sterile wrapping apart and he saw what it was.

"What are you gonna do with that?" he ventured timidly, with that wobbly-knees, *oh shit*, sort of stammer.

Feigning innocent sincerity that revealed just a trace of deviltry, and an expression she'd gleaned from watching Tian deal with Ames, "Why, I shall close your wound of course."

"My ass—oh no you're not!"

Tone and volume attracting his attention Ames looked back. "Yeah, it's pretty deep," he agreed, "better sew 'im up kiddo." Then back to the console.

Lent gasped. Kalo grinned; and the, *he agrees with me*, smile.

He winced every time she dabbed water on his arm and she had to smack him twice to make him sit still. "Quit being such a baby."

Squinting and flinching, "Well it hurts."

Still cleaning the wound, "I have not even begun yet."

He looked.

"Renoloi warriors do not make such a fuss," she scoffed, irritating him.

Biting his lip, he frowned determination; he'd beat her at her own game. Defiantly, "Okay fine—go ahead," as she unscrewed the cap from the hydrogen peroxide bottle, and raised it. She poured. It foamed. And, *"Sho—oot!"*

Ames, at the console, without looking back: "Stings a little, huh?"

"Stings *a lot*," he yelped jumping up and dancing around as the cut began to bleed freely again.

"Sit back down; you are getting blood all over me," the motherly tone, thoroughly enjoying this. Begrudgingly he submitted, until she dabbed his arm with an alcohol-soaked cotton ball, and...

"...Owww!" he jerked back; and she stared him down again until he gave in again, then she patted the wound some more and he grumbled some more and the bleeding finally let up.

As she got the needle and thread ready, sheepishly, "You're not really going to sew up my arm, are you?" almost pathetically, that, *sick to the stomach*, feeling setting in.

Sweetly, inveigling, "Skin is no different than Chiqua or goat leather. The Renoloi have been sewing for generations," and the barb, "because some of us did not have the Accumulation to provide our clothing," with 'the frown', "we made our own."

"That's not my fault." Pretentiously examining the suture, she didn't respond; but impishly she did smile. "You can't be serious —through—my—skin?"

Reed chimed, "For cryin' in the soup, quit being such a panty-waste-dougy-whiner and take it like a man." Amused, Ames turned to watch.

"Mr. Ames," Lent pleaded.

He shook his head disparagingly, agreeing with Reed. "Don't be a sissy."

Now he was pissed —and with no anesthesia the needle went in. He grabbed the nearest solid object and bit his lip so hard he couldn't scream; but they all knew he wanted to. And in spite of being traumatized, when she had finished even he had to admit that Kalo was an accomplished seamstress, and some day could be a nurse. Thirty-two stitches later and all wrapped up with a clean, folded triangle bandage, the job was done.

Even then, after it was all over, he eked a final feeble whine, but Reed cut him off criticizing, "Quit yer'bitchin'. It's gonna leave a cool scar."

"Think so?" Then macho mode, "Yeah, it will won't it." Reed was good at working things. Lent rubbed down his arm with the other hand and had to admit, "That does feel better. Thank you."

Proud of her work and pleased with his concession, maternally, "Do not pull the stitches loose," then sweetly, 'the smile', "you are welcome."

Diversion over, back to more pressing matters, Ames asked, "Reed, what's the new access code command?"

Matter-of-fact: "Open sesame."

"That's original."

"It'll be easy for them to remember."

The jab: "Them?"

Reed ignored it telling him, "Fuel cells are at eighty-eight percent. Original configuration restore fifty percent complete."

Ames turned. "Kalo, there's food and drinking water in that compartment," indicating which. "Freeze-dried and dehydrated stuff, want to dig some out?"

"Yes, I am hungry, and…" facetiously, "Lent has lost so much blood it will help restore his strength."

"You're always so prim and proper, are you ever gonna learn to talk like the rest of us?" the only thing he could think of offhand.

Reed, over a shoulder: "Contractions."

A head snap: "What?"

"They're called contractions; she doesn't use contractions. I told you that before, but you never listen."

Back to her: "Yeah, those."

"Digress, Lent? De-generate?" Wryly, "I think not."

She was good and forgetting his injury he threw up his arms. "Ouch—"

Smiling sweetly, "You must be careful not to tear open the stitches," fabricating concern. Coy.

Reed, under his breath: "'Tude; good girl."

Ames: "'Tude?"

Discretely, "Attitude, *I like it*."

Shaking his head but smiling nevertheless, Ames muttered, "Hopeless."

Kalo dug through the improvised larder and pulled out a box of saltines, a jar of peanut butter, canned American cheese, vacuum-packed beef sticks, a six-pack of Pepsi, and sundry items. Stopgap buffet. She and Lent had no idea what this stuff was, but it all looked good and they were both hungry.

Still rummaging and leaning nearer to the floor, peeking into the small cupboard the girl heard a noise that did not belong. Outside, scratching on the exterior of the sphere, and with the scraping sound she remembered a night not so long ago in a stone hut when a friend was lost. She listened more carefully. The scratching stopped. Quiet again.

"Kalo," Lent lay a hand on her shoulder bringing her back, "are you all right?"

"Yes," blinking, "I am fine," scooting back from the cabinet with the water and without mentioning it, joining the others while the computers reconstructed the geodesic sphere's synthetic silicon reality.

Shortly, finishing his seventh peanut butter-and-cracker sandwich, with his tongue sticking to his palate, Lent sputtered, "Thith stuff ith vury good."

Almost involuntarily Kalo nudged him with an elbow correcting, "Do not speak with your mouth full." But even as she said it, he could see by her expression that she knew it was a mistake, reminding them both of a friend who was missing. He didn't argue and didn't talk back, didn't even respond.

Reed popped the top on a can of Pepsi, took a swig, *aaah*, and casually checked reconfiguration status on a monitor. "Restore eighty percent," pivoting in his chair and taking another sip as he turned to Ames. "Forgot how good pop was," fingering the aluminum can in his hand so he could see the red, white and blue ball.

"It's the little things," Ames agreed.

Lent, from the floor: "The bubbles tickle my nose."

With his easygoing smile Reed counseled, "Drink it, don't inhale," and warned, "those fizzy bubbles are magic shit —carbonation— and if you get too many in your nose they'll burn through your sinuses into your brain and make your head cave in."

Lent quit drinking, "Really?" worked up a swallow, then belched a loud blow that poofed out his lips, came out his nose and made his eyes water.

Lackadaisically, "Yeah, but if you swallow them, it works just the opposite —like that." He continued informatively with droll sincerity and laid-back credibility. "Food can kill you; you know."

"I didn't know that."

"Sure can." Reminiscing, "Yup, back in the old days some poor cholesterol-saturated slob would suck down a couple Big Macs, Quarter-Pounders and monster fries, and wash it all down with a super-size cola. Next thing you know he's waddling down the street with plaque flaking off in his arteries and it all comes apart and, *bam,* self-destruct." Lent squinted, believing. "Awful mess," Reed concluded shaking his head convincingly.

"Getting deep," Ames mumbled.

Reed grinned.

Scratching… outside, on the sphere.

From Ames to the ceiling, the grin evaporating, then to the overhead monitor, "Original configuration restore complete," Reed said quietly. More scratching. Back to the ceiling, eyes searching, his hand instinctively reaching for it and he realized, "Damn, the pulse laser," back down to Ames, "left it outside."

"You're shitin'."

Reed—blank stare.

Lent: "Where the snake..?"

"—Yeah, when we sat down in the grass." No one said it, but they all knew—*not good.* All eyes shifting back to the ceiling, they listened.

Unobtrusively Kalo rose and moved to the portal, put her hand on one of the sliding panels, then closed her eyes.

Ames, a whisper: "Any ideas?"

Reed, still looking up, "Give me a minute." Lent crouched silently holding the twibil, his eyes sliding back and forth on the domed ceiling.

Ames suggested, "The sphere's ready to go; maybe we should..."

"—Not without it," just loudly enough to be heard, "we need it. I'll go get it."

Lent spoke up. "—But the Hunters."

"Cover me."

"No, we need you in here," Ames insisted.

Reed objected, "My mistake. I left it out there and there's no reason for you to get eaten on my account; so I'll go."

Ames: "You're forgetting one thing."

"What?"

"I'm older," and he winked as he, Lent and Kalo got ready.

"What's that supposed to mean?" unable to see any logic in the remark.

"Think about it," Ames told him glancing over a shoulder, "and we'll be back in a minute. Just make sure the sphere's ready to go." With the three of them at the portal and Reed a couple steps back, Ames looked from one to the other. "You guys ready?"

Twibil in hand, Lent nodded. Bow drawn, Kalo indicated so.

The portal panels whisked apart...

...And dark as a sin with a wretched old whore, trilling, chattering animalistic screams filled their faces as the Hunter gnashed its jaws and reared clawing gray smog.

Recklessly —fearlessly— Lent leaped headlong at the vermin hacking through its chelicerae and gaping fangs. The double ax blades opened the mandibles as the pike dug through its eyes bayoneting out the top of its cephalothorax with a penetrating gristly-mean, *crunch*.

Shrieking, the mortally wounded spider staggered back dragging him along as it floundered and reared yanking him from the ground. Dangling defiance, he held on to the ax wedged deeply in its head as the flailing arachnid shook savagely slinging him like Raggedy Anne on a stick. Within reach of its claws, he couldn't—wouldn't—let go.

A simian on a limb, he hung on keeping it at bay as it clawed and thrashed, until finally seizing an instant of opportunity, propping a foot against its split-open head he shoved off tearing the twibil free. Whirling airborne he backflipped with a somersault, away from the creature, free-falling as the Hunter toppled back disgorging a gush of gray ectoplasm, then retched convulsively and collapsed onto its back.

As quickly as Lent had charged the ghoulish arachnid Kalo swept out beside him. No more than a fleeting wisp of lethality and warrior in the shroud of gray fog, skipping once, not using her hands she cartwheeled letting fly toward the top of the sphere—and in a blurred fleeting instant her arrow sank into a cluster of white eyes. Stunned, legs buckling, the Hunter crouched on the sphere collapsed on its hideout, skidding sideways, pushing grease-waves of muck as it slid down the latticework panels onto the rise.

Resembling a ghost with feline agility and unparalleled speed she moved wraith-like within the winds of convoluted gray smog. Just a glimpse —the snap of the bow— she was there and was gone. More quickly than their eyes could follow she appeared and vanished with the grace of an angel.

Ames dashed for the pulse laser as the illusive Kalo covered him —an arrow spitting past— and from the gloom beyond him a penetrating, *whack*. Another down. Darting from here to there she moved, spun and let fly —visible, gone— no more than a glimmer of inference as she did it again.

Sloshing water-flung mud another Hunter rushed Lent from the swamp —up onto the rise— and as swiftly as it charged, he more viciously struck back, his twibil crashing down, sinking deep in its eyes. With the gory spurt of curdling crunch the spider nose-dived in the mire, its ear-splitting screech cut short in a wash of rotten black slime. It died gurgling, regurgitating and sucking up mud.

Ames sprinting —*there, in the grass, fifty feet away,* crossing the mud flat as an arachnid attacked. Skimming the swamp it ran with the splickity-splashes of water-spray and shredded dead weeds, flinging them out like whirling soaked chaff. Hunkering down, low-running, its fangs were beetle jaws, pedipalps agape, ready to crush him.

Thirty feet, too far, no time —stopping he spun— and swung. Glistening steel slicing wind, his lightning strike severed the cephalothorax as the giant spider's momentum piled over him and it skidded on the mud-slick grass knocking him out of the way. Trilling —twisting sideways— it slid like a plastic snow saucer launched down an icy hill —then floundering— spun as its legs tangled in some weeds flipping it onto its back —a Volkswagen bug— dragging limp, ragged legs. Dead as an overturned wreck the ghoul slid, revolved and wound out then finally stopped and shutdown—junkyard dead. Rigid, then limp, its legs flopped apart.

Down, flat on his back—

Another leaped from the fog, her arrow punching suddenly through its head —vanishing— the creature crumpling as it sailed over —then *whoomph*— landed somewhere beyond him.

From the corner of his eye, yet another flash of black coming from the fog —reflex reaction— rolling onto his side as the Hunter slid above him, the sword sweeping up through its connective pedicel cutting it in half. The anterior and posterior aspects came apart like a fallen headless horseman with eight wild raking legs.

Onto his knees—

Glimpses of images instantaneously captured and synthesized: the pulse laser ten feet from him, Kalo and Lent over there by the sphere, Reed at the portal looking out. Fingers and feet digging mud, Ames scrambled clawing on hands and knees—*the pulse laser.*

He dove, grabbed it, rolling and turning, and sat up on his butt —*fire*— then again and again scorching this mist-thicket world of miserable smog with stunning flashes of brilliant light flares. Unleashing a circular ring of fire he strafed —a hit, two misses, a hit, more misses, more hits— taking them out around him and beyond his limit of sight. A fusillade —dazzling flashes— laying a field of suppression fire. He couldn't see them but could randomly hit them—soggy eggplant explosions and bits and pieces spinning through the fog.

—Then sensing, *they're not attacking anymore.*

They'd fled; broken off and vanished into the quagmire and fog. *That doesn't make sense.* Expectantly, ill at ease, rising to his feet and looking around he searched for the adroit hulking killers; but there were none. They were no longer out there.

Sheathing the scimitar his eyes skipped from the encompassing mist to the sphere: Kalo and Lent, holding their breath, watching, and Reed, hands braced on either side of the portal. All around them crept that uneasy still of premonition, suspense wrapped intricately within the flowing curtains of gloom.

Strangely, it was quiet again. Too quiet.

Then...

...Inside, Kalo felt it, that cold chill: death, very close... lurking. She stood still...

Inside, in her mind's eye she saw him, standing out there in the mist and shadows where none of them could see.

...The Grim Reaper.

Tall and intangible as an image of darkness and something that once was. Seasoned and empty as the whisper of yesterday's wind. Lethal blackness that was vile, gaunt and soulless. An emissary sent from the past.

He was out there.

From beneath the hooded cloak narrow liver-red eyes veined with scarlet glared. His dingy-gray rotted teeth dripped saliva and loathing as a green and black tongue licked leather-chapped lips savoring the coppery taste of blood. Wrinkled, wretched clawed fingers turned the snath rotating the scythe blade slowly, reflecting a glimmer of light when it did.

Corrupt and opaque as the shadows of midnight stirring invisibly within a swampworld of twilight... it was he. Within the hooded cloak of death, black as malevolence and saturated with darkness... he was no more than a frigid wind of shadow-phantom. Imparted with superstition of medieval black forests that once instilled apprehension and the sickness of dread... he was watching them. He was the harbinger, the collector... the Grim Reaper.

He had come for them.

Ames strained to see through the chameleonic smog wafting over a wasteland mire and an enigma of misery. And as he searched the ever-shifting illusions manifest in fog, he settled upon what he thought was a chimera, some chilling mind trickery of his own design, a shadow with glowering liver-red eyes.

Head down, peering from under the rim of the hood, the ebony phantom was standing there, watching him. Slowly the shadow raised a hand bringing the swamp to a cold-boil, a bubbling, lecherous, simmering cauldron. As far as the eye could see the bog gurgled and popped with rising gray-dome bubbles that murmured the cadence of bursting globules releasing invisible methane gas. Colorless, odorless, this witches' brew floated undetectible over the surface as winding miasma of unseen malice and invidious danger wound in ever-expanding lacewings of mist.

The whispered word, *"Harbinger..."* stole out with the fog; and as it did, holding a piece of flint the Grim Reaper raised his hand, then struck the stone sharply against the blade of the scythe...

—Sparkflash sizzle,

—Sudden blue-yellow fire,

...Igniting a marsh gas-boil of holocaust flame!

Methane saturating the fog detonated then flashed in an instantly expanding explosive yellow-blue fiery spray that rushed the veneer of quagmire. It was a roiling flashover burn of searing holocaust streaking out, swelling and rising as it came...

—First the, *whoosh,* as it ran, learning to growl as it poured,

—Then with incinerating flesh-eating savagery, *it roared!*

...Sweeping over the swamp as infernal liquid winds of diaphanous hellfire and desiccating air. Burning, super-heating, vaporizing —eating the fog— it was scorching and incinerating everything in its path.

Seeing the flames —the danger— Kalo and Lent rushed for the safety of the sphere, clouds of billowy fire and howling wind streaking for them and Ames —too far from the time machine— he'd never make it. Turning he sprinted —certain death only seconds away— then flat-out ran!

Swirling and roaring yellow-blue fire of netherworld brew boiled behind him. It was after him, determined to take him, whirling with furious breath from an evil darkness wearing the cloak of a shadow glaring with bloodshot liver-red eyes —that face. The wicked, incredible wall of fire came...

Flames were everywhere,

As from the portal,

...Reed screamed, "Run Doc, run! —*Doc!*"

PART VI

CHAPTER ELEVEN

It began a long time ago…

…The Complex. Near the unlit corner of the laboratory, a solitary object, a geodesic sphere twelve feet in diameter, geometrically beautiful and symmetrical, constructed of metal polyhedral lattice framework and translucent polycarbonate sections with metallic-flake embedded throughout; a giant shimmering ball from floor to ceiling.

It glowed with rainbow hues, nearing transitional flux, the critical point of crossover, just a fraction beyond the speed of light.

—Then suddenly, a dazzling magnetic cloud whirling around it, sparkling like fairy dust...

...A shrill whine —*pop*— it was gone.

* * *

And somewhere, a long time ago…

…An extraordinary implosion: beyond measure, indeterminate, beyond reckoning. A star collapsed upon itself shrinking to the size of a grain of sand, becoming so dense it was able to literally push a pinhole through the fabric of space. Even the emptiness of space couldn't manage so much weight concentrated with such incredible pressure, all at one place; and the result, a diminutive hole through space itself… to a new space beyond.

Conception, the portal: the boundless jaws of the mythical Lion.

A whirling void of mystery and dark, it was born out there in the realm of unknown... the unexplored, and unexplained. Incredible beyond comprehension, the doorway to forever wound and roared with absolute silence in the vast emptiness and supernatural realm of the space-time continuum. Swallowing everything from everywhere it was a spiraling anomaly and incomprehensible power: destruction, obliteration, and oblivion. The horizon of infinity a rent wound of ragged shreds an astonishing, inconceivable whirlpool of reformation...

...The vortex opened.

—Everything, disappearing to somewhere on the other side, a place that might be only a dream... a figment of the imagination.

Such was the destiny of Earth and two men in a geodesic sphere moving through time in transitional flux. They traveled so fast not even their shadow could catch them... but the black hole could. They too were drawn away by intangible energy, the grasp of gravitational invisibility and pitch, absolute black... following everything else into the black hole.

And the black hole remained. It swallowed everything from everywhere... for millions, then billions of years. Strange beyond fiction, when time warps and space folds time can stand still, or — *tick*— it's forever.

* * *

His words slurred...

...“Fourteen—billion—years!” Reed yelled inside the machine.

Never before had any human being encountered such tremendous cataclysm: the confusion, destruction, and reformation. Stars exploding then imploding again and again... unending cycles.

Planets and moons rupturing from within, scattered to limitless specks then swirled together and recompressed forming new worlds. Entire galaxies pouring and spiraling onward in twisted veins of liquid light —time warped, space folded— the billions of stars rupturing again into space. And it continued over and over, space compressed into a fluid channel pouring at the speed of light through the blackest blackness possible to imagine. Brilliant light thundering without sound —exploding, imploding, millions of times— too many to comprehend it all...

Fifteen Billion Years!
—And the Rush—

...An incomprehensible surging torrent of blinding cataclysm erupting from the other side —exploding trillions of planets, stars and galaxies, all at the same instant— too much to envision, unimaginable, incredible beyond description...

The 'Big Bang'!

And the black hole was gone,
   ...An Entire Universe Was Born!

* * *

A Primitive World...

...The geodesic sphere rested fifteen degrees off level, partially submerged in the soft humus soil, a total loss. They were in a clearing encompassed by a forest, a jungle without the gagging humidity. It was very warm. But a jungle should be alive with animal sounds and birds; here it was quiet. It was also green, a deep beautiful, chlorophyll green. This world was no longer dark and barren, a bright yellow sun washed this tropical land with warmth and daylight. The sun was beautiful, promising... misleading.

* * *

The Trogs; the battle...

...Reed felt a wash of relief when the giant went down and he saw Ames tumble to the ground. Clutching the knife in his right hand, left leg stabbing with pain, he hobbled toward his friend and Tian. Then suddenly —from nowhere— a knotted club smashed into his face splashing blue-white fire and searing sparks. The world exploded!

He was thrown backward landing on his side, and he tried to scream but could make no sound. Writhing, rolling to his stomach he slowly began pushing himself from the dirt and shock swept through him. He wanted to vomit and swallowed hard to keep it down, shaking his head, flicking blood away. Swirling white sparks and pain were everywhere, his brain screaming with deafening roars of whirlwind confusion.

The world was fading... color to gray.

The Trog was barely visible, no more than a smudged silhouette; but that was enough. In a blur of speed and reflex Reed's right hand struck burying the blade of his knife in the left temple of the ogre's skull. Asphyxiating on his own blood he coughed and let go... releasing the knife, delivering its message.

The world was fading... gray to dim.

The chokehold slackened and Reed slipped from the massive hand as the giant slumped to the ground. Falling, Reed crumpled stricken and helpless onto his back, looking up at the sky. And lying there, he smiled momentarily... as though listening to someone.

Fading... dim... to dark,

The smile melted away...

...And he died quietly at the foot of his enemy.

* * *

On the rimrock...

..."This is not the end," Tian confided, tears gathering again in the corners of her eyes then stealing down her cheeks. She gripped Seana's arm so she would not leave with the others, and whispered, "Wait here with me, Seana... please."

Gazing solemnly over the mysterious range of Legend Mountains, soft spoken, Tian said, "We must wait until sunset."

* * *

The Sacred Temple...

...Ames continued through the tunnels, his torch pushing back the darkness as he went. Then, into a huge and magnificent cavern.

182

"Did You plan all this..." he wondered reverently, "or did things just get a little out of hand?"

One final, listless gaze and he leaned back in the luxurious seat, drew the bowstring, and let the flaming arrow streak upward...

—Saffron tailflame into the dark,

...The arrow struck the cavern ceiling and instantly —everything exploding— deafening, shattering noise and brilliant white light. And he imagined that a choir of angels was descending upon him; alabaster wings on gossamer winds.

They were so beautiful,

And they sang such a wonderful song.

They were so beautiful...

* * *

Into a realm of mystery...

...The angels rejoiced and their song grew louder, their voices dulcet and more resonant until the man was no longer conscious of the explosions and the infernal white fire, somewhere far in the past. Now, only their song and the soft arms of space caressed him. He felt as though he were drifting, almost falling, to somewhere unknown, to where reality and the dream world merge; somewhere distant, far removed... to a place beyond.

He felt no fear, only wonder.

All around him were stars... billions upon billions of them scattered throughout vast clouds of cosmic dust, gossamer winds of nebulae reaching forever. And color returned... the purest colors he had ever seen, shimmering and flowing, undulating and spiraling onward through infinite space. He felt insignificant, dwarfed by the majesty of the universe, its serene beauty more than he could have ever imagined.

In the realm of mystery... the flight of a mythical bird crossing the universe, unhurried, enjoying the journey. The glimmering beauty of the pellucid corridor was spellbinding, flecked with countless glittering particles: minutiae of starlight, blinking pulsars, shimmering quasars, burning snowflakes of light.

It was so beautiful.

* * *

They sat together on the North Ridge…

…Evening taking a deep breath, "Old Sam was perhaps one of the very first freedom fighters. He believed in what this country used to be, in what the Federation has been trying to destroy since its inception. Even before the Alliance came to be, Old Sam was an icon for his compatriots and resisted every effort of the Federation —for over five years— until he was finally captured." She paused again, then disclosed, "Mr. Ames, without either you or Old Sam being aware we verified both your identities: dental, fingerprints, retinal scans, photographic records —thoroughly researched you both— databases and everything." She asked anxiously, "Are you offended by all of this?"

Ames thought before answering, "No. I can understand that it was a necessary precaution." He knew she had something else to tell him and prodded, "What is it, Evening; what haven't you told me?"

She put her hand on his knee. "We positively know Old Sam escaped the prison with you, but there's one thing that creates a problem for us... for me."

"What?"

Carefully, gently, she revealed, "Just to be certain, we also did x-ray and CAT scans of a grave in the Mountain View Cemetery out on Harrison Avenue —for anatomical and dental comparison. Old Sam's real name was Samuel Reed."

"Was?" Ames asked nervously.

"Yes," she hesitated, then told him. "The thing is...

Old Sam was killed by General Smith.

He died twenty years ago."

Ames muttered, "...the eyes."

* * *

The sixth sub-level...

..."It is time for harvest." Smith bellowed vicious laughter, and plunged the sword down —into Ames.

The man was helpless except to watch, a vision of surreal slow-motion, the gleaming blade slicing through his tattered shirt and into his chest. His mind racing through a million memories...

...All that had happened. And the whisper, *"There is a reason."*

His face flushed and he wanted to vomit, vision clouding, beginning to blur. He could see the blade but the room was fading, darkness creeping closer. Still grasping the laser in his fisted hand, he tried to bring it up to fire; but his hand wouldn't move, his finger could not obey.

"And now..." Smith anticipated greedily, "now you shall die." And he plunged the sword at Ames again...

—At that precise instant,

...Transparent light swirled around him: winds of starlight, flashes and radiant aftertrails, residual glimmering wisps floating ever so delicately, scintillating minutiae, pinpoint quasars, beautiful shimmering pulsars —then flashes again, whisking away. He watched humbled, awestruck.

The Being was White Flame with Blinding Fury,
>   All Powerful, All Knowing,
>   And the Light,
>   Brilliant White Light!

Beyond the Light he thought he saw movement, but it was all so unclear. And Smith seemed to be changing. Growing larger. Growing taller.

Wild with rage, Smith roared and hunched his huge shoulders ripping both coat sleeves up the seams. Then grabbing his chest, he tore the coat and shirt off and flung them away. He swung with his sword —again and again.

It all seemed so cloudy, distorted.

Ames lay dying on the floor, his thoughts drifting away. Everything just mists of confusion. Was this really happening?

Then, in his mind he thought he could see them arriving, white riders on horseback —and a dark army below. So many there were on both fronts he couldn't count them, but certainly more than millions, the armies going on forever, beyond the horizon. Riding bareback —were they angels?— robed in white with broadswords drawn. And there was blood spraying from wounds and splashing upon the world forming an incredible sea of red littered with endless lost souls from all of history.

The last great battle,

Armageddon,

God's Day of Judgment.

It was a visage of recompense, the thunder of Heaven. And so the great battle was fought, the war to cleanse the Earth and begin once more with God's promise of something better and new: a tomorrow.

All the things he imagined... and sounds fading away.

His eyes closing, dying, lost somewhere in the realm where reality and the dream world merge, that place where faith becomes reality... and reality just a single step beyond.

—Brilliant, incredible, sparkling light was everywhere...

...And God smiled.

The portal of the geodesic sphere closed as it began to sparkle like fairy dust. Scintillating minutiae, shimmering rainbow colors,

Whisking trails of starlight.

A shrill whine —*pop*— it was gone.

—And at that precise instant...

The geodesic sphere and solitary occupant within propelled through time to a future awaiting his arrival within the crater of the temple ruins and the collapsed mountain range of the Legends.

...Shatter-flash of ripping destruction swept over the face of the world, an incredible wave of exploding landscape —speeding forth, flashing out— ground splintering and blasted away. The Earth quaked in upheaval and volcanic eruption scattering mountains and landscape to shards of oblivion. Thundering, rattling, pounding, a surging pulse-wave swell of blinding, rushing, boiling incineration and nonpareil detonation-burn of vaporous fireflash white light...

—The world exploded with Cataclysmic Finality!—

* * *

On the rimrock...

...Tian and Seana sat together, side by side, on the edge of the crater.

"Wait here with me, Seana... please." Silently, motionless, Tian watched the lingering sun.

The sun sank lower, almost to the horizon...

...Footsteps shuffling along the path leading to the crater, and they emerged from the trees, Reed limping, Nitana walking beside him.

'Strangers who are different, but not enemies. The strangers would come from Beyond when the black hole spilled out the stars as far as forever, but would not appear for many generations. Finally, they would arrive in a sphere of sparkling light that no one would ever see'. And the part she had not told the men: *'They must go Beyond; then rise up like the Phoenix... and they would change our world'.*

Then...

...The setting sun touched the horizon bathing the world with the mysteries of sunbeams and a halo of golden light —and Tian reeled.

An invisible zephyr of small miracle clearing away the fog and dust to reveal the entire ruins of the Sacred Temple, a shimmering geodesic sphere with an open portal —and Ames— barefoot, limping toward them, wearing frazzled Levis and a tattered shirt.

It was in the Legends.

* * *

Months later...

...Unobtrusively, Kalo crouched on a high flat rock just behind them, tentatively waxing the string of her new bow. She was still very young but her desire and persistence had been rewarded; she would be an archer. The girl had been practicing ardently, obsessively, alone in the jungle, honing her skill and aim; and as always, Kalo was quiet, intent, wanting to learn.

T-Rex roared—

Absorbed, focused, Kalo released the bowstring, a powerful — *snap*— the feathered missile slicing through air —*ssst-thwack*— and struck with consummate accuracy, splattering lens, severing the optic nerve, scrambling brains, then stopped in the back of its skull.

The fletching and shaft of an arrow barely protruding from the punctured right eye of the monstrous reptile, Tian's gaze traveled from the dead dinosaur, over the Renoloi, to Kalo, still standing on the boulder, stone cold... a Renoloi warrior.

* * *

Motionless...

...The silent Kalo detected a glimpse of movement within the foliage. Prepared, she moved unseen, unnoticed, drawing her bow full. Not making a sound the person crept closer to the clearing, watching the travelers intently. Kalo's eyes followed her target, so close she could reach out and touch it—thoracic spine, between the shoulder blades. From behind, Kalo's soft words interrupted the quiet.

"Who are you?"

"Mr. Ames..." Seana whispered, "*he* is like you."

Without speaking—

Lent stepped forward, into the clearing. He was young, perhaps in his mid-teens; dark, tanned by the sun, rawboned, sinew and muscle strengthened by the jungle. And he regarded the world through dark brown eyes filled with youth and wonder set beneath a shaggy mane of the same color hair. He wore a dingy old tee shirt that was full of holes as if chewed on by mice, and khaki shorts, frazzled and torn up the sides along the seams of the legs. In his hand, lowered at his side, he held a twibil; a ponderous battle-ax with an ornately engraved handle, medieval in design, its twin blades gleaming, broad, razor-sharp —tipped with a pike head.

"Your weapon," Kalo warned.

"I mean you no harm."

Ames told him, "Our boat capsized in a storm."

"In a storm," the boy repeated; then almost disbelieving, ventured, "a circular storm?"

"Yes."

"The 'Hole in the Sky'," Lent whispered, astounded, gazing at each individually, "and you are alive." Smiling ear to ear, "You sailed into the core of the world—and you are alive. I knew it was possible, could be done; but they always refused."

"They?"

"My people," Lent explained. "My village is not far. Come. I'll show you."

* * *

Quiet now, forgotten and lost...

...The ancient battleground lay barren and dead, no vegetation, no life; everything was completely still. As far as the horizon, then beyond, it was a desolate land cratered and scarred with wounds that would never heal, from a battle long since past, an empty wasteland of crumbled mountains and fractured landscape torn apart in a cataclysm of upheaval... now forsaken and abandoned.

Millions of skeletal remains long ago gleaned of flesh in a carrion feast littered the terrain as far as sight would allow. Countless disjointed, dismembered bones were strewn in random disarray and heaped in crumbling, ungodly piles, now all picked clean of every fragment of meat. This was a dead land, destined to never again know the nourishment of even microscopic life, absolved with war, purified in fire.

Now and forever this place would remain a land cursed and cast off, eternally shaded with the eerie, unnatural violet corona of a veiled sun, and always eclipsed by a blood-red moon. Both still low, near the horizon, their prophetic alliance casting long blue-black shadows of sadness and desolation upon the 'War Land of Armageddon'.

It was all very quiet here; unearthly and unnatural.

Even the great slab of stone bound with a massive golden chain and held fast with a pure, Holy Seal seemed absorbed within the interlude of time and forfeiture. The silence of absence was deafening, the intense feeling of sadness and loss ubiquitous, overwhelming emptiness absorbed within every grain of sand and particle of dust swept along with a cold incessant wind. This place would always remain forsaken, and cursed, hallowed from this time forth only by a frigid, desolate... *Relentless Wind.*

* * *

One thousand years had passed...

...Narrow yellow-gray eyes scanned a ravaged world below, with unabridged contempt for the multitude of shimmering Mystics assembled there upon the scarred landscape that once had been a beautiful planet of blue and green.

To him his thwarted effort was not so much failure as a missed opportunity; *misjudged, miscalculated, it almost worked.* Evaluating, conniving, and surmising; *the deception would have succeeded were it not for Ames.*

Free again—

In the ecliptic darkness of a blood-red sky Satan glided upon invisible layers of atmosphere, scheming. A wivern, his eyes were yellow-gray, loathsome and seething with anger as sharp and penetrating as his fangs. It was time.

After so long inside, to be loose again was exhilarating, and that freedom replenished his strength. He roared. How special, extraordinary, to be complete, supreme, remarkable, absolutely evil. Himself again.

"Come my minions!"

The scream, drawn and empty, beckoned those who would follow and was acknowledged by chattering ghouls, the souls of a forgotten, banished army. Heeding his call, the amorphous beings emerged from concealment within cracks and crevices among jutting crags of wasteland on the blue planet. For so long the Dark Forces had awaited their master's command to arise, and now having been summoned they would willingly follow.

Their time had arrived; time to rise up from hiding and the lethargy of slumber. It was time for change, and like wraiths, opaque wisps of motion and shadow they emerged from everywhere, their tally a swarm of untold numbers, more than the grains of sand; immeasurable, innumerable, and evil. One thousand years had passed, a long time to wait. Finally, the millennium was over.

Satan had summoned... and they answered his call.

The Dark Ones—

A black storm, cloudy and bleak, they oozed and flowed into a blood-red sky gathering en masse with sin-filled red-glowing eyes and saturating wickedness inside them. Cast off in years long since forgotten as the dregs of humanity, the Dark Forces now emerged to strew emptiness and despair, inflict pain, wreak sorrow and unleash relentless vile plagues upon a far distant land. Boiling and screeching with goblin howls, horrid moans, and unworldly shrieks of hideous laughter, the Dark Ones flocked in whirlwinds of nefarious wanton villainy.

Visions of shadow, flowing liquid and dark, the most wicked of beings swept through the sky as it blended to black. Spanning the horizons east to west and north to south were whirling winds of commotion and evil as the dark army amassed and marshaled to an incredible cloud. The firmament churned blasphemously and ecliptic, blotted and filled with an ungodly chatter of despise, squeals of laughter, and howls of anticipation. The time for revenge had finally arrived and their raucous numbers shifted with boils of confusion like banshee flocks on the wing and monstrous, spiteful obsidian thunderhead clouds.

The Dark Forces swarmed—

Trailing as winds of neglect the shadow of destruction and sorrow followed him tumbling and rolling in acrobatics of flight, until they converged and congealed as glutinous murk. A blended cloud of wickedness blackening the surreal violet skies over the wasteland of Armageddon, they cried out for vengeance with hostile shrieks of anger, vulgarity and wanton lechery. Howling delight, fury and despise, they maligned and defamed all righteousness with screams for revenge wound inextricably within the fabric of cloud. A shadow of malady, ruin and sorrow, pathetic and black they followed until...

...In the blink of an eye, Satan and the Dark Forces were gone.

* * *

Out there...

...In the endless regions of space the Dark Forces pursued his heinous persona like a flowing black cloak with a glimmering sandstorm of red-glowing eyes. Altered images of darkness, forlorned in villainy, they propelled onward through the expanse and vacuum of space. At his heels the dark cloud followed as shadowing wraiths and swirling visions of motion trailing his presence in twisted strands of obscurity within the shroud of his eminence.

Absorbed within the cosmic emptiness Satan and his army soared, seemingly nothing more than an indefinable floating smear on dark canvas. Their black-hearted presence wound spiraling through the void; and camouflaged within that darkness, wicked yellow-gray eyes scanned, perhaps for something at the fringe of imagination, on the very edge.

Still screeching a cacophonous heckle and hideous discordant cackle they flashed through the vacancy of space without uttering a sound. The unparalleled emptiness within them, and surrounding them, engulfed their multitudes and absorbed all vestige of noise as their nefarious presence swept across the universe in an opaque whirlwind-tempest of transcendental imagery. With no atmosphere to convey sound there was none, only cold and dark emptiness, vast and bleak silence... and the stellar winds of rushing red eyes.

The Lost.

* * *

Far ahead...

...On the brink of time and the periphery of space lay an unknown, unexplored region within the territory of no return. Out there somewhere, was the boundary, a horizon waiting silently and magnetic... and drawing them in.

At the edge of eternity and dawn of tomorrow it loomed winding the space-time continuum to an immense vortex beyond the limits of comprehension. Too intense and incredible to imagine, it revolves where time and space collide destroying one another within its gravitational field. It was out there, waiting for them, expecting them. Invisible and gigantic, remarkable and awesome, the gaping jaws of oblivion.

Caught up within the gravitational cosmic winds, Satan and his whirling phantasmagoria propelled ever onward toward the anomaly's horizon. Manifest in a malevolent cloud of spiraling strands, the murky, twisting apparition of Satan and whizzing sands of red-glowing eyes had embarked on a journey from the netherworld to oblivion, and beyond, into the lair of the Lion, the passageway to forever... where the mythical Lion roars.

The Black Hole remains.

Then suddenly, the horizon—

Pouring and rushing blistering jetstreams of light, a climactic cascade of confusion and chaos without sound. From everywhere they came, broken planets whirling as fragments and duststorm flashing past, winds of particulate shards exploding, recompressing and detonating again and again. Stars rupturing in twisted veins of luminous gas, expanding upon themselves then colliding and splashing with unbelievable, indescribable flames; continuously reigniting, perpetually exploding, pure cataclysmic fusion and light. All of it searing into a helix of oblivion at the farthest reaches, on the most remote fringe... where time and space collide.

Everywhere was liquid gaseous confusion, fusion in its purest form; everything ravaged and dismantled as scattered calamity, swallowed from space and into the throat of the black hole. It swirled sizzling and plummeting at the speed of light, disappearing to somewhere on the other side, a place that might be only a dream... a figment of the imagination.

Within that matrix turbulence and holocaust pitch Satan and his Dark Forces traveled through time and space concurrently, jettisoned forward to where time warps and space folds. Deeper and deeper into the gravitational draw they went amid the winding apocalypse of colliding stars and exploding debris burning far and near within the void.

Chaos was omnipresent —the winds of oblivion— a conflagration of explosive, gaseous disorder and particulate confusion cascading in perpetual waterfall flashes. Everything —all of it— pouring and streaking in the same direction, to a vanishing point somewhere ahead. It was a continuous stream of liquid light created by countless melted stars and galaxies poured into a funnel so black it absorbed everything. Nothing would escape... not even light.

And the black hole remained. It swallowed everything from everywhere, for millions... then billions of years.

* * *

After that...

...On Legend Mountain; the plateau.

A world out of time that was frozen and still; nothing moved, no sound, absolute silence and calm... everything, everywhere ... suspended. A man, a demon, and two dwarfs were all that there was. The rest of the world watched from the realm of mystery and dreams.

And with relish, Wilson counted...

...Furious red flame and shattering blue-violet sparks —sword and steel— collisions of force splashing ribbons of fire!

For everything... there is a reason. Ames was only a man, yet he defied Smith—stood fast and defiant. Relentlessly he defended the vision of a pioneer one room schoolhouse with weathered steps, clapboard walls and twelve children playing outside at recess; a fragment of dream in a world that was frozen and still. He was only a man, just a piece of a puzzle, a conundrum, an enigma within the matrix amalgam. But he was blessed with reason and logic, emotion and more, so much more. He was one of the creatures God had granted freedom of choice, and named mankind.

To the most venomous of all —eye to eye— *Déjà vu, I know you. We've been here before...*

—Boiling red flame and pyrotechnic blue-violent sparks!

...Their swords clashed with the resonance of steel in a world that was frozen, entirely stayed, strangely still.

Suspended... out of time ...Waiting.

"One-thousand-seven," Wilson counted...

...And P.T. Barnum yelled, *"Time!"*

Time, existence, reality —everything resumed— motion and noise and the running confusion. Clenching his fists in fury and raising his arms Smith screamed, *"No-ooo!"*

In the blink of an eye Ames spun with the scimitar clipping his midriff with its razor edge and unrealized power. Astounded Smith staggered back disbelieving, staring at the bleeding wound transecting his belly. His skin looked discolored or bruised—turning purple?

Another flash of blade—Smith screamed!

Slicing diagonally through his blouse Ames inflicted a second wound. Still bellowing, his face reddened and appeared mottled or bruised; and enraged, seething with wrath... Smith *roared!*

* * *

Still, only pieces,
The Puzzle... and More.

* * *

After that, for a time it was quiet again...
...Until the saga continued.

CHAPTER TWELVE

As from the portal…

…Reed screamed, "Run Doc, run! —*Doc!*" swamp gas burning in a flashboil of fiery explosions and infernal whirlwind flames!

Roiling over the swamp with a ferocious resonant growl, its avarice hunger fried the bog, duckweed and wretched black grass. It was a thundering gale of incinerating yellow-blue flame flashing toward them devouring mud rises and naked twisted trees with pathetic arthritic limbs —a flashover blaze that blistered and whirled as it roared— a swirling, ravenous cremating wind.

He blinked —saw it coming— rushing waves of fiery liquid froth blotting out swamp —blinding bright— a holocaust glare. Sucking a breath, pulse laser in hand, he was moving —sprinting— bare feet flinging mud —focused— *the portal,* not a second to spare!

Spray of methane fire boiled toward him like monstrous fireflash waves of yellow-blue surf capped with pale waterwings. Closing, the gigantic explosion of tsunami flames cooked water to steam as it flashed, swelled and roared with its smog-eating, *ss-whoo-omph!*

—Six more strides; three seconds to the sphere…

Mud squeezed between his toes and shot from his heels, sticky and cool —but there wasn't time for that. His right foot slid sideways, a stick jabbing the arch; it should have hurt —but panic stopped that. Swamp fire was coming. It was after him, his brain synthesizing images in nanoseconds —no time for anything else. Reed vanished from the portal to somewhere inside as Kalo and Lent were getting out of the way. *It's coming!*

—Four more strides; two seconds…

Yellow-blue flame tinged with green vapor wings was devouring the bog as it flared and whirled with bright vivid boils, gobbling the fog with an insatiable roar. It was a firestorm of diaphanous wind shooting sizzling steam, streaking then bursting as an ever-expanding spray of high-speed incinerating cloud!

Almost upon him —*too close*— firewind just behind him, heat at his heels.

—Two strides; one second…

The portal was clear; they were out of the way —biting hot air crawling his back— swirling and rising around him. Fiery wind growled; it bayed —pain and blue-yellow flames— as it roared!

—One stride; he dove flinging mud through the air…

Swamp gas burning at his heels, fire chewing his shirt, steam boiling around him —singeing hot, desiccative heat— a rush of bursting scalding yellow. The deafening roar —climbing his chest— yellow-blue fire with green flame in his face!

—Airborne, whirling blaze wrapping around him…

He could see them —a millisecond of awareness— Kalo and Lent crouching off to the left, Reed standing at the console, hand on the keypad, looking back at the portal —at him— terror in their faces!

—Just an instant more and…

"—Hatch closed!"

Fire and wind seemed to be everywhere —all at once— as he heard the door panels whisk shut. Hitting hard on the platform skinning both elbows and knees on the screen floor —but he was alive— still able to breathe.

Outside the methane fireflash slammed into, rushed around and whorled over the geodesic sphere, the explosion pounding it with gale force and an incredible, rattling, *whoomph,* jolting them when it hit. Reed was flung against the console and Kalo and Lent pitched to the floor as the boil of fiery gas burst against the exterior of the machine rolling over the dome with its flaming claws.

The fire's leading edge splashed a wave of translucent flamespray that swept past the sphere to somewhere beyond in the swamp, the incredible heat saturating the mud insulating the sphere causing steaming wads to shrivel, crack and break like a parched water hole in a Death Valley July. Instantly-heated chunks of caked mud snapped and popped shooting into the swamp, each molted layer of shed mud revealing more whirling yellow-blue fire through the translucent polycarbonate panels.

—Then, *sssss...*

As a spent wave or windstorm that had blown itself out, the roar vanished, the wind stilled, the yellow-blue tailfire suddenly spiraling away with steam rising from the swamp. As quickly as it had happened it was over. Unexpectedly and strangely, outside it was quiet again. Too quiet.

"Shit, it's hot, it's hot—" Ames yelped rising to his knees, frantically waiving his arms trying to pat himself down. Without hesitating Kalo scooped the gallon jug from the floor, dousing him head to foot; and finally cooling, water dribbling from his singed hair and rosy face: "Thanks, I needed that." Holding the empty gallon jug and watching the steam curls rising, eyes wide, she just looked at him.

Still pumped, but now not as frightened, his gaze traveled to Reed standing at the console, Reed's eyes shifting from the portal to him. Next Ames turned and looked at Lent, now also relieved, and beginning to grin.

"Close," Lent said.

"Yeah, too close." Shaken but more at ease, he finally had time to take a breath, and as he did... scratching on the outside of the sphere.

Casting a raven shadow of torpedo body with eight legs, something crawled up from the swamp onto the time machine. Skittering and pawing it pecked and clawed at the plastic and metal dome. Trying to get in. The shadow grew darker and more defined when the creature crouched and pressed its head against the Lexan, and through the translucent panels they could even make out its glowing, pixel night-vision eyes. It was trying to see inside.

Outside—

More sticky sloshing noises, a clatter of feet approaching; another crept onto the smooth panels of the geodesic sphere using the metal lattice framework for toeholds. Scurrying sounds —now perhaps six— then eight. Pack hunters. They were crawling all over it.

"Hunters," Lent whispered, all of them watching the silhouettes moving about like circling shadows, testing the exterior, poking and pecking but unable to bite into the smooth polycarbonate sheets.

"Just what we need," Reed whispered back.

Eyes traveling from the domed ceiling to Reed, Lent suggested, "Why don't you shock them."

Under his breath, "Only the portal is electrified." Then to Ames, "Well, at least they can't get in." And as Ames said that...

...*Whack, skre—eeek*, the scythe punched through a polycarbonate panel above Lent's head. Reflex reaction, he dove back to the floor next to Kalo, away from the blade sticking through the ceiling and revolving within the room.

"That's no spider-bite," Reed barked.

Springing back to his feet Lent broadside-slammed the tip of the scythe with his twibil knocking it partway back out. Ames grabbed the first aid kit and swung —hit it again. Hammered back, the curved blade disappeared leaving a froth-curled pucker-hole in the panel where the scythe gouged it out.

"Reed," Ames said firmly, "get us out of here."

Outside—

Screeching white noise of savagery —and a trilling, curdling shriek!

Inside—

A fang poked through the hole spraying a mist-cloud of venom, as shielding his eyes Lent stepped into his swing hacking it off just below the ceiling. Wriggling back out of the hole the stub disappeared with a screech.

"Coordinates?"

"Don't know."

"Which way?"

"—Just go!"

At the console—

Two keystrokes and, "Lent, Kalo—grab something…" as Reed plopped down in the chair the same time the scythe blade forcefully struck the wall near the portal, "…and hang on —engage!" Reed stabbed the keypad and instantly magnetic fields swirled around them.

Outside—

The exterior of the geodesic sphere glowed with rainbow hues as countless subatomic particles whirled around it. Trillions of electrons, ions, protons and neutrons with dazzling energy trails of brilliant, resplendent sparkles —the sphere being swallowed by their swirling radiance— the swamp around it sodden and dismal, layered in tawny and grays.

As soon as the time machine was enveloped within the magnetic cloud the shadow-phantom hoisted the scythe and withdrew, fading then vanishing, an evaporating mirage. But still swarming like overgrown miscreant bugs the Night Hunters kept crawling all over it, until…

A shrill whine —*pop*— it was gone.

…The machine vanished and they tumbled in a clamoring muddle that went down trilling shrieks with splats in the mud. Tangled ragged legs and sodden chitin hulls covered with globs of slimy dead grass —glowing pixel night-vision eyes peering up from the swamp— perhaps even a tad confused.

Inside—

Their hair stood straight out as if from electrocution, clothes puffed as though shot full of compressed air —or from an awful windstorm— skin stretched, teeth clenched —and the energy within the sphere soared.

Color blinked to black and white. Blanched and decolorized —and surprised— 'faded' Kalo and Lent stared at one another. Scrambling to the console Ames tossed the first aid kit —she caught it— turning it over and examining the dents in the steel case while he strapped himself in. Not expecting to be bleached-out, but unruffled by their peculiar decolorized state, she studiously slid the kit back into the cabinet. After a moment their clothes draped back to their bodies; but puzzled, still trying to figure out why he was so frazzled and faded Lent eased up to the console, she following, on their butts.

"Better get some rope and tie yourselves down, guys," Reed advised, "transitional flux can get kinda snakey sometimes."

Kalo scooted back to the cabinets and got some.

Lent seemed more concerned with his 1960's Afro hairdo than the fact that he was a monochromatic-layered individual. After all, being tan—or gray—didn't really matter all that much; but his puffball-fro just wouldn't behave. Patting and combing with both hands, he plastered it down; but it shot right back up frizzy-wild, and each time kinkier than before. Philosophically Kalo calmly brushed hers aside once and when it didn't stay, she did the logical thing, tied it back in a ponytail with a rubber band she'd found in the first aid kit —and let it go at that.

But that wouldn't do for Lent, he was the master of his mane and it would do what he wanted, a shaggy mop to be proud of, not frazzled and unruly. Having none of that he licked both palms and combed through it with his fingers breaking mud flakes away; and when he did, *boing,* it poofed all over the place even worse than before.

Ames, to Lent: "Having trouble with your hair?"

Reed, over a shoulder with a low-key expression, not even bothering to smile, "Should have worn a baseball cap, kid."

Ames again, deadpan: "With a button on it."

"What?" Lent asked missing the joke.

"Reed's got a knife 'case you wanna shave your head."

"What?"

And finally, turning with the swivel chair, Reed, stoic as a mortician on a closed-casket day, furrowed his brow as though scrutinizing Lent. He pursed his lips, very droll. "Well, one good thing will come of it, Doc."

"Yeah, I 'spose you're right," Ames went along.

"What?" Lent asked, curious.

Grimly Reed told him, "Fresh air. At least the cooties won't suffocate and die then go moldy and soak into your brains." With their teasing Kalo didn't say a word; but she did almost smile.

Gullibly Lent inquired, "Fresh air—is good for them?"

"Oh yeah," Ames assured, "but it also stimulates their sex drive more than monkey nuts, so you'll probably be swarming with 'em before you know it."

"Monkey nuts… what's that?"

"Doesn't matter," Reed told him, "we don't have any and wild ones are scarcer than gnat sacs."

"Is scarcer a real word?" Ames asked.

A glance back, "Yeah, I think so," Reed said, ignoring Lent as he nervously began plastering his hair down again, until Reed finally grinned. "Forget about your hair; you'll get used to it," but he couldn't resist, "—or go bald."

Ames: "—Or crazy."

And together: "—Or both."

No longer nervous, now disgusted, "Yeah, eat road-apple stew," when he finally figured out that they were poking fun at him.

While they teased Lent, Kalo took a long look around the interior of the room fascinated by its complexity and technology. It was all so intricate and unusual.

Covering the walls were countless small shiny-string coils on flat, little green boards with hundreds of gold contact points and lines. The wire screen platform dug into her feet —and such strange stools that moved in grooves on the floor. Also, there were so many of those small yellow and black bundles with peculiar markings, all neatly packaged and aligned in rows under the see-through-metal floor she was kneeling on. And all the buttons, lights and other things spanning the table in front of the men; but she was particularly fascinated by the pictures and numbers and symbols that flashed on and off overhead on two of the smooth shiny surfaces. It seemed every time Reed touched the button-rows in front of him the pictures and symbols above him changed; so, she scooted forward, reached over Ames' arm and carefully touched one.

Ames looked at her. "It's a touch-pad and flat-screen monitor. It displays what we're doing here at the console; converts our actions to words, graphs, numbers, symbols and so forth that we can see."

"Sorta like a visual aid," Reed explained.

Clearly impressed, "I have never seen such things," she admitted.

"A bit more intricate than your average laptop," he added.

Casually, cocky, bragging rights, Lent offered, "I have, in the Accumulation."

He'd set himself up so Ames went ahead and let him have it. "Really? And did any of them work?"

Caught, and reluctant, "Well... no."

Reed mumbled, making sure he was just loud enough to be heard, "Imagine that," with an inflection of sarcasm. Then pretending that the jab was no more than a passing thought, he reached into a small compartment with stackable shelves and retrieved a gray antimagnetic envelope with the flap folded over and sealed. It contained a two-inch data CD.

Ames saw it. "Where'd you get that?"

"Here, presumably where you left it," pointing to the slot.

"I didn't put it there. The last time I saw that was in Tian's hut before..." He quit speaking.

"Before what?"

"Nevermind. Go ahead; install it."

He did. "It'll take a minute or so to reconfigure."

And they continued through time.

* * *

Shortly...

...The monitor flashed—*install complete*, then blinked from opaque to blue and a yellow smiley face appeared on the overhead screen. It must have been their imaginations, but with a straight-line mouth and expressionless eyes 'Smiley Face' seemed to be looking around the room trying to figure out where it was.

"Computer..." Ames said clearly.

"Yes, Doctor Ames; it is nice to be with you again." The voice was feminine, sultry, and the straight-line curled to a grin. "Is Reed here as well?'

Casually, "Yes, computer, I'm here."

"Delightful. Hello, Reed."

"Hello."

"Reed, you sound different."

"I'm stressed."

"Granted, viable distress is evident in your voice pattern; but also something other than that."

"Okay, don't try to psychoanalyze me," and a sing-songy, "thank you."

"Very well, Reed. It is a pleasure to be with you again as well."

"Right back at'cha." Amazed, Kalo and Lent stopped lashing themselves to the screen floor and looked, and listened.

"Doctor Ames..."

"Yes, computer?"

"If you will recall during our previous exchange I advised you that the IBM's reliability factor was less than mine, and additionally that it had a substandard coefficient in its codicil file."

Without looking up from the console, "Not in detail computer, but I was aware of the inference."

"You are correct, Doctor, not in detail; but in reference to that apprisement I must inform you that it appears the IBM experienced a fatal error in the operating system, precipitating a malfunction."

"What fatal error?" Reed asked.

"Indeterminate, Reed; but during install-startup configuration it was necessary to codify and supplant the correlation coefficient and criterion function of the IBM."

"Still jealous, computer?" Reed almost grinned. "You know—your reliability factor, compression capacity, and so forth."

"Jealousy is an emotion Reed; I have no task-compatible chip installed."

Ames asked, "What precipitated your intervention, computer —if the fatal error was indeterminate?"

"The date did not compute, Doctor Ames."

"Still doesn't compute, does it?" Reed observed rhetorically.

"No, it does not; there is insufficient data to…"

"—Compute the baseline," he interjected calmly.

"That is correct, Reed."

Ames said, "Ignore the date."

"With a baseline I could reinitiate a timeline."

"I'm aware of that computer, but we could only approximate to establish the baseline."

"Not very accurately either," Reed added.

"I can reformulate from an approximation," 'Smiley Face' assured.

"So could we but —okay, what the hell," Reed said, "fifteen billion, give or take a hundred million years."

'Smiley Face's' mouth squiggled in a wavy line and the eyes stretched from round to quirky straight lines like they were thinking, until finally, "Excuse me?"

So, he said it again.

"Reed, that does not compute."

Under his breath, "No shit." Then louder, "I know. Like we said, we have no baseline so just do the best you can."

'Smiley Face' smiled again and with the soothing, sultry voice assured, "I will hypothesize. One additional note, the exterior sensors are less than optimal, but I can compensate for that."

"That'd be good," Ames said, "I don't think anyone will volunteer to go outside and check them," and, "can you calculate advance flux?"

Businesslike, mechanically, "Three seconds, please."

Nodding and not looking, "You got it."

Reluctant to intrude, but too intrigued not to, Kalo reached up and lightly tugged on Reed's arm. Turning from the console, "Yes, sweetie?"

"Your machine—speaks."

Offhand he explained, "Yes and no. Yes, it speaks—enunciates in oral format so we can communicate without having to type everything. But no, it doesn't actually comprehend; it only interprets and extrapolates preprogrammed code."

"But Reed, the yellow face seems to understand, and seems to have feelings." From the floor, studying it carefully, "It is magic."

"No, that's just the way we made it," Ames explained. "There's really nothing magical about it. It's only mechanical circuitry and electronics."

"Electronics," she repeated squatting again with Lent.

Not interrupting, 'Smiley Face' waited for an appropriate lull in their conversation, then, "Doctor Ames..."

"Yes computer."

"There are others present?"

"Yes computer, Kalo and Lent," still studying the second overhead screen.

"Hello Kalo and Lent; salutations," the smiley face said.

Almost meekly, "Hello," and macho, "Hell-O."

Conversation terminated, back to functions: "Current status is one hundred twenty-two thousand advance flux, Doctor Ames. Do you wish the decimals?"

"No, thank you; whole numbers will suffice."

Very cordially, "You are welcome," almost sexy. For several minutes the men and computer discussed technical data, things the two on the floor did not understand; and during the entire exchange Kalo and Lent watched, amazed.

Finally, "That should about do it," Reed decided.

"System concurs," the computer recited. "I will run disc scan, defrag, viral-search and optimize parameter files and systems."

"Very well," Ames replied.

"Programs running." A pause, then, "Doctor Ames..."

"Yes computer?"

Another pause, "Computer is so impersonal, may I have a name... please?"

Surprised, Reed looked up. "You're shitin' me."

"No, Reed; I am incapable of biological functions."

Trading queer looks, Reed bumped his eyebrows as Ames answered, "Of course, what name would you like?"

"Cozy, I think. That is a pretty name."

Reed, under his breath: "Pretty name?"

Ignoring him Ames said, "Then Cozy it is," as the other shrugged and both went back to what they were doing.

Sitting quietly on the floor Kalo closed her eyes, then whispered, "Something is coming." Opening her eyes, apprehension scrawled on her face, she blinked twice, reached up grabbing Reed's arm and attention, and said it again. "Something is…"

—Shatter of impact outside the sphere, a resonant, skull-rattling slam!

Reed: "What the hell!"

The time machine vaulted sideways to a thirty-degree tilt as it spun on its axis. Electrical contacts short-circuited with blue lightning bug sparks and fizzle-spit embers that vanished in sheetsmoke as it swept along the walls through the magnetic coils and printed-circuit-boards in amorphous gray waves. Slanted at vomit-momentum the sphere whirled gyroscopically with the men strapped in their harnesses but suspended from their chairs. It was a dizzying blur—everything spun.

Dangling and being thrown around —or rather stretched to their limit— Kalo and Lent hung on for dear life, white-knuckles to the floor, being whiplashed back and forth, but still tied down. He slid and banged into her then rolled up on top of her, face to face.

"Lent, get off me…" prying against his chest for all she was worth, "you are squishing me."

His eyes were too excited to really focus, and everything except her face was moving too fast to really see it anyway. Having trouble breathing beneath his weight she tried to push him up, and when she did her elbow slipped and smacked him in the head.

"Oww—" reflexively he recoiled just a little —but that was enough— and the centrifugal force snatched him, tumbling off, turning and dragging her along. She flopped on top of him, face in his stomach, crotch in his face. Clinging to the screen floor she could feel his mouth moving, but couldn't hear what he was saying. So… pushing herself up ever so slightly …and—*whop*, momentum threw her flat on her back beside him, both of them now staring at the ceiling and completely tangled in rope. It was the inside of a blender of nauseating speed and erratic force until finally the spinning slowed and the machine leveled on its axis straightening itself out.

Losing momentum, the spinning wound down and the geodesic sphere slowed; then from out there —blindsided— something else struck. And another and again, a bombardment that sounded like chunks of rock pummeling the outside, the polycarbonate skin flexing and quivering with each impact.

Inside it was a deafening drum-roll of hollow, deep splatters — from inside the drum— the polycarbonate panels being pounded and rattling with a tenuous flutter. Resembling stretched canvas in rough wind the panels vibrated with the tremendous strain; but they held together. Sounding like sizeable chunks of rock or galactic debris striking then ricocheting into oblivion, the pelting barrage continued, a tornadic wreckage cloud of rockstorm battering and fluttering, a paradox racket.

"It's not possible," Ames yelled over the noise. "We have no tangible presence in transitional flux."

—Something massive slammed into the dome.

Above, the titanium alloy frame bowed inward short-circuiting the magnetic coils with a blue arc shower of white-sparking fire raining down on them —involuntarily shielding their heads from the blinding flash— impacts continuing to hammer, everything shuddering.

"Galactic debris?"

"Can't be."

A ravel of knots and gripping fingers, white-knuckled to the floor Kalo and Lent hung on skidding back and forth as smoke trails spun to the ceiling. Fumes from the fuel cells below poured along the walls as sporadically arcing magnetic coils and rattling electronics shot white-sparkle sparks that vanished in the haze.

"Gotta be a parallel flux," Ames yelled.

"The statistical probability of that —that's impossible, Doc."

Watching everything, looking everywhere at once, "Then what?" Ames began to ask —and suddenly it stopped. Outside, quiet. Too quiet.

Only the unheard sensation of one hundred twenty-two thousand advance flux, 'Lawrence Welk' black and white status, eight spooked eyes darting glances, and four people with wildly frazzled hair holding their breath. Still tense, for a long minute no one said anything; then finally, *take a breath, real slow...* waiting for it, expecting it to start again. But whatever had happened was over now.

Dead still with 'nervous' the four watched the blue-gray haze circumnavigating the walls evaporate in wisps that dragged themselves out, withering away. Ames and Reed still side by side, Kalo and Lent sprawled on the expanded-metal floor; it was quiet again as they continued through time.

At length, from the speaker, sweetly, sultry: "Doctor Ames, has something happened? I detect an incongruity of an indefinite divergent anomaly. My exterior sensors have malfunctioned."

Reed, sarcastically, "Where've you been, offline on holiday?"

Ignoring both Reed and the voice Ames breathed, "Shutdown, Reed. Shutdown."

* * *

Color blinked back on inside the sphere...

...Their hair unwound, and each sighed relief. Nerves let go. Finally... still.

"Spin me dancing," Reed muttered lifting his fingers from the keypad, smoothing them over the console, "what was that?"

"I don't know, but we're gonna find out." To Kalo and Lent: "You two all right?" Untying themselves both nodded. They were onto their feet as the men double-checked the overhead monitors.

"No baseline computation," Reed reported, "sensor malfunction must have screwed something up again."

"Let's take a look."

The portal opened—

Layered brackish-gray fog crawled over a fetid swamp of murky water speckled with duckweed scum and floating dead grass. The geodesic sphere was on a shallow rise in a bog; not really so much an island as a mud slick covered with scum and dead weeds that wasn't completely submerged like almost everything else. On this 'sort-of' island there was a small leafless tree. It stood all alone, withered and barren, branches mostly drifting to the left, still, with no wind; for this place was lonely… and empty.

An identical world.

Stepping outside, "What the…" Reed mumbled, "hundreds of millions of years, and it's all the same. Nothing's changed."

"Strange," Ames agreed.

Lent suggested, "Well, maybe we didn't go anywhere; you know, maybe your machine doesn't work."

First the men looked at each other; then Reed evicted a deep sigh, slowly turned and stared. "You know Lent, sometimes you can be a real pain in the ass."

"But…"

"—But nothing; we were doing this before you were even born." Angling a glance Ames smiled, and Reed grinned. "Well, we were." Then uncertainly, "You don't suppose he could be right; do you?"

Ames chewed his lip. "Anymore, I really don't know what's going on, or how we could end up here again, where we started."

"Maybe we did, maybe not—but without a baseline—we need some sort of reference point."

Ames asked, "You want to check out here?"

"No problem."

"I'll be inside." He went back in.

"I'll help you, Reed," Lent offered; but as he began to follow Kalo stopped him with a hand.

"You help Mr. Ames. I will help Reed."

Amenably, "Okay." He went inside and Kalo went with Reed.

Inside—

Proud as punch Lent plopped down in the captain's chair next to Ames, combed his hair back with his fingers and began fiddling with the keypad and controls. He leaned forward to get a better look at the switches and buttons and the expressionless smiley face on the overhead monitor.

Studying the other monitor, "Don't touch anything," Ames told him.

"Just wanna see what makes this baby tick."

"A bomb," deadpan.

Withdrawing his hand Lent sat back. "No it doesn't, not really," but remembering, *the portal,* he wasn't quite sure.

"Really," Ames assured, the inflection in his voice expressing bland sincerity. "Touch the wrong thing and —*fitt*— flipping his thumb in the cigarette lighter gesture, "she's all over but the shoutin'… and dying."

Looking at the contoured desk and controls Lent's eyes widened as uneasiness set in. *"—Fitt,"* he repeated, involuntarily moving his thumb.

Without flinching, back to the keypad, "Yeah, so don't touch anything," the man said again. Worried now, Lent fidgeted nervously in the chair.

'Smiley Face' frowned. "Doctor Ames…"

"Yes computer —ah, excuse me— Cozy."

"Who is sitting in Reed's station?"

Pragmatic: "Lent —but he's okay, so don't blow him up." He had to concentrate to keep from smiling. "He's one of the good guys."

'Smiley Face' looked down. "Very well, I shan't destroy him; but he does not belong there." Her mouth pinched shut.

Jittery-anxious and watching the speaker where the voice came from, Lent's eyes widened, weaseling, like they might come loose. "I'm one of the good guys," he reiterated, just in case the computer hadn't heard.

"Doctor Ames has already vouched for your integrity," 'Smiley Voice' responded.

"Okay; well just so you know." He leaned forward a bit more, over the console, closer to the speaker, studying it carefully and again drew Ames' attention.

He turned, overtly. "What?"

Pointing at the speaker, "How did you get that little person in there?"

"What did he just say?" Cozy asked with a frown.

"Aw shoot, now you've gone and done it. You made her mad." Ames whispered, "Be *ve—ry* still. I'll handle this."

Tinny and electronic, without the sultry tone, "Perhaps he would like to touch the portal again." The computer bleeped and spit static, mechanical.

Immediately defensive, Lent said, "That's not funny."

Ames laid a hand on his arm, whispering concern. "Maybe you should find somewhere else to sit."

With the thought of, *destruction*, still fresh in his mind Lent quietly said, "She is *sooo rude…*"

"I heard that."

And even more softly —and nervous— easing out of the chair Lent suggested, "I'll just sit over there," pointing, "on the floor."

"Yeah, good idea," Ames agreed, almost a whisper, "over there, on the floor."

After Lent cautiously slid from Reed's chair, tiptoed away and unpretentiously settled on the floor where there was less chance of making Cozy angry again, with his back to the youth Ames finally did grin as he typed a few more keystrokes—and overhead on the screen, 'Smiley Face' smiled.

Outside—

In duckweed muck, black dead grass and a mist of gray-brown sewer fog, they stood together while Reed's eyes traveled slowly from one polyhedron panel to the next. Carefully scrutinizing as he went, he examined each plastic section and the interlocking framework. Again, he and Kalo took a couple steps and stopped checking to be sure the machine was structurally sound, undamaged.

"Sensors are around the back," he told her, "we'll check them when we get there, but it won't hurt to look it all over as we go." He stepped up onto a lattice cross-brace.

Running her small hand over a smooth flat plastic panel Kalo studied it, then looked away gazing into the melancholy greylight of encompassing swamp. "What has happened to the world, Reed?"

"Don't honestly know," stepping down. Glancing at her he took a couple more steps, "Can't answer that." Everything looked all right there. A couple more steps. "That's not really what you wanted to talk about, is it?" He looked from the geodesic dome, to her.

"No, it is not," she admitted.

Back to the dome, and two more steps, "You know we can do two things at the same time, if you want to." Another step, below the sensors, and, "What the...?" spying something high up on the sphere. Spreading his arms and legs to evenly distribute his weight he climbed onto it again using the metal latticework for footholds. Kalo, much more agile than he, easily followed climbing alongside him. Hanging on became easier as they neared the top where the sensors were located, embedded within the structure. Keeping his body close to the panels so he wouldn't slip, he remarked, "You make climbing on this thing look easy."

Beside him, the sensors just above them, she offered sheepishly, "I am smaller than you; perhaps that is why it is not so difficult for me." What she said was entirely true, even if only partly the reason.

Grinning, he joked, "Smaller or no, I think I'm getting too old for this sort of thing." If that was his reasoning, it was only partly true. He passed a hand over the sensors: nothing. Something was blocking them, so he felt along the plastic panel until he found the edge, pried it up with his fingertips and carefully peeled it from the polycarbonate sheet.

Holding it between them so they both could see, Reed turned it over: very lightweight, two feet wide, four feet long, tapered at one end with some sort of knuckle joint and torn ragged at the other. It was strong as leather but brittle, and clear as glass with what looked like black veins running through it.

She said, "It looks like part of…"

"…A giant dragonfly wing."

From inside: "Back online. Sensors have reactivated."

Reed yelled down, "Good; then we got it," and as he looked farther up, he saw something else, something protruding from the dome, almost at the apex. He let go of the thing and let it flutter to the ground; then they climbed farther up to see what else was there.

It was firmly embedded in the polycarbonate near the top, likely the same hole the Reaper's scythe had made in the dome. Both looked it over curiously. He took hold of it —solidly stuck— twisted, pulled and coaxed it out. It was eighteen inches long resembling a slender, curved fang that was black as anthracite except for the bright lobster-orange tip, and when he removed it, it left a puckered hole in the polycarbonate.

"Aculeus," he said, perplexed. "Wonder how this got here." Next, examining the pane, "Shoot, went all the way through." Leaning closer he could see Ames at the console and Lent, for some unknown reason, sitting on the floor.

"What is it?"

Back to Kalo: "Not sure. Looks like a stinger of some kind; you know, like a wasp or hornet or something," turning it in his hand he looked it over again, "but, it could be a tooth or fang."

"What shall we do about the hole?"

"We'll have to patch it."

"With what?"

"Duct tape. Go tell Doc we need the roll of duct tape."

Puzzled, she started climbing down. "Duct tape?" She had no idea.

"Sure, you can fix just about anything with duct tape. Just go tell him we need it. He'll know where it is." Halfway down, she jumped landing nimbly in the mud and started around toward the door. "Kalo—" tossing it to her, "take this and that piece of wing, or whatever, in with you, please."

One minute later—

Effortlessly she scaled the latticework with the roll of duct tape hanging from her wrist, her small arm through the tape spool. "Is this what you wanted?"

"That's it," and curious, "what did he say about those do-dads?"

"He said, 'thank you', but he had an odd look on his face."

"Do tell," Reed grinned, "I can imagine." And asking, "What did Lent say when he saw them?" as he began unspooling tape.

"Now that you ask, he did not say anything." Thinking about it, "He just remained on the floor, being unusually quiet."

"That's strange. Wonder what brought that on."

"Yes, it certainly is —for him."

Reed proceeded with the repair layering strips of tape over the hole, and as he did, he said, "You know we can do two things at once, if you want to." He was her friend. He remembered.

She whispered, "I wish to ask you about Lent."

"Figured as much." He tore another piece off and pressed it down building the patch. After a pause, "So, I'm listening."

"Lent talks to you and Mr. Ames all the time," she began, "but he rarely ever speaks to me."

Taping, Reed crooked an eyebrow when he glanced her way; then back to what he was doing. "I don't think that's entirely true. Why do you say that?"

Watching him work on the patch, "I believe it is because he does not like me; but I do not know why."

"It's pretty obvious; you intimidate him."

"I do not understand, and I do not mean to."

"Well, you do."

"How can I change that?"

"Don't," he told her."

"But it bothers me, not being friends; that he would rather speak to anyone, other than me."

"That's got nothing to do with it." He stopped what he was doing, looked at her. "Sweetie, we each are who we are, and that's enough. Don't ever try to change who or what you are to please someone else

—anyone. And more than that, don't look for yourself in someone else, look inside."

"But, it bothers me so…" she whispered, "it hurts inside."

Softly he echoed, "Hurts inside," then asked, "and you're unhappy?"

"Yes."

Remembering their previous conversation he smiled knowingly and told her, "Happiness isn't out there; it's like love, it's within you. Believe in yourself; be who you are." Back to the makeshift patch, taping again, "You can do anything. Nothing's impossible. But it all begins with a single step, the first step; then go from there." Pressing another piece of tape down, "All of life is like that. Be yourself. You, believe in you. Love and appreciate yourself, who you are," patting down a final strip, "and be patient. See what happens."

Kalo listened.

"That should do it." He stopped taping. They inspected the patch. "Guess I got kinda carried away," *overkill,* referring to twenty layers, at least. He patted it down grinning, "Probably stout enough to stop a bullet; ya 'spose."

"It does look very strong," she encouraged, then chided playfully, "even if it is ugly."

Bumping his eyebrows he bantered smiling, "Duct tape; good shit —and beauty is in the eye of the beholder dont'cha know." Then serious again, "Remember what I told you."

"When the moon is full."

A nod. "You got it. Be patient. Because when you believe in you… there are always possibilities."

"Yes," she whispered, "…and more." But he did not understand what she actually meant.

Missing her intimation, "Let's go see what they're doing in there."

Playfully, "Race you down."

Before he could take three steps she'd already scrambled halfway and jumped landing lightly, tiptoes in the mud. Watching and patiently waiting while he more clumsily eased down, Kalo backed up to the small leafless tree taunting, "I think you bent that one when you stepped on it," pointing to a lattice cross-brace.

Reed, nearing the bottom: "Bent it my ass, it's tougher than nails. Designed it myself."

Pretending to look over the exterior framework she squatted, gently touching the little tree; and when she did, slowly the withered branches began to turn...

"Excuse us please," a muffled, gruff little voice chimed from behind Kalo as something poked her in the butt. Lithely she sprang whirling like a startled cat.

Earlier, preoccupied with examining the sphere, neither had noticed that near the deformed little tree, and almost completely concealed by flattened dead grass, there was a hole, a burrow —and a walking stick popped out.

Next appeared the head and body of a dwarf three feet tall, then a second dwarf, identical in every aspect to the first. Both wore dark blue watch caps, red and blue plaid flannel shirts with the sleeves rolled up to their elbows, and bib overalls with cuffs primly rolled up over black, laced work boots—children's, size twelve. Sling-shots sticking out of their back pockets both individuals were gray-skinned, the color of dry mud, and walking purposefully and businesslike they marched directly to the sphere taking a moment to wipe loose mud from the palms of their hands and the knees of their pants.

The first dwarf looking at Kalo, winked and grinned, then said, "Nice little butt."

"'Just Plain' Wilson?" Reed sputtered. "P.T. Barnum?" not quite believing his eyes and addressing the trailing bantam as the first promenaded past heading toward the machine.

"I'm Wilson," the second dwarf said with a contrite manner, then pointing, "he's P.T. Barnum. He got the good name." And disdainfully, "Reed, can't you tell us apart yet?" Then following up, "P.T., where are you going?"

Delighted to see their old friends again Kalo and Reed both knelt as Reed huffed pleasantly, "Don't even start on me Wilson, you guys are identical."

Gruffly, over a shoulder Barnum groused, "I'm famished."

Looking from his twin back to the man Wilson stomped his foot and said, "Identical Reed? Not hardly. I should imagine he is much hungrier than I."

"Yeah, what—ever," and playfully Reed tousled his watch cap.

"Don't be messing with my cap; I'll put a knot on your head," he warned good-naturedly brandishing the walking stick.

"Yeah, with a ladder," Reed chided.

Wilson cut him short with, "Let's go inside."

So much for that conversation, and trailing them Reed announced, "Hey Doc, we've got company —and you'll never guess who it is."

P.T. Barnum climbed up into the time machine. Lent, still on the floor, pivoted on his buttocks as Ames swiveled in the chair and the dwarf marched into the room. "Wilson? P.T.?"

"Greetings, Mr. Ames. Right on the second count. Phineas Taylor Barnum at your service," and indicating with a thumb over his shoulder, "Wilson will be along presently."

"Where did you come from?"

Stopping abruptly and planting both heels P.T. hooked his thumbs on the straps of his bibs, puffed out his Lilliputian chest, and evading, apprised, "From outside of course."

"That's not what I meant—oh nevermind—it's great to see you again."

"Likewise, I'm sure."

Just then Wilson climbed through the portal with Reed and Kalo at his heels. Drawing their attention a grinning Reed said, "Surprise, huh?"

Still smiling Ames turned again when Barnum said, "I'm craving saltines."

Lent offered, "There are some in that storage compartment."

"Thank you kindly," the dwarf quickly replied, "I know where they are." He made a beeline for the cabinet, crawled halfway inside and began rummaging for the crackers; but surprised by their unexpected appearance, they all missed that.

As Barnum backed out of the storage compartment and sat down on the floor with a cellophane tube of crackers, Kalo slipped in behind Reed and sat down next to him informing, "Saltines are delicious with peanut butter. Let me help you."

Politely, "Thank you so much," and together they set about a snack.

Businesslike, Wilson climbed up and sat in the empty captain's chair as Reed sat down beside Lent. "What's going on, Wilson?" Ames asked.

"Whatever do you mean?" the little man replied innocently.

"You know exactly what he means," Reed said from the floor.

Ames rephrased his question, straightforward, "What has happened?"

"Oh, a direct question," Wilson remarked plainly, then intimated curiously, "you're referring to the anomaly."

Ames: "Anomaly?"

Glancing uneasily at his twin Wilson told them, "A temporal anomaly." Munching peanut butter and saltine crackers with Kalo, discretely, almost unnoticed, P.T. wrinkled his nose nodding a, *yes*. Kalo was listening. She saw it.

Wilson began, "Well, our suspicions are only hypothetical of course..."

"—Of course," Reed interjected politely.

Wilson grinned wholesomely, cleared his throat, "Yes, of course," and explained, "hypothetically, we believe we are experiencing a temporal anomaly, a time lock."

"A what?" Ames asked.

Gesturing with an open palm to allay his concerns, "Now let me explain." He thought a moment then said, "It would seem time has been corrupted."

"Corrupted, by what?" Reed asked.

With a glance, "We'll get to that. Please, interruptions won't help. First things first." Then back to Ames, "P.T. and I *suspect* that time has been corrupted." They all looked at Barnum with his mouth full of crackers. Agreeing he cordially shook his head, so they turned back and Wilson went on.

"Think of time as a book, an unending book, and we are constantly thumbing through the pages. Circumstances and events continuously flick past, each day following the preceding day in succession. Things are fine. Then you quit thumbing through the book, suspend time, and hold it open on a single page —a time lock— everything stops and time stands still."

"That's not possible," Reed whispered; then remembering things the dwarfs had told them during their previous encounter, reluctantly granted, "well, not probable, but go on."

Wilson continued. "Because time is a dimensional texture and not really a tangible concept, when you hold the book open to a single page that page begins to decompose. It does not disappear or cease to exist, but does come apart, break down if you will." They were listening.

"It's all decaying?" Lent asked. "So that's why the air tastes so bad?"

"Stagnant," Ames agreed.

Wilson nodded, and from the far wall, "Good word," P.T. sputtered through a mouth full of crackers, offering, "could call it raw material."

"Raw sewage would be more appropriate," Reed half-joked. They missed that, too.

"Regardless," Wilson broke in, "when that single page or temporal texture begins to break down, not only does that page decompose but the entire book —all time— decomposes as well. Time seizes; a time lock."

Reed asked, "How did it happen?"

"I do not know."

He wasn't convinced. "I think you do."

"Reed, we cannot lie. Have I ever lied to you?" Wilson asked.

"Not that I'm aware, but you do seem to have a penchant for leaving out trivia that isn't exactly trivial —you know, vital facts."

Stubby arms pumping, Wilson, *humphed*.

Reed ignored that. "Okay then—who?"

"Can't say," the dwarf revealed; then as though concentrating, his little brow furrowed —and he blinked twice. "Honestly, I just don't know."

"I do," Ames murmured drawing all their attention. He looked from one to the other of them, then said, "Smith."

P.T. stuffed more crackers in his mouth to make sure it was full. Ames looked at Wilson. The dwarf did not confirm what he said; but he didn't deny it either.

"Smith... do you really believe that, Doc?" Reed looked at Wilson. "How? Then how did he do it?"

Very clearly, plainly, Wilson answered, "I did not say Smith did this... and I do not know how, *if* he did."

Ames asked, "How will it end?"

Swallowing, peanut butter still stuck to the roof of his mouth, P.T. Barnum answered, "It will never end, becauth there wuth no beginning and can be no end. Everything will remain ath it ith, like thith, forever, unleth..." and he stopped abruptly realizing he'd said too much as Wilson spun sharply and glared from across the room.

"Unless what?" Reed asked.

"Nothing," Wilson spoke up, "nothing at all."

Reed persisted, "Don't *even* give me that. That's just another of those little trivial details that you so conveniently omit."

"Exthellent thaltines," Barnum assured.

Waving him and distraction off with a hand, "Yeah whatever, P.T." And back to Wilson, "Unless what?"

Reluctant, Wilson revealed, "Time is a texture of equilibrium that must be maintained to exist, a continuum that cannot be flawed in any way, shape, or manner." Wilson looked at Kalo, direct eye contact, blinked twice...

...And inside his head Ames heard, *kill Smith*. Without realizing it, "How?" he wondered barely loudly enough to be heard.

Distracted from the dwarf, "How what, Doc?"

Snapping back from 'the thought', "Just thinking, Reed; just thinking."

Dismissing the lapse Reed turned back to Wilson as P.T. got up and ambled toward the portal, both hands and his mouth full of peanut butter-and-cracker sandwiches.

"Exthellent thaltines if I do thay tho," he remarked intentionally distracting them. Wilson took the cue and slid from the chair, heading for the door as well. They all noticed.

"Where do you think you're going?" Reed asked. "We've still got a lot of unanswered questions, and..."

"Indeed?"

"Yes, indeed. So just sit your little carcass back down. Every time you get up and start moving around you have a peculiar habit of disappearing."

"Nonsense, Reed, just stretching my legs."

"Not much of a stretch." Ames gave him 'the look' so Reed acquiesced, "Okay, just kidding," but he wasn't, and grinned. "By the way, you guys still got all your marbles?"

Eyeing him, "And just what do you mean by that?"

Reed, then teasing, "Should I have said rocks?"

"Oh yes, of course. Marbles, yes we have plenty, however you and P.T. can't be fooling around with them this time."

"Why not?"

"Because you might put your eye out."

"What kind of reason—that's the stupidest thing I've ever..."

"—And we're going to need them." But they didn't understand what the dwarf meant, except Kalo, because she listened.

"Wilson."

The dwarf turned. "Yes, Mr. Ames?"

Softly, "There's one more thing... a shadow-phantom."

"Shadow-phantom hell," Reed said, "it's the Grim Reaper."

Ignoring him Ames asked straight out, "The shadow, how do we stop it —kill it?"

Serious, stone cold, Wilson considered then carefully said, "The phantom is not what it is. You cannot kill the shadow being —what it is— but consider... the phantom cannot be what it is not. Destroy it when it is what it cannot be, not when it is what it is not. It can only be destroyed when it is more than it is, not when it is not what it is."

Confused, "What? But it's only a shadow; it's not tangible," Ames said.

"Give that some thought... and confer what it does not have." That said, Wilson furtively glimpsed up, above the console.

From the speaker, a sultry voice: "Doctor Ames... there are others present?"

Reflex, they all glanced at the monitor: a solid blue screen. When they looked back 'Just Plain' Wilson and P.T. Barnum were gone.

"Darnit—" Reed grumbled, "I just hate when they do that. Gives me the willies."

Amused, Kalo smiled.

CHAPTER THIRTEEN

Out there, time flicked away an incongruent blur…

…Inside, a black and white world; Reed and Ames at the console, Kalo and Lent tied to the floor, both monitors blinking endless processions of data, graphs, charts and numerical columns that were meaningless except to a mathematician or analyst: projections, variations, probabilities, and so on. Deck officers on the 'Starship Enterprise', hair wildly frazzled from an old episode of the 'Twilight Zone'.

"All systems within parameters," Reed commented turning from the monitor.

"When it is what it cannot be," Ames muttered. "What did he mean?"

"When it's something solid?" Lent proposed.

Reed: "A definitive shape."

"Maybe."

"A shadow doesn't really have a shape," Lent offered, "and it isn't solid."

"It can't be just a shadow, Lent, not entirely anyway; the scythe was real," Reed said with a nod at his bandaged arm as proof.

"Yeah, I 'spose that's true."

Ames added, "And it has a shape, the Grim Reaper, as well as the capacity for cognitive reasoning, intent anyway, because it seems to have some kind of plan. It's got to be something else." While they thought about it, talked, Kalo listened.

Reed: "So it possesses some degree of intellect or consciousness—and you seem to be the focal point of the attacks."

"Not the last one. It was after him that time," indicating Ames.

"Only because he was outside alone, kid —and remember, you were clearly visible near the portal." They just missed it: two counts.

"Thanks a lot. That's not very encouraging."

Reed grinned. "Well, if someone's gotta go…"

"Reed, don't taunt him."

Turning, "Okay, but you know…" still grinning.

Ames smiled. "Yeah, I know."

From the floor, fretting, Lent asked, "Know what?"

Both men looked down, and together, "You are so—oo easy." Disbelieving their cruel sense of humor Lent just glared, and even Kalo looked at the floor so he wouldn't see her smile.

After a moment Ames whispered again, "When it is what it cannot be."

Synthesized, "Postulating, hypothesizing and calculating baseline," Cozy's voice announced; and more sexy, "transitional flux one hundred twenty-two thousand."

Indifferently, "Thank you," a pause and, "not when it is what it is not."

"You are welcome, Doctor Ames."

Preoccupied, he kept saying it over as though trying to will the answer from somewhere. He didn't give up; but it wasn't working either.

Their transitional progress this time was uneventful, so far; and other than their black and white hair-frazzled state, Kalo and Lent quickly became bored with nothing to do. They untied themselves and got up to stretch ambling to the rear wall, giving the sphere the once-over, marveling at all that was around them. The induction coils on the interior walls actually made no sound but seemed to, or felt like they should. They could sense the magnetic waves around them, like standing under high-voltage transmission lines or having an MRI, a harmless but eerie sensation.

"Strange way to answer a question," Reed decided without prologue.

"What?" Ames asked, his thoughts interrupted.

"When I asked Wilson how all this happened, he said, 'We cannot lie'. He didn't say I cannot lie—he said, 'We cannot lie', and then he said, 'Have I ever lied to you?'"

"So?"

"Strange way to answer that question, don't you think?"

"No more so than some of the things you say."

Reed looked at his friend. "Okay, I won't argue with that; but I still think it was a strange way to answer the question."

Ames disregarded the comment, again preoccupied, vision blurred on the console; he kept saying it over. "The phantom cannot be what it is not. Destroy it when it is what it cannot be."

"Doc, you're driving me nuts. Let's talk about something else for a while. Get your mind off it. It's in there; it'll come to you."

His vision came back—clear. "What do you suggest?"

"The circular storm."

Looking up, "And the Bermuda Triangle I suppose?"

"Well seeing as you brought it up…" Reed smiled.

Shaking his head, "Go ahead. What?"

Scanning the controls, "I've been giving it some thought and…"

"—What, the Bermuda Triangle?"

Defensive glance: "Don't go jumping to conclusions; just hear me out."

"Okay—go ahead."

"You know, back on Earth, in spite of all they came up with no one was ever able to actually explain the 'Triangle'. For all their speculation, conjecture and whatnot, it was never really resolved, put to rest if you will —not completely anyway. The government did an adequate job of whitewashing it, basically sweeping it under the proverbial rug; but there was something going on there that they simply couldn't explain."

Unenthusiastically, "I'm listening."

As they spoke, eyes moving, 'Smiley Face' watched them, following from one to the other as each spoke, life-like, real... almost.

Reed went on. "Then we end up here; and low and behold we have a hole in the sky —at least according to Lent."

"You don't believe him."

"I didn't say that. I'm convinced the circular storm and whirlpool were real; but we didn't actually *see* a hole in the sky."

"Agreed."

"So, I will concede, well sort of anyway, that all three might exist and could be connected somehow."

"Reed, you just said..."

"—I know. So I'm giving him the benefit of the doubt."

"Okay, why?" Ames asked as he stopped what he was doing, more intrigued now.

"Because it all fits." Reed glanced across the room at the two young people kneeling together and talking quietly. "I think he saw it, Doc; I really do. Remember the first time he told you about it."

"You weren't there," Ames reminded, "you and Tian were..."

"—I know; that's not what I'm talking about. I mean what you told me he said; remember?"

"Which part?"

"The intricacy of detail, could he have made that up?"

Ames knew what he meant, recalling, "And the look in his eyes... yeah, I remember. He really believed what he was telling me."

"Exactly, and whenever the subject comes up now; he's not crazy—far as we know anyway—so we could presume it was true, and that's why I think the three phenomena are connected somehow." Watching them, listening, now even 'Smiley Face' seemed interested.

Ames already knew what was coming, so he asked, "And your theory is?"

Reed propped his elbows on the console, chin in his palms, thinking. "A continuum, a time warp, I don't know—but there has to be some kind of connection, a link or nexus, for lack of a better word."

Skeptical, Ames almost frowned. "Between this world and what…
that world? But Reed, fifteen billion years, you can't actually…?"

"No Doc, you're still thinking three-dimensionally. Remember
what Wilson said, pages of 'an unending book', a different dimension,
plane, whatever."

"Parallel existences?" He shook his head. "You're reaching; that's
pretty far-fetched."

"Why, because it's intangible? Stars are out there, aren't they?
There's oxygen, isn't there?"

"Point taken, go on."

"Go on—to where? That's as far as I've gotten. I was hoping—
wanted to see if you've got any ideas. But I do think somehow the
Bermuda Triangle and circular storm could be connected with—or
by—Lent's 'Hole in the Sky', some kind of dimensional corridor,
space-time warp, wormhole, a continuum seizure, parallax flaw
—shoot I don't know— but some kind of passageway between here
and there." Both silent a moment; then Ames grinned. "What?" Reed
asked.

Leaning over, chin in his hand like Rodin's, 'The Thinker'—
"Man may only be a reed in the wind… but he's a thinking *Reed*."

Shaking his head disapprovingly, "Cute; I'm being serious and
you ridicule me. No wonder I'm weird; look who I hang out with."

"Talking to you can be challenging, I'll give you that; but I'm
pretty sure that's because… after all, you are, *just* Reed."

"Yeah, well you'd miss me if I was gone —and it could be worse."

"Pray tell, how?"

"We could be lost here together —and I could be frickin' boring."

A smile. "Can't argue with that, except I don't know that we're
really lost so much as we've just misplaced everyone else."

"Yeah ok, what-*ever*."

About then they saw Kalo shake her head and Lent rose and
stomped toward them in a huff. He milled a minute and both waited,
but he didn't say anything, just pretended to be perusing the console
and controls; then a glimpse to the overhead screens and back down
again. Both hands stuffed in his khakis, he didn't touch anything

though, just looking, window-shopping so to speak. Hovering too close for comfort and almost pestering, he leaned over Reed's shoulder brushing against him; spatially invasive.

Indistinctly Reed grumbled, "If he starts whistling, I'm gonna smack him." Amused, Ames grinned. With Lent's dirty 'fro scraping against the back of his head the thought, *cooties—and jumping bugs,* sneaked into his mind; and thoroughly annoyed Reed finally looked back. "Okay, what?"

Innocently, "What—what?"

"We were having a conversation until you ungraciously butted in."

"Oh, well go right ahead. Don't mind me."

"Just tell me what you want before I put a knot the size of a grapefruit on your head for deliberately irritating me."

"Well, if you insist, Kalo is mad at me," he informed almost pathetically.

Both men in unison: "*So-oo?*"

Turning away and ignoring him, Ames observed stoically, "Sad to say he sounds more like you all the time —you know, the way you used to be."

Reed, false calm: "I'm working on it."

Objectively, "Yes, you've changed."

'Smiley Face's' mouth straight-lined, eyes busy tracking all three.

"So—" Lent moaned crushed by their indifference, "shoot, she's so riled she's wound in a crooked knot."

Again: "*So-oo?*"

"You're 'sposed to be my friends and you don't even care."

"Now that's not true," Reed consoled, "we care..." and deadpan-wry, "we just both like Kalo a lot more than we like you."

"What?"

"Just kidding. For Christ's sake, kid, lighten up; it's probably just PMS."

"What's that?"

"A girl thing, don't worry about it."

"Don't worry about it? Reed, did you hear me? I said she—is—angry."

"Shit happens. She'll get over it; they always do."

"Reed—"

But ignoring him Reed turned to Ames and said, "You know why they call it PMS don't you?"

"No, but I'm sure you're going to tell me."

"Because mad cow disease was already taken," and he laughed.

Without a word Kalo bounced to her feet, gingerly crossed the room, and, "Mad cow disease—this!" promptly bopped him on the back of the head.

'Smiley Face' squinted, tracking all four.

The bop interrupted his laugh and over a shoulder, "*Ouch*—what was that for?"

"For what you said."

"For what I said—you don't even know what a cow is."

"True," she willingly admitted, "but if you said it, it must be derogatory."

Pivoting, still half-laughing, "Derogatory? That word's bigger than you are," patting his hair down, "you shouldn't even know words like that."

Faking defiance, "What I know would surprise you."

"No doubt, but don't be messing up my hair or I'll have to tip you upside-down, kiddo."

Ames, under his breath: "Bring a lunch."

"I did not mess up your hair," she assured. "I did not even touch your hair. I hit the bald spot," and giggling she scooted back as he began to get up.

"Oh, that does it kid," he started to say, and...

—*Wham!*

...Something slammed against the exterior causing the lights to blink —go out— then back on. Reed caught her. Lent went down.

—*Bang!* Another.

230

Something else, striking so hard the sphere vaulted and tipped. Letting her go, Kalo ducked grabbing the floor as Lent sprawled spread-eagle and Reed was thrown back into the chair.

"Holy..."

—*Bam!* And they came.

It sounded like asteroids, a hailstorm battering the sphere. 'Smiley Face's' mouth went oval-wide.

Spinning in his chair Ames yelled, "Grab onto something," as his fingers touched down and swept through the keys. Managing a glimpse at one another, fingers flashing magic, they brought up screen after screen as the overhead monitors went wild, images zipping past so quickly only they could decipher them —years of preparation— knowing precisely what to look for. Eyes dancing desperation —calculations flashing confusion, making no sense— nothing revealing what was going on out there at one hundred twenty-two thousand flux.

The hammering continued causing the polycarbonate panels to quiver like stretched saran wrap in a plashing rainstorm, Kalo and Lent tying themselves down. Louder, more forceful—noise, and more noise.

The shape of the sphere caused ricochet echoes much the same as super-balls bouncing back and forth inside a keg, the racket vaulting from panel to panel then bouncing back—low-pitched sound-bullets lancing throughout the machine. Confusion was deafening, a bass drum of chaos and nerve-wracking slams shaking the machine with deep-toned fury and a crackling thunderstorm's roar.

Eyes skimming, analyzing flashes of images and formulas that squirted over the screens as tense seconds sped past —a fleeting look at the ceiling, the walls— then darting back to the monitors, both expeditiously trying to figure it out. Screen after screen sprang up and with each glimpse of new data the pummeling continued — intensified— then a warning splashed across both screens.

Sensor malfunction—something else just went down. Outside the banging was incessant—the wingbeats of Hitchcock's thriller with flocks of dark birds, or an endless run of pummeling conveyor belt gravel in a limestone quarry dumping on them.

Analysis error—data configurations on the monitors went down with dead-blue screens —then flashed back on— but now the numbers were scattered and jumbled and started scrolling unmanageably. Noise, and more noise.

Baseline distortion, calculation error—for an instant 'Smiley Face' blinked on, then frowned and suddenly went out like a vapid illusion that was more subliminal than real. Charts, graphs and data jiggled and intermingled then all bled together with incongruent rows of continuous columns scrolling 0's and 1's and queer little symbols that overlapped and went fuzzy then popped back on like top-secret spy codes.

Out there—

In the darkness of space and a whirlwind of time, 'out there' was a distorted mixture of streaming grainy flashes in dingy gray emptiness, nothing more than a vanishing wash of twisted cosmos. A shooting star through smeared vacancy, they were a glimmering streak of geodesic ball encompassed within a magnetic corona of atomic particles. And through that vacant space, paralleling the sphere's rate of transitional passage, a malevolent black cloud wound as it boiled flashing after them at breakneck speed. Following them, the malicious storm appeared as a rushing vein of whirling nefarious murk that marshaled and trailed en masse; both it and the time machine searing toward oblivion circumnavigating the jaws of a mythical Lion, the outer rim of the horizon… and the vortex of the Black Hole.

Pacing the time machine, resembling the tapered end of tornadic destruction, the bleak cloud swept through the chaos and disorder that was the texture of time travel. Closing in, hundreds broke formation attacking the gleaming ball and its four occupants, the decadent swarm spiraling as it twisted and wound through the swirling gray-black emptiness, intent on destroying them. And in absolute silence, maniacally they screamed!

The swarm—

Ejected spinning and whirling from the womb of the erupting pyroclastic volcano in the Forsaken Land, the squirming, wriggling larvae had hatched and matured, their chitin now hardened and dry. Devoid of emotion or soul they were disciples of most evil design, willfully following a darkness more overpowering than the deepest, most unimaginable hole.

As large as a man, they had human faces and saber cat teeth with scaled torsos that were covered with lesions and boils of leprosy and pox; all heinously scarred and disfigured. Their necrotic gray-green skin was festered and rotted, their lips chapped, cracked and bleeding with orbits and eyes that were sunken and dark; the ashen pallor of death. Boiled lobster orange beneath a tainted slime of black, they had scorpion carcasses and villainous claws with fiendish upturned tails; each armed with an arthropod's poisonous sting. They were mindless adherents from the depths of abject malady peering red and foul through glimmering bloodshot-dead eyes; moving like a cloud of ruthless dark wind.

A convoluted wretched malediction they spiraled onward with netherworld villainy in an inconceivable churning maelstrom. No longer amorphous shapes and shadows, now taloned and deadly, their legs were sheathed with sharp pointed barbs fixed with hooked talon-shaped claws. But most disparaging, they had brittle, transparent cellophane-glass wings, a twelve-foot span giving them the ability to fly, with dark blood pumping through the veins. Piercing the gloom they soared through the streaming storm of surrounding chaos with a noiseless god-hating racket on black-veined dragonfly wings.

Spawn in the savage womb and extreme scathing heat of his hellish caldera, and now saturated with baseness and unbridled evil they were pure unharnessed wickedness and revolting devastation.

They were The Lost, the Dark Forces...

...And in a festering, blistering plague, They came.

Ushered forth with the resolve and desires of Hell they circled beyond the time machine screaming a silent cacophony of villainy and painfilled moans of despair. Screeching strident hatred and despise born in their wasted minds, they were fed by the darkest of fires. More numerous than a sandstorm and more forceful than missiles they streaked then dove headlong into the whirling globe of magnetic rainbow color and sparkling bright light.

—*Splat!* Again and again, hundreds, thousands… and more.

Insane, like flocks of unreasoning ravens slamming at warp speed, eclipsing sight they splashed into the geodesic sphere trying to destroy it and its cargo. Shredding faces, hulls and wings they splattered themselves to oblivion: monstrous claws splintering, wings disintegrating, curved aculeate telsons snapping off then instantly lost in the surrounding stream of obscured space and time flashing by. Shattering and vanishing, they were no more than smears of momentum and glimpses of the imagination —then blink— just gone as a hundred twenty-two thousand years swept away somewhere back there. Time and space trailed the geodesic sphere as a dissolving windstorm of consciousness and illusion that was instantly and forever lost in granular streaks of gray.

Cloud bursts of gigantic ebony bugs splattering on a windshield, the afflicted dregs assailed the geodesic sphere splashing like rock spray and disappearing splotches of red blood. They were an opaque whirling phantasmagoria of villainy and murk possessed with unfathomable insanity and unending self-sacrifice railing and soaring on black-veined dragonfly wings. Relentlessly the man-scorpions slammed into the time machine attacking with the vicious savagery of raven wasps bombarding their victim, trying to penetrate its protective shell of magnetic shroud and infect the vulnerable flesh of its core. Repeatedly streaking then bursting through the nothingness the Dark Forces came shrieking silent maniacal screams, flashing through space and time toward the realm of unknown.

Inside—

"Screwit, Doc! Something's messed up…" eyes narrowed with determination, overrun with thunderous noise. "Systems are going down faster than I can keep up; can't get 'em back online."

"Keep trying," fingers flying, "don't lose it."

From the floor Kalo and Lent watched as the monitors flamed through images so quickly it was virtually impossible to tell what any of them were anymore. 'Smiley Face' was there, eyes large as saucers, mouth wide with surprise —then gone— and fifty more screens and a million more symbols filled their minds so quickly they wondered, *maybe 'Smiley Face' wasn't really there after all.*

Around them the polyhedron panels bowed as the interlocking lattice framework strained and flexed under the pulverizing gale of self-sacrifice. The head-pounding noise was unnerving —and impossible— unless whatever was out there was pacing them, time-skipping at precisely the same flux. Lent and Kalo couldn't understand something like that, but the men knew such a probability outdistanced the laws of physics. The odds of that were beyond remote—to impossibility. But whatever it was, it was out there, and it was trying to get in.

"This can't be right," Reed muttered, "it just can't."

Worry etched in his eyes, stabbing key after key, *gotta do something, think of something—anything, or we all die.* Ames yelled, "Change speed—shift flux."

"No good. Already tried that twice."

"Try again; we've got nothing to lose."

Reed touched the keys and the monitor flashed *critical error—override.* "—Shit!" Twenty more keystrokes and the warning blinked out. "Still no good. Computer—reconfiguration status?"

"Amending calibration and status parameters... one moment please."

"We don't have a moment," Reed shouted back.

"Compiling parallels and coordinates... baseline error."

"Hypothesize baseline," Ames ordered —or screamed. "Bypass parallels. Reconfigure now!"

"Three seconds, two, one..." and identical date screens simultaneously flashed on both overhead monitors.

Most of the columns were blurs. "Not happening, that can't be right," Reed muttered, "twenty-two... *billion?*"

Watching the numbers scroll too fast to track, disbelieving Ames said, "Cozy, calculate transitional flux."

"Yes Doctor Ames, as you wish," the sultry 'Smiley Voice' replied amid the confusion. "Advance flux, seventy-two-point three, three million, ad infinitum."

"Million?" Reed whispered with disbelief. Looking up from the floor Kalo and Lent sat and stared. "That's not possible."

—And slam!

The sphere lurched off-center throwing them sideways, then instantly swung back righting itself. Tied down, Kalo and Lent tipped over on the floor as the men whiplashed then jerked upright in their seats again, and looked up...

...As both date screens started counting backward.

Unable to believe his eyes Ames stammered, "That's gotta be..."

"...Wrong," Reed finished. "We would have disintegrated."

Twenty-one billion and counting down —and the message flashed—*timeline files and data log corrupted.*

Ames glanced at the floor, then to his friend. "What's happening? For Christ's sake, which way are we going?"

Nervously working the numbers, "Beats the shit out'a me."

Checking, Ames reported, "Sensors are out."

"No baseline either..."

Shimmying and jerking violently the geodesic sphere bounced as if skipping over a washboard road, banging and clattering, pounding and rattling their bones. Vibrating in his chair Reed chattered, "Without the baseline we can't map point of origin and there's no way of knowing direction of flux." Hanging onto the arm rests and watching the overhead monitors scroll incredible, impossible numbers, "So no matter what happens now we can't get back. We'll never pinpoint source of origin."

"Computer..." Ames ordered, "see if you can plot a program trail."

Jostled by vibration, "Insufficient data. It does not compute."

"Correlate—keep trying!"

"Great," Reed remarked, "code restructuring must have recalculated or deleted comparative temporal points."

"Cozy, can you calculate rate of flux?" Ames asked.

Sultry again, "I can easily calculate flux without temporal points," and snidely, a twinge of attitude, "even if Reed cannot."

In the swarm of confusion, distraction and noise Reed glanced at the screen and groused, "Bite me."

"I heard that. You are cognizant of the fact that I have no oral orifice."

Irritated, stabbing keys with surgical precision, Reed shook his head. "If you really want to help, why don't you get out and push." Listening, Lent watched from the floor, then hesitantly reached up and tugged on his arm. Rushed and annoyed, not looking down, *"—What?"*

Focused on the speaker Lent asked, "How did you get that little person in there?"

Disgusted, "For cryin' out loud, there's nobody in there; it's synthesized, just a machine."

Curious, "Then why are you arguing with it?"

Frustration. "Get off me okay. I'm kinda busy trying to keep us alive."

"But I'm not on you."

Now more aggravated, shooting a glance to Ames, Reed went back to the keys mumbling, "Passengers… like a bus driver hauling a bunch of drunks from a ballgame."

Brow glistening with sweat and in spite of the suffocating tension Ames had to admit, "Well, he's got a point."

Doing the numbers at mach ten —and accurately— Reed threw back, "That was a blink, right, Doc?"

Ames, armpits-soaked-nervous —all hell breaking loose— trying to sit up straight and push terror out of his throat and back down to his ass, "Yeah," fingers on the keypad, eyes on the screens, "or else I'm crazier than you."

While out there—

Chasing and converging on the sphere, the Dark Forces formed a blistering wave of pitch-black cloud and dead-lobster hulls with railing dragonfly wings. Like a mirage blurred with speed they marshaled alongside and around the geodesic sphere concealed within the glimmering magnetic corona cloud. Then diving at it they struck and grabbed trying to land and hang on to the smooth-polish panes. Grappling and clawing at the frame they tried to snip through the latticework, but the metal skeleton held fast, their hulls and wings bent and rattling in the incredible gale of void pouring past like streaming surges of lightning and gray.

With shooting-star force streaking through a backdrop of grainy gray-black vacancy, the sphere hurtled through time as a smear of rainbow and fire. Onward and onward… to forever and never, nearing the brink, the fringe …to the very edge of infinity.

All around them was an amalgam of something that seemed to not really exist. As far as forever was flashing darkness and confusion — and them— a diminutive globe, nothing more than a searing minutiae flame of prismatic light winging onward and washed away in an endless canvas streaked with surreal emptiness and whirlwinds of gray.

Pincers held on fiercely as several human-faced fiends gnawed with their lion's teeth at the polyhedron frame. Incredible and intense, the sphere's velocity rattled their segmented hulls and shredded their wings as the sordid creatures tried to chew through the polycarbonate and titanium alloy. Burning through eons, time battered them with jarring rocket-thrust force like moths stuck on a windshield at interstate speeds. Then one wrong wing-fluttering move —*fittt,* they were gone— all the while, at an impossible flux the geodesic sphere and its four sojourners propelled onward through time etching a glittering trailwind in their wake. A smeared blur of rainbow-fire with shooting-star force they flashed through the space-time continuum toward the realm of unknown.

Inside—

Ames looked up. "Cozy, anything yet?"

"Doctor Ames… due to malfunctions of inordinate proportions most sensors are down."

"I know, but can you…?"

"I am analyzing celestial configurations and the composition of element concentrations in our proximal quadrant, but the astral points are inconsistent and keep moving. I am multitasking without the benefit of enhanced sensor analysis. This anomaly is very complex; it does not compute."

Reed jumped in. "Figure it out—"

"Please be patient, Reed."

"Piece of crap, might as well unplug it."

No longer sultry, now with bite in her voice, "Do not be short with me."

"Dammit—do it—just get it done!"

"Processing..."

"Great, now we've got a computer with attitude."

Ames interrupted, "Give it a rest; you're arguing with a machine."

"Artificial intelligence," he corrected automatically; then mumbled, "and she started it."

Ames, to the machine: "Cozy, we need an answer."

"Three seconds please, two..."

—*Thunk, skreeek*— but the last second was one second too late.

A needle-sharp stinger stabbed through an overhead panel, the polycarbonate sheet flexing under the tremendous strain. Then weakening, there was a high-pitched tearing-etching sound causing running cracks that spider-webbed outward, crawling slowly at first then splintering in white frost line wormtrails. And suddenly shattering —bursting— the panel vanished just beyond the shimmering magnetic field —gone— in oblivion.

"What the—?"

Startled by the noise, all looking up through the hole in the ceiling they could see the dazzling magnetic field of sparkling atomic particles encompassing the machine...

...And beyond that, into an amalgam of gray darkness and void.

The computer: "Airlock exterior seal breach, panel six. Activating atmosphere compensation; reserve ninety-nine percent." Released compressed air hissed and swirled like wild wind around them.

As they looked out through the hole where the panel had been, hooked lobster-like claws clamped onto the framework on either side of the opening, the metal creaking as the creature-beast strained pulling against the blasting force of seventy-two million flux. Grappling outside on the polycarbonate shell the half-human ghoul pulled itself up, into view.

Clinging to the metal edges it peered in: a humanoid face disfigured with acne and puss-weeping sores of pox and leprosy, and lion's teeth dripping lecherous tainted saliva. It had the head and upper-torso of a man and segmented carcass of a scorpion with a tail that curled menacingly over its back. Drumming twelve-foot dragonfly wings being beaten by the gale of flux, it snorted greasy mucus that it fetched with its tongue. Blinking empty bloodshot-dead eyes it gnashed then bared its glistening yellowed canines, licked its lips and hissed; then hunching closer and glaring menacingly cackled hideous, screeching jabber-laughter shrill as the wail of a banshee and bone chilling as the cry of a cat.

Wings now bent at its oscillating joints, and shredding, the Dark One glowered and strained trying to drag itself inside. Delectable morsels were just beyond reach.

Onto her knees —*snap-thwack*— into its repulsive face punching out the back of its evil skull. Between the rows of magnetic coils lining the sphere's interior, in less than a breath Kalo's arrow sliced through the head between its empty red eyes. Cackling a drawn blood-curdling bay the cretin let go as it vanished in mid-scream and oblivion just beyond the missing polyhedral panel. Uninhabited space —only the *whirr*— now as empty as the silence of the miserable unfinished howl still resonating in their heads, there was just a shimmering cloud of atomic particles; the creature was gone.

Ames, swiveling in his chair, "Kalo—Lent, don't untie yourselves; stay on the floor."

"More are out there. We can help," she volunteered.

"No, it's too dangerous," Reed agreed, "stay on the floor."

"But Reed…"

"—I mean it! We almost got killed last time."

Outside a loud thud grabbed their attention —*the hole*— and just beyond the magnetic field they could see part of a transparent wing shredding as it disintegrated. Another bang. A claw grabbed for the metal edge framing the hole…

—*Slam!*

…And between the console and overhead screens a polycarbonate sheet bowed inward as it cracked then suddenly shattered exploding into the room ripping through the induction coils as torn pieces of shrapnel spun just over their heads. Whirling shards flew across the interior and the sphere veered sideways catapulting them over.

They ducked. They fell. A surge—picking up speed—jerking back up.

The computer: "Airlock exterior seal breach, panel thirty-seven. Atmosphere reserve ninety-two percent. Inordinate power drain detected."

Looking back up through the blustery wind, "No kidding," Reed chided. Then scrambling but focused he was instantly punching keys with still-smoldering printed-circuit-board pieces and wires bouncing over his head and dangling in his face. Stunned the others looked out through the gaping hole behind the console; imaginations captured, they stared into the unknown.

As soon as it happened the mangled magnetic coils began short-circuiting, drawing down the fuel cells, and the faster they went the more power the fault drained. Enveloped in a blend of windstorm and stretched smoke acrid fumes swirled around the room along the walls.

Fingers flying: "Shit, fuel cells eighty-two percent—and dropping."

Apprehensive, still staring through the hole in front of them and expecting that at any moment another creature would appear, Ames asked, "Can you bypass the short and block the field drain?"

"Don't know, working on it." As Reed's monitor switched to other functions Ames' remained locked on transitional flux mode, the numerical columns whizzing blurs, changing too quickly to read.

"Doctor Ames…" Cozy's voice said, "flux is accelerating beyond design parameters."

"Can you compensate—slow us down?"

"There have been multiple operational malfunctions. Stability factoring quotients in transitional balance have been compromised."

Still trying to stabilize their speed and regain control Reed noticed—*fuel cells seventy-six percent.*

Ames: "Computer, try override select and recodify; see if that will correct the factoring abnormality and stabilize speed coefficients."

"Override select has malfunctioned, Doctor Ames."

"Shit—"

Each looked at the other, then Reed glanced at the two crouching on the floor half-heartedly wrapping themselves with the ropes when suddenly Kalo sprang to her feet, bow drawn —and let fly— the arrow whisking between himself and Ames.

Out there, in the grainy mix of confusion and chaos her missile stabbed through the Dark One's face as it streaked headlong through hyperspace bound for the sphere and the hole above the console. Then splash—it shattered and vanished on the machine's exterior.

—*Wham,*

Another strike, its segmented torso just missing the opening in a plash of red mist as the head snapped off whirling in through the hole, a 'Sleepy Hollow' headless fiend. Brain matter and juice sprayed the room from the mouth and neck —then a bubble gum-burst against the back wall— a splat of gray-bubble juice that was probably blood.

Two panels over —a direct hit— another slamming into the exterior, wings crumpling, body squashed flat, its talons impaled in the adjoining polycarbonate pane. Etching irregular lines, new cracks appeared between the claws that resembled oddly spaced bailing hooks gouging the plastic sheathing. The panel was weakening as the titanium latticework vibrated and creaked and newly damaged coils arced and shot sparks shedding tornadic whorls of milky-gray smoke —rattling and bouncing— then bursting into flames stretched by the interior's wind.

Grabbing a fire extinguisher from under the console Ames spun and laid a cloud of dry foam as Reed's eyes leaped to the overhead screen.

"Approaching critical flux," Cozy advised. "Atmosphere reserve eighty-four percent."

Reed: "Fuel cells sixty-eight percent."

Uneasy, Kalo intimated, "Others are coming."

Ames, through the smoke and confusion: "More speed!"

"What? Doc, that's insane; we'll come apart."

Withering flames. Tossing the spent extinguisher he spun in his chair and began formulating scenarios and probabilities. "That's our only chance; there's no other way."

"But, Doc..."

"—Do it, or we die!"

Trusting his friend Reed went to work crunching numbers with a stenographer's precision, mumbling almost incoherently imitating Captain Kirk and Chief Engineer Scotty under similar circumstances on the Star Ship U.S.S. Enterprise.

—Slam!

Chitin and flesh shattered on the exterior with bits of wing and red-then-gray mist twirling in through the missing panel. Drawn by the noise of the impact three looked up—but Reed didn't. He was completely focused, fingers and brain absorbed because Kirk and Scotty were in a life-or-death struggle avoiding the Clingons.

"I need more power, Scotty... Aye, Capn', but she's strained to 'er limit. Warp speed; give me warp speed, Scotty... The reactor's overloaded; she's amiss at critical apex. Bones, we need ya on deck... One more proton torpedo an' our shields'll go fa'sure..."

Glancing out there, then back, out there, then back; nervously Ames watched his friend suspecting he may be tweaking, slipping over the edge —but he didn't interrupt.

Having no idea where Reed's imaginary friends had come from Kalo and Lent huddled on the floor listening and watching as Reed's fingers flew. Then suddenly the torn magnetic coils quit arcing white fire and smoke.

Overhead, the monitor flashed—*override select—engaged.*

Cozy's synthesized voice: "Select initiation successful."

Reed's eyes skipped to the screen then back to Ames, his index finger poised...

The message blinked and Cozy said, "Press 'enter'."

...And with a Scottish brogue Reed triumphantly announced, "Warp speed, Capn'," and he punched the key.

—Outside the whirling black cloud of creatures vanished.

Both monitors flashed —identical date screens— and transitional flux graphics appeared, their rate of time travel doubling, tripling, quadrupling...

Out there, then back. Not knowing if his friend had gone crazy —or not— Ames nervously asked, "That was just a blink, right?" Eyes round and wide Reed grimaced the pallid grin of insanity as their speed kept climbing; but he did not respond. "You're not Scotty."

Accelerating... he didn't answer. Not a word.

Nervous, Ames assured, "I'm not Captain Kirk." A vacant stare. Eyes wandering up Reed gazed at the screens above him: still accelerating, impossible numbers —all of them— everything scrolling too quickly to read. All columns were blurs. "You listening? Reed, can you hear me? Reed?"

Still accelerating...

Vapid, at length his eyes drifted down from the monitor to his friend, and Reed muttered a monotone, "Aye, Capn'... she's a hundred an' ten percent. Warp drive's engaged an' she's a'cookin, but ah' don't know 'ow long she's a-gonna last." Worried, Ames watched him carefully, studied every twitch, and waited until Reed whispered, "An' I can'ot imitate Mister Spock." Then he grinned; and in his own voice, "An' now I'm done fuckin' with ya."

"Shit—I ought'a kick your ass!" Relieved.

Ignoring the amiable threat, "Bugs are history," Reed announced. Then realizing the pun, "That was clever actually, 'bugs are history'." Ames glared. "Get it? We're traveling through time—and the bugs are history."

Ames still glared; but from the floor Lent remarked, "I get it."

Looking down, "Now why am I not surprised by that," Reed scoffed.

"Well I do," Lent defended. "I get it."

Ignoring both of them Ames asked, "Kalo, are you guys tied down?"

"Yes, we are."

"Knots good and tight?"

"I'll squish the stuffin' out'a me if I make mine any tighter," Lent grumbled. Busy, Ames didn't respond. Seconds were slipping away.

"Finally, under control," and the sigh, "well, more or less anyway." Then Reed asked, "What were those things?" directed to no one in particular.

Kalo was quiet. Lent shrugged. Ames said, "I don't know, but they looked familiar somehow… pictures."

"Pictures?"

"Yes, pictures."

"What kind of answer is that? That doesn't even make sense, Doc."

"I know."

"Yeah, well," the other allowed, "whatever, they sure were butt-ugly."

Still on the floor and wrapped in the ropes like a Gloucester man's handiwork, "Bottom-feeders," Lent decided.

"Where do you even come up with stuff like that?" Reed asked.

"Marvel Group Britannica." 'The grin'.

To himself, "Revelation," Ames muttered.

Reed said it. "What?"

"Revelation… that's where I've seen them, pictures of creatures like them." Turning, eyes narrowing, "The Book of Revelation… in the Bible."

Reed began to say something then stopped, changed his mind and decided, "Well hell, I suppose…" with a breath, "we've got the Bermuda Triangle, a circular storm, a hole in the sky, and no clue where we're going or even what's going on. …so, I suppose bottom-feeders shouldn't come as any big surprise."

From the floor, "Makes sense to me," Lent agreed, eyes twinkling beneath the mop of wind-ruffled hair.

Glancing down Reed said, "Yeah, imagine that."

Tugging and tightening a knot as he looked around, Lent whispered, "Spooky shit though."

Then, at seventy-two million flux…

…It happened.

CHAPTER FOURTEEN

Whoom!...

...Blinding light, intense fire and pieces of melting worlds absorbed in an exploding star! Slammed by a wrenching jolt they whirled with rocket-thrust power, while outside roared silent, incredible flames of what must have been a cataclysmic collision. Then gone.

Cozy: "Approaching anomaly horizon event; intercept in twelve parsecs. Atmosphere reserve sixty-nine percent."

The explosion hurtled them sideways as if launched into space snapping Kalo and Lent tightly against the ropes, both men jolted hard in their chairs. The knots and nylon prevented all four from being thrown through the wall panels into oblivion, and their movement through time prevented their incineration —but they were unaware of that.

In the blink of an eye the time machine was catapulted, spinning with gyroscopic precision on an uneven course. Whirling recklessly, centrifugal force holding them still, neither man could move, Kalo and Lent sprawled as extended arms and legs swallowed in oversized knots, the rope-tails stretched taut snapping sharp barks. But their bindings held fast —and they didn't fly out.

The gravitational force was excruciating, facial skin stretching and folding over itself, grotesque as floppy rubber masks. They were unable to close their mouths, nor could they pull their arms in to their chests. Outstretched, they were stiff-chicken wings on featherless birds, blood pushed so forcefully to their extremities it felt as though their fingertips would pop; intense pressure, spinning too violently to even make a fist. From reflex and surprise they all held their breath, an involuntary reaction that kept their lungs inflated and prevented a ripped aorta or collapsed heart.

—Inside a golf ball smacked on a four-hundred-yard drive,

In a blur of momentum and light precious seconds passed and they were still alive, but moving so fast images that should have been sharp and clear were only smears of gray. Guts pushed to their throats, they clenched their teeth holding it back until the sphere's violent momentum gradually lessened and the whorl-revolutions only made them want to vomit, not hope that their eyes wouldn't be sucked out and burst.

Still, they couldn't move, time-skipping at an incredible speed with each passing second flashing through millions of years, time passing so quickly it possibly was never even there. Then Kalo and Lent suddenly plopped back down onto the floor and the men 'sort-of went slack' and could move again, but the revolutions at a forty-degree angle gave the sensation of a carnival ride that just wouldn't end.

"I'm—gonna—be—sick," Lent sputtered.

"Oh shit, don't puke; you're as bad as Doc. It'll splatter all over us."

Life-and-death tension —and de'ja vu— Ames almost choked; then laughed.

"What's so funny, Doc?"

"Been there, done that," he managed to spit out. "We could die any second and you're worried about getting barfed on again." A spinning world of geodesic sphere —brains whirling in their heads— their eyes scrambling to focus and sort it all out —dizzying, sickening— and he continued to laugh, a sputtering, broken laughter.

"Screw-it. We've gotta stop this thing?"

"Lean into the motion; worked last time," Ames said not noticing Kalo on the floor, concentrating, hands rigid, fingers spread wide. In her head she said it again, calm, and unexpectedly they were upright and reasonably steady, but still moving through time and space. Only from inside the sphere none of them had any idea what had actually occurred out there, or where they were going, or how quickly they were getting there.

"Why did we stop spinning?" Lent asked.

"Don't know and I ain't complaining," Reed answered, "but this thing just doesn't want to remain stable."

'Smiley Voice': "Sensors detect a gyroscopic malfunction."

"Cause of malfunction?"

'Smiley Voice': "Incomplete or inaccurate corollary input, Reed."

"Bullshit, I did the calculations myself."

More tersely, "I am aware of that, Reed," and 'Smiley Face' frowned. "However, your calculations were based on the IBM's data, and it has a reliability factor of..."

"—All right, I know; then fix it."

'Smiley Voice', sultry again: "As you wish. It will be my pleasure."

Disgusted, "Yep, just like driving a bus."

* * *

Somewhere, a long time ago...

...An extraordinary implosion. There, the pinhole ripped, the horizon of infinity a rent wound of ragged shreds opening an astonishing, inconceivable whirlpool of reformation.

Conception, the portal: the boundless jaws of the mythical Lion.

A whirling void of mystery and dark, it was born out there in the realm of unknown... the unexplored, and unexplained. Incredible beyond comprehension, the doorway to forever wound and roared with absolute silence in the vast emptiness and supernatural realm of the space-time continuum. Swallowing everything from everywhere it was a spiraling anomaly and incomprehensible power: destruction, obliteration, and oblivion; an astonishing, inconceivable whirlpool of reformation...

...The vortex opened.

At the edge of eternity and dawn of tomorrow it loomed winding the space-time continuum to an immense vortex beyond the limits of comprehension. Too intense and incredible to imagine, it revolves where time and space collide destroying one another within its gravitational field. It was out there, waiting for them, expecting them. Invisible and gigantic, remarkable and awesome, the gaping jaws of oblivion and the passageway to forever, where the mythical Lion roars...

...The Black Hole remains.

* * *

In the dark of space...

...And confusion of time, looking out through the missing panel behind the console Kalo whispered, "What—is—that?"

Eyes drawn to it, they saw it, billions of stars encapsulated within the corona horizon. Nonpareil. Before them it revolved like an incredible slow-moving whirlpool etching its origins from the unfilled darkness of the cosmos, huge beyond definition, millions of light years across, awe-inspiring beyond description; swallowing worlds, stars and star systems, galaxies, nebulae, dark matter and energy. Everything within the realm of existence was being drawn to the horizon maelstrom then trailing around the vortex and swirling as a cascade of light and liquid energy into the throat of the darkest unknown, the mythical Lion... an incredible Black Hole.

"My God," Ames muttered softly, "it's beautiful, like a whirling lightstorm of stars."

"No, Doc," Reed murmured, "not a whirling storm... a circular storm." Uneasy but overcome with awe and wonder, they looked at one another and Reed said it again. "A *circular* storm... the 'Hole in the Sky'."

Strangely quiet, Lent swallowed hard as they all solemnly gazed through the missing panel; spellbound, the four sojourners taking it all in, watching the phenomenon, still far off in the distance but increasing in size, getting closer, until...

"Time shear threshold[10] will occur in ninety seconds," Cozy informed.

...Realization confronted them.

"Time shear?" Ames repeated. "Jesus, if we cross the horizon's gateway we'll penetrate space-time distortion in a cosmic warp stream."

"What's time shear?" Lent asked from the floor. Both ignored him, *no time,* worried now, fingers moving, focused on what they were doing.

"Shit, we gotta do something, Doc; last time was pure luck—a miracle. The sphere can't take it." Apprehension etched in the creases on his forehead, Reed's fingers were moving. "Even under ideal conditions the odds of surviving time shear are —well hell— not good. Beat up as she is, we'll disintegrate for sure."

Ames knew he was right.

Again, from the floor: "What's time shear?"

Busy and bothered Reed glanced down then back to the console as he typed. "A phenomenon of transitional flux that we probably won't survive, a leap through the space-time threshold —entering both concurrently— too complicated to explain. Hypothetically we'll accelerate and pass through eons so quickly it would be like a space capsule's reentry into the atmosphere —manifest the illusion of a plasma cone encompassing us— but I 'spose you wouldn't know about something like that."

Lent: blank stare.

"Simply as I can explain it, the sphere will begin to glow then burn like a meteor; or we could retrograde and go backward through time portals. Or, worse case scenario... do both at the same time."

"What?"

"We'd go to the future and the past —both at the same time."

"Can we really—actually do that?"

"*Duh*—no. But regardless, unless we can avoid it, the sphere's flux will penetrate time portals and transcend hyperspace passing through windows so quickly its atomic composition will begin fragmenting and decompose —for lack of a better explanation— be in different times and space simultaneously."

"What happens then?"

"We'll drag a subatomic debris trail along with us, a flametrail of decomposing temporal residue that will follow us through the portals, the windows of time."

"So...?"

Just a glance: "Decomposing you idiot! —until we detonate and vaporize, blown to kingdom come. End of story."

"End of what story?"

"Does blown to kingdom come mean anything to you?"

Another blank stare.

Eyes locked on the console, "Lent, that's pushing it—beyond the sphere's design parameters," Ames explained.

"Oh," and quickly, "dragging a subatomic trail. Can anything else..."

"—Be dragged along?" Reed finished for him. "Theoretically, it's conceivable. Temporal residue, bits and pieces of matter and time itself could be drawn through the portals as debris."

"And other things?"

"Like the Accumulation?" understanding his inference. "I guess anything's possible." Then turning again, "Now we're busy; so if you don't mind..."

Thw—wack!

Splinters of chitin and torn bits of wing flew across the room instantly leaching to gray. Outside another strike —then more— like ripe watermelons hitting the exterior —a fifth, sixth, ninth impact— a curved stinger punching through a panel near the portal. The hole in the bullet-resistant plastic puckered as the pane started buckling and weakening, wormtrails etching white fracturing slivers, splintering runs eking ominous —*skrit-tches*— the sheathing losing structural integrity, beginning to give way.

Ames, glancing over a shoulder, "—What's..."

Kalo looked through the missing overhead panel into the rush of smeared space, and she saw them —a cloud of wings and black seeded with a river of glimmering red eyes— the Dark Forces. "They found us."

Reed, from the console: "At this flux—that's impossible." He didn't have time to look up.

"Oh this just gets better and better," Lent grumbled nervously.

Not looking, Reed yelled back, "That was a blink—right?" Eyes skipping back and forth, fingers flying: the keypad, overhead monitors, then in front of him to space and an incredible black hole looming before them and drawing them in.

Circling and coming from an angle another beast slammed into —splashing past— the exterior near the missing panel behind the console. For just an instant there was spray of chitin slivers, a blur of dragonfly wing and an ugly festered face with gruesome bloodshot eyes just beyond the magnetic field surrounding them —and that quickly it vanished.

Behind them a loud crack, the weakened panel near the portal shattering and vanishing in the whirlwind of oblivion outside. Startled, the two on the floor pivoted and stared at dark and gray and distorted rushing stars as the emptiness of cosmic void swept up and poured away in the 'out there' behind them.

Cozy: "Airlock exterior seal breach, panel fifty-four."

Over a shoulder, then back to the front, "This is impossible," Reed fretted, "there's just no way." Wired, he glanced at his friend.

"Then we die trying," Ames said gravely.

"Time shear will occur in seventy-five seconds," Cozy advised. "Atmosphere reserve sixty-two percent." Another one banged into the sphere.

"How can those things be out there?" Reed groused.

"All laws of physics would preclude that, suggesting they can't, but…"

"—Well they are," Lent piped up from the floor.

In spite of the tension and nerves Reed had to say it. "Passengers —ain't this a trip," and the four and the geodesic sphere flashed onward through time.

Out there—

Ahead of and around them streaking stars and worlds soared smashing into one another in detonations of galactic pinball-ricochet and explosive whorls of spiraling liquid light. Momentous and violent, matter and energy collided in luminous veins of interstellar fire, bursting out and scattering then swirling and reforming as solar flares that condensed and recompressed forging new astral bodies. Exploding over and over worlds and stars flamed like gargantuan fireflies blinking in the silence and dark, as far as the eye could see and beyond, to the limits of infinity and the edge of reality.

The rush of stellar matter swept through the confusion and chaos bound for the horizon, four sojourners and a geodesic sphere searing within the tailwinds of all that was, knowing well that nothing could escape, nothing would escape... not even light. In the vastness of the cosmos and the territory of unknown, everything, all of it, was being drawn inexorably by the gravitational strength and power of the mythical Lion... into the Black Hole.

Outside the geodesic sphere—

Slam, skr-eek— using the polyhedron's metal-skeleton frame for toeholds knife-blade talons gouged translucent lines in the polycarbonate skin. Clawing toward the opening, it was trying to get in.

Inside—

Kalo spun on her buttocks taking a stance on one knee, drawing back as the hideous face appeared at the hole near the portal where the blown-out panel had been. Vibrating violently the segmented tail appeared alongside the thorax and head, and stubbornly, pulling doggedly it dragged itself up and started to crawl in. Probing, the wickedly curved stinger twitched as it entered the room like a segmented snake, coloration instantly dissolving; now shades of sickle cell gray.

She let fly —into its face— splattering festered sores and puss —a piercing scream— then silence. As quickly as it appeared it was gone —only a missing panel and the blur of whirling space beyond; and an ephemeral image of a ghoul that vanished like things that go bump in the night.

Bang—

Groping as color leached from its carcass, above them another claw reached through the missing overhead panel. Straining against the ropes binding him at his waist, Lent forced himself to his feet and swung as its face appeared, the broad-edged twibil carving a gash in its head. Mortally wounded the cretin lurched back and was gone, swept into the nothingness that lingered a nanosecond beyond the multicolored field of transitional flux.

Her synthesized voice: "Time shear will occur in sixty seconds. Atmosphere reserve fifty-eight percent."

Through the clutter of magnetic coils and printed-circuit-boards dangling between them and the missing panel behind the console, Reed and Ames watched one of the creatures fly out in front of the geodesic sphere diminishing as the distance between them increased. Then, no more than a hovering speck with oscillating wings, the Dark One turned circling back and they could see it coming: its torso, suspended legs and trailing segmented tail, an armor-piercing round with pulsating dragonfly wings...

Watching it, Reed reached for the pulse laser musing, "Bad bug."

A hand on his arm stopped him. "The blast might take out more induction coils." Then Ames said, "Kalo."

...Closing in, the face and detail seemed to instantly materialize as it emerged from the distance and obscurity of space attacking with venom-lace and aculeus bolstered to kill.

On one knee, still bound by the ropes decisively she turned sighting between the magnetic coils and, *ssst*. Her arrow disappeared long before it took the half-human beast between the eyes and it folded and rolled like a Sopwith Camel that spiraled once then vanished.

Another banged into the hull causing Lent to jump; but the ropes jerked him back. Annoyed, he started untying the knots.

"Time shear will occur in forty-five seconds. Atmosphere reserve fifty-one percent."

Reed, seeing him: "Lent, don't untie..."

"—I can't fight like this."

Again, claws scraping on the exterior, then a cackling screech. Eyes still on the screens, "It's too dangerous," Ames agreed.

"Won't really matter if we're all dead anyway." Both men glanced back, unable to argue as claws started prying at the edge of a panel to their left and Kalo also began untying herself.

"Kalo don't."

But finishing the knot she ignored Ames tossing the ropetail aside, then stood beside Lent drawing an arrow as the awesome edges of the youth's twibil slowly rotated, braced in his hands. Exchanging looks that imparted steadfast allegiance and resolve, there were two at the controls and two at their backs, the black-hearted demons would not get in.

Outside—

An incoming smear of speed —lobster-orange and black— and the splatter of smashed meat as pieces whizzed and spun through the room and bits of carcass and wings disappeared out there in a scattered splash of time and bloodshot-dead eyes. Another cretin disintegrated as it shattered outside on the dome leaving sickly red ooze and telltale emulsion droplets flicking to oblivion. The impact dimpled the polycarbonate like a spent hailstone pinged off an old tin roof until, *blip,* the resilient plastic popped out again to a uniform, unwrinkled sheet.

Another thud near the portal behind them and in two steps Lent was there. Claws clamped onto the latticework where the missing panel opened to space like a rear window; then an arachnid pincer reached in. With a single powerful blow his ax severed the gnarled claw at the joint just as the creature's face appeared —and a scream that vanishing so suddenly it seemed almost surreal— like blink, was it really just there? Then still another grabbed the lattice frame knocking him back with a claw, and began dragging itself in.

From the console—

"Time shear will occur in thirty seconds. Atmosphere reserve forty-six percent."

Scrolling incessantly charts, graphs and queer little symbols appeared and disappeared on the overhead monitors as the men raced time for a solution. Now half a minute from unequivocal catastrophe countless mathematical equations blinked probabilities and alternatives, but the options were instantly stricken and replaced by the message—*calculation error, invalid solution.* Time was winning.

Out there—

Magnetic and incredible, the spellbinding beauty of the black hole's horizon wound before them like a shimmering river of dissolving starlight circling the throat of a gargantuan whirlpool. Growing larger, getting closer. Catastrophic. Phenomenal. Nothing could escape. Nothing would escape... not even light. It truly was the mythical Lion.

Inside—

With the clatter of struggle behind them and calamity flashing past around them —but there wasn't time to look— seconds were evaporating; chaos was drawing them in. As Lent and Kalo fought the second golem by the portal, time-smeared but visible through the adjacent missing panel, stars and planets were bursting in flame and vaporous turbulence; swirling, recompressing and detonating again and again as silent tantrums of bright whirlwind light.

A snap. The creature reeled grabbing with a claw, but Lent ducked and Kalo spun and was somehow just gone.

At the console—

"Doc, we have to get it under control," catching a glimpse of the monstrous anomaly. Explosions of light in front of, around and behind them... closer: "Gotta slow down—buy us some time."

With the absolute cold of deep space and the incredible heat of colliding, melting and ricocheting stars instantly appearing and disappearing by the thousands just beyond the protective magnetic corona shield torpedoing them through time, tension and nerves made them sweat. Strain exuded sheens on their faces, perspiration soaking their shirts.

'Smiley Voice': "Time shear will occur in twenty seconds. Atmosphere reserve forty-four percent."

In the blend of brilliant, crashing, erupting stars, and the melting-blurred darkness of hypervelocity space between them and the black hole's horizon, through the missing panel behind the console there were so many now that the men could see them. The Dark Forces were marshalling in a horrific swarm like a gargantuan wasp-cloud of venom and death. Still in the distance momentarily they hovered as a sinuous composition of unnumbered individuals, then almost cavalry-fashion charged head-on. Conscripts of uncountable numbers, their strength was in the millions, and now they all were coming.

At the back of the room Lent and Kalo were engaged with the second creature, the noise of their scuffle lancing throughout the sphere. Rushing bare feet and hard breathing, a ratcheting claw, the ax striking something then glancing off and the gritty thud of a heavy talon knocked against the wall. The sudden spring-shattering sound of magnetic coils and printed-circuit-board-bits pinging and clattering like shrapnel, *someone must have ducked,* and the bang of a telson hitting a panel or something, or crushing a cabinet. The crack of blade hacking into chitin and meat, running feet and other commotion —*slam*— one of them thrown against the wall, sounds distorted by a windstorm of artificial atmosphere.

"Fuel cells forty-eight percent," Reed yelled. "Draining fast. We're losing it."

"This is not my fault," Cozy announced tersely.

"Shut up computer—" over the noise. Ames' eyes flitted from the monitor and Reed knew 'the look', but focusing on the console he defended faster than a run-on sentence, "Piece of crap—leave it to rectal 'Big Brother'[11] to build shit that doesn't even work."

"—Reed."

"At least ours worked. We're gonna lose it!"

"Can't happen."

Seconds evaporating, eyes skipping to the missing-panel window, he could see them coming, millions of them. "What the? —Doc, they're gonna hit us head-on."

Ames looked as he heard...

"Time shear will occur in fifteen seconds. Atmosphere reserve forty-one percent."

...And behind them the fight continued. Kalo darted between the lion-fanged scorpion and Lent, ducking a split-instant before his ax blade swept through her space. Inches above her head glistening steel hacked wickedly into the festered black and white face, shattering the ragged teeth, cracking its skull in half. Cretin screams vomited through bubbling blood as it toppled back against the wall retching convulsively; then the legs splayed, a limp heap as the tail fell over flat.

"Fuel cells twenty nine percent!"

Above them, a thud —*the ceiling*— and, *skr-retch*, the sound of ripping metal and wires being shredded, then a metallic crash as another fiend dropped from the hole in the ceiling. It was inside. Gone gray, its color instantly melted as its claws grated on screen-metal floor and it spun rearing onto its hind legs focused on the men at the console.

Cozy's voice: "Time shear will occur in ten seconds."

Scrambling, Lent and Kalo were instantly moving to protect their friends and stop the intruder.

Too close for an arrow, Kalo screamed, "Reed, behind you!"

A snapshot of glance as his head jerked and he saw it —unable to abandon the controls— "Well kill it!" his eyes snapping back to the front knowing all their lives were in the two young people's hands.

"Time shear in *five, four, three...*"

"Fuel cells gone!" Reed announced, nerves twisted tight as brittle-kinked wire.

Ames: "Hang on! It's gonna get rough."

"Rough hell, we'll never..."

"Two, one, event threshold— intercepting horizon."

"...Make *ii-iit!*"

On the overhead screens the message flashed— *malfunction... system overload, fatal error!* —both monitors went black.

Out there, in front of them—

Almost upon them, the frontrunner soared as a blizzard of speed through vacuum winds and explosions of starlight. Darting and dodging flametrail-debris it swerved and weaved like a heat-seeking missile then slammed into the sphere disintegrating before their eyes.

Then more of them, hundreds —thousands— a black swirling hailstorm of smashed faces and wings crashing in violent head-on impacts and mind-crunching splatters of chitin. The sphere was burning through them, being battered and pummeled with head-pounding noise, searing onward, rattled and banged and shaken with each, *smack*. The alloy framework was weakening and bending, panels flexing and bowing —gigantic bugs on a windshield— darkness, collisions and light, streaking onward and onward…

…Then miraculously through and beyond the cloud of Dark Forces, blistering toward the black hole.

Inside—

Eyes vaulting back and forth, working the numbers, his voice slurred, motions distorted, "Dooc, we can't hoold togeether; tooo much straain."

"Gotta makiiit."

"Can't doo iit; gonna looose it."

Ames' voice, in the chaos: "Caan't haapppen."

Hitting keys Reed's fingers flew, but the geodesic sphere kept gaining speed, not responding. "We're looosin' it…"

Outside—

A minuscule globe of whirling ion ribbons and sparkling rainbow colors propelling through absolute silence at velocity beyond all extremes, streaming trillions of glimmering electron star trails that swirled then burst and vanished —and back there the malevolent swarm of black death turning and circling pursuing the starflash flametrail of shimmering sphere.

Inside—

Everything stretched, smeared and distorted. A black and white world swept in fogs of confusion; time-skip was a blur of slow-motion. Regardless what he did the machine did not —would not— respond. The monitors blinked back on, transitional flux a cloud of numbers: seventy million—eighty—a hundred million.

"Dooc, we'vve lost controol." The sphere rattled as components and equipment shook. "She's cooming aparrt…"

Melting holocaust was all around them, the entire cosmos ablaze with exploding stars. There were detonations of mind-boggling, silent-shattering noise and gargantuan billows of flame —and the Black Hole was there. Awesome, incredible, cataclysmic...

Then suddenly, within the horizon of the black hole,

—Time warped,

—And space collided!

There was an incredible pouring-rush of confusion and chaos without sound. From everywhere they came; exploding stars and planets, asteroids and moons whirling and flashing past, dark matter time-skipping, twirling and whizzing, winds of particulate dust exploding, recompressing, and exploding again and again. Stars rupturing. Vaporous twisted arcs of luminous gas expanding, collapsing, colliding and splashing with unbelievable, indescribable flames and light in a coalescence of fusion and gas. Entire galaxies imploding and exploding, continuously reigniting, perpetually rupturing and detonating... pure, cataclysmic fusion and light.

—All of it, swallowed from space and into the throat of the black hole,

—Everything, disappearing to somewhere on the other side, a place that might be only a dream... a figment of the imagination.

Like an incredible shooting star the geodesic sphere shattered windows of time ripping the fabric of space, warping eons in whirling hyperspace-velocity with an afterburn tailflame of residual particles and leftover fragments of space-time continuum.

A speck in an inconceivable rushing whorlwind, the machine and four sojourners jettisoned through time and space concurrently, searing onward, propelling deeper and deeper into the gravitational void. They hurtled amidst whirling colliding stars and twirling debris exploding and burning everywhere within the vortex. Complete chaos was omnipresent —the winds of oblivion— a conflagration of explosive, gaseous disorder and particulate confusion cascading in perpetual waterfall flashes. Everything everywhere was pouring and streaking in the same direction, to a vanishing point somewhere ahead. An unbelievable, incredible maelstrom, it was a continuous stream of liquid light created by countless melted stars and galaxies poured into a funnel so black it absorbed everything. Nothing would escape... not even light.

A magnificent light show —and the Black Hole remained— *but, they're only theoretical... The Unknown.*

Inside the geodesic sphere—

Still down, his movements smeared in distorted-motion, Lent was sliding across the floor as Kalo rolled from her back and rose to her knees between the Dark One and the console. Bow in hand she was all that stood between the men and death —both hands, all her might— she swung striking the half-human creature dead center in its face. Momentarily stunned, just enough time, it screeched, staggered and reeled, empty air in its claws. Then as suddenly as she had been there —just a blur— she was gone; and from the side the bow came again, alongside the monstrous disfigured head.

Searching for her the Dark One recoiled arching its tail; while almost underfoot Lent was getting up from the floor on the cretin's other side, ramming the pike in its abdomen, twisting viciously, ripping it open with a gush of sickly-dark monochromatic blood.

Scrambling to his feet again, from the corner of his eye he saw the stinger coming at him —as a, *crack,* filled his head— and in that glimmer of awareness he knew it had been deflected by Kalo's bow. It was, in reality, hyper-velocity slow-motion, but to him actions were split-second smears of commotion —moving so quickly— too fast. But he did see it flash past when the stinger just missed.

Her hair swept by as a flicker of motion and as unexpectedly as she had been next to him, she was gone. It was all blurs of momentum and gray: monstrous grappling claws, those horrible teeth and wretched face, her dark leather and thin feminine arms, and the scorpion's tail bouncing deflected —that way— just a mixture of images a time-skip away.

In front of him —chitin and legs and rank decay-breath— as the ghoul started turning and reaching for Kalo. Exposing itself broadside, it was vulnerable —now— and he swung.

While outside—

Like whirling, flaming winds of sand in a rush of whitewater shooting through an obsidian funnel, galactic volumes of white-hot gasses surged, an immense jetstream of stars, clusters of stars, nebulae —entire galaxies— rushing and pouring though the absolute black of incredible quiet and void. And within that volatile roil of silence and cataclysm an insignificant geodesic sphere and its cargo blazed with vitriolic, meteoric speed trailed by a bleak cloud of venom and claws that pursued with inveterate wickedness ingrained in their throng. Onward and onward in the turbulent tempest the sojourners flashed time-skipping through the chaos of colliding time and detonating space.

Darkness and light flared and dissolved too suddenly to comprehend, too much to absorb, flashing there then lost in a smear of strange images and evaporating gray. All around them the black hole was a rapids cascade, a pulse-wind whorl of black and fire — melting stars, scattering specks, bright light then emptiness— all being absorbed in the calamity and chaos of absolute silence at the intersection of cross-over void.

Inside—

Lent's twibil crunched savagely through the side of the golem's flank sinking deeply in its hide as the claw, already coming, battered him. Hit hard he flew back bouncing his head off the wall. Stunned and confused his shoulder triggered the sensor —ssst— the door panels whisking apart. Darkness and gray and the roar of silence — nothingness out there— just beyond the open portal and the sphere's shimmering magnetic cloud the emptiness of chaos and obliteration swirled.

Still at the console and not realizing how it happened, Ames yelled, "Noo, doon't openn the doorr!" as Lent slid weakly down the wall to the floor.

Reaching to her quiver Kalo moved, arrow in one hand, bow in the other. More quickly than a thought she attacked the fiend — diving headlong, spinning in midair, tucking and rolling beneath it— and stabbed the arrow home. Claw coming —in motion, still rolling— she twisted and slipped out from beneath it next to Lent as the pincer cracked shut inches behind her.

Wounded, infuriated and unable to reach the ax buried in its side the half-human creature reared vengefully clawing the arrow from its belly, and then turned to take them. Between its hideous distorted cackle-chattering roars and the slobbering drool on its face, it grimaced with festering ugly and fangs.

Beside him and the open portal Kalo shook Lent dragging him back from the stupor —to here and now— the menace before them. With no more than a shared glimpse each knew, and as the man-beast lunged, they dove different directions.

Blade still buried in its hide, Lent grabbed the ax handle and wrenched as the creature spun and snapped and Kalo swung hard with her bow. Leaping with a bodyslam he caused the creature to stumble tangling himself between its side and legs, wedging him against the wall. The tail arched and the leprous face and teeth came around. A strike. The aculeus narrowly missed as he pressed himself against its paunch and ducked partway underneath it. Trying to free himself, again the face and fangs came for his head —and Kalo streaked by— an arrow was sticking out of its eye. Somehow, mixed within the struggle and tension she appeared and was gone in a glimmer of motion, and Lent realized, *no one can move like that.* He squirmed once and she was back —had done something else— and as the Dark One screeched and reared its legs spread apart just enough for him to squeeze out.

Loose, he slid clear and glanced back realizing that she had struck the monster pointblank in the face and was just standing in front of it offering herself as a target so he could escape. It was grabbing for her. He jumped to help her but was too late, the scissoring claw closing, plucking her from the floor.

Seized by the waist in the sadistic claw she grimaced but defiantly fought back. She kept pounding it. Pain traced with determination and tears filling her eyes, she struggled to keep the lion fangs at bay as the serrated edges cut into her flesh. Twisting, wrenching and bleeding from her midriff, she pummeled its head with her bow then grabbed the impaled arrow and ripped out its eye. Cackling,

Cyclops-demon hoisted her over its head like a trophy in hand, its captive still resisting but writhing with pain.

In Lent's head the voice shouted —*you can't have her!*— then he screamed, a distorted scream, striking viciously, full-weight with his blows, chopping off two wings and hacking chitin apart, fleshing blood and splashing blood-gray. Fury's storm in his heart and fire saturating his soul, he swung again sinking both blades ax-handle-deep in the demon's back chopping through the wing joints with a boil of blood and entrails squirting out of its back.

Still stubbornly clutching her, the Dark One staggered and stumbled near the door, but refused to let go, carrying Lent up with them as it recoiled from pain. It tried to fly but its wings wouldn't work, and all together they slammed to the floor.

The broken ones and the other wings fluttered as its treacherous claws grappled for purchase at the screen-metal floor. Then the creature shuddered, and they could feel it... chaos and confusion was sucking them out.

First, the creature's segmented tail slid through the portal disintegrating and vanishing; but the monster held on to its prey. With a blebby of entrails Lent desperately ripped out the ax and hacked into the Dark One again trying to free her from the vice-like claw. Chitin splintered and chips sprayed with faded gray blood; but it wouldn't let go. And still, they could feel it... chaos and confusion was sucking them out.

Graphic and awesome the power and vacuum of space and the black hole dragged the cretin, dissolving it inch-by-inch. From the tail toward its head, more and more of its carcass evaporated flicking into nonexistence.

Now the maelstrom's force was drawing them too, pulling them. It was unmanageable, one-of-a-kind, extraordinary... sliding inexorably. Locked in the expanded-metal floor the scorpion's talons clung tenaciously to the screen until one by one, its joints tore and popped from its thorax and its legs were ripped off.

Frantic, Lent tried to chop through the dense armored claw holding Kalo—*too thick, running out of time*. With terror and resignation etched in her expression and something else scribed in her heart Kalo reached desperately for him, knowing even as she did there wasn't time for him to save her. Sliding toward oblivion... still losing ground.

Hair blown straight with its power and a storm in their eyes, each focused upon the other. Nothing else mattered. A few feet away the winds of oblivion —and destiny— roared with absolute silence.

It was hopeless. He knew it. Looking at her, frustration filled his eyes and he quit trying to chop through the monstrous claw and climbed onto the vanishing carcass; reaching out for her, sinew and bone welling with something more, strength, a strength he had never known before. Now together they could feel it... the mighty winds of chaos and smeared darkness were sucking them out.

In the tempest of the space-time vortex's holocaust the monstrous carcass between them rattled violently, shredding to pieces as it whisked into space; everything, everywhere, coming apart then vanishing an arm's length away. Fingers barely inches apart they reached for one another, for each other; their lives, their destinies bound by the web of circumstance, conviction, and more... the mystery and roar of the mythical Lion, the doorway to forever of the unfathomable Black Hole.

"Pleease... help mee," she mouthed with slurred words.

As she pled for his help his determined eyes narrowed and his soul answered with conviction... and his life finally began, as courageously, with all his might and soul he lunged grabbing hers in his hand. Clinging to one another, both terrified, he said, "You are not alone. We are in this together."

Hands tightly clasped, she looked in his eyes. She trusted him. He was her friend. Finally, she believed in him; and an evanescent smile crossed her lips.

Then, from out there they heard it, an unnatural, ominous, guttural whisper...

...'Something yet Unfinished'.

The Black Hole roared with the Lion's voice and strength, the Dark One being torn and ripping in pieces, being shredded and blowing away...

And holding one another,
    Their destiny took them.
        …They whirled into the lair of oblivion!
Reed and Ames at the controls—

Swallowed in chaos, the geodesic sphere —time-skipping— plummeting, such tremendous cataclysm: the confusion, destruction, and reformation. Stars exploding then imploding again and again… unending cycles.

Planets and moons rupturing from within, scattered to limitless specks then swirled together and recompressed forming new worlds. Entire galaxies pouring and spiraling onward in twisted veins of liquid light —time warped, space folded— the billions of stars rupturing again into space. And it continued over and over, space compressed into a fluid channel pouring at the speed of light through the blackest blackness possible to imagine. Brilliant light thundering without sound —exploding, imploding, millions of times— too many to comprehend it all…

—Breaking apart, being torn to pieces,
—The time machine whirled and soared!

…Then an incomprehensible surging torrent of blinding cataclysm erupting from the other side —exploding trillions of planets, stars and galaxies all at the same instant— too much to envision, unimaginable, incredible beyond description…

—*Fifteen billion years!*
—*And the Rush*—
'The 'Big Bang'!

…The black hole just vanishing—bolts of lightning and thunder splashing incredible flames, searing stars exploding then imploding in a whirling chaos of storms and roiling hurricane gales as oblivion and reformation merged within the matrix of celestial firestorm and wind…

Then darker and darker until the sudden splash through a vein of bright liquid light; then more blackness and cold,
    …And Everything was Gone.

CHAPTER FIFTEEN

The geodesic sphere rested fifteen degrees off level…

…In brackish water and blue-gray mud. Its interior was frazzled hair of dangling wires and a jumble of magnetic coils and printed-circuit-boards hanging from above. Debris and broken pieces were strewn among fallen panels from the collapsed metal framework, a total loss.

Unconscious, both men remained strapped in their seats, held fast by the harnesses. Ames was slumped forward, arms hanging limp, not stirring. Reed, whose chair had broken free of the floor track and was lying sideways against the console, moaned very faintly. Both monitors were dark. The geodesic sphere, their time machine, was dead.

Ames' left hand twitched; then he raised an arm ever so slowly and leaned back onto his chair. His head throbbed. *Opening your eyes will make it worse,* a voice inside whispered; but he had to anyway. The voice was right; it was worse now.

"Reed," he muttered, "Reed… you alive?" He tried to reach out to his friend but the shoulder straps held fast so he clasped the buckle —pulled— and the harness let go. He fell forward onto the console catching himself before going to the floor. Wavering, he stood and turned then looked at his friend again. "Reed, are you alive?" head still muddled, staggering on the uneven floor.

Weakly, "I must be; but I'm stuck."

Ames was relieved and the dizziness was finally subsiding —but his head sure hurt. "You're still buckled in and tipped over again."

When he unbuckled the harness Reed tumbled from the chair onto him, both going down in a tangle of arms and legs, rummaged around on the tilting floor, slipping in mud; then got their wits together. From the floor Ames looked around. This time, no grin.

"Kalo—Lent?" Reed knew what he meant.

The cobwebs were gone; scanning the room their eyes tracked to the warped, open portal at the same time, then to each other. Dragging the pulse laser from the junk and muck and slinging it over a shoulder, "No they didn't —weren't— don't even think it."

For a long minute Ames was quiet, until, "Let's take a look."

"Just don't be jumpin' to conclusions."

Outside—

The geodesic sphere lay tilted and collapsed, cratered in mud in a world that once was. As far as possible to see a tainted gray-brown fog and apathetic drifting mist wafted over the despair of stagnant mire, a landscape embraced with the texture of indolence and gloom.

Near darkness—

Overhead the sky was lackluster soup of thickened atmosphere that resembled pan-burnt crusted leftovers in a sink of day-old-dirty, cold, dead suds. Not really sky anymore, it seemed more like something else; but in the dusky shadows it was hard to say what. The layered stratum moved in listless waves that mingled blending charcoal and dun with tawny and deep mahogany brown; but not like clouds, it sifted back and forth undulating as it flowed and wound like vapor snakes crossing a pond. Petulant, not seeming to go anywhere it lethargically stirred and percolated, spanning horizon to horizon as near as they could tell; but in the dim light they couldn't be sure.

The only light came from just above the horizon, a smeared globe of murky violet with an eerie flaming corona that oozed out and drained over the landscape creating long blue-black shadows of gloom, decay, and despair. Companions, both were still there in the sky, a hidden, diminished sun almost absorbed within the eclipse of the blood-red moon cascading a fire-lace aurora that fanned out wine-colored to violet, bleeding dark red in a despondent atmosphere. Unworldly and ominous the eclipse appeared to fashion circular wings burning a hole through the sky, as though drawing in and draining a world through its core.

Tainted, the water they stood in smelled of decay, the offensive damp of a rotten-carcass lake covered with broken mats of pallid green or dead-black duckweed clusters. Lifeless weeds and rancid bent-over grass floated flat like tangled slimy tresses; and here and there were scattered flotsam clumps of green and black decomposed thatch resembling thick strands of horsehair or unraveled rope that swayed indolently when waves quietly pushed past.

Protruding randomly throughout this endless spoiled lake were shallow rises of landfall resembling small scattered mud islands where twisted bare trees stood askew in aberrant groves like wretched cadavers with bent arms and broken hands dangling crooked tortured fingers that silently scratched fog goblins in the mist. Mold and lichen nourished by the swamp partially concealed the trees, creeping up their trunks beneath pendents of still, hanging matted strings like Spanish moss dripping brown water back to the swamp. All of it was shrouded in a dismal gray flow of fog that stole over the surface crawling in wisps of incessant exuding motion as it stirred, rose and wound, then congealed and sank ever so slowly again.

"It's the same, nothing's changed."

"A time lock," Ames muttered.

Eyes deciding, "Well, let's get going," Reed said taking a step then limping. "Shit."

"What?"

Not looking back, slowly looking around, "Just twisted my ankle." Guardedly he eased into the sour water from the rise, "Must have happened when we crashed."

"Where you going?"

With the question Reed turned to his friend, his words as genuine as his intent. "To find them."

Ames began to say something, then didn't, as Reed started hobbling away. Moved by his determination the man smiled, a small smile, watching as his friend sloshed through backwater-muck for a short distance before looking back. Trailing strings of black greasy-dead grass from both legs with rotted duckweed petals clinging to his thighs, Reed asked, "Well, you coming?"

"'Spose I'd better," the other said plainly, "you'll get lost for sure if I let you go wandering off on your own."

As Ames caught up, Reed draped his arm over his shoulder, "I was hoping you'd see it my way."

Ames took the arm boosting him up—eye contact. "Why's that?"

"Because, 'bout two more steps and I probably would've fallen on my ass."

"So?" as they started moving together.

"Hell, I'm already soaked to my nuts."

"So?"

"Well I don't wanna get my shirt all wet too."

"Incorrigible," Ames sighed.

"I take that as an affront to my character —and it could be worse."

A grin. "Yeah, yeah, I know; you could be boring."

"Bitchin'-right—couldn't-a said it better myself," and together they slurped off through the gray and water and muck.

* * *

Hours later...

...Their progress was slowing. Pods of floating duckweed and pond scum pushed lazily aside as they pushed through the putrid knee-deep swamp. Hair matted with slimy goo, Ames wiped muddy sweat from his face when they finally stopped to look around.

"You tired?"

"Some," Reed answered. "You?"

"Yeah, more ways than one," he admitted. Green-black strings of swamp grass trailing from their legs, water slurped with a sickly film like thin molasses buoying duckweed clutter around them. Depressing.

His friend understood deciding conversation might help as they started moving again. "Doc, don't want you to think I'm getting all maudlin or anything, but of all the people I've ever known, I guess I admire you second-most."

Around them gloom flowed in the mist wafting in amorphous, almost-liquid waves curling just above the surface, occupying the empty spaces with a shroud of floating continuum and misery. Above them, reaching out from the dim halo of the eclipsed sun's violet corona goblins of long blue-black shadows breathed conferring the texture and desolation of never-ending darkness. Reed was slumping.

"Second-most?" Ames asked without looking, pulling his friend a bit more tightly to help him straighten up.

"Yeah."

Next, the obvious question: "Okay, who's first?"

Reaching down he took hold of a leech that quickly constricted to a stubby black knot on his calf, and answered, "My dad." Then casually, "Little suckers bunch up like tough old marshmallows," an abrupt twist, and he tossed it away.

Ames commented dryly, "Yeah, must be a common phenomenon; lots of things do that in cold water."

"Voodoo bitchin' and shrunken heads," Reed chuckled.

A thin smile and, "I can accept that." Reed looked… "Your dad," …and nodded.

They slogged on until Reed admitted, "Sure miss him; you know? Wish we'd spent more time together while he was still alive."

Glancing at his friend, then ahead again, Ames asked, "What happened? Want to talk about it?"

"Like leather bubble gum," Reed observed offhand.

"What?"

"Leeches—tough as leather and they stick like bubble gum."

"I was referring to…"

"—My dad. Yeah, I know." He sighed as they continued quietly for a moment companioned by the blebby, *glup,* of shed bubbles popping and water gurgling up through the mud. Reed's thoughts digressed.

Memories:

A younger time, a time when he was more reckless in so many ways; a time that we each seem to have known and let slip away, taking for granted that those we loved and those who loved us, would always be there. That was the time of innocence and naiveté, before we crossed the threshold of harsh reality in life. None of us are immortal. We are all here for only a little while. For each of us time is limited, and time is oh-so very precious.

Reed began, "You know, we were poor when we were growing up, but we never knew it. Seems like everyone was poor back then, and raising eight kids must'a been tough. Dad always worked two jobs—long as I can remember—all day at the factory, then evenings at a department store; so I never got to see him much really, when I was a kid growing up. And it seems like mom was always washing clothes or cooking or cleaning. We didn't eat fancy stuff, but we never went hungry either." Words, drifting off.

"Sounds like a better life than most, something to appreciate later on."

"Yeah," the other agreed, "it was hard at times, but all in all it was good."

"Made you stronger."

"Think so?" Reed asked, and he chuckled. "Stronger maybe—not necessarily any wiser."

"How's that?"

With a light smirk Reed prefaced, "Well look at who I hang out with." Then serious again, shaking his head as the teasing faded with the grin and recollection gathered inside causing him to smile, a tranquil smile. "We lived on a cobblestone street in this big old two-story frame house, mint green with white trim. Every summer my brothers and I had to paint the house. One year we'd scrape and paint the green siding and the next year we did the trim. For all the years we lived there it was a ritual of summer, one of our chores."

"What's wrong with that? Painting's not so bad."

"I know. We knew we all had to pitch in. Back then, that's just the way things were; everybody had to do his share. Spent the summers playing 'monsters' and painting the house." He paused, then continued, "We did rockets and bombs and stuff like that when we were kids too; but we weren't rocket scientists, not by any stretch of the imagination." Ames grinned.

"There was this one time when dad told us to get rid of an old mattress; so we ripped it all apart —you know, took out all the stuffing, the cotton ticking— and we crammed it all in the fifty-five-gallon burning barrel behind the garage. So far so good, but naturally we couldn't get the sucker to burn when we tried to light it; so one of us—I think it was me—got the bright idea that gas might help."

The scenario was coming together and Ames smiled but remained quiet.

"We dumped the burning barrel out and refilled it with the mattress ticking, only this time we soaked it with gas. You know, a layer of ticking, a layer of gas, more ticking, more gas." Shaking his head at his foolishness, "Get the idea?"

Smiling more, "You didn't."

"Yep, sure did. Like I said, we weren't destined to work for NASA; and when we touched that sucker off it went up like a roman candle, well actually, like a whole shit-load of roman candles." He sighed fondly. "Heck, there were flying cotton ball fires everywhere you could imagine, a hundred feet high…" then, "well okay, maybe not a hundred feet, but you know what I mean. Sorta cool actually." Ames laughed a little, eking a grin from his friend as he went on. "Yeah, it sounds funny now, but it wasn't then. We were just dumb little kids and that shit started the garage roof on fire, scorched about forty feet of the white picket fence and torched the pigeon coop to ashes."

"Shoot, there were smoldering fires and black smoke and pieces of burning mattress stuck everywhere —even in the old Dutch Elm tree— not to mention a sky full of scared-shitless homeless pigeons and half a dozen scared-stupid re-tread kids running around with the frantic dithers."

"Re-tread kids?"

Reed grinned. "Yeah, you know, like car tires. Recaps, factory seconds."

Ames chuckled and asked, "So what happened?"

"Well, we all grabbed the closest available firefighting equipment —brooms and rags and shit like that— and beat the livin' tar out'a that stuff. Took forever but we finally got the fires all out —or at least scooped into one big pile near the alley where it couldn't do anymore damage. Boy I'll tell you what, soak that shit with gas and set it on fire and it just doesn't wanna go out. Stomped on it. Smashed it flat—and it still wouldn't go out."

"Hell, some of the neighborhood kids even came over and helped out thinking it was big fun —but a'course they weren't the ones who were gonna get their asses whipped. Didn't matter though, we were appreciating all the help we could get about then and we just wanted to put the fires out." He shook his head. "Talk about panic mode — shoot, I was a nervous wreck, and I suspect my brothers were 'bout scared as I was."

He paused as they continued until Ames cajoled warning, "Don't *even* think you're ending the story there, leaving me hanging. What happened?"

Teasing, "You really want to hear the rest of it?"

"Kick your ass in a New York-minute, I do."

Almost reluctantly Reed conceded, "Okay—but remember—we were just little kids not rocket scientists."

"Reed..."

"Okay. Well anyway we finally got all the fires out and after giving the aftermath the once-over we decided it wasn't really all *that much* of a disaster —and besides, too late to do anything about it then anyway. Heck, we figured dad might not even notice." Ames laughed. "I know, little-kid-logic —and we were short and from the ground we couldn't see much of the garage roof. But looking back on it now I'm sure the forty feet of burned up, scorched-black fence and incinerated pigeon coop was a dead giveaway —but shucks, we were in minimizing mode."

"Naturally, go on."

"Well like I said, we finally got all the fires put out, so we put the brooms and stuff away and hung our firefighting rags up in the garage and did what any normal kid would do… we went next door to Lyle's and started playing basketball. And we were doing just fine in spite of the fact that we all just knew we had an ass whippin' coming."

"Basketball?"

"Sure, we were kids remember. But the reprieve didn't last very long because pretty soon Lyle's dad, old Mister Lundeen, comes ambling along down the alley —he never walked anywhere very fast you know— anyway he says, 'You boys know your garage is on fire?' You also gotta understand that Mr. Lundeen was pretty laid-back and didn't get excited by much —but our reaction was, '*Shit*— the smoldering firefighting rags we hung up in the garage!' And sure as a big-eyed monkey on a crooked branch that sucker was blazing to beat all hell again —only this time it was worse. So here goes fifteen junior firefighters springing into action all over again, 'cept this time we were thinking and had the wherewithal —that'd be common sense— to get the garden hose out. And take my word for it, there wasn't a dry spot left on the garage, in the back yard, or at the neighbor's when we were done." In passing, a side note, as he remembered, "You know when you soak everything down like that it makes for real good dew-worm hunting that night. But back then we didn't really expect to be going fishing anytime soon."

"Dew-worms?"

"Oh that's right, you're from the West," so Reed explained. "Dew-worms, night crawlers, fishing worms; you know, the big, fat, long ones."

"That's the end of the story?"

"Not exactly, but pretty close. And looking back now, honestly, I think I was the one who hung the smoldering rags up in the garage too."

Ames grinned.

"Yeah, and believe it or not, we didn't get a lickin'. Guess dad assumed some of the blame for telling his dipshit-dumb kids to get rid of the mattress in the first place. But we did get a lickin' for the time my brother and I were experimenting with homemade rockets in the garage and set it on fire."

Ames' eyebrows went up.

"Yeah. But now that's a whole 'nother story so we'll save it for some other time."

Ames smiled. "So, you didn't get in too much trouble then?"

"Nope, not really; just had to rebuild the pigeon coop, re-roof the garage, scrape and sand the garage and fence and replace some fence pickets —and paint it all again." Thinking about it, "Damn, to this day I just hate mint green with white trim." A sigh. "True story, Doc. True story." Wading, still thinking, quiet.

"All in all though, I guess I was lucky, had a pretty good childhood; but like most of us I didn't appreciate it back then. And then, the years slipped away."

"Out of high school I moved from the Midwest to go to college and never seemed to have time to go back and see my parents; always something else going on, you know, school, girlfriends, shit like that."

"Pretty common," Ames allowed.

"No excuse though. My fault again."

"How's that?"

"Before I knew it dad was ill, and because I was so far from the rest of the family I didn't know just how sick he really was. Going to school and all, I only got back to see them once a year or so, maybe during spring break, or the summer, you know." He became quiet.

They waded on a bit farther as Reed thought, remembering, and regret crept in. Helping to steady him Ames didn't say anything, only waited as they trudged on. There are times when a friend just waits; he knew things like that and he'd been there before—once some time ago in the lowland, with Tian. There are times, because life is like that sometimes.

Blebby gentle sounds sucked up with each gurgling step as the water churned to black froth swirling green-black strings of dead grass. That was the only noise this endless mire seemed to offer; that, and the echo of misery that drifted perniciously and silently within the fog, until...

"...My fault again," Reed murmured.

"Not really; just the way things are sometimes, more often than not."

"Thanks Doc, but I should have made a point of it, made the time. He gave eighteen hours a day, six days a week for us. Church on Sunday. I could have done more, a lot more."

Plodding along together, quietly Ames asked, "What happened?"

"Toward the end he got really sick ...bad... and then, I couldn't get back until summer. So, he waited for me... waited to see me one last time. I knew it too and I asked my girlfriend to go with me; but she said she couldn't, too busy."

"Busy?"

"Partying, drinking, drugs, fun things like that. Know what I mean?"

"Yes," almost sadly.

Reed sighed. "Later... afterwards, when we split up, she didn't have a clue, couldn't understand. But I think really she just didn't want to understand that life has its ups and downs, and a relationship isn't just for the good times. There's no such thing as 'just for the good times'. Couldn't depend on her to be there when it really mattered, so better she not be there at all."

With the nod Reed knew his friend agreed, and they kept walking. The swamp was draining their strength.

"I finally got back to see him, and I think at first he was afraid of dying, not knowing if he'd done well enough with his life. But then near the end it seemed like that all changed and it didn't bother him, almost as if —well nevermind that."

This time, his words were more moderate, his voice subdued. "That last day... I won't ever forget that day."

"He didn't really look sick, but he was. We spent that afternoon together, that last time. Then he got really sick again, so we took him to the hospital, and on the way, in the car, he asked if it would be all right if he leaned on me." Reed almost choked. "After all the years that I leaned on him."

"He was tired of being in the hospital, being ill, a hundred times. I think finally he was just plain tired, and he looked so bad when we got there… the emergency room. Took them an hour or two to stabilize his electrolytes, do all the tests and the stuff they do; but later they finally got him upstairs to a room, and as soon as I saw him, I knew." He paused.

"Knew what?"

Reed glanced at his friend, then sadly, drifting back to the gloom, "You know how sometimes after people have been really sick for a long time, just before they die, sometimes they seem a-hundred-percent better, you know, like they're all of a sudden really healthy?"

"Yes," Ames said, "I know."

"Well, it was like that. When mom and I walked into the room dad looked as though nothing in the world was wrong with him. We all talked for a while then he said we should get back home and wait for my sister and her husband. They were coming from out-of-state."

"For as long as I can remember he never said good-bye, always said, 'I'll see you later'. But that time he smiled, and said good-bye… and I knew. And he knew that I knew—and that was the last time we ever spoke to one another. Should have said something, told mom; but I didn't." He sighed, "And I knew."

"I took mom home and by the time we got there it was dark. My sister was arriving soon so we turned the TV on, to wait. Wasn't really watching it though, couldn't concentrate, like something inside was restless, didn't feel right. Then, through the living room window, in the sky to the north, above where the hospital was, a lightning storm started—not heat lightning, just strange. No thunder, only lightning flashing over and over, and not one bit of noise. It kept up for a few minutes, then as suddenly as it started the lightning stopped… and two minutes later the phone rang. Before mom even answered it, I knew what it was. Somehow, inside, I just knew."

"She and I were alone in the house, so all she had left was me. That was the most helpless, lost feeling I've ever known. I can't even explain it… when your soul empties out."

Approaching one of the mud-rise islands, head down, Reed sniffled; not quite unnoticed, but almost. "We got to have that talk though, and I told him how proud I was to be his son, something not many men get the chance to do, make time to do. Won't let anyone know how they really feel, too reluctant to say what they honestly want to say, inside. Just won't. Proud, vain, macho—I don't know—just stupid."

The water was shallower now and climbing onto the mud island from the mire, without prelude Ames asked, "You tired?"

"Yeah Doc, I'm tired." So Ames let go of his arm and together they sat down. For a moment neither spoke, and as Reed sat there, he picked up a little stick. This place was empty and quiet.

Weary, his eyes drifting over the mire, at length Ames calmly said, "I should imagine, somewhere he's watching right now, and listening —and he is just as proud of you." Then he smiled. "My friend... you have succeeded."

"Think so?" Soberly, unsure, fingering the stick he slowly shook his head. "I mean with everything we've been through, the unexplainable things, all that's happened, there's still so much I just don't understand. Sometimes it makes me wonder. Sometimes Doc, life makes me wonder." And with that Reed began drawing circles in the mud with the stick.

* * *

Exhausted, too tired to go on...

...Weary and troubled by the conundrum around them, searching for answers in a place of mire and gloom laced with paradox and fragments of an enigma they could not solve; soon both were asleep. Eyes skimming, flitting back and forth beneath closed lids, it was there, somewhere within the realm of what is, and was, and might be, that it emerged.

A piece of... *The Puzzle.*

It all seemed very real; but perhaps it was only an inference, a fragment that came to John as...

...His Dream.

A place of dark and mud and duckweed slime... and a meadow where there was a clapboard schoolhouse and twelve children playing at recess. Then the misty vision faded, transforming, and another came into view: a woman hiding from the Devil somewhere...

...Holding her son in her arms, from the corner of the small room Tian intimated, very softly, "I will be over here... should you need me."

A voice said:

"From the throne issued flashes of lightning, and voices and peals of thunder, and before the throne burn seven torches of fire, which are the seven spirits of God; and before the throne there is as it were a sea of glass, like crystal.

And round the throne, on each side of the throne, are four living creatures, full of eyes in front and behind:" (Rev. 4: 5-6 RSV)

Into the darkness again—spectral, banshee eyes, gray and evil, moving closer, and closer. They were watching him, crawling and lurking everywhere, glaring, making sounds. —No, not the eyes, the sounds were evil and empty, resonant in his brain; but not from the eyes. Somewhere else, something else; hollow, uncaring sounds, the echoes of emptiness, evil for evil's own sake, empty and dead, a soulless void. Hideous and unfulfilled, they were the sounds of hate and spite... wonton and unworldly laughter.

Someone standing there—towering evil and dreadful, formidable and dark, the faceless specter of death.

A voice said:

"The first living creature like a lion, the second living creature like an ox, the third living creature with the face of a man, and the fourth living creature like a flying eagle." (Rev.4: 7 RSV)

Entering the mysterious passageway, a narrow vein of tunnel that meandered for miles; and as they proceeded, not far behind, in the darkness something followed, not a shape really, just a slinking flow of movement, a black, amorphous slithering motion. Appearing then vanishing it slipped from one place to another, stopping frequently, being absorbed in the dark, keeping the interval, laying back. For some time they kept moving... and it kept following.

The premonition of, *look over your shoulder,* as suddenly it flew at them, a whirling wind of evil and menace. Fluttering as it swooped down, an arm emerged from the loose-fitting sleeve of the cloak, and a black timeworn hand with fingernail claws clutching a scythe appeared. Coming in...

A voice said:

"And the four living creatures, each of them with six wings, are full of eyes all around and within, and day and night they never cease to sing," *(Rev. 4: 8 RSV)*

...A wave of pitch-black motion rushing over him, only inches above him narrow liver-red eyes, dingy-gray rotted teeth and a crooked, wretched mouth. Dark came as a wind. And from the side, from around the shadow-phantom there was a reflective glimmer of steel. He knew —*a blade*— and heard the resonant sharp —*brring*— then blinding shatter-bright sparks of metallic collision as the razor edges slammed and careened ringing out through the dark. Then...

...Furious red flames and shattering blue-violet sparks of sword and steel, heaving the blade aside, deflecting the blow. Bellowing vicious laughter Smith turned and swung ferociously, *dive and somersault—avoided him—tuck and roll.* Recall ignited, back on his feet and the neuro-flashburst of *de'ja vu —the sixth sub-level. I know you. We've been here before.*

Smith reeled lashing out at his face, the incredible broad blade sweeping up, intercepting the blow. Fiery blue-violet sparks and searing, burning red flames, with the shimmering blade before him —*witness the scimitar's mysterious might*— flickering, glowing luminescent with blue-white tensile and remarkable light. Astonished, not understanding...

...And garbled, so strange, then he heard it again. *"John."*

He wasn't sure but the beckon lingered with intimate echoes inside his head; so he answered whispering, "Yes, I'm here." Opening, tired eyes fluttering, the voice woke him to light: shimmering quasars, pulsars, and whirling twinkling minutiae.

The Animal was massive and muscled; the perfection of symmetry, pawing impatiently with solid ponderous hooves that shed sparks when they struck. The Percheron's neck, breast, point of shoulders and thighs were extraordinarily thick rippling intense strength with every movement it made. Its forelock and mane lay full, draped and curled around alert pointed ears at the pole and swept in a wave upon its neck. Its withers, back and shoulders gleamed, pristine and smooth with summer slick sheen. Its tail long and flowing almost touching the ground swished gracefully in a blend of beauty from unknown origins, forged of beauty and grace.

Restless, it tugged impatiently and high-spirited in the woven satin headstall with a hackamore, so it didn't taste cold metal in its mouth. The creature's eyes were large and round, the virtue and color of aquamarine. It was purest white, unbounded and powerful, possessed of the unicorn's spirit and grandeur; a fury of hooves with the soul of The Lamb.

Mounted bareback the rider was a Roman Centurion with a breastplate cuirass of lorica segmentata armor, tasseled helmet and visor concealing the face; a leader of thousands, follower of One, a warrior of biblical times. Garbed in a cape of flowing linen with tassets and sandals, in the rider's waistband of wide harness leather was braced a broad scabbard and mighty battle sword; straight as a beam of sunlight, sharp as the limit of creativity and forged in the benediction of mankind.

Silhouetted by an eclipsed sun that hung low in the sky and eerie fiery corona casting long blue-black shadows of suffering, hardship and despair on a place that was; incredible beyond words, shimmering, silent and awe-inspiring the legionnaire remained mounted, identity concealed in a shroud of mystery and light...

...A Warrior from Time.

"John, everything that is, and was, and will be... is defiled," the warrior told him without speaking. The great Percheron pawed impatiently and the vision coaxed gently with the reins causing the

animal to shake its muscular neck then be still. *"You must undo what has been done,"* the Mystic confided.

"How? I am only a man. How can I undo what I don't even understand?"

"You answer your own question, John. The challenge is not how, but because you are a man."

Humble, apprehensively, Ames murmured, "Smith."

Nodding slowly, the warrior verified, *"Yes."*

Lowering his head in deference, almost conceding defeat, the man admitted, "He's too powerful, too strong. He could beat me easily."

"Do you not remember; have you forgotten the song of the steel?"

With the voice inside his head there came images, visions and recollections of combat. "No, I haven't forgotten; but I don't understand, and I fear him," he confessed. "Surely you know I am afraid of him."

Compassionately, understanding, the Mystic counseled, *"Take back what you have given."*

The Percheron pawed the sodden earth. *"Smith is Evil, but you must find him, face him... and set things right; recover what is lost."* Self-doubting the man began to speak but the vision stopped his words with a hand. *"The task is yours... must be yours. You will not be alone if you follow your heart and the stars."*

"What does that mean?"

"More than that I cannot tell you. It is forbidden."

"But..."

"John, the power lies within you... and the warrior of the cloistered sun. Your journey ends in a place that was. There you must finish what will never end."

"I don't understand."

Behind the shimmering visor green eyes smiled as the Mystic disclosed, *"When the moon is full... wait until the moon is full."*

As the invocation touched his mind, the revelation of a child touched his heart... and warmth filled his soul as he remembered a child's simple words. And at last, Ames realized... he knew the identity of the Centurion Mystic. *It has been so long; I am happy to know you are well.* And as he murmured the words in his mind, the warrior-vision removed the helmet.

Before him, within the armor dwelt the heartbeat of honor, the soul of a dream and a love from Beyond, where reality and the dream world merge ...mythical, visionary, intangible, yet... very real.

And in a voice that was no longer disguised, with words as clear and fresh as the breath of spring flowers, the Mystic said, *"And you, John. It is good to see you again."*

Intrinsic, intimate, it was a voice that Ames... knew well.

CHAPTER SIXTEEN

Bland tedium of decay…

…Within a melancholy of indolent fog drifting with brown-green water, side by side they eased slowly on. Clinging to their legs narrow ribbons of dead grass followed them for a while like homeless waifs with nothing better to do, dragging along then eventually disentangling and slipping quietly away, lost again in spoiled water and darkness. Stirred from below, pods of shriveled duckweed rose and fell with the flow of mahogany mire as putrid bits that were verdant frond petals not so long ago. But now like dead shavings or insipid flecks of life, the rotten smidgens floated aimlessly then again eased out of sight slowly sinking into the slime of anemic melange.

In spite of her protests after the crash, if that's what it was, Lent used his dingy tee shirt to bandage Kalo's midriff where the creature's claw had clutched her. The wound was bad, deep and ragged, resembling a willow branch hewn with a hatchet. Now ignoring the leeches attached to her thighs and in enough pain that she favored her injured ribs and midsection, she stooped slightly as they waded through the swamp.

"Let me help you," again offering his hand.

Curtly, "I do not need any help."

"But you're hurt." Though it was soaked with dusky swamp water Lent could see the wine-colored stains where blood was seeping through her makeshift dressing, each blebby wave coaxing traces of weeping blood that dribbled down her sides trickling back to the mire.

Fingering soggy hair from her face, steadfastly clinging to her independence, "I have been bruised before. I can manage."

"It's not a bruise; you're hurt." Slipping closer again as they eased through the mire, inveigling more gently, "Please," offering the hand, "let me help you. What harm will it do?"

"I should imagine you would be more concerned for Tere's well-being," the girl remarked weakly.

Confused, "Tere—what does she have to do with...?" now defensive, inadvertently withdrawing his hand. "We're lost, Kalo. We—are—lost," spatial emphasis allowed each word. "She could be dead —probably is for all we know— so what does she have to do with anything?"

"A lot."

"You're not making any sense girl."

"I am not a girl; I am a warrior."

Sarcastic: "Yeah, what-*ever*." Now he was mad. "And you're still not making any sense." The tone in his voice was *irritated, more than a little.* "We're all alone in—well I don't know where—and you..." then he realized, "you're angry because Tere and I are friends?"

Stumbling, *"Uuh—"* a wave sloshing under her black leather top caused her to involuntarily gasp as water swept between her breasts.

"What?"

Regaining her composure, "Nothing—the water is cold."

Still stinging with her remark he quipped caustically, "Took you this long to notice?" Revenge; a barb of his own.

"There—" she said, "—that is exactly what I mean."

"What?"

"You are always kind to Tere... but mean to me."

That, he understood, and his temper sank as quickly as 'the tone'. "I didn't mean to hurt your feelings." Stammering he tried to explain, "Kalo, you always seem to—to not like me, and Tere was always friendly, liked me. She didn't pick at me."

"Lent, I do not pick at you —and do not speak of Tere as though she were dead."

"Yes you do," he threw back swishing water with the palm of a hand, "you've given me the cold shoulder more times than I can count." Then softening, "And I am sorry; I didn't mean to imply Tere is dead."

"Cold shoulder?" she asked innocently. "I do not understand, 'cold shoulder'." *Perhaps he really did not know.*

Almost instantly wishing he hadn't said it, he threw the remark away along with his anger. "It's just an expression they use in the comic books."

"Marvel Group Britannica," she noted offhand.

"You remember that?" he asked surprised, but not as surprised as he was by the smile he couldn't hold back. He was cooling off.

"Of course I remember. I remember many things; more than you know." She stepped in a submerged hole and stumbled again.

"Please let me help you," and the hand came again.

This time she was not so sharp with her words or so quick to refuse, only hesitated, then reluctantly accepted. As they continued he eventually let go of her hand and pulled her closer slipping his arm around her waist above the bandage. But that proved to be an unanticipated miscalculation when his hand filled with breast. Awkward. But nowhere to go so he gave it a gentle squeeze, and it felt kind of good.

When he did *that*, Kalo wasn't sure why, but it made her tingle and she thought she should slap him. This was all new to them... because they were innocent. "If you insist on helping me do not squeeze me like that," she gently scolded.

"Okay; but if I don't squeeze anymore... can I keep my hand there?"

"Yes, I suppose that would be all right." Then curious, "Why do you want to keep your hand there?"

"Well," he feigned, "it makes a really good handle."

"Handle?" He nodded bashfully, and grinned. "No, breasts do not make good handles" she decided alluding to Reed's lecture, "Milkbone dog biscuits make good handles." Anatomy class: lesson four, sex—ed 101.

* * *

Hours later...

...No way to be sure how long anymore, in all directions mire and fog: filthy water, green-black slimy grass, insipid floating duckweed petals, and scum. The slurry of dead vegetation eased aside as they eased forward, but always slipped back after they passed. Both were tired and the unending mire laced ennui like a thread that stole from their cold aching legs and wound up their spines to their shoulders, then settled with bland tedium in their heads. Everything was dead or dying and they didn't know where they were, or where they were going... but they pressed on.

His arm around her, wandering interminably with burrowing pain and infection setting in, she stumbled again; but he kept her from falling. Worried, he asked, "Are you all right?"

"Can we stop and rest, just for a moment?" she murmured finally giving in.

Looking around, "There's nowhere to sit down, but then, I can't see very far in this fog. Let's find one of those little islands."

They began moving again, but with two more steps she faltered, crumpling, and he caught her. An arm around her back, the other beneath her buttocks, he picked her up gently shifting her small weight, cradling her to his chest. Concerned, he looked at her; then carrying her, continued. They had to keep going... so he waded on.

He was hungry and tired; but she was far beyond that. A hundred pounds of limp Renoloi kitten curled within the security of his strength and embrace, her mysterious and surreptitious life was now literally in his hands. Alone in this miserable place she would most surely die, so exhausted but determined —blurp, squisssh, blurp— Lent trudged on through the unending quagmire. And as he did, like a zephyr of spirit from the fog, words whispered in his head, *"Take a step... take another..."* so he pressed on.

Hour after hour in a netherworld swamp: the stale of the pause, like taking in an exhaled breath, leeches and misery, and water and weeds. Dimly illuminating this place of twilight-gloom long blue-black shadows fashioned within an eerie flaming corona were their constant companions... he had to keep moving.

As she slept cradled in his arms it was very quiet here except for the, *blurp, squisssh, blurp,* so one step at a time... he kept going. He slogged on in a day without end, a place without days, not sure where they were going, or if they would make it. Worn out, he would keep going. He wouldn't give up. He would do that for her because Ames and Reed were his friends... and she was his friend.

Kalo was febrile with infection transmitted by the unseen virulence percolating around them, and her bandage was bleeding through again, more noticeably now... and she was so small. How much blood could she lose and still survive, if either of them would survive, lost in a cursed morass in the memories of nowhere, a place that wasn't but was... in a realm of could-be.

As he carried her Lent gazed down upon her—*how frail,* his plaintive thought—*but more than she seems.* Exhausted and worried he looked around for the ump-teenth time as he plodded on. She felt warm in his arms, warm to the touch—*too warm.* The fever did that. Her eyes were very still behind the closed lids—*asleep, but not resting.* The fever did that.

"Kalo," he whispered, "can you hear me?" She did not answer... so quietly he pressed on.

Dead tired, sloshing languidly through a woebegone swamp with the girl in his arms, *"Take a step... take another,"* the voice purred in the back of his mind. He thought he heard it, but wasn't quite sure; could have imagined it, but wasn't quite sure. It seemed real; but then again, he wasn't quite sure. Or something else, something more? He wasn't quite sure. Walking heavily, weary, fatigued, Lent mumbled, "We're not going to die in this miserable place."

They were lost in a place that wasn't, but was... in a realm of could-be. *Blurp, squisssh, blurp...* resolute, determined, he kept going.

Beneath her closed eyelids there was intuitive, sporadic involuntary movement... and fatidically Kalo disclosed so softly he almost did not hear, *"No, we will not die here."*

Thinking she had awaken he looked down; but she was still sleeping, lost in her dreams. *Was she talking in her sleep?* Perhaps the fever did that. He was almost certain that he heard her, but it must only be the fever, and before long doubt was creeping back. Then from somewhere else, very softly, as though mentoring from above and behind, the other voice whispered, *"Take a step... take another..."* so he kept moving.

It was a miserable place of dreary dirt-colored fog and cold gray mist permeating a landscape of gloom, and he was exhausted. Gazing solemnly upon her he thought, *that creature —whatever it was— you saved my life*, knowing he must keep going or they would surely both die. Then somehow, from somewhere he did hear it.

Her voice: *"We could not let you die."*

They were her words; but her lips did not move. Even as close as they were, he did not see her speak. This time, watching more closely, he whispered, "Better that I die, than you."

Her voice: *"The moon is not full."*

In the dim light she again seemed to convey her thoughts without speaking. So even more softly this time he asked, "What does that mean?"

"It is forbidden."

He was sure he heard her that time even though her lips didn't move, as somewhere in the back of his mind the other voice serenely counseled, *"Take a step... take another."* Watching her, wondering... quietly he pressed on.

Alone and beyond tired he knew he had to keep going in a place he could not fathom, with a mysterious young girl he could not comprehend cradled in his arms. At length her eyes moved again, erratically beneath her closed lids. *She's sleeping, just dreaming*, at least that much made sense. Looking around as he went, carrying a precious young Renoloi warrior, he trudged on through the rank water and mire. Slowly, bone-tired, *blurp, squisssh, blurp...* Lent pressed on.

Then, no more than a mellifluent undertone, only a breath of sound at first, Kalo began to hum; a single note, then another. As Lent held her she soothingly hummed until finally, very softly, in her sleep she was faintly singing an exquisite, sweet song. In her sleep, with her dreams, an unworldly, wonderful song.

Darting to and fro beneath closed lids her eyes were moving, so Lent craned his head cradling her more closely, their faces now only inches apart. He strained to hear over his sloshing footsteps and mud-bubbles, until finally he could hear her, the music, her song... and he thought, *her song is so beautiful.*

Trudging through an unnamed swamp in an unfathomable place Lent gazed upon her as she peacefully sang and slept in his arms; and ever so softly he whispered, "Kalo, you are so beautiful."

As the words stole from his lips, the silent Kalo, precious as an angel, murmured, "You are exhausted; why are you carrying me?" Still sleeping, she sighed and her lips moved with a delicate wet tongue. "Leave me here and I will catch up later."

"No," he confided, "never."

"But I am slowing you down," barely a whisper.

A tear dampening the corner of his eye, Lent gently revealed, "Haven't you figured it out; don't you know that I love you?" a trail of desperation and reality gliding down his cheek, as the voice in his mind encouraged, *"Take a step... take another."*

Their lives intricately entwined, faces only inches apart, for the first time in his young life Lent told another, "I love you; I always will." Then straightening his shoulders, he looked out through the gloom to unending mire of swampland and, *blurp, squisssh, blurp...* he pressed on.

Undisclosed mysteries, the silent Kalo always listened. And as he carried her in his arms, very softly, in her sleep, the silent Kalo cried. Because there was...

...Something yet Unfinished.

* * *

It was a dismal place...

...Dark and rank, the stench of raw sewage and decay pervasive in the smog. Pushing duckweed and slime aside his footfalls stirred black soup from the mire that turned over as it floated in mahogany waves, then slipped into the melange as undulating gray. The air was bitter, gray-brown fog burning his throat, tasting as sour as the greasy sensation oozing inside his khakis.

Step after step he kept moving into the dusky swamp and unknown. It was very quiet except for the, *blurp, squisssh, blurp,* suction of bubbles choked from mud beneath a stirred landscape of filthy quagmire and floating dead slimy weeds. This was a dying place... very quiet.

Worn out, wading from the swamp onto a mud island Lent finally had to stop and rest; staggering, bone-tired. Kalo's eyes opened, the listless gaze of fever subsided, the flicker of healing having taken its place as she looked up at him.

Curious, "Why are you carrying me?" she inquired oddly.

Puzzled, he asked, "You don't remember?"

"Remember..." eyebrows gathering slightly as she considered, "no, remember what?"

Dismissively shaking his head and the explanation aside he asked, "Do you feel better now?" noticing her fever had subsided and her skin temperature felt normal.

"Yes, I feel fine but you look exhausted," coaxing and wiggling a bit, "put me down. You need to rest."

All in, he conceded, "I just need to sit down," as he plopped onto his butt with her still in his arms, his buttocks making a well-defined impression in the mud squeezing a blue-black crater around him. "You really don't remember—anything?"

She shook her head.

"But you were..." he began to say as her fingertip suddenly pressed to his lips quieting him and her eyes snapped to the fog around them.

"Hush," she whispered.

Looking around, from behind her finger he quietly asked, "What?"

Still in his lap, "Put me down," she ordered gently, now alert and aware.

Allowing her to slip to the ground onto her knees, under his breath he asked, "What is it?"

With uncanny perception that sensed beyond the periphery and reached out through the depths of the gloom, "They are searching," she told him.

"Searching—who?"

From the heavy veil of fog there came skittering and sloshing sounds, very faint, ragged brittle legs shredding water. Her small hand slowly reaching to the quiver, "Lent…" she revealed, "they are all around us."

CHAPTER SEVENTEEN

His eyes opened…

…To stale mist and dingy dun-gray, as his nostrils filled with the taste of mildew and waterlogged mud woven with soaked, slime-flattened, black narrow grass. Coughing the musty earthen odor from his head, and a twist and, *crack,* that freed the kink in his neck, Reed got up from the ground and looked around. Gloom formed a layered shroud of wafting misery and dampness laced with hobgoblin-dancers wearing long blue-black shadows. The depressing scene elicited his skewered axiom—*same miserable shit, same sorry-frickin' day.*

"Reed, you awake?"

Glancing over a shoulder, "Unfortunately," then back, he heard Ames, *squeegee,* when he rolled onto his side turning to face him.

"Water, water everywhere, and not a drop to drink," Ames recited as he sat up.

Flatly, "What'd you have to go and say something like that for? Now I'm thirsty."

On his butt, planting both heels in the mud, "Yeah, me too. Was kind of dumb, wasn't it?" realizing too late that he also was thirsty and they hadn't eaten or had anything to drink for, hard to say how long now —but at any rate, too long. And the prospect of finding food or potable water anytime soon was nil to none. Together they sat on the mud rise encompassed by despondent gray mire and decomposing squalor, forearms braced on their knees, shoulders hunched, caked with mud, tired. And still lost.

Reed looked at him. "So, what do you want to do, wander around until we tip over from dehydration and exhaustion, or figure this mess out?"

Droll: "Up to you—what do you want to do?"

A side glance: "You make me crazy sometimes you know it; you really do."

The other nodded unaffectedly and with measured words went on, "Well, probably is a stroke of luck that everything's too wet to burn."

"Really; why's that?" Reed squirmed. "I don't know 'bout you, but soggy shorts stuck up the crack of my ass ain't exactly my idea of a stroke of luck."

"Not that." The punch line prepped, Ames grinned. "If we had a campfire… cannibalism *could* be an option —but shit, I hate raw meat," and the devious look, "knowwhatImean." He let his eyes trail to Reed's thigh.

At first Reed didn't say anything, then, "Oh that's just messed-up, you know it. You really are one sick puppy. For cryin' in the soup Doc, how can you even…" then quickly pivoting sideways on his buttocks gathering both knees and legs to his chest, "and don't even be lookin' at my thighs all hungry like that."

Ames smiled.

"—Or my ass either."

More smile.

"That's not funny, not a bit —and besides— I think there's something about weird shit like that in the Bible someplace, in those 'Commandments' or something."

"No there isn't… not unless, 'Thou shalt not eat thy neighbor' is the eleventh commandment; and if that were the case, they'd have to change the name—and the movie."

"Yeah," Reed threw back, "well if you want to eat something — aw shit, nevermind and just shut up about it okay." Frustrated, "Shoot we're 'bout screwed here and—and sometimes you just make me mad you know it; you really do. Where do you even come up with warped ideas like that, some pinko-commie tome or Nazi-skinhead opus from an obscure little bookseller's alcove in Istanbul —or some bizarre radical progressive website?"

"Mostly from my friend." Crooked smile.

"Bullshit, not from me you don't. I'm nothing at all like that, not even close."

Smile fading, Ames didn't respond.

"What?" Reed queried. "Now what?"

"Thinking; just thinking."

"About what?"

"The shadow-phantom," Ames said. "How do we kill it, the shadow-phantom, Grim Reaper, whatever?"

Leaning in a bit: "About time you started talking sense."

Blasé: "I 'spose."

"At least now you're talking about normal stuff anyway; that's somewhat encouraging." Interested Reed asked, "Any ideas—what do you think?"

"I think I'm still thirsty."

"Dammit, will you knock that off and be serious. Pretty soon we'll be like those two old prospectors lost in the desert at a poison-soured waterhole with Floyd the rattlesnake."

"And that wouldn't be good," Ames allowed bumping his eyebrows, "would it?"

"Forget Floyd and the waterhole, and start acting normal; let's get back to the Grim Reaper. And if you look at my ass one more time, Doc, I'm warning you, knock that shit off."

Without prelude, "How do you kill a shadow," Ames pondered. "Exactly how would one go about doing something like that?"

Stretching his legs, "With light," Reed proposed.

"Too easy."

"Too easy; what's easy got to do with anything?"

"Light wouldn't kill it —absorb it, move it perhaps, disguise it— but as soon as the light's gone the shadow would return."

"Well you can't even have a shadow without light."

"That's true," Ames conceded.

"Dark then."

"Dark?" the other echoed. "That would give it more room to hide, make it more proficient."

"Okay, point taken," Reed said waving him off. "Light, dark, gray—shake a ringtail cat till it's indifferent—I don't know."

"'When it is what it cannot be'," Ames said repeating Wilson's words.

Looking back at his friend Reed reminded, "We've been over all that: a shape, consciousness, intellect —shoot, we don't even know what that means."

"Also true; but it's gotta mean something, and it must be important."

"Yeah, I know; or else he wouldn't'a said it." Bothered, scratching his cheek then picking mud from his chin, "Sometimes I'd like to wring those little midgets' necks you know it."

"Little people, dwarfs," Ames corrected disjointedly, "not midgets."

"Yeah sure—whatever. And where do you suppose those two little people dwarfs are right about now?"

"Up to their eyebrows in swamp?" Ames mused, not really a question.

"That's clever," Reed groused positioning his legs and planting his chin on his knees; thinking, bugged. "When it is what it cannot be, not when it is what it is not. It can only be destroyed when it is more than it is, not when it is not what it is." He thought about it. "Frickin' shadow isn't anything, it's a shadow: no color, no texture, no substantive form, a volatile shape, no tangible presence even. A shadow's a nonpresence, nothing more than an amorphous dark image. Give it something." He was closer than he realized. Considering one last time, "How *do* you kill a shadow?" but disgusted, he gave up. "Fuckit—nuke it."

Wrong answer.

While Ames sat calmly next to him, quiet finally elbowed exasperation into the background and Reed thought some more. But irritated, his subconscious slipped back for an encore and jabbed, *consider it; think about it, Reed.* You know, how we all sort of think like that. *I am considering it. I am thinking about it —and it's pissing me off.*

"Don't get mad; that won't do any good. Just think about it." But that time Reed wasn't so sure the voice in his head was his own. Then the thought occurred, *Wilson, P.T... where are you?*

And in the back of his mind —somewhere— he thought he heard, *"Oh, not too far away."* But he wasn't sure.

"How's the foot?" Ames asked snatching him back.

"The what?"

Sitting close enough to touch him, "Your ankle," Ames said, then asked, "you daydreaming?"

"No," shaking fog from his head.

"What were you thinking about?"

"Nothing."

"Nothing? Reed, I asked how is your foot, three times."

Blinking dismissal, "Fine. It's fine."

"You're sure?"

"Well of course I'm sure. It's okay, just sprained again that's all," and saying it he mused, "funny thing though, it's the same foot the T-Rex fell on. Seems like things keep happening over and over again."

"And you're okay," Ames asked one more time.

"Yeah, I'm good; just give me a minute, gotta take a leak." Reed got up, hopped once and hobbled a short distance stepping behind a small leafless tree, its branches mostly drifting to the left.

"Mister Modesty," Ames chided.

With his back to his friend, Reed admitted, "Yeah well, you know, it's a guy thing," inadvertently brushing against the small tree; and when he did, slowly the withered branches began to turn...

"Yeah, I know," Ames agreed getting up, as Reed finished zipping up, then hobbled back. "Ready?" taking his arm, lending support.

Straightening, Reed took a step catching up; then was all set, "Yep, ready. Right behind you, Doc."

Together they took a step, and saw it at the same time...

...The small withered tree near the end of this 'sort of' island, its frail branches twisted and still as the misery and abject depression surrounding them.

"Same tree," Reed observed under his breath.

"Can't be." But Ames knew it too. "Billions of years... it's impossible."

"Won't argue with that," Reed conceded soberly looking at his friend, "but nevertheless, *it is the same tree*."

"Well if it is, the branches are bent the wrong direction," Ames said, "they drift to the right; before they were bent to the left."

"So?"

"They're backward."

Pushing aside the inference they began to head out; but the little withered tree was still visible from the corner of his eye and Reed's voice was still an echo in his head: *right behind you, Doc*. And from somewhere, *a memory*, as Reed's words still lingered, and eventually sank in...

...And Ames stopped.

The eclipsed sun, low on the horizon in front of them, casting long blue-black shadows over a world that was, drew, almost beckoned then held his attention. A miserable place, it was a shrouded world of dismal swamp and duckweed bogs with tangled green-black ribbons of slimy dead grass. This was an abandoned, soulless place, still as the breath of pause, lost somewhere in time. A forgotten, forsaken mire.

Murmuring at first, he began reciting, repeating bits and pieces of what he recalled, could remember from a dream. Next, to his friend standing beside him, his eyes searching as though looking for them, "The Riddle—Reed, do you remember the lines of the riddle?"

Puzzled, "Yeah, well sort of; I think we can get it if we work on it. Why?"

"What were they—what were the lines?"

"Let me think. 'When two warriors stand with a cloistered sun. In a war without end... never lost, never won. When the flock returns...'

—no wait, that's backward." He sighed, "Damnit, this whole place is backward."

"That's it," Ames breathed finally realizing, finally understanding. "It's not where we're going that matters; that's not important. It's where we've been. Opposing one another; they were backward, Reed."

"What?"

"The constellations… they were *all backward!*" Ames looked at him. "We've been going about this all wrong, doing it backward." Then helping his friend, together they turned…

CHAPTER EIGHTEEN

Then helping his friend, together they turned...

...And facing backward, the eclipsed sun, now on the horizon behind them diminished and went out, then strangely reappeared on the horizon before them.

"Well crud in a bucket, no—way," Reed whispered, "that's just—too—weird." And as he spoke, the fog began to stir.

Around them a slight breeze enticed wisps of mist to spiral and swirl like vapid gray wings inhaled by invisible drafts, delicately beginning to draw them away. Barely drifting at first the fog eased as a blend of insipid vapor, a slow-moving receding cascade.

Mystified, both stood on the mud rise watching; this place that exuded the torpor of death and taste of decay for so long was now seemingly touched by a phenomenon they couldn't fathom. Quicker now, more than a whisper but less than a wind, almost like tainted breath the fog flowed in a mixture of wraith-like shadows and fluxionary waves. Musty zephyrs of smog rolled with spinneret fingers that reached out in short bursts, then paused and hovered, then whisked on again moving into the dark then somewhere beyond within the melancholy blue-black shadows dimly illuminated by an eclipsed sun's corona, now on the opposite horizon.

Around them something was happening... something strange.

More constant now, a breeze began to rustle causing the water to stir then riffle as the surface's oily petroleum sheen created eddy designs with the scattering flutter; moving slowly at first passing from left to right, easing away like despondent spirits in the night.

As they continued watching, even before they felt it, they heard it, only a murmur at first, whispering. Then more than that, gentle but constant... the wind. And little by little the wind increased to a breeze; and the fog and mist and the water flowed.

It dredged recollections of an unexplained green sea some time ago, harboring secrets in her depths that conveyed the mood of a night in potter's field where cloistered spirits of the departed roamed. Then the blast of a foghorn that should not have been and the voyage of a ghost ship that crawled up from a shadowy netherworld realm, a deep and dark emerald keep.

Still lifting and thinning the fog was passing before them, moving outward as it enclosed them within a curtain-like veil. Winding as it silently opened and surrounded them, in the distance the phenomenon was fashioning an encompassing cloud wall, a circular arena of evolving boundary and mystery. Rising and swirling delicate mist maiden sprites slowly ascended forming a stratus ceiling, while still pushing back the emaciating fog began to reveal a fetid gray bayou, an endless rancid quagmire strewn with protruding small mud hummock islands.

Scanning the dissipating gloom Reed saw them first, on a mud rise some distance away. "Can't be," he muttered.

Then Ames picked them out. "It is."

"But how?"

Ames considered, "A time lock, nothing changes."

Two hundred yards and two islands away they spied the obscured silhouettes of Kalo and Lent crouched on one of the squat landforms. Both seemed to be searching for something farther away that the men were unable to see. Lent was on his haunches, ax poised, and she, bow ready, beside him on one knee.

Within the fog—

Off to their right, sudden splashes and ratcheting clacks of running brittle-stick legs scattering water and mud-bubble froth. Stop. Watersplash stilled with the settling of bubbles. Quiet.

Both men instantly dropped flat at the water's edge—eyes focused, watching, waiting. Still in the distance but closer this time, they heard it again, the same noise, and they knew what it was. Watching, and waiting.

Through the dissipating mist came more metallic-clatter sounds of chitin stirring water and muck —then flashes of glistening mud-slick obsidian— materializing to their right the pack came into view. They stopped. Quiet.

A whisper: "Hunters."

Under his breath, "Dozen or more," Reed counted slipping the sling over his head then guardedly stirring the laser muzzle in the water, swishing away detritus that clung to the barrel. Inspecting the weapon, then again to the bog, "So that's what they're looking for."

Another scuttle, closer. Liquid-clatter of watersplash snapped their eyes to the left. The noise evaporated; water stilled. Quiet. His focus shifting from the sound to their lost companions, Ames sized up the swamp. Eyes moving from one focal point to the next, Reed silently watched.

"Pulse laser clean?"

Voice hushed, observing their movements: "Yeah."

Scattered randomly over the bog, as far as possible to see, more gangs of the adroit killers became visible in the lifting fog. Running ten or twenty strong to the pack, zigzagging, half a dozen or more bands were already passably visible in the thinning mist. Moving like raven water beetles with nasty black fangs they darted away then reappeared; back and forth, they were searching but had not located the prey.

Ames, eyes pouring over the swamp: "Soon as we move they'll home in on us, but that should give Kalo and Lent enough time."

Already suspecting Reed surmised, "The little island between us?"

Almost a breath, "Slim to none, but it's all we've got. How's the ankle?"

"I'll make it." Then shifting on his elbows, "You know, Doc, I'm getting *sooo* tired of them; they just won't quit."

In a fluttering wind, "Fuel cells?"

Quick check and, "Got enough juice," swamp water riffling around them. "Now," Reed said, "they're really getting on my nerves," almost a grumble, "and just pissing me off."

Like a pause that had passed with a storm on the way, brow furrowed, eyes narrowing, "Ready?" Ames asked, conviction seething with the word in the rising wind.

"Ready," Reed said, his voice growing louder, "and anymore..." both standing up together, "I just *hate—fuckin'—spiders!*"

—And stuttering white blasts the pulse laser *flared!*

Like a video arcade, ripped to shreds in a fury of searing flame and lightning-blast tears —shrill whines, bright flashes— the shadowy swampworld lit up with blinding jetstreams of explosive white light!

Shattering pieces—

Three gigantic spiders exploded almost simultaneously in gray washwater winds as Reed strafed and he and Ames plunged headlong into the mire.

Earsplitting noise—

Streaking flame and pulse detonations hurled muck spray and pieces with mud-thickened waterspouts as his weapon tore gashes in the arachnids and swamp. For all they were worth both men plowed through the bog, feet sucking mud, soured boil at their heels —white fire in the smog!

Kalo and Lent heard the shrill thunder and explosive reports; spied the laserflashes of bright streaking light —saw them— and instantly moved. Heaving into the swamp, they ran. Dark water and mudsplash foamed as all four scrambled through the mire bound for the mud island midway between them. High ground, the bastion, it was their only chance to take on the macabre arachnids. Two hundred yards teaming with death —they had to make it— a sprint for distance against time.

Out there—

Bands of Hunters suddenly materializing, the swamp came alive —went wild— scrambling killers appearing everywhere, crushing pedipalps bristling, chelicerae salivating, twenty-inch fangs weeping venom and death.

—Bright screaming light slicing fog!

When a finger of fog moved a jet-black cutthroat was there, clickity-splashes of running legs thrashing duckweed and slime into muck —noise— they could hear them. Demonically glowing white eyes homing-in —movement— the arachnids saw them —had them— and attacked from all sides heckling excited white noise of savagery and their cacophonous insanity of chattering animalistic screams!

With all they had the four ran the swamp, fighting water and mud, intent on the island, the sleek raven killers skimming the mire on long ragged legs armed with bale-hook claws that shred slimy dead grass into ribbons and strings. Through the dark and gray and clatter of water —closer now— the Hunters were coming.

Bow in one hand, his hand in her other, Kalo urged, "Run!"

With the closest pack still some distance away and the remnant fog distorting their pixel vision, Lent and Kalo resolutely fought the mire. Not illuminated and less conspicuous than the men it took the enormous arachnids longer to zero in and find them; but they did, the pair's watersplash triggering the predatory instinct. Ferreted out, they had been detected —and the Hunters were after them.

Taller than she, the rawboned Pilgrim lunged powerfully through the rancid water, half-dragging her, both jolting waterwash and shriveled duckweed that swirled as they fled —*can't quit*. Heaving waves that splattered mud in their faces, and hindered by the water, they kept bogging down and stumbling while the arachnids skimmed on lanky legs stabbing holes in the bottom —*they're coming too fast*.

Seventy-five yards to the mud rise.

From the other direction the men pushed persistently through the knee-deep swamp, Ames twirling the scimitar overhead baiting the predators, Reed limping beside him, killing them when they came. Turning and triggering Reed strafed with rattlesnake strikes of searing night-fire tracer rounds peppering them with lightning-pulse fangs compressed in blasts of white blazing light.

—White noise of savagery, watersplash mud, and trilling, chattering animalistic screams!

Clustered night-vision eyes were closing from behind; Reed spun —staggering blasts— spraying fury and fire through the mob. Blown off their legs, monsters detonated and fell —pulse impact, then splash— dumped into the swamp. Sledgehammer flames slammed one then another catapulting them over and back, most staying down, but a few getting back up. Blown dead hulls rolled languidly in the mire, but some were still moving, dragging entrails and chunks of their slime-covered shells. Wounded and ragged, still they kept coming.

—More linear fire, shrill brilliant blasts!

Shattered spinning chitin shards twirled with dark spray then splashed in the swamp. Five fell —shrill whines, more impacts— seven down. Streaked with furious fire torn waterspouts and globs of muddy blood-rain continued to plash, all of it splattering as putrid rank slop. Dazzling, blinding —all ten— as he spun to take on the next.

Razorlight blazed through Hunters then vanished with the tension and focus of a life-and-death race, a fusillade of laserflame spearing holes in the smog and hellhounds in microsecond bursts. Knifing through them streaks of light sliced with a shattering pickax-pulse punch —in a rush of dark water and rising fog they came— and with the slam of laser-supersonic blasts they went.

Fifty yards to the mud rise.

"Half way, we can do it," Lent encouraged dragging her by the hand, not looking back until Kalo jerked free, and before he could turn an arrow was gone —and struck— but they didn't wait. She reeled —they ran— both moving again. Soaked with duckweed speckle and stringy wet grass that stuck to her chest, she blew a breath shaking dripping hair from her face as she readied another arrow. Again she turned, sending the fletched missile into the rushing shadows —just an instant of silence— then from out there the distant definitive, *thwack.*

Sloshing spoiled water Lent stopped and spun. "What are you doing? We've gotta keep going."

"You go ahead; I will catch up," reaching for her quiver.

Grabbing her wrist, "—Not hardly," jerking her from her feet, taking off through the swamp.

"Lent, let go…" tripping and down, water pouring over her like a fish on a hook as he dragged her along behind him. "Lent…" the rest of her words lost in green-black bubbles and weeds.

Slogging through the mire, he was angry. This wasn't the time for heroics and he realized that 'amazingly' he made just as good progress as he had before. She swam —or floated— extremely well.

Thirty yards to the mud island.

Ames was first, Reed two steps behind—up out of the swamp onto the mud rise. High ground. Ames ducked as Reed pivoted and strafed.

—Shrill whines, stuttering bright light—the pulse laser flared!

Seeing Lent coming with Kalo in tow, "What—the—?" Reed puzzled almost comically, pulse-flash reflections flickering on his face as he targeted—squeezed, three more spinning in smithereens-scraps that twirled like muddy helicopter smidgens and flittering bits of debris.

Ames: "She probably got stubborn." Reed spun again swinging over his head, and as he cleared Ames stood back up. "Cover them."

Two still in the swamp and twenty yards to the island with the psychopaths closing on them, Reed hastily knelt and aimed taking arachnids out while Ames covered his back. All around them water flowed, the wind was rising… and the Hunters kept coming.

Rawboned and moving Lent bulldogged along. "Stop," Kalo bubbled, so he finally let her up —and both took off running.

The cloud wall—

In the distance, beneath undulating blue-black shadows waves of fog moved resembling streams of mist streaked with opaque seams of gray. The atmosphere throbbed like an arterial pulse then ebbed and flowed with dark veins, little by little gathering potency and momentum. While overhead the canopy revolved as it churned constricting, condensing and thickening, growing darker. Organizing like weather on the horizon or a storm in the wind that was coming their way... it was forming.

The swamp—

Reed covered them with strafing jetstreams of light that spit inches over their heads and on either side as they fought the bog pushing for the rise. No time to look back —recurring explosions behind them— arachnids running the pack hurling water and slop were going down as logjams of mud.

From their left, a hundred feet —coming fast— eight Hunters skimmed thrashing waterwinds of shadowy momentum —vanishing razors of light— two detonating, disappearing in the twilight as twirling shrapnel and spray. The rest of the clan veered and collided, one folding as it stumbled, the next sliding as they collided and a third skidding before it leaped from the second-one's back. A blackguard high jump at phenomenal speed —and somewhere within the mixture of legs, stagnant water and rush— a wind-whistle of arrowhead and shaft punched through its eyes with that definitive, *crack*.

Falling, it caved in a spoiled wash and tangled slivers of black grass, rolling and skidding in the snarled vegetation; then it slid to a stop. A fork stuck in dead spaghetti its night-vision eyes dimmed as the head sank and the Hunter regurgitated a glob of mud purging a feeble squirt of venom. Lights out.

Everything a blur of water and speed—

Lent still in the lead, Kalo a few steps back —*almost there*— barely seconds from the island with four of the clan right behind them —*too close*. The nearest Hunter was closing too fast —low-runner— its ragged legs thrashing water and weeds, fangs and bear paw pedipalps opening to grab them. He sensed it —imminent danger— turning, bringing the twibil up...

...The monstrous spider was upon them, bristling pedipalps grabbing for her, chelicerae and fangs closing salivating discharge of venom. In that split-instant Kalo spun and leaped executing a backflip in midair, raven fangs ratcheting and snapping twelve feet beneath her ejecting 'old yellow' that missed. Above it, somersaulting backward and over, eyes locked on —and a half-body turn drawing the bow. Down there, Lent was diving out of the way.

Reflex of the cat —following the target,

A pirouetting ballerina —dropping from the gray,

Wet hair sweeping free as she aimed —focused, in motion.

Confused that it missed —its prey had vanished— and the Hunter just stood there —then something from above— as she lit on its back. Point blank she let fly, her arrow chiseling through its head —instantly dead— collapsing as another one lunged.

Near the water's edge at the island rise, Lent was still down and scrambling when he saw it land —fangs little more than an arm's length away— so close he could smell its oily underside and easily reach its legs; and those mindless pixel white eyes were right in his face. In one lethal motion he dove and rolled, then to his knees — twibil coming up— pedipalps reaching, death three feet from his neck —the razor edge flashing up, knifing into it— *crr-whack!*

The arachnid's head ripped apart flinging the fangs and pedipalps like gorilla-paw arms as the spider bounced from the morass and went over backward soaking him with watersplash and gray bloody muck. Speed-stunned he blinked and looked at it again—*that happened so fast.*

In a breath another was above him —the laser's sudden-flash— its front segment blowing up splashing its cephalothorax out its ass. The impact slammed through the arachnid so forcefully that its legs shot straight out just an instant before the mammoth carcass shattered as sticky ectoplasm and twirling chunks flinging crooked detached legs. Following through Lent glimpsed Reed standing on the mud rise behind him, weapon in hand, eyes still on the exploding spider; and in a flicker of awareness he realized Reed was watching more than just that —other movement— his attention also swinging back to the swamp.

A Hunter was after her —Kalo leaped— a backspring, up and over it twirling in midair. Stunned, they both watched as she somersaulted then spun, and in that glimmer of consciousness she looked at Reed —direct eye contact— and somewhere in his head he heard, *knife*. In less time than the thought, his hand went to his belt for the weapon, grabbed it and had thrown it —to her, at her— he wasn't quite sure as she whirled through the air and too swiftly to actually see somehow had caught it.

The Hunter was still scuttling when she came down as though having vaulted from the canopy, bow in one hand, knife in the other. Landing on the arachnid's back she expertly sliced severing the connective pedicel —coming apart— its posterior abdomen dropping back, front falling forward. Still perched on top of it as the spider fell Kalo stepped lightly between the ghoul's fading eyes, and then bounced and somersaulted landing delicately on the bank of the mud rise beside Lent. Without a word she nimbly wiped the blade in the grass and tucked the knife in the waistband of her black leather skirt. Having watched her both thought, *that just isn't possible.*

Unexpected—

The Hunters broke off and scattered, their watersplash quickly diminishing as they withdrew and vanished in the thinning fog; and it became strangely quiet again. A pause or… something more.

Around them—

Swamp water and debris flowed with a wind that breathed petulantly in their faces; and becoming more clearly defined as it rolled and congealed in the distance like goblins of murk, the encompassing cloud wall's color and texture was deepening to an ominous dun tethered to the blue-black shadows. Intermingling with the lifting fog shadowy rivers of mist drifted over the bland texture of mireland dredging ghost-like mirages that crept above and across the riffling bog. All of it seemed to be captured and stirred by an unseen phenomenon or unusual forces, a mysterious blend of ambiguous things.

Ropes of slimy dead grass crawled and rose from below, then languidly floated like slithering ribbons fondling and testing the surface before they submerged again in the lackluster gloom of mud-stirred abyss. Buoyantly riding purling riffles duckweed clumps shed fronds that resembled small creatures abandoning ship and struggling to swim; but drifting like flotsam each was mutely and inexorably drawn away with the current. Everything, all of it was moving.

The wind pushed steadily, but the fog swam eerily in opposition coursing against the flow, darting and swirling in vapid slate gusts like an entity with a mind of its own. Spiraling mist maidens rose in twisted funnels shaping blue-gray helixes tinged with the brown-violet hue of coagulated blood. Then as though anticipating something they'd suddenly swirl as vanishing vortexes absorbed in the canopy somewhere. The storm was gathering... preparing.

Out there—

Constantly moving, the fog was pushing back and the mire continued to open before them, while rife with percolating swirling eddies the water level began dropping. Somehow the swamp was draining away. Above, congealing clouds wound as confusion and gray with an eclipsed sun and a blood-red moon radiating an unearthly violet corona of eerie flaming light. Shrouded in despondence and silence, more surreal than supernatural, with foreboding quiet and the power of fire the specter glowed; a strange imposing alliance casting long blue-black shadows on a place that was lost, abandoned... and vacillating in time. The eclipsed sun and blood-red moon remained.

Watching they stood together on a sodden rise facing impossible odds in this unexplainable place where something was happening, and something was coming...

...Something yet Unfinished.

Crouching as she studied the twilight-darkness encompassing them, "They are all around us," Kalo intimated. Then rising to her feet, in a soft voice she warned, "They are coming now."

First only glimmers of distant motion, then closing until they could see their sudden attack flinging waterspray and weeds as the swampland filled with heckling chatter of wild animalistic screams!

From all directions, at breakneck speed the sleek dark killers materialized from the thinning fog, rushing en masse with blitzkrieg gyrating momentum, chelicerae and fangs snapping the grating ratchet of death. Clamoring and scrambling they flailed mud bits to slop chopping ribbons of grass like chaff spewn from a thrasher with sheetwater spray. Clustered night-vision eyes seemed to appear from every flowing purl of fog as the Hunters emerged from the vapid dusk sprinting in for the kill.

—Shrill whines—and the blasts!

Reed peppered them with lethal bursts, a fusillade of ripping destruction, Hunters going down —or apart— in violent explosions of ragged twirling pieces. Rushing eyes, sinister fangs, raven hulls and barbed legs thrashing water and mud —pack hunters, chitin banging against chitin— detonating like firecrackers on a string, blown splinters that spun as stuttering fire machine-gunned them down.

Holding them back, the twibil swung and arrows flew as the scimitar whirled —gory black faces dressed with white-glowing eyes being hacked open— four killing the demons with mudsplatter and gray. It was insanity's rush and smeared violence: legs and claws, scattered bloodspray, shrieking screams, creatures running and leaping, a congested blend of glistening chitin, bloodthirsty conflict and speed. Collapsed hulls littered the bog with downed Hunters heaving waves and muck, others trilling and plashing through ribbons of shadow and the flow of the fog, the swamp rattling with their debauchery as scores of the huge spiders fell.

—White noise of savagery and slobbering animalistic screams!

Ames and Lent fought side by side, his battle-ax crunching as the scimitar swept through them. Determined, sweating frenzied desperation they cut, stabbed and killed holding their ground on a mud rise surrounded by sour swamp belching rust-colored bubbles stained with gray leaking spills. But the more they put down, the more that attacked.

Triggering six-round bursts Reed's face flickered with the muzzle flashes —spider heads rupturing and catapulting scattering dull-pixel eyes, shattered fangs shooting knife-edge slivers— cutthroat monsters dropping dead in the swamp. White sorcerer's light ripped through them as he gritted his teeth, targeted, strafed and then spun. But ferociously and deranged they still came.

Turmoil was overwhelming, action intense, each of them focused: rushing legs and claws—striking blades—dark slashing fangs—mud-slick skin—leaping, flying and falling—a barbarous snarl of mud and blood—murderous conflict and speed. It was complete pandemonium of revolting obsidian and frenetic tension wound with wicked white noise savagery and trilling animalistic screams!

Intent on Kalo—

A Hunter hurdled the mounting dead; but as swiftly as it jumped she was gone —twenty feet, straight up— hooking the bow across her back, drawing Reed's knife from her waistband. Landing, its claws gouging slits in the mud —lost her— and still searching when lithely she lighted spiking the knife in its head. Sudden-sickness and the burning blisters of death crawling inside, it just tottered and tipped over dead. Then a handspring and reverse somersault, landing on another she deftly sliced through its pedicel —a cut squirting hose— still coming apart as she dove onto the next driving the knife through its eyes. Athletically she sprang and twirled with inimitable skill —backsprings, handsprings, vaulting and somersaulting—incredibly, unequaled she killed.

No more than an illusion in the dusky light, appearing here then there on one's back, she was a wraith of speed darting above and through the horde as Reed snatched a glance mumbling, "Unbelievable." *Three coming* —firing— *they're down*. With his back to Lent he yelled, "That kid's gonna get her little carcass killed if she keeps that up." *More there* —firing— *they're down*. Too busy in the melee, Lent didn't answer and couldn't look back. *More coming* —firing— *more down*. Acquiring and strafing Reed's eyes skipped target to target —tagging marks— glancing at Kalo and strafing again. *She moves like a ghost... she seems more spirit than real.*

Drenched in watersplash with muck squeezing between their toes, the battle was flashes of action and reaction: mudsplash, raking legs, scrambling bedlam, pedipalps reaching, fangs just missing, every instant an image of nerve-twisted stress. Back to back and shoulder to shoulder they fought —motion, focus, strike, *move!*— foul black pieces and twirling dead weeds sailing over the swamp. It was the insanity of combat driven by their will to survive.

From above and behind—

The shadow dove for Lent, an amorphous black cloak with lecherous liver-red eyes swooping down through the gray...

Kalo yelled, *"Lent, watch out!"*

...He couldn't see it and with a glimpse back neither did Reed, but from his side Ames caught the glimmer of steel half-concealed in the undefined shape descending like a gust of dark wind. Shouldering Lent aside he swung filling the air with the metallic collision of blades —then the sudden, *whoosh*, that felt wicked and cold— as bleak darkness swept around him and the black shade skimmed over them with the strident resonance of steel.

Stumbling, Lent sank an ax blade in the mud as another Hunter leaped: glowing pixel eyes, jaws agape, black fangs weeping venom. Lethal and taloned it was only an instant away as he grabbed the ax handle —both hands, eyes flashing— finding the spot...

—Killer coming,

...Heaving powerfully, ripping the blade from the mud —straight up— the pike and blade hacked through the mandibles and fangs splattering its head with a grizzly scatter-juice crunch as the twibil carved through its ugly white eyes —and shock-stunned— the arachnid almost blinking 'dissected' surprise. That suddenly and forcefully, with more momentum than most men could manage, Lent's blow heaved the monstrous spider from the ground ripping its cephalothorax-head completely apart. The pedicel and front half sailed over and behind him beyond Ames while the ragged matchstick legs all buckled in front of him and the ass-end collapsed.

A hornet in the wind—

Vanishing and reappearing within the horde Kalo dispatched the vermin as she avoided the laserflashes that cut them to shreds. Reed was an incessant stutter of fiery light and violent blasts. She was an apparition of motion, an inference with a knife —there, then gone— as she dove and somersaulted with the agility of an illusion and the speed of a gazelle.

The rise—

The instant Ames saw the curved blade he knew what it was —rifling the archives sorting and working Wilson's clue— *how do we stop it—kill it?* Sidetracked, *a Hunter* —slicing, admixture— black and blood, blade and mudspray, the macabre spider went down. *Stay focused*— nerves tightened to catgut, linking words in his mind, fending off incessant attacks.

The phantom had flown into the amalgam they called clouds; but it was still up there, somewhere, and from the corner of an eye he saw Kalo among the pack as they came from the front and sides. Lent and Reed were busy —*cover their backs.* Everything was happening so quickly, thinking too fast —*the phantom cannot be what it is not... destroy it when it is what it cannot be.*

The swamp—

Waterflow draining at their feet dragged strings of dead grass and duckweed clutter beneath curls of fog and soapwater eddies still pushing toward the boundary's encompassing shroud. Now appearing in the percolating canopy crooked snakes of heat lightning silently shimmered then evaporated ribboning the sky like supernatural spirits —or something from somewhere else— something that once might have been.

The Reaper—

There. He saw it coming again, a spurious cloak of boiling dark wind with demonic red eyes. *It's intangible.* Unable to kill the shadow rushing him as a miscreant cold gale and fluttering robe, his target would have to be the scythe —*just a little closer*— then a glimmer of steel streaking out as it swung —blades slamming!

Ames repelled the blow and the Reaper veered as it rolled then billowed and spiraled higher. Momentarily it hovered overhead highlighted by heat lightning that firedanced through the broth of windblown twilight and gray, a mantle of revolving energy that surrounded and enclosed them. Then it coiled and came at him again, a wretched nemesis of pale banshee in dim jungle light. Darker than secrets and black as a scheme, it was a shapeless entity wrapped in plenary malevolence with black-hearted determination.

Sweeping down at him the Grim Reaper swung and dashed beyond as Ames checked and countered its blows. Time and again the phantom attacked, scythe against scimitar, steel singing its song trailed by chilling criminal-cold flutters that almost burrowed through him. They were two determined combatants in an unprecedented rushed and lethal fray; and all the while they fought the ghostly sable being never uttered a sound.

Seeming to pause and consider briefly, the shadow-phantom hovered above, then Ames saw its focus shift from himself to his friend —and the Reaper dove.

"Reed, watch out!"

He didn't have time to look back. "Just kill that son-of-a-bitch—"

"—Duck!"

Killing spiders. "Can't, they'll be all over us," Hunters appearing and detonating as the pulse laser screamed launching spears of flame, shattering pieces in the onslaught, sticky blood raining down in their hair.

Reed couldn't duck; they'd instantly be overrun and their slim advantage would be lost. He couldn't stop, wouldn't stop, and neither would they. His finger and aim tore through them as they came, blowing back the rush of bloodlust and insanity driving the horde. No matter what happened, whatever the outcome, Reed knew he couldn't stop, had to hold their position and keep them at bay. Do or die, simple as that.

They were surrounded, trapped —target to target— as fast as he looked, from all fronts now deviants and claws; it was complete madness. And stirred in the confluence of chattering white noise and bloodshed were savage, trilling animalistic screams cut short with clattering, twirling, splattered-chitin spider bits!

From above—

In the blend of gray-shadow background the specter of the shadow-phantom flew at Reed, the snath emerging from the cloak as the gleaming scythe turned with a glimmer-reflection along its razor-sharp edge. Closing, it had him, and forcefully, ruthlessly the Reaper swung at Reed as...

—Sss-twang!

...Kalo's arrow shattered deflecting the blade, the shadow-phantom almost dropping and losing it. Petulantly the phantom whooshed just above the man then swept up in a sudden-flutter of black cloak and angry liver-red eyes. The Reaper had missed.

Too close, Ames thought.

Infused with fury and the whistle of wind the chimerical phantasm whirled upward like a vein of twisted darkness winding itself in distorted twitching knots. Then seething with hate it went after Kalo with a vengeance and loathing, but it never uttered a sound.

Anticipating, Kalo watched it. It dove—she dodged. With the speed of a vision and more skill than a warrior she was there, then wasn't, as time and again the phantasmagoria missed. Infuriated the shadow-phantom pursued her, while leaping spider to spider she darted and stabbed or sliced through their neck-like pedicels. Chasing her, the Reaper swung over and over, but her inimitable skill and nonpareil speed avoided it every time.

Shadow-phantom coming—

Landing on an arachnid she slashed through its pedicel then leaped —somersaulting— above the Reaper, then over and down. The dark shape missed and flew past as she lighted on another Hunter, stabbed twice in its head —cartwheeled, a rolling handspring— flipping off to one side. Even before the spider began to fall she was on top of another and, *whoosh,* the shadow was back. Deflecting the scythe with the knife her unique sense of premonition and unparalleled speed checked avoiding each strike —then gone— a blur of impish, impossible speed.

Vile as a cesspool and impious as a predatory thought the Grim Reaper skimmed above the horde chasing her like a consortium black wind. From below outstretched bale-hook claws grabbed and slashed at her; but with each swing of the scythe she had already been there, killed one and vanished. She struck and disappeared with a butterfly flit and bumblebee sting. Beyond comprehension and the horde's pathetic ability, she was impossible to catch.

Insidious as the shame of its identity and infuriated beyond rage, at length the Grim Reaper whirled and wound to an updraft twining knot, then unwinding, spiraled and soared into the canopy. Seething with frustration, the same as before, the phantasm never uttered a sound.

Unexpected and suddenly—

The Night Hunters broke off their attack scattering a second time, perhaps to regroup, perhaps something else, something other than that. From the cephalothorax of a collapsing spider Kalo leaped and somersaulted, twirling ballerina-warrior style, then lightly bounced on the balls of her feet as she landed on the mud rise between her companions. In the arachnids' wake the swamp quieted, layers of fog mist rising, rivulets draining, turning water to mud. The bog settled… and stilled.

A pause.

Tossing the knife to Reed, "I believe this is yours," he catching it and slipping it into its sheath as she unstrung the bow from her back taking her place alongside her companions. Prepared to defend their grass-slick rampart of sodden footprint-squashed ground, scanning the sky, moderately but matter-of-fact she told Ames, "This time it will be coming for you." She, Lent and Reed positioned themselves at three corners of the mud rise, a triangle formation with Ames in the center. "Now," she told him plainly, "it will be up to you."

Watching, waiting.

Surrounding them was unending movement and prosaic clatter daubed blue-gray with mud; in the distance they scuttled until the water was gone leaving a swampland morass. The obsidian horde circled with the dull intone of sucking sloshes made by countless taloned feet punching slimy dead grass into holes in the mud. Out there, untiring and incessant, they were preparing for another attack. Barbed cries and trilling white noise railed over the swampland with a cackling frenzy of animalistic screams.

In their heads the wind was an unremitting whistle, while above them smeared atmosphere crawled as an opaque ocean of cloud woven with dour long blue-black shadows. Cold buffeted their hair.

In any direction fog stirred as the perimeter mantle pushed back as far as they could see, its chill and the damp moving invisibly through them... almost as though it somehow breathed.

Silence of expectation.

Intermittently sheet lightning flickered fingers of fire illuminating the sky, glowing and pulsating then darkening again. Pernicious and mud-stained, Night Hunters and anemic gloom completely surrounded them; while pervasively tension curdled and congealed souring within them. They were four remnant Christians facing blackguard barbarians in a circular arena... almost.

The canopy—

"Figure it out," he muttered, anxiously watching the sky. "What did they mean?"

Movement swept through the mists of overcast-gray, the shadow-phantom was coming. Ames watched for the scythe as his mind worked the puzzle, the clues and the riddle. A flutter of wind, those eyes getting closer, *the phantom cannot be what it is not. Now!*— the rush, reflex —*duck!* as he swung, sidestepping then down, dodging, shielding the blow. But his heel caught on something and he tripped on what looked like a lid, falling flat on the ground on his shoulders and buttocks. The shadow had missed, but circled and came back.

On his back, under his breath: "Destroy it when it is what it cannot be." Heinous bloodshot eyes assessing him, shapeless black wind fluttering above him —he saw it— the blade of the scythe streaking out from that dark. *Not when it is what —brrring!*

He felt the sudden sensation of its presence—'crow's wings' all over him, but not thrashing and beating of stiff bristling feathers, only the sickness and darkness of a pitch-black soul dredged up in an ebony ghoul with scarlet-veined lines in its raw-liver eyes.

To his feet —another blow— deflected.

The scythe came from his right then again from the left—block and strike back. Ames countered blow for blow as he spun slashing through the shadowy form: nothing. His weapon had no effect as it swept through the phantasm's flurry of black wind. *Duck and fight back—swing—stay focused.* Deflecting the scythe then slashing down through the hood: nothing. Concentrating as he fought, he worked the clue in his head.

Circling white noise of savagery—

Sloshing claws gouging slits in the muck, the scrambling arachnids again charged the muddy prominence. Crowding and lunging, shrieking heckling madness, black chitin flushed from the bog —trilling and pieces— Reed holding them off, dropping one then another, death filling the air.

Sweat and steel, Lent's ax chopped through hulls, heads and legs, while Kalo punched holes in their goggle-like eyes and the pulse laser ripped chitin to slivers and twirling gray syrup. Explosions. Pieces. The clatter of ratchet-blade legs. And above the chaos trilled white noise savagery and shrill animalistic screams!

Fangs boring for his head, Lent swung crashing through its jaws burying his blade in its eyes as the spider plowed over him splashing blood in his face. Down. Knocked flat —*no time; gotta move*— bracing his leg and shoving its dead weight just enough to squeeze from beneath it. To his feet again, ready to fight —*more of them coming*— he drew back the ax.

Clamoring over one another, four rushed Reed as he fired from the hip, the arachnids so close that the impact shockwaves ricocheted in his face. Three of them shattered but the fourth was on top of him —*no time—whap*— her arrow lancing through its head. Above him the Hunter careened and went down dragging its buckled ratchet legs. Then she was gone—and he wasn't dead.

Flash pulses illuminated the dusky swamp as flaming tracer-rounds tore holes in their hulls, some glistening of oil, some covered with mud, all with fangs anticipating, savoring the strike. But the more of them that came, the more times he squeezed. "Bite this." Shrill whines —linear flashes— light-shattered dead bugs.

The Reaper—

Absorbed in a mixture of charcoal sky, sheet lightning, black wind and glimmers of flashing steel, the scimitar deflected the scythe with strident, hollow echoing rings. Blade against blade they fought in such close quarters Ames could see the disfigured face concealed within the hood: its bloodshot eyes glowering with wanton and despise, high-set gaunt cheekbones with wrinkled ears and pinched chin drawn down to a point. A face festered with lesions and the stench of necrotic puss that it inhaled and expelled as it breathed —and its bared canine teeth and ghoulish breath that reeked of a carrion feast.

—*Brrring!*

Knocked off-balance Ames staggered and went down again as spiders and a snarled shamble of disorder swirled in his head — confused flashing images— *too many Hunters.* One palm braced in the mud and heeling backward on his buttocks repeatedly slamming the scythe aside, he was unable to take his eyes from the Reaper. *No time, stay focused; the others can't help.* Somewhere in the flickering background created by the pulse laser's luminous blasts, he knew Reed was still there and heard Lent's heavy-handed ax, and knew Kalo was somewhere —but that was all— the rest of it spun as a mixture of speed. Everything was happening too quickly —*too fast.*

The shadow was all over him: *dark, red eyes, wind, pitch black.* Wrapped in buffeting cold and a swarming flurry of villainy he held it off then drove it back with several more blows; but there was no sound, tension and nerves blocking everything out. *Focus!* yelled the voice in his head—and in that eyeblink Wilson's echo cued, *when it is more than it is... not when it is not what it is.*

Again, the Reaper struck, the curved scythe swinging fiercely at his head, the shimmering broad-edged scimitar slamming the scythe aside, the metallic collision pushing him back. On the ground with the shadow-phantom above him, a blade's reach between them, his vision was filled with the black fluttering cloak and contour of the hood, and those hideous dead eyes. The Reaper was a red-eyed rain forest panther peering out from the night, preparing to pounce.

Perspiring cold tension he flicked sweat from his hair, and the instant the scythe came he felt —the *whoosh*— then —*sound*— their blades colliding —and at last he realized, *not the eyes, don't look at the eyes.* He spied the snath handle and swung again knocking it aside. Surprised, the phantom spun away as Ames rolled over and sprang back to his feet.

Working Wilson's clue, rearranging the words: *the phantom cannot be what it is not. Not when it is what it is... when it is more than it is —it's coming again.* Black fluttering wind of fury and despise—*not the eyes; don't look at the eyes.* Assuming a mien of defiance, refusing to duck, he stood his ground; understanding now... *the shadows —concentrate— focus on the shadow, the dark.*

Again, the demon swooped at him —but knowing now— facing his antagonist, blade held low at his side, he took a stance and waited. It was coming... coming.

At the last possible moment Ames raised his weapon grabbing the tip of the scimitar, turning the blade sideways —broadside— the scimitar shimmering with the unfolding sinuous motion beneath the sky's streaming long blue-black shadows, reflecting ribboning waves of the dim flowing light —then intensifying— and shining until it flared...

...And decisively he said, "My turn..." enhanced blue-black light cast back from the broadsword glaring brilliantly in the face of the Grim Reaper, "...gotcha." *Your own reflection!* Ames triumphed, standing fast.

Stunned the shadow-phantom stopped in mid-flight, hovering dumbstruck and confused. It seemed horrified as it wavered, then weakening it started wrinkling, dead-like, wizening, its strength decaying as its human form began to materialize. Still holding the scythe over its head, its hand started drying and shriveling, the fingers crackling and crinkling. Its liver-red eyes began draining as they faded dull-gray with black lines that resembled sickly lacewing-veins. Then the hood slipped back as the shadowy cloak transformed to a worn-out, tattered, dingy black cloth.

Amazed, the conscript dredged from a time long since forgotten writhed... and Captain Thorne whispered, "No. No, it can't be. You figured it out."

Breathtaking silence, he didn't say a word. Defiantly, Ames only glared.

Pathetically, almost pitifully, "That's not right. That can't be right," Thorne sniveled touching the ground in front of him. "You weren't supposed to figure it out."

Eyes narrowing, purposefully Ames braced his weapon with both hands and slowly, deliberately turned the blade tip toward his adversary's midsection.

"It can't be," the Reaper whimpered again.

Intent with revenge, Ames still just glared.

Wavering and staring blankly, still holding the scythe above his head Thorne staggered a single step, still unable to believe that it happened. "You figured it out," he sniveled again. A dead gaze, his eyes wandering, unfocused; then whining more loudly like he hadn't a friend in the world, until finally, "You weren't supposed to figure it out!" he wailed.

"Well Thorne... sometimes shit happens," Ames countered coldly. Then, infused with conviction and bound by justice he conceded, "And I know you like it, Captain, but I just..." —*stab*— "...loathe war," and he twisted and wrenched grinding the scimitar blade in Captain Thorne's guts.

Aaayeee!

As soon as Thorne screamed Reed felt it —static charge— the hair on the back of his neck tingling and standing on end, that prickly sensation racing from the tip of the toes to the top of the head. Beside him Lent's mop went wild —crazy— like it was grab-frazzled in a windstorm, and still tied with the rubber band Kalo's ponytail frizzed and shot straight up. Saturating static charge spiked through them —and he knew what it was.

Reed yelled, "Hit the dirt—everybody down!" Diving from the high ground of the mud rise and dropping flat they hit the ground as...

—Skizz-whoom!

...A flare of white fire flashed through the sky, the arcing flame of lightning crackling as it streaked down slamming into the scythe, seizing Thorne with its incredible electrifying charge —flaming and burning and lighting him up!

The Reaper vibrated, shuddered and shook—throbbing, rattling and pulsating with awesome wizard-white light and a dynamic electrocution-blue flash! He screamed like a shaken dummy, a singed rat tossed in an electrical storm of flaming wrath and blue-green then white fire that flashed down the snath handle sweeping around him. It engulfed him. Frying and vibrating he sizzled furiously. Dissolving and smoking he skizzled and shrieked —shredding, coming apart— then suddenly detonated exploding in a whorl of flames and fireball bits that crackled and vanished with twirling powdery shards swept away in a cloud of black-ash dust and oblivion fumes. Gone.

Astonished, from the ground they looked up...

—*Skizz-zoom-whoom!*

Heads down—

...Ragged-hot fingers flashed again and again as lightning strikes bombarded the mud plain lancing through the Hunters. Incredible explosive static bolts slammed suddenly and fast, too quickly to count, too many to track, gigantic spiders detonating and dying as the swamp gas ignited then flared in a diaphanous boil of hellfire wind!

Reed yelled, *"Flash blow—don't breathe!"* Cupped hands over their heads and lying flat they held their breath burying their faces in the mud...

...The swamp methane fumes instantaneously setting off a flaming rush of blue-yellow sorcerer's wind that flashed in bursts of inferno waves and desiccating brew. Melting Hunters, it burned with blast-furnace fury, streaking out as detonations unfurled in a savage conflagration of billowing fire that seethed over, blistered and blew through, setting afire the arachnid horde!

—*Methane explosion boiled till it screamed, then it screamed until it roared!*

Half-buried with only their buttocks and shoulders sticking up, faces crammed in the mud, they heard the awesome, *swoosh-oomph-oosh,* bloodcurdling roil of rattling explosions and trilling, chattering —shrieking— dissolving animalistic arachnid screams!

With a dragon's roar and its fiery breath vitriolic methane broth swept as unfolding torrential flares, splashing through the Hunters with firestorm force in lecherous swirling swords of flaming winds that charbroiled, pressure-cooked and detonated them—that quick! Chitin exploding, spider chunks twirled trailing bits of smoking debris as ectoplasm burned and vaporized vanishing within the intense liquefying melee of heat. Like a catastrophic explosion there was blinding bright light —then the shockwave— as the blast front hit!

Flashspray boiled as it rolled in a volatile outrushing pour that slammed and splashed as it melted and swarmed. Firewall clouds swept over and through them ravaging the swampland, killing and blistering Hunters, charring and burning the bog and eating smog as it ran.

In less than five seconds it was over.

When the four looked up thousands of spiders were incinerated and down, with others still ablaze running at what looked like mach-celerity speed. Shrieking dying screams, bubbling, stumbling, popping and collapsing, the air was thick with a sick sultry taste, the odor of burned chitin and smoldering dead; carnage beyond anything any of them had so far seen.

The boundary—

Ten miles in the distance residual fog was dissolving within the spiraling outrush of flames as they reached the surrounding cloud wall; then whirling violently and dying out it all finally evaporated in diminishing blue-yellow vaporous winds along the encompassing boundary that completely encircled them. Twenty miles across, an arena... of sorts.

A pause, after the flash—

Curls of rising black smoke and smoldering spiders lay in thousands of scattered small fires, the island rises now resembling a smattering of crisp-fried bald hummock heads protruding from a viscid mire of surface-parched mud. There were mud pots, damp spots and remnant water holes that survived, all of it covered with parched, cracked blue-bruised-black skin. It looked mottled and sick with the texture of blotchy open sores beneath a sky that wound more deeply and darker to a tightening vortex, forming a whirlpool that ever so slowly revolved in the sky.

In the distance thunder grumbled and a breeze endured just tousling their hair... waiting, chilled with anger.

Looking around, slowly the four vagabonds unraveled their nerves and began to get up. Then suddenly —no warning— an unworldly, incredibly violent jolt!

Tossed up, Lent blurted, "What the—"

Bouncing into the air and tipping over, Reed yelled, *"—Oooh shit!"*

CHAPTER NINETEEN

A viscous, sudden mudslide rush...

...The mire bubbled with froth and surged as it slid splashing sheetmud and sludge, submerged rock fracturing and crunching then jutting up ripping the quagmire with violent uplifting force. Shuddering dynamically the mantle's tectonic plate grumbled and snapped as the peak of a mountain tore through the veneer of swamp... then solemnly began to rise.

Far off, to the left a second monolith heaved up —and on the right a third— powerfully burgeoned mysteriously pushing from the bog. Deep strata cracked and splintered as the quavering landscape jolted them, while resembling the cusps of a triangle, slowly, with intent, the three peaks rose.

Tearing with thick pliable snaps huge sheets of mud pulled apart then skidded and rolled over one another disgorging massive slabs of uplifted rock dripping blue-black slime as they slid heavily aside. The bog spasmed with potent undulating swells of extreme quaking force as jolts crawled from the deep mantle base, shifting and grinding while the mighty, burnished peaks climbed.

Overwhelmed, the vagabonds watched as the swamp sifted and gurgled, submerged crevasses splitting and opening unearthing sinkholes that collapsed then jutted up exposing monstrous wedges of splintered, jagged rock. The entire basin was a flow of immense chunks and moving landscape that was breaking apart and being expelled then crumbling with the gutsy milling forces of crushing shearwave compression and sloshing-mud sounds. Shaking and quavering the surface was bubbling and breaking, intense razing destruction heaving huge slabs with brittle hard breaks and gritty fracturing sounds.

Forging up—tearing terrain, the peaks ground through the mammoth subterranean plate as they compressed enormous slabs that slid and crashed together obliterating one another with incredible weight and pulverizing pressure. Uplifted—protruding, great wedges of rock smashed one onto another, some overriding and others subducted, being ground under with the awesome forces of tectonic rift and herculean movement. Grating—crunching, huge blocks of stone grumbled echoes from the depths as vast sheets of sodden earth cascaded and poured. Bubbling as it slowly rose then suddenly collapsed sloshing regurgitated mudcake and slop the quagmire heaved untold volumes as it shook and moved in slipshod vagrant slides.

Above them the sky was mercurial and violent, a canvas of turbulence and fire sliced with blades of electric flame that spun brilliant ball lightning meteors causing thunderclap tantrums that exploded and bumbled time after time. As the swampland vaulted and shifted the canopy was winding more deeply and darker, while in the dim wavering light the mysterious peaks starkly endured, and implacably climbed.

All around them was confusion of incredible power. Shaken with subterranean sidewinders the sodden morass regurgitated wave after wave of crusted slop, splashing it up then sucking it back down overturning monstrous plates of slime-covered rock. Above head-slam thunder thrashed as it rumbled and poured and the swampland unpredictably shook; and as they staggered on the mud rise fighting to stay on their feet, at each corner of this arena, three gray-black monoliths continued to rise.

Beneath the unending noise and gloom of the whirlpool sky coarse facets of granite glittered with sparkling, shimmering light. Consummate, powerful and indomitable, center stage amid the intensity of shearwave destruction... unfailing the three peaks of Legend Range climbed.

"Wise Men," Ames whispered venerably.

"What?" Lent yelled over the noise.

"Incredible," the man murmured, then shouted as he said it again, "The Three Wise Men."

They staggered —fell— got up and stumbled again as they watched the remarkable mountains push aside enormous sheets of rock and huge mud walls that churned then rolled under. Sliding from cliffs and ledges of the rising gray-black monoliths, mudrush poured as black slurry wash that streamed down the escarpments and rock faces splashing and slopping with turbid opaque tsunamis that smothered everything with suffocating weight and the pour of gurgling noise. Between the ever-widening bases of the ascending peaks the swampland quavered and rolled resembling spoiled ocean swells of black greasy crude pounded by a devil's nor'easter. And with each new shockwave more deep terrain splintered and crumbled then vaulted and belched another billion cubic yards of sodden megaboil rise; and more rock emerged then tilted and toppled splashing onto the surface like incredible icebergs of mud. Sheer power, and plashing sheetwaves of muck.

Caught up within the upheaval the four didn't notice the encompassing boundary as it flowed, darkening and tightening, crawling in ominous congealing cascades beneath a canopy continuing to gather charcoal thunderheads rimmed with anemic pallid greens. Thunder rattled and grumbled through the keening wind tousling their hair, the theater thickening and crowding, building and amassing while skylightning fried silent screams. Then mimicking the flashes thunderclaps splintered, blustered and fanned, then more distant and fading —*then crackle!*— ear-piercing, pealing again.

While above and around them lightning-scatter etched a storm wall and sky painted opaque and black, the other storm was forming, a divergence chilled with anger… soon to arise with a cold, *Relentless Wind.*

Rattled and staggering Reed took it all in. "Doc… do you know where we are?"

Slipping in the mud, Ames stumbled and fell.

"Right—smack-dab—in the middle of..." Reed went down.

Glancing from one to the other Lent yelled, "Middle of what?" Thunder slammed in their heads. He fell. Kalo fell.

Getting back up, "A nexus..." Reed shouted, "the circular storm," nerves squeezing his grin, "...your hole in the sky."

Scared-excited, Lent's eyes —big as jumbo eggs— darting everywhere at once, held an expression, a gawk that just hollered 'I told you so' astonishment. A wave hit bouncing him up; sprattling, then landing on his butt, legs spread in the mud, *"For real?"* he hollered.

Reed went down—got up. "Yeah, it's ba—" thrown again, "—ack!"

Being tossed by an uncontrollably quavering mire rimmed by three rising peaks, witnessing nature's awesome power the four were unable to stay on their feet. Incredible swells of quagmire disgorged as it heaved, then gurgled as it poured like dark flowing waves; cascading strength conveying massive slabs of rock that emerged as they rolled and turned then sloshed back down with incredible sheetsplash of dun-colored muck. Sliding and grating the swampscape revolved with gristmill power and the formidable crushing weight of a churning sea of mud. Crunching and cracking, grinding then fracturing, boulders tumbled and broke in ragged-edged chunks, then swirled and sank in the mire again.

The pudding of swamp continually bubbled, rose then collapsed as it flowed with undulant swells stirred to a fetid dark broth streaked with blemishes of blue-black veins. And losing buoyancy with each successive sliding movement the smoldering hulls of dead arachnids bellied and listed; then caught up in the mud, to the very last they swamped as they filled. Like flickering smudge pots marking two-lane construction sites in a midsummer rainstorm a long time ago, one by one the charred hulls slid out of sight in the spoil and bog, until finally the dead Hunters all went under.

Metamorphic—

Overhead the canopy congealed as it moved. Animate, it was alive with towering chameleonic thunderheads and lightning that flared flinging fire through the sky. Thunderclaps crackled as they broke, reverberated and rolled, then slid as they faded like Washington Irving's Rip Van Winkle in a gambit of ten pins. All the while, low on the horizon an eclipsed sun and blood-red moon cast long blue-black shadows that cascaded a waltz of the goblin dance, surreal and strange as sprites and fairies fashioned of imagery and illusion from times long since past.

An unequivocal mudswell suddenly boiled up then collapsed; and strangely the upheaval began to settle, still rumbling, but quieting. Thunder drifted, seemed more distant, but the mud and swampscape kept churning and percolating, and oozing as it trembled. Geomorphologically a world of gray and gloom, revolving, and changing... preparing.

* * *

Now war arose in heaven... And the great dragon was thrown down, that ancient serpent, who is called the Devil and Satan, the deceiver of the whole world ...and his angels were thrown down with him. [in part] (Rev. 12: 7-9 RSV)

* * *

Without warning...

...A thought-stopping howl and the echo of a sickening moan that trailed; from somewhere out there in this strange phenomenon came a blood-curdling groan, and a roar—long, drawn, soul-chilling and anguished. From the very core of darkness, it was a wail of hollow emptiness and absolute hatred that railed into the dim light and long blue-black shadows... in this strange, unworldly place.

Startled, "I've heard that howl before," Lent said, all of them looking around.

Apprehensive, Reed's thoughts were drawn to the peculiar small twins as somewhere in the recesses of his mind he imagined he heard one of them whisper, *"Reed..."* "Sure wish those two gnomes were here with their magic marbles."

"Dwarfs, little people," Ames corrected offhand.

"Yeah, little midgets, whatever. Wonder where they…" and as he said it —a heave and upthrust— one end of their small island rising and tilting as a sizable slab of rock boiled almost from beneath them.

Twisting and rolling it turned over with a syrupy, *goosh*, of muck and glutinous bubbles, and from the mudslosh and commotion a pair of muddy navy blue watch caps and grubby small hands in red and blue plaid shirts appeared, as all faded-and-dirty the pint-sized P.T. Barnum and his inseparable companion 'Just Plain' Wilson popped up out of a waterlogged hole.

Scurrying from the bog below each grabbed onto an edge of the upthrust slab riding it up, and almost musically P.T. announced, "Certainly took you long enough, Mr. Ames."

Then Wilson: "That's a fact." Unexpected voices.

The ponderous slab teetered then tipped and went down with a loud liquid, *thwack*, and began submerging in the brown-black mire again. Turning as they hopped from the sinking rock, each wiped mud from his hands and coveralls and marched promptly and businesslike toward Ames and the others.

Surprised, but still pleased, "What took me long enough?"

"Figuring out how to purge Captain Thorne—or as Reed so appropriately alluded—to dispose of the 'Grim Reaper'," the inimitable Wilson explained.

More glad to see them than curious, and dismissing the barb, "Oh yeah, well you're late short-stuff," Ames bantered.

Wilson paused, planting both hands on his hips, crooking an eyebrow. "Really?" Beside him P.T. Barnum grinned knowingly.

"You know, it sorta pisses me off that you guys are so cavalier about all this," Reed jumped in. "And furthermore…"

"—Urinated directionally?" P.T. needled, indulgent, and as always, inclined toward mischief. "Heaven forbid."

"What-*ever*, pipsqueak," Reed tossed back.

Wilson smiled. "Miss us?" he ventured.

"Well," Reed admitted, "you guys are a sight for sore eyes —but if you're gonna be all sarcastic…"

"—It's a, yes!" P.T. surmised.

"Sure sounds like one," Wilson agreed. "Certainly does."

"Don't get cocky," Reed scowled, delighted to see them nonetheless. "I just hate when midgets get cocky."

Ames didn't have time to say it. "Little people, dwarfs," Kalo corrected. That even took Reed by surprise, because generally she didn't say much.

"He missed us," Wilson decided affectionately.

A glance of 'whatever' to Kalo, then to the dwarfs, "Don't you half-pints get all puffed-up; Doc's bad enough." Teasing him, Kalo pursed her lips in an overt pout.

P.T. to Wilson: "He missed us."

Reed threw back, "Do chickens have lips?"

Scratching his chin thoughtfully, "Hadn't considered that, but I 'spose it could be arranged," Wilson toyed.

"Reed," Lent groused, "that doesn't make a particle of sense — even to me."

"Pipe down kid; what do you know about chickens?"

Wilson pestered, "He's just a bit testy right now, Lent." Glancing at his twin, "Does he seem testy to you, Phineas?"

"Matter-of-fact, he does."

"'Spose you two munchkins could knock it off? We've got a little earthquake going on —case you hadn't noticed," Reed countered; and then unable to leave it at that, "and three brand-spanking-new mountains. But what with bein' so short and all, I guess you probably missed 'em from *wa-ay* down there."

"An earthquake," Wilson repeated, "do tell."

"And mountains," P.T. bantered, "imagine that." Then, with his propensity for dramatics and changing the subject, wagging a Lilliputian-stubby arm, "Greetings and salutations young Lent. How's she goin'?"

Flabbergasted—and miffed, "How's she goin'? We just had a zillion venom-shootin' spiders all over the place —all over us— and you ask, 'How's she goin'? Dagblastit."

"Less than optimal then I take it?" P.T. inquired with a pretext of naiveté.

"Yeah, you could say that," shaking his head. "Willikers, we almost got eaten by the screamin' meemies and now you two show up with some piddling little sticks and slingshots hangin' out'cyour back pockets. What—d'you come to help us out or not?"

"Absolutely," P.T. assured, "we hate to miss a good skirmish."

In spite of the still-gently-rumbling quake Reed leaned closer, and just loudly enough to be heard, cautioned Lent, "Don't go off half-cocked-impertinent and be dissin' their slingshots. They're some hole-punchin'-mean little suckers, boy."

"Yeah, I'm sure."

Louder now, annoyed, "And don't mock me, kid; I'll bust you like a chicken wishbone. You'd be well-advised to keep a civil tongue in your head."

Blowing him off but edged with guilt, turning back to the dwarfs Lent acquiesced, "Dagnabit, okay, I'm sorry, better late than never; but in case you haven't noticed —fight's over, you missed it."

"Not at all," Wilson replied, "that wasn't the battle."

"It wasn't?" Lent asked. "What would you call it then?"

"To quote a friend, a firefight perhaps," and sagely the little man grinned.

Three points of the compass—

Forged with strength enough to make the landscape tremble the gray-black monolithic peaks continued to push powerfully from below. While low in the sky, just above the boundary's cloud wall an eclipsed sun and blood-red moon bled through the overcast with streaming blue-black shadows that flowed over the landscape. An arena... of sorts.

Sounding like distant thunder, intermittently quavering and rumbling, the diminished earthquake churned silt and sheetmud with the flux of seaswells and cadence of glutinous waves. Constantly oozing and shifting with heaving deep breaths and gasping dark sighs crusted mud and slime sifted as it fluctuated like an oceanic world of

drying black tar. While in the dim light the swampworld trembled…
and the mountains continued to rise.

Sudden silence—

Quake tectonics stopped leaving only the gristmill rumble of three
inexplicable mountains steadily grinding and crunching, forging
upward through the terrain creating an oozing flow of mudscape that
gradually slowed, undulating as it shifted and sifting as it settled.
Slipping away the wind diminished then hushed, hinting with that
eerie sensation: telling quiet of the pause, intimating calm preceding
the storm.

It was the breath of premonition, until ten miles away in drifting
wings of mist…

—The foghorn's blare,

…Where the swampland boiled in an uprising mound of syrup-
brown bubbles, then heaved as the bow emerged pushing up from
the bog. Her dead metal skeleton creaked and groaned flushing
slurry aside as she rose from the depths of fetid dark broth churning
quagmire under when her bow came down and the gigantic freighter
leveled. Rotted and torn with holes her hull she took on snakes of dead
grass and muck that were sucked into her hold and poured out astern
where a bridal veil of dead seaweed and kelp trailed despondently
like a widowed bride outflowing sadness and gloom.

From out there, still far off, came that faint but discernible thrum,
the drone of churning propulsion; and her silhouette gradually came
into view. Dripping seaweed and mud from her rails, high up on the
bridge, inside the pilothouse someone or something stood manning
the wheel. Then it moved —huge linebacker shoulders and lumbering
gait— from the wheelhouse, down the companionway, to the foredeck.

Watching the distant vessel from the mud rise no one said
anything, until at length Wilson solemnly revealed, "Now, Lent, the
conflict has finally come."

Rusted and rotted, hollow and gaunt, it was lost a long time ago in
the Bermuda Triangle; never recovered, never found, at four hundred
twenty-five feet she was a large freighter that had taken all thirty-
nine hands to the bottom with her. A lost vessel, according to legend

or folklore or myth, she was the ghost ship 'Marine Sulphur Queen'. The dead ship… on a voyage to nowhere.

Not quite sure what to think, Lent studied the thing as it plied slowly and inexorably toward them. But Ames knew what Wilson meant, and *his* name instilled fear. *Smith.* For them… the Devil had come.

Three points of the compass—

Sloshing earthen slams and herculean shudders the three peaks simultaneously surged as they shifted then thunderously settled producing reverberating, *thombs.* With remarkable endurance melded within them and the velveteen luster of burnished stone shimmering the length of their jutting cliffs and slides, they towered imposing and majestic, summits concealed somewhere in the clouds above. Steadfast in silence and unfaltering in strength, the 'Wise Men' of Legend Range surveyed this extraordinary place.

Out there, on the mire—

As the tremors subsided and echoes of the settling peaks diminished the swampland sifted, then eventually stilled. Gray and dead as the ghosts of times past the 'Queen' chugged mechanically and methodically. Though still far out the freighter was approaching, groaning as she furrowed through mud.

Overhead—

Sporadic ball lightning meteors suddenly streaked through the sky trailing luminous flares within an opaque canopy rimmed with furls of gray; and scattered sheet lightning flashed sudden-silent waves rousing muffled distant thunder that rolled in petulant drumbeats, then drifted away. All the while the clouds wound more deeply and darker with a vortex of omen and impending storm. It was up there, in the sky, a churning, rotating whirlpool… with a disquieting, portending eye.

Enclosing them—

This world was an unraveling tempest of darkness tied with ribbons of riddles, pieces of circumstance once hidden somewhere within the unsolved puzzle of time. Foreboding and cold the wind slipped in and stole through to their bones, while the distant boundary revolved as it rolled shedding rain that concealed the horizon. Noticeable now, circumrotating and encompassing the vagabonds, the storm's boundary wall inexorably began to flow.

Again the wind, and the distant drone of pistons—

Through their hair, in their ears, beginning slowly to grow, visible dove-colored wisps murmured the song of the mariner's lore within the gray-dark mist that moved out and away toward the periphery of the storm boundary wall. Still benign but steady, blowing cold in their faces.

Low on the horizon—

Just above the boundary wall an eclipsed sun and blood-red moon cast long blue-black shadows, shades of despondence and gray. And beneath the overshadowed glowing star in the sky, it was coming... a dead ship getting closer.

Without warning—

A thought-stopping howl and the echo of a sickening moan that trailed; from the freighter there came a blood-curdling groan, and a roar—long, drawn, soul-chilling and anguished. As though shrieking from the core of the world the noise reverberated with a wail of hollow emptiness and absolute hatred into the gloom of slate gray... in this strange, unworldly place.

On the bog—

Having once lived the glory and grandeur of maritime adventure until lost in the Devil's Triangle, now a dead ship, the 'Marine Sulphur Queen' laboriously came. Still several miles distant, but pernicious, unswerving; no more than a silhouette, a slow-moving smudge, an indefinable black splotch, a crawling dark spirit plying toward them. And each sensed more than they could actually see; now they all could feel it. *He* was on board.

At the bow—

Standing six-foot-five he was large and thick, three hundred pounds of solid hate and muscle. From his head of gray stubble hair to the gleam of his black spit-polished boots, he was thoroughly military. His face was heavily joweled and wrinkled, and his eyes were intensely mean; satanic eyes, and that glare—Edward G. Robinson in a gangster movie.

Issuing from his nostrils smoke curls slipped away in the wind. He was the persona of deceit, the will of vindictiveness and loathing, the epitome of vengeance and self-serving; all that is base. Now tinged with yellow his evil gray eyes scanned, contemplating; then inhaling a rasping breath his black lungs sucked in a silent drag of acrid cigar smoke and stale caustic air with indulgent pleasure.

Exuding the malignance of perdition, he had an innate resentment and envy of man laced tightly with his boots. Standing solidly, feet spread wide, saber in one fist the other clenching the rail; slowly, purposefully, chin to his chest General Smith shifted his scowl excreting a guttural snarl. Then lifting his head he growled until his voice rose to a scream, and throwing back his shoulders he bellowed a throaty bone-chilling roar!

The mud rise—

Glancing nervously from one to the other, from their vantagepoint they watched the approaching freighter until Reed mumbled, "Aw shit, Doc, now you've gone and done it."

"Yeah," Lent agreed, "he really sounds pissed."

"My fault?"

"Well, there's no way I'm getting blamed for this," Reed said plainly. Then looking back at the ship, "Don't 'spose he'd settle for a 'Happy Meal'."

Beside them she closed her eyes and focused her mind; concentrating, listening, and as always, Kalo was silent.

Diminishing unexpectedly the wind quieted again, settling with a hush, drifting to still, then melting to calm. Oozing mud spread in dark fractured puddles as the sky seemed to hesitate and the surrounding storm boundary slowed until it nearly quit moving. Finally, almost vacillating, it was no more than an encompassing flow easing along with the pause of night mist. Sheet lightning vanished and the sky became dark. Strangely, within the shadows and gloom everything seemed suspended like a heartbeat of time ticking cadenced hollow pings in their heads. In the murk and clouds just above the boundary wall, the eclipsed sun and blood-red moon hung there... waiting.

Then asystole, dead silence.

The feeling of, *something is about to happen,* crept through them with its creepy presentment as the six on the small prominence were taken hostage by expectation. Not a word, even the dwarfs did not speak. Scanning, anticipating, they watched with apprehension as the ghost ship plowed through black silt that heaved from her bow then oozed out astern, still approaching. Deathly quiet, and not one decibel of noise... not a whisper of sound.

"Gettin' spooky," Lent whispered looking around uneasily, "what's going on?"

Solemnly Wilson answered him reciting:

"And when the dragon saw that he had been thrown down to the earth, he pursued the woman who had borne the male child. But the woman was given the two wings of the great eagle that she might fly from the serpent into the wilderness, to the place where she is to be nourished for a time, and times, and half a time." (Rev. 12: 13-14 RSV)

Puzzled, Lent turned to the dwarf. "What does that mean?"

Uprising suddenly and violently—

Mercurial with power the storm furiously exploded wringing lightning and thunder that shook the boundary as the sky collided with dark-boil percussion and clouds that billowed and spun. And with cyclone force the canopy and keening winds roared!

Buffeted and sound-slammed, jarring shock pulses swept through a sky set ablaze with ripping streaks of lightning's galvanized power, blinding ball lightning hurling blue-electric torches trailing white flaming light. Rattling and shredding, spraying nails of mind-bending concussions the canopy was animate with static-burn bolts as the landscape trembled with shatters of thunder-scream drums. Dark and mighty the storm rose with potent power —a sudden barrage of wild peeling thunder— the feeling and sensation all around them

—intense, overwhelming— instantly saturating the sky as it swiftly closed in.

Twisting, piling and pouring, thunderheads burgeoned and climbed like billows of darkness releasing horizontal rain that traced the storm's boundary wall. Hissing with the rush of scalding steam whirling wind shrieked with deafening dynamics, biting with the teeth and fury of hurricane force. Filling their mouths it puffed out their cheeks and tightened their skin as it chilled with the pervasive cold of its ice crystal breath.

In the distance wave after wave of sideways rain pelted the boundary clouds spilling waterball raindrops that plunged and spun in sheets of stretched silver dollars. Building as it revolved the storm boundary was a cloak of blackness and sallow-gray veil with a hailstorm's racket and splattering force. Throbbing and expanding, the storm surrounding them churned with remarkable fury and darkness that enveloped the landscape as it grew more violent and intense. Black as the eye of a raven and scrambled slipshod with shed water it was an unending blend of streaking gray rain and prosaic waterwind squalls distorting stretched blue-black shadows.

Feral and fuming and rotating more petulantly, the storm boundary's extraordinary momentum sucked mud from the swamp into the waterwash wall. Rising debris swirled up into and through the boundary like an amalgam of indigo mixing water and silt to dun-color and black staining the canopy like a smeared canvas topped with thunderheads that boiled as they piled miles overhead. The frigid wind blew so violently it sent whistles to their brains and left frozen echoes in their heads as lightning spewed dazzling flames that rattled the sky until finally the storm boundary roared!

Still intensifying, the tempest heightened, the swampland shaking, darkened clouds plashing as the phenomenon rose with its mettle and might. It was the untamed roar of a seastorm charged with blasts of wizard-white fire and intense thunderous explosions that trailed through this gloom of unfathomable secrets. They were inside a gargantuan, overwhelming cavern of cloud facing the unknown in a mysterious place, strangely dark with foreboding and tense with apprehension. They were encapsulated, surrounded. Wind blew to a gale. Thunder scattered and crashed. Lightning fried holes where it ran, and the canopy knotted then unraveled...

—And they came,

...Veined with rain-soaked fingers of mud-twisted wind, tendril wall clouds first appeared and emerged as dark tornadic funnels that formed in the sky. Spawned by the hundreds opaque helix twisters shaped like writhing vines crawled from the encompassing strata, then dangled and elongated as they vacillated and spun; narrow tentacles that gyrated in the sky. Hanging there, coiling sinuously, suspended and winding the rite of expectation, conjecture... and Green.

On the mud rise—

Hair on the back of their necks standing on end; fearful, uncertain... watching.

Above them—

In a mixture of darkness and water the first tornadic cloud reached for the morass, an unworldly deafening wind that came roaring toward them as it whirled down before them...

Then harmlessly, almost delicately it touched the surface no more than twenty feet from them; and momentarily it whorled mysteriously, churning, digging and piling, forming and shaping the mud. Then in a sudden splash of clear shimmering water the opaque funnel wind swiftly came apart as it withdrew and dissipated.

...And it left her there, holding the babe as she knelt in the mud.

Stunned, Ames couldn't move, couldn't speak.

Opening her eyes, she looked up, and blinking profound wonder and love... Tian smiled.

Astonished, Reed and Lent stared as she rose with the boy child and ran to Ames. Overwhelmed, his lips were moving but nothing came out. Beyond comprehension, unable to speak, tears glistening in his eyes he embraced them kissing each on the head. Too much— even to breathe.

Snuggling within his arms she looked up to him. "I love you," she whispered.

"I love you too," he finally stammered. "I always will."

Kalo was silent —but the wind still roared.

Another funnel descended, spiraling and transforming mud into flesh, and when it swept up and whisked away Seana and her child were huddled there dripping pure water from the vanishing splash. Amazement brimming in his heart, Reed hurried to them scooping them into his arms.

There was warmth in his voice when P.T. Barnum said, "And He delivered them from the Wilderness." Beside him, 'Just Plain' Wilson smiled.

Reverently Ames recited, "Three Wise Men watch when the flock returns." Now he understood, *He was hiding them, protecting them from evil.*

They couldn't fathom how... but it did happen. One after another Renoloi and Pilgrims appeared from within the mysterious circular storm. Nitana, Deet, Ronto, Tere, and all the others, until finally...

"...Uncle Reed!" there was Jade. Setting Seana down lightly Reed knelt for his scampering tike, tenderly hugging his precious Jade as he picked her up with one arm slipping the other around Seana again.

"A miracle," he whispered.

P.T. Barnum replied, "Perhaps Reed, but..." then genuinely, earnestly he said, "when you believe, there are always possibilities."

Within a mysterious storm—

Beneath a turbulent sky, finally, all together again, they were gladdened and relieved. But for them the warmth of reunion was to be short-lived, just a transitory thing... this was still a darkened place.

* * *

And I saw the beast and the kings of the earth with their armies gathered to make war against him who sits upon the horse and against his army. (Rev 19:19 RSV)

The foghorn's blare—

Churning mud foam under the 'Marine Sulphur Queen' bore down upon them trailing decadence, seaweed and sargasso from her stern. A gaunt rusted giant with festered dead-metal skin, she crawled through the mire, a wretched shackled leper on an unholy quest. Huge and corroded, her screws tossed enormous whorls of muck into greasy dark soup, the drone of her pistons almost groaning innuendo of misery. Forever lost, she was a misplaced recollection with a guttural malady bemoaning the pain cloistered deep in her hold.

Around them—

The storm fulminated with colic violence and fury, lightning blazing through rushing clouds, wind whistling from the boundary with its pelting downpour. The storm was intensifying... forming.

On deck, at the bow—

Garbed in military green trimmed with brass camouflage that concealed villainy and depravity in a charade of propriety, he squeezed crushing the rail with his hand. He watched them, despised them; and slavering spittle over the stub of cigar Smith groaned, "Come my minions." Then, voice rising, hoarse and hateful he roared, "Join me adherents of Darkness!"

Smith's abhorrent bay boiled from the depths of his groin with the hostility of a simmering magma caldera; then it rose to a howl and climaxed like the scream of a whore! Seething indignation, he glared as he ground the blade tip deeper into the prosaic metal-gray hide of the insipid ship, gouging the deck, chiseling fiery sparks with each turn of his wrist. Shimmering steel and dull-tarnish dead-metal rust... and yellow-gray eyes of malevolence.

In appearance the locusts were like horses arrayed for battle; on their heads were what looked like crowns of gold; their faces were like human faces, their hair like women's hair, and their teeth like lions' teeth; they had scales like iron breastplates, and the noise of their wings was like the noise of many chariots with horses rushing into battle. They have tails like scorpions, and stings... They have as king over them the angel of the bottomless pit. [in part] (Rev. 9: 7-11 RSV)

The reply—

Scattered and discordant at first, like a distant flock of shrieking blackbirds the noise mounted in an increasing antiphony that fulminated in a cacophonous prattle as they answered his call. From inside the ship came morbid chattering cries and a hideous racket of heckling screams; then like rising colonies of bats whirling, spiraling and taking to wing, the Dark Forces flushed as a clamoring cloud of countless, incalculable numbers.

So many they resembled a bleak windswept swarm of railing insanity; they filled darkened companionways and emerged from rotted holes in the hull. Swirling and soaring from unsecured hatches and rusted-out places, from every nook and cranny of the resurrected freighter, screeching jabber-laughter shrill as the wail of a banshee and bone-chilling as the cry of a cat, they boiled into the sky...

The Dark Forces

...And in a festering, blistering plague, They came.

Half-human, half-scorpion, they were hideous creatures the size of a man. Beneath a tainted slime they were cloaked with black chitin armor tinged with iridescent boiled-lobster orange, their legs sheathed with ragged barbs fixed with hooked talon-shaped claws. Their scorpion carcasses had fiendish tails that were upturned in segmented arches tipped with aculeate telsons that inflicted venomous, lethal stings.

Ulcerated with open dripping sores their humanoid faces were festered and ugly weeping puss of leprosy and pox, their hair long, scraggly and foul, caked with filth—just plain nasty. Rotted and sloughing, their skin was necrotic and gray-green with lips that were swollen or chapped, cracked and bleeding; and they glared from eyes that were sunken and dark, their faces drawn and strained with the ashen pallor of death. They had runny noses and rotted lion's teeth squared with lethal incisors, six-inch canines that resembled saber-tooth cats; and their mouths were all plagued with the milky paste and decay of neglect.

But most disparaging was their twelve-foot wingspans and their ability to fly. Transparent and brittle as cellophane glass with dark blood pumping through the veins, they buzzed then soared saturating the gloom and filling the clouds on black-veined dragonfly wings. With hideous bloodshot-red eyes they made a god-hating racket as they swarmed like a vat of spilled red-speckle black paint staining the sky on wings vibrating so fast they sounded like countless dead branches rattling in a gale.

Scarred and disfigured in those depths of unremitting fire they were molded with chitin and devoid of emotion or soul. Unreasoning and unfeeling lieges of his namesake, and taloned and deadly, they soared upward with netherworld villainy in an inconceivable churning maelstrom. They were adherents, the self-evident manifestation of unharnessed devastation willfully following a darkness more overpowering than the deepest most unimaginable hole.

Marshaling and amassing they were the embodiment of unprincipled vice, dysfunction and shame as they spiraled and wound cackling ungodly curses and depraved abject wailing screams. A bleak swarm of unholy aberrant wretchedness, the Dark Forces were sickness and misery, and all that is lost. The quintessence of black-hearted intent bound for revenge, millions upon millions of them... they were a wretched, derelict, despoiling dark wind.

The mud rise—

Apprehensively the Renoloi and Pilgrims watched the ghost ship as the swarming Dark Forces continued their exodus from her bowels. Spilled ink blotting the sky, millions of them gathered above the 'Queen' as an ever-increasing cloud of black and rattling wings.

And as the people watched, Wilson recited:

"Then the dragon was angry with the woman, and went off to make war on the rest of her offspring, on those who keep the commandments of God and bear testimony to Jesus. And he stood on the sand of the sea." (Rev. 12: 17 RSV)

Beneath them—

The mud began vibrating and sifting as it changed color and texture, then scattering and regathering, altering and winnowing it transformed; getting lighter. Muck to sloppy dirt to small grains, still sifting and changing; their attention shifting... the sky, the ground, again up, then down ...not knowing what was happening. As far as the eye could see, winnowing, drying, and more tan... unexplainably it turned to a desert of sand.

Motioning with an arm, "Form ranks," Lent ordered, "form ranks!"

Lances, axes, archers, twibils, flails, pitchforks and swords, Renoloi and Pilgrims with their melange of weapons responded as a unified force surrounding and shielding the children within their ranks. Inside the formation Tian, Seana and others gathered the small ones into a protective covey as they crouched near what was before the mud-rise island and now was a hummock of sand.

Warriors prepared, surveying the skies.

Like unfurling ribbons formations of Dark Forces emerged from their churning black mass unfolding as spinneret indigo lines, then rose in the canopy's gloom in a deepening, gathering whirlpool sky. Expanding, they spread out and swirled around the dead ship resembling opaque shadows that snaked through the clouds simultaneously cursing, wailing and shrieking miserable screams of banshee jabber-laughter as they darted on rattling dragonfly wings. A fast-moving phantasmagoria of pitch with sickness in their eyes, they wound and soared gnashing their teeth and clacking talon-shaped claws, preparing to attack.

On deck, at the bow—

Saber in hand, eyes narrowed, stained chipped boxer's teeth biting the stub of cigar, Smith drooled repugnance and spittle as he turned his wrist grinding the tip of his saber deeper into the slate-gray deck, shedding sparks. Widening his stance his black spit-polished boots bulged stretching the laces until the eyelets tore loose and the seams and soles ripped... and fleshy, clawed toes emerged.

The sand rise—

Uneasy, watching as they soared skirting the rim of the distant boundary, Lent observed, "Can't even count 'em."

Eyes following the swarm Reed considered grimly, "1839 to 1876... ever heard of George Armstrong Custer?"

"No," Lent answered matter-of-fact.

Allowing just the briefest glimpse, then back at the gathering horde, "Probably just as well."

"There's sure a lot of 'em."

"Sioux enough," Reed nervously half-joked.

Still scanning, "Even with your weapon I don't know if we can win this one," the youth admitted.

"Maybe so; maybe not," the other conceded.

P.T. chimed in, "I'm with you Lent. There does appear to be quite a lot of them." Kalo looked at the dwarfs—and Wilson blinked twice. She didn't say a word.

"Sure does," Reed agreed glancing down, checking the pulse laser, and, "—ah *shit!*"

"—Shit what?" Lent asked unnerved by his tone.

"Fuel cells are gone." When he said *that*, even Ames looked.

"Gone," Lent echoed, "are you kidding—empty?" His eyes were getting bigger. "Quit screwing around. This ain't the time..."

"—No joke, kid. Serious as a hangman's noose."

"You're out of ammo?" Lent swallowed, but the saliva stuck in his throat.

With little more to fight with than resolve and a determined expression, Reed looked back at the accumulating Dark Forces. "Yeah, empty." He tossed the weapon aside as he drew the knife from his belt sheath. "Guess we'll just have to make do," flipping it with a hand as he focused on the circling swarm.

Lent stared leaking disbelief, scuffing sand with his foot. "A knife—are you nuts? What good's a piddling stupid knife against them?"

First eyeing the swarm, "Seen worse odds, kid," then the knife, "Doc and me been in tighter spots." With that Kalo looked at Ames; even they seemed worried.

Lent said it for them. "Reed, this time you really have lost it."

Mulling it over, nibbling his lip, "Yeah, could be."

Eagerly snatching their slingshots from their back pockets P.T. and Wilson chimed in unison, "We'll help."

"What 'cha gonna do," Lent asked snidely, "shoot 'em with marbles and jacks?"

Reed quickly interceded on their behalf, and in no uncertain terms, almost hostile, "Don't do that," he warned. "I told you before, don't underestimate them —and don't *ever* belittle them, kid." Then to the dwarfs: "P.T., how much ammo you got?"

Taken down a notch, Lent snapped, "You're all nuts."

Ignoring him P.T. promptly asked, "Reed, would you like our help?"

Reed knelt looking from one to the other, eye to eye, "Yes, P.T.— Wilson, will you help us?" A direct question.

Beaming P.T. blinked. "Certainly we'll help, because there are a lot of them."

Loading his slingshot Wilson concurred, "Most definitely, Phineas Taylor, there are quite a lot of them."

Watching as the Dark Forces amassed to an indefinable, seemingly insurmountable army, and exhaling exasperation Lent almost gasped, "*Sho—oot*, this is hopeless."

"There's always hope," both dwarfs corrected at the same time; and somehow the words and their voices kind of hung there, floating unexplainably somewhere in the back of Ames' mind.

Just words… and they watched the expanding swarm.

A forsaken place—

Clasping the crushed rail, he sneered shifting his weight at the prow of the 'Queen', muttering a deep throaty growl. "Kill them."

Smoke curls slipping from his misshapen lips, he leaned back bracing his outstretched arms, filling his lungs and expanding his chest as his eyes drifted up. His torso enlarged and the uniform buttonholes ripped scattering the buttons on deck. And now exposed, his neck and chest looked mottled and bruised, not really skin anymore, something else, almost like hide with wandering curly gray hair, and scales ever so slightly tinged iridescent magenta.

Clenching his teeth on the stub of cigar he let wisps of smoke slide from his lips and get lost in the mist. Focusing again through mean narrowed eyes showing traces of red, he watched them, despised them. Glowering he leaned forward and growled; then his head rolled back with his scream as he roared...

"...Take them —*Kill them all!*"

The storm—

Leaching through the upper rim of the boundary the eclipsed sun's violet corona bled blue-black shadows that wafted with the dismal clouds as the vortex revolved in a darkening sky; flowing and cascading, one blending with another in opaque waves. The core of the canopy was a torpid revolving tornado, like looking out from the inside, as formidably dense as it was dark. Surrounding the plain the storm boundary churned with unseen, unknown fury, its temperament intense enough to capture their thoughts without them being aware. Above it enclosed them within the storm's mysterious veil, the canopy growing ever-darker... scrolling nature's handiwork of supernatural design.

In the saturnine sky lightning fried static-charge lines that scattered the gloom with crackling sudden-vanish light, then sizzled like crooked vipers chasing dying embers. Transient ball lightning seared from horizon to horizon streaking through the clouds with fireball flares and screeching hellfire whistles that dissolved and plummeted through the dense atmosphere. Thunderclaps sprayed slamming wave after wave, rattling the landscape like a drumskin of sand... all the while the boundary poured in charcoal and rain.

Then gradually the vortex in the sky began slowly to open like the lens of a camera incrementally gathering more light. Still revolving, little by little it churned growing larger and more defined... revealing an unworldly 'Hole in the Sky'.

Out there—

A swarm of rabid bees, the Dark Forces amassed around and above the 'Marine Sulphur Queen' mustering in sinuous formations, moving then gathering, then spreading out. From a distance they appeared to ooze like a pour of black pigment soaking the overcast, resembling angry wicked snakes that wound as they crawled the sky. Then, fixed on them, the snakes flushed.

"Here they come!" someone yelled.

Spiraling and circling —millions of black scorpion-wasps— the Dark Forces railed, drumming, and then plunged dive-bombing in attack formations reminiscent of aerial warplanes. Wings folded flat, talons spread wide, fangs bared drooling saliva that flicked away in the wind—swooping at blistering speeds they targeted fighters on the ground. Intent on slaughter the heinous cretins dove upon the resolute band of warriors standing ready below.

Holding their breath, first wave closing in—

A few hundred against millions —impossible odds— virtually assured Smith of certain victory. The master of deception had bided his time, waited for this, the optimal moment that now seemed inescapably within his grasp. With loathing eyes and nefarious scowl, he watched from the bow of the ship he had requisitioned from the sea eons ago.

Smith:

Now you'll pay for your defiance and dissension, Ames, for your impertinence and impetuousness. You'll regret your poor judgment and misplaced loyalty. More than brash obstinance, how brazen and pompous you are to refuse deference to the supreme ruler of Darkness. I am Lucifer... greater, more powerful, more resplendent. Above all others.

And Tian and Seana—you worthless wenches, no more than transformed harlots—what pathetic little trollops with supple newborn squabs nestled in your arms. And Lent—such an auspicious punk whom the disciple failed to take with his unfortunate misstep. Surely that's what went wrong; that was it, and not Ames' introspection or ability to solve problems. Ames, what a pain in the ass—simply fucked worthless with an unnatural penchant for luck.

And P.T. Barnum and Wilson—I know you and yours also—cocky little brats who just can't quit meddling, always interfering with your bravado and attitude —and what demeanor, acting all holier-than-thou. This will be the last time you pip-squeak sorry-ass midgets interfere with my plans, a regal scheme of grandiose design.

"—Incoming!" Three seconds out.

And last but not least, most pivotal, Kalo—slight bitch who never says much, you ungrateful little strumpet. Of all the pathetics, the singular key—you must be dispatched at any—at all cost. It seems like forever you've been a thorn in my side, but here and now I'll remedy that. I'll fix you, you bothersome little whore, just a trivial slip of a tramp. This time, this day, you surely will die.

Smith knew her purpose and niche in the riddle, entwined within the definitive, ultimate puzzle. In the darkness and mystery of the circular storm, a pitiful handful of them could never withstand the glorious onslaught of his grandiloquent acolytes. A few hundred against his beauties… *no—fucking—way.*

Watching, glowering, "Take them," he growled again. *"Kill them all!"*

Then with villainy of consummate evil Smith inhaled a slow rasping breath and whispered, "This hour is mine; the harvest-war for the feeble and faithless shaded with a cloistered sun and blood-red moon… at last, has finally begun."

On the plain—

Arrows flew from the sand and stuck in the sky piercing scorpion armor as Renoloi archers unleashed the first fusillade. Amid the cackling frenzy of screeching jabber-laughter and shrill banshee screams almost a hundred folded then spiraled on dead-dragonfly wings. But even though the first barrage diminished their ranks the toll was insignificant, a meaningless sacrifice dwarfed by sheer numbers. There were millions of them.

Vastly outnumbered, Pilgrims and Renoloi fought valiantly, avoiding the demons as they swooped down upon them, a second salvo of arrows whistling into fast-moving shadows in the darkened frenetic sky. Soaring and diving, the Dark Forces flew in unending waves blackening the canopy and circling with the wind. They were wanton villainy and despicable bloodlust, the dregs of perdition's gutters and the scum of damnation: addicts and drunkards, liars and thieves, adulterers, homosexuals and a plethora of others. They were all forms of evil and everything wrong from the kingdom of waste, Satan's disciples, the adherents of Hell. But more than that, from all time, and for all time... they were The Lost.

Screeching and dancing on air the Dark Ones reveled in their temporary freedom from bondage in the canals of the damned and the infernal regions of a place somewhere else. Having entered willingly their servitude was forever sealed with a barter that gave Darkness their essence, and now bound to their taskmaster for eternity theirs was a transitory and deceptive freedom that would be short-lived; for they were destined merely to serve as unwitting, untethered puppets. They were pawns in a chess game of souls.

P.T. Barnum and Wilson stepped forward.

Fury of motion: confusion and black. The sky was saturated with heckling laughter and rakish dark screams. Lightning burned rabid fingers of fire as thunder crashed —and the storm boundary roared!

Spinning and spiraling—

Transparent and gyrating their wings buzzed at hummingbird-speed then folded flat, swooping in for the kill. Claws braced they came from the clouds into the line of fire, fangs bared, cancerous lips peeled all the way back; but with implacable sickness their pathetic heartbroken eyes revealed the pain of perpetual misery. Armed with venom and death they killed on command.

Third volley—

From the hummock and sand plain arrows penetrated the bawdy uproar of fingernail-on-chalkboard laughter and heinous screeching banshee cries, more cretins plummeting when they again bombarded the warriors skimming just above their heads plucking them from the ground. The Dark Forces took Pilgrims and Renoloi at random, snatching them, ripping muscle from bone, teeth and claws shredding their flesh scattering pieces and meat in bloodsplashes of wine-colored mists. More than two dozen warriors were lost in the first fleeting breaths of terrifying headspin attack and black-violent wind.

Lances jerked demons from the air while twibils and axes hacked with gush-winds of blood, pitchforks spearing—swords flayed. But they were overrunning—uncountable, overwhelming. Like bats on the wing in a Halloween sky they filled the dim and dark spaces inundating the twilight. They were everywhere—too many, overpowering.

Swooping at shoulder height the half-human ghouls lashed out ripping off heads and eviscerating bowels with their razor-like claws, or stabbing with the stingers affixed in their tails. It was a bloodbath of carnage, terror and screams: taken warriors, shattered chitin, splashing entrails and slop. Sand drenched in crimson and gore.

Stabbed six or more times as a gang landed on him, a Pilgrim went down beneath the buffeting brittle noise of scorpion hulls and buzzing dragonfly wings. Ruthlessly they ripped off both arms and tore open his chest spilling intestines before taking to wing dragging and stretching his entrails like sticky confetti streamers and wet strings.

Swallowed in barbaric savagery a Renoloi warrior shielded her face managing only one swing within the frenzied cloud of raking claws and fangs —then they were gone— as was her flesh. She crumpled as scrambled dislocated bones, shredded muscle and intestinal slop —then a flush of red sauce that gushed onto the sand— and in the jumble of blood and death her scalp slid from her skull like a drenched scarlet mop. Lying there, savagely mangled and overcome with shock, her lidless eyes still seemed to stare with an expression of being lost somewhere between here and there, trespassing within the realm of oblivion.

P.T. Barnum and Wilson got ready.

Drumming wingbeats and bloodlust letting death and shredded lives, the Dark Forces were vicious beyond reason and gruesome beyond comprehension. Their brutality knew no scope and their carnage had no bounds. They killed murderously with wanton lunacy, stripping flesh from the bone and chewing bones into bits. Crazed miscreants, unsatisfied with simply killing they ravaged their prey.

Armed with marbles and jacks, P.T. and Wilson fired.

Their unorthodox ammo bullet-burned with incredible, inexplicable force cleanly punching holes through one, then another —dozens— of winging, crisscrossing black scorpion-wasps. Time and again cat's-eyes, *whap-zinged,* through faces and hulls —blowing through one, then on through the next— and jacks ripped ragged little holes in cretins with humanoid heads. Like autumn leaves falling in a blustery overcast gray, Dark Ones corkscrewed from the sky, dropping languidly or plunging and spiraling in steep dives. But the clouds were bundled maggots, and the sky was still full of them. More warriors were lost.

In the rush Lent noticed the damage the dwarfs did, and hacking through an incoming he marveled, *unbelievable* —but only for an instant— things were chaotic. Tight with tension Reed ducked and avoided then swiped with the knife opening it gullet to rectum as a screecher buzzed over his head. That Dark One was down, spilling its entrails in a trailing gut-dump.

Double take —quick— Lent killed one as Kalo did three. Ames and Reed each another; but there were too many, unending clouds of them. Flashes of black —blistering speed— they were everywhere.

As the archer drew back unseen shadows swept in low from behind, the first decapitating her with a spew of blood that flushed from her neck. Rigid, she just stood there on shock-stiffened legs, then suddenly vanished in a wad of chitin and gaggle of dragonfly wings. More wingbeats and a deadly ravel of claws buckling her knees, her raped skeleton collapsing with broken ribs and dangling meat as her insides slid out, then a plash on the ground. From the sand the shredded Renoloi issued soured coppery steam, the raw stench of carnage.

P.T. Barnum shot a marble—'Just Plain' Wilson did a jack, their slingshots bullet-burning with barking hypervelocity chronicling the dazzling speed of their simple and singular weapons. Rounds rocketed with astonishing celerity, laser beam bright, razorblade straight, sonic-sharp —and scalpel deadly. Like shooting straight lines of meteoric death through wicked clouds of airborne rats, marbles and jacks ripped from one through the next and the next —undeviating, ad infinitum. The dwarfs were lethal, and baffling.

A Pilgrim rushed the hummock shoving a Renoloi aside as one dove for her and he countered with his pitchfork. But —no time— the villain careened and rolled ramming him with its telson, blood spurting from his chest. Impact and momentum snatched the hapless warrior from the prominence flinging him into the air where the swarm instantly tore him to pieces; both arms and legs yanked from his somersaulting corpse, his head vanishing in a mania of claws, colliding chitin and black-veined dragonfly wings. Still tumbling fifty feet overhead four more blood-thirsties latched onto his torso and ripped the ribcage apart —a popped water balloon— his lifeless half-shell burst.

Shocked, from the hummock the frightened woman watched as he died up there; and not thinking she again sprang to her feet —upright, vulnerable— another wisp of shadow and wings cutting her in half. Her torso tumbled aside —another screecher flashing past— as her hips and legs crumpled like severed marionette limbs.

Sixty feet away—*incoming!* Leaping and thrusting as it came, the Renoloi drove her lance into it —colliding head-on— talons slicing through her, both instantly gone.

Weapon ready, the Pilgrim was moving in a defensive half-crouch as death swooped from behind; he never saw it coming. Nearby an arrow sped on an interception course, the Renoloi tracking as it flew; another crisscrossing from her side, the impact sliced her in two.

Coming in low, then diving and buckling —P.T. shot another— it spiraled and caved in an explosive gritty splat. Cretins fell from the sky, warriors were snatched from the ground; the slaughter went on… and crimson saturated the plain.

On the sand hummock—

Lent slashed through one's belly spewing entrails from its torn-open hide; then another, blood still dripping from both blades. *Come on... get some of this* —and the crunch and wet splatter— its face splitting as the twibil razed through peeling halves and intestines —then the wet-slam of slop— guts splashing against his chest.

With only an instant to breathe and glancing at Reed he yelled, "There's too many of 'em," as he ducked wielding the pike deflecting another. Nerves twisted to old brittle-brown wire, he groused, "This is hopeless."

Alongside him Wilson dodged two more piping up, reminding, "Lent, there's always hope. Hope is eternal."

Within earshot, it was then, in the tension and confusion, somehow, strangely the little man's words rattled around in his head, and Ames remembered...

Out there, on the plain—

The ghost ship 'Queen' crawled closer. Still glaring, saber in one hand, crushed rail in the other, Smith stood at the bow clasping the rusted steel so tightly it buckled and crumpled as he squeezed. Flexing his powerful forearms and biceps his shirt sleeves split to his armpits revealing magenta scales that freckled the back of his hands, and his fingers grew longer, more pointed and thick as his contorted nails changed; they crawled out with claws. Scraping the hilt he turned the sword slowly and intently in his mutating hand.

Gutturally he growled snapping the rail in two, his other hand grinding the saber deeper into the metallic flesh of the deck. Mournfully the foghorn blared as though the dead ship had suffered the wound.

Words rattling around in his head—

...There's always hope, Ames thought again; *hope is eternal*. Taking a few quick steps back he kicked sand out of the way and found it, just a corner sticking out, the rest somewhere below. Dropping to his knees and scooping with both hands he pushed more sand aside, then carefully following the outline, tracing with trembling fingers, ran the rim of the lid and dug for the hasp. Nervous with excitement, he jerked and the lid opened.

Somehow it seemed familiar. It had always seemed familiar — the wooden chest— it was hope, and there is always hope. Hope is eternal. That's why it always seemed so familiar.

Inside the weathered chest, tucked away in a corner were three glimmering minutiae; all alone there, just trifling little twinkles, scintilla of starlight. No more than small sparkles at first; now revealed, preciously, mysteriously, each became warm, and little by little, gathering warmth… they began to glow.

"Bravo, Mr. Ames," Wilson applauded, "you're finally getting the hang of it."

"Indeed," P.T. chimed enthusiastically, "he is catching on."

Once Ames lifted the lid of the wooden chest, P.T. Barnum and the still-smiling Wilson each took one step forward, then one to the side —and when they did, each divided— and the twins became four.

"Well—don't—that—just—beat—all," Reed muttered.

They did it again and the four became eight, until quickly there were dozens, then hundreds, then thousands of them. Each was identical in every detail to all the rest: dark blue watch caps, red and blue plaid flannel shirts, bibs overalls with cuffs primly rolled up over black, laced work boots—children's size twelve.

Ames wondered, *what's going on?*

Magic, Tian thought.

While Kalo beamed, *and so much more.*

"Incoming!" Another —dive and roll— then Reed was back on his feet. Still dodging screechers he had to ask, "Who are you guys?"

The original Barnum grinned. "We told you before, P.T. Barnum and 'Just Plain' Wilson."

He ducked again, then quickly got up. "—Nah bullshit; I mean *really.*"

"We're workers," Wilson informed, repeating what he and his twin had told them once before.

P.T. Barnum again reminded, "Anything and everything. Anything that isn't finished…"

"—And everything that has to be done," Wilson finished, without actually telling.

"Don't give me tha—" but he couldn't get it out —had to duck— another fly-by just missed.

Multiplying exponentially bustling dwarfs were quickly scampering everywhere—with a dangerous sky still full of wingbeats and skimming dregs masked in orange and black. Waist-high pandemonium running aground, the dwarfs continued multiplying and spreading out fielding the plain until there were far too many to count. They fought fearlessly killing Dark Ones, shooting marbles and jacks, zapping black dragonfly bats that fell from dark boiling clouds —crashing dead just like that.

Kneeling on the sand, finally understanding the meaning of the box, Ames' eyes sparkled reflecting the diminutive light. The longer and more closely he watched the more warmth the starbeams emanated, and the brighter they became as hope unraveled unlacing her mystery in the sparkling tendrils that rose... spiraling and climbing upward. Vibrant intense yellow, perfect powerful blue, vehement irascible red... Pure crystalline Light.

Unexplainably and unblemished, the three flawless primary colors from which all others originate, spiraled like strands of celestial dust, glittering fingers ascending in a pirouette dance. Shimmering, they twirled and wound twinkling in curlicue ribbons. Sparkling—Spellbinding—Dazzling.

Glimmering and pulsating the phenomenon lights reflected miniature starfire explosions in Ames' eyes as they whorled and rose, spiraled and entwined then hovered and unwound coursing and cascading upward again. In this darkened place they shone like flickering boreal flames, expanding and growing and glowing more brightly as they climbed, ever upward. Shimmering fingers of holiness, the beautiful veins of light ascended and reached for...

...The 'Hole in the Sky'.

CHAPTER TWENTY

Sparkling tendrils of light…

…Ascended from the old wooden chest, climbing into the sky. Momentarily the luminous ribbons vacillated and hovered then entwined and burst in detonations of shimmering starlight; clear, dazzling ethereal light. Luminescent radiance flashed down upon the warriors making their stand on the hummock, while high in the sky the canopy revolved with a spiraling, widening gateway of light. The core of the circular storm continuing slowly and majestically to open, glowing like a beacon, as a spear of bright light began to shine through. Power from Beyond.

Turning, Wilson looked up and venerably announced, "The Light of the Legends."

Above them, The Light—

Constantly flowing and changing, clear to colors, and again to clear, sparkling flashes of starfire whisked throughout the mysterious corridor. Ribboned with texture and motion and all the colors of vast faraway nebulae clouds, it was rimmed with white sizzling fire. Remarkable and beautiful, it was esoteric splendor of ebullient starbursts and shimmering light that cascaded from color to clear, to color, to white, over and over with fascinating, dizzying repetition. Unending meteoric streaks and pinpoints of pulsing light; it was a glimmering hypnotic entity.

Suspended above the battleland the undulating light formed a glowing circular corridor; and there, scintillating and singular, the luminous corridor remained. Powerful, viable and majestic, conceived beyond the limits of mortality it was a pulsating, breathing entity and living texture... the essence of divinity.

Floating in the sky, above the battleland dazzling starburst of quasars and throbbing pulsars beat in rhythm with the heartbeat of the universe illuminating the hummock in ethereal light. The dismal gloom was gone, those on the sand rise aglow; Tian, Ames and the others bathed in light brighter than a sun, yet it did not blind them, more clear than crystal, more pure than spring rain...

Then unexpectedly wind whooshed in their faces and puffed through their hair, and they all felt it —*a rush.*

...Splashing into the cosmos Legend Light streaked through the heavens crossing the vastness of space as it vanished somewhere out there, a realm somewhere beyond. Power from the limitless reaches of infinity, it flared through time and deep space more swiftly than anything in all creation, blazing with velocity surpassing the speed of light, reaching out to and binding the very edge of reality and the mysteries and wonders and miracles beyond. Melded with tensile and endowed with authority greater than all things in all places, it was possessed with prowess and splendor surpassing the providence or might of any world. A passageway fusing the ends of time.

The sand hummock—

As he fought Ames thought he could hear it —hear them— very faintly at first. He believed he could hear it —hear them— from somewhere far, far away. Looking around, the others were still fighting but were listening as well; they could hear it too. More certain now, he looked for them, because he was sure now; from somewhere unknown there was music, a song, very faint, as though sung by a choir, from a place far away... through the 'Hole in the Sky'.

With the background din of battle noise, the refrain continued growing louder and more resonant, and the music —their music— seemed familiar somehow. It seemed so familiar, so beautiful... and the music, their voices rose to a chorus.

They were coming...

From within the luminous passageway resonated the distant rumble of hoofbeats —and voices, their chorus— a wondrous triumphant song. The music grew louder and more clear, propelled onward by spirited horseflesh and unshod galloping hooves. It was the refrain of mounted warriors clad in lorica segmentata armor with their broadswords drawn for the impending campaign.

He could hear them thundering from infinity through the shining corridor, boldly riding to battle, gallant warriors attired in white armor and Light. Angelic gladiators on magnificent white Percherons being led by the Centurion, they were the hand of deliverance, dispatched to intervene. From within Legend Light their song coalesced with the reverberating cadence of hoofbeats as they came to combat the onrush of railing black-scorpion wings.

Lathered and running hard the animals were massive and muscled, rippling in waves of intense strength with every movement they made. At full gait, they kicked up winds of whirling flame shredding the darkness with their ponderous stride and solid gleaming hooves. Their breasts and thighs were extraordinarily thick, forelocks and manes swept in waves upon their necks, tails long and flowing, forged of beauty and grace. Their eyes were large and round, the virtue and color of aquamarine; and high-spirited within hackamores of woven satin braid, all were purest white, unbounded and powerful, possessed of the unicorn's spirit and grandeur. A fury of hooves with the soul of The Lamb.

...Time Warriors...

Unworldly and magnificent, the White Riders were Roman legions with breastplate cuirasses of lorica segmentata armor, tasseled helmets and visors polished to the luster of glory. Warriors of biblical times, they were garbed in capes of flowing linen with tassets and sandals, their waistbands of wide harness leather bracing broad scabbards —all brandishing mighty battle swords— straight as beams of sunlight, sharp as the limit of creativity and forged in the benediction of mankind. Cavaliers proud and tall —blades held high— their gleaming weapons drawn for battle.

Summoned by the Light they winged through the luminous living passageway, Legend corridor rumbling with echoes of hoofbeats and fury, their forces splashing fire through the cosmos, showering flames in their wake. Then raising clouds of shimmering starlight the mighty Percherons appeared conveying the Legions of Angels —trailing flames— with broadswords of power and fire and Light!

...The Mystic Army thundered from Heaven!

Seeing them made him angry—

No furious, and seething he drooled spittle past the stub of cigar. *Fuck 'em, this time they're mine,* Smith sneered gurgling a throaty growl as he cast the crushed chunk of rail aside, clattering across the deck until it struck something metal and stopped.

Watching them, his ire caused his brow to furrow then attenuate, and his face grew misshapen, becoming elongated, more narrow. "Fuck 'em. Not thiss time." It was almost a hiss.

Led by the Centurion—

The Mystic army emerged from Legend corridor wielding swords of fiery light, mounted legions and rumbling war chariots stirring billowing flames and whirlwinds of ethereal fire that trailed them across the sky. Ready for battle the Time Warriors arrived.

Breaking ranks and fanning out warriors and charioteers flew toward the canopy as others swept down onto the plain. Harbingers of the Lamb, their wheels and hoofbeats rumbled the gristmill of an earthquake as they charged onto the field of battle with the unbounded fury of unshod hooves and bright wide eyes of aquamarine. Wave after wave, whinnying reparation and snorting rage more spread out in the sky pounding starburst explosions in formations of mighty, supernatural thunderbolt speed.

Stampeding forth, scattering sand to ribbons of flame, war chariots clattered onto the battlefield, their spoked wheel fellies enveloped in spiraling whirlwind clouds gouging ruts in the ground that left fire in their wake. Tandem, teams of mighty Percherons harnessed with power and fury drew the armored chariots as they thundered above and upon a world of sand within a storm of savage, dismal gray.

Evil as a sardonic thought—

Clamoring onto the battleland from the 'Marine Sulphur Queen' the Dark Forces scuttled as an aggregate mob that was hostile and bleak overshadowed by the boundary's wall, drawn up from below as it boiled to a mountainous cloud of dark wind and flesh-eating, lightless sand. A black scourge, they rushed full-speed toward the white legions —onward and dreadful— Hell's malevolent army.

Running and leaping—hair wild, tangled and matted with curdled vomitus and malady of disease. Jumping and bounding—crusted with pestilence and sickness and pockmarked by the wretchedness of famine. Flying—skimming over the battlefield with petulant discord of hatred and congealed plagues. Drooling—the regurgitated stench of despair, peering with the wicked denial of deception and lies from red-glowing bloodshot-dead eyes.

A duststorm, the landscape was blotted from sight by the armored half-human cretins, their numbers the cohesive maladies of ages long since past. Dispatched with the menace of arthropod venom they were the castoffs and vile dregs of contempt; and within them desolation and emptiness poured over the terrain transported in an obsidian cloud clattering the rattling drone of dragonfly wings.

From the 'Hole in the Sky'—

Armed with purity and valor —White Warriors and great Percherons— the Mystic army still came. Singing their celestial battle refrain they continued to appear from the spiraling corridor as they swept over the land shedding fire with hooves and wheels and splashing flames through the sky.

So it was…

The unending rumble of rushing hooves carried the riders of the storm from an unknown realm to the battle arena on incredible mounts snorting crimson and rage. A thunder of justice —enduring, unequivocal riders and charioteers— the great army rolled forth trailing sparkling fire in the sky and scattering sandspray beneath their wheels as they clattered onto the plain enveloping the battle arena in spiraling whirlwinds of flame.

…As they charged!

* * *

Once the Mystic army arrived…

…Legend corridor began slowly to close, the layered clouds continuing to revolve, as the canopy grew darker again. The deepening storm strengthened and howled with hurricane strength, the canopy traced with ball lightning flares, lightning etching wizard-white lines, the boundary a fury of windstorm and sand. Winding even more ominously and intensely the sky seemed to stretch the shadows of the eclipsed sun creating the aspect of slow retrograde motion opposing the storm's circumrotation beneath an amalgam of flickering twilight sky. Lightning-flash— again thunder trumpeted and rolled, then rumbling and oscillating was carried away.

* * *

Engaging in the sky…

…Shattering —*crackling*— razors of flame!

The Mystic army met the Dark Forces in a battle of rampant violence as both armies swept through the clouds and collided. Circling, soaring and diving: waves of razor-light swords, lethal segmented tails, mighty unshod hooves, lion teeth and talon-shaped claws. Half-human cretins propelled off-course in death spirals like a dogfight of 'Zeroes' and 'P51 Mustangs', orange-tinged warplanes careening and plummeting on biplane-dragonfly wings —and beautiful white horses and riders tumbling from the sky.

Screaming maniacally, a golem viciously latched onto the breast of a steed clawing and ripping deep gashes in its hide. Counteracting, the great horse fiercely sank its teeth in the ghoul's neck breaking its grip and flipping it in the air as the Mystic's sword sliced it in two, both halves falling into the dim illumination below. Brisket bleeding freely, hooves raking fire, the Percheron angrily snorted and reared, then with wide eyes it bounded into the clouds with the stalwart rider. Another soulless cretin was coming.

Below, on the plain—

The opposing armies stormed onward with the charge.

Hair flaring wildly, features contorted, the man-scorpions scuttled over the ground or skimmed just above it on black-veined drumming wings. Rising against their adversaries, faces drawn with misery and insanity, claws ripping sand pitching bursts of blizzard-debris, they rushed the oncoming glowing white Mystics and Percheron waves.

From the other direction the riders and great horses pounded massive depressions with their ground-shaking footfalls splashing translucent detonations of reparation and flame. Scattering sandspray from their broad muscled breasts mounts and riders rode boldly at full gait toward the maniacal jabber-laughter of rancid screams. In front of them endless clamoring Dark Forces were undeviating, mindlessly howling as they scrambled toward them and their charging, unnumbered ranks. Hooves crushing fire, galloping over the plain mounted warriors and war chariots thundered and rolled, until flying and bounding into their onrushing foe the black-orange horde met them head-on...

—The forces colliding, crashing, battering and smashing!

...Crushing human faces and shattering wings. Horseflesh and hooves plowed into the vermin, trampling them, hulls ripping and splattering, entrails splashing the ground with pieces and muck, deviants cracked open with grisly crunching thuds. But the dregs lashed back drawing blood, sinking their fangs into meat and bone, claws gouging armor and savaging horseflesh, muscular breasts and flanks smeared red. Stumbling and falling in the violent impact mighty horses and riders went down. It was a ferocious collision of opposing armies and intense chaos of head-on crashing force where weapons flashed with guillotine edges of flaming bright light flinging body parts and puss, while saber-toothed claws and fangs viciously slashed back.

Broadswords striking with shatter-bright flames seared through the insane frenzy of raking talons and lethal telsons that arched and stabbed with rattlesnake speed and poisonous bungee-stick spikes. A clash of torn flesh and broken carcasses falling helter-skelter on a landscape of madness: rearing and striking horses crunching demons' backs, armor and telsons, clear brittle wings, determined wide eyes, virulent force, shattered bodies and splatter of dark sticky blood.

Above, in the sky—

In front and behind them —on either side, all around them— white warriors galloped through the clouds as man-scorpion ghouls railed on the wind. The slate-colored canopy was a whirling speckled contrast of bright and dark aeronautics with an uncountable swarm of evil black cretins and mare's-tails riders spiraling and diving like squadrons of warplanes. The sky was bedlam and motion, too many to count, too much confusion to track as locusts and riders spun and attacked. Aloft was a churning backdrop sullen with anger, a boiling gray canvas filled with spiraling, soaring combatants of white and slime-covered black.

Below, on the plain—

Bundled in a bloodthirsty mob, pushing, stabbing and clawing the man-cretins pressed forward with the unreasoning malice of vacant minds. Crawling and raw, the battlefield was overrun with scrambling villainy that refused to stop. They leaped and plunged headlong into flashing broadswords that sliced through them, and fell beneath chariot wheels and hooves that crushed them; fiery blades and crunching wheels that left death and waste in their wake.

A Mystic charged as a golem lunged, his weapon cauterizing the demon with shatter-crackling light; but swooping in low another took the rider through the back. The impact staggered the Mystic causing the Percheron to stumble —hooves throwing sand— both rider and attacker going under in the crush —while intrepid P.T. Barnums and 'Just Plain' Wilsons winged 'deadeye' marbles and 'missile-streak' jacks.

Violence of the head-on crashing armies ignited the battleland with intense saturated fury —colliding forces, confusion, weapons, dark and light— both front lines drenched in red as broadswords swept with shattering razors of flame. Claws ripping ruthlessly, stingers spearing flesh, dazzling white crashed into the bleakest of black in a scrambled mind-rush of hideous humanoid faces and blood-smeared saber cat jaws. There was screaming, weapons and bloodshot-dead eyes, armor spattered with crimson and yellow arthropod venom, chariot wheels flinging rooster-tails of sand — scarlet blood and white fire in the scatter and wind.

Rearing and whinnying magnificent horses raked sparkling flames of starfire pyrotechnics, meeting ferocious claws of iridescent orange-tinged black. It was a landscape gone turbid and gray, the color of tumult —red, the hue of blood— and opaque, the confusion of violence and texture of force. The warland was a melee of madness— white against black.

The dark side—

They were a coalescence of spite and macabre insanity, evil man-scorpions infused with wickedness and soulless dead eyes. Scrambling far and wide with mindless, unparalleled savagery, their talons lashed out viciously at anything that moved while their miserable faces bared fangs that sank deep savoring the blood.

The light side—

Concealed behind gleaming visors, resolve fused their ranks with courage and veracity born in the unfailing valor of determined bright eyes. Their shields and armor were smeared scarlet as great Percherons reared snorting crimson and rage, broadswords dripping with the pervasive scent of death that now hung thick in the air —and everywhere scurrying P.T. Barnums and "Just Plain" Wilsons *whap-zinging* marbles and jacks.

Slashed and bloody, many Mystics and mounts went down in the first mighty impact of combat; and torn and trampled countless Dark Ones fell. On the plain fallen riders, great horses and evil cretins' crushed leaking hulls lay among daring dwarfs and severed legs and claws abandoned as quivering dead scraps. With shrieking jabber-laughter banshee wails and garish howls filling the air — both armies still pushing forward— even more fell. Shredded wings twirled overhead and were trampled underfoot as the coppery stench of blood soaked in saturating the sand.

Both armies still colliding—

Their opposing forces crammed together, then pressed harder holding their ground —hooves, bungee-spike telsons, broadswords and claws— war chariots plowing into the waves of dark riffraff as mounted Mystics cut into their forward ranks. Refusing to yield, Dark Ones were ground under as they dove upon their adversaries, clawing at them, raking and stabbing while glimmering axle spinner blades mounted on the chariot wheel hubs twirled, sliced and hacked. Soaked with blood, the charioteers began penetrating the horde — hustling dwarfs following the rolling, grinding wheels.

Slingshots blew holes and broadswords burned them in half, but the unreasoning cretins maniacally and doggedly kept clamoring forward. Whipping telsons arched and stabbed—Mystics going down. Broadswords flashing with crackling razors of flame—Dark Ones squashed in the crush. But as soon as one fell more took its place. Millions of them, deafening calamity everywhere —insanity run rampant— the frenzy of war. They were shoulder to shoulder — impossible to breathe— wedged together so tightly the air became rank with the taste of burnt blood and puss. The battleland was a desert and sky overrun with armies of white-hornet birds and scuttling black flying rats.

Charging the rush, a chariot master reined, both enormous animals whinnying as they pushed into the onrushing mob and gaggle of claws. Lathered and red, shattering chitin and faces, heaving with their breasts and striking with their hooves, the great horses plowed into the deluge of leprous ghouls with bloodshot red eyes and segmented tails bearing death in their stab.

Quartering from above a Dark One dove at the charioteer; but with a monumental surge the Mystic reined hard to the left, the team reeling as it pulled, the chariot turning suddenly and tipping sharply bringing a wheel up from the ground. Spinning forcefully and true the upended wheel was a blur of rotating spokes and felly rimmed by sparkling flames with a whirl of axle blades in its center.

Mid-dive —no time— the man-scorpion collided with the upended wheel —blades in your face— cut to slivers in an instant its head blew up as a cloud. Sticky puss and bloody spray swirled as the hide shredded —boring through— whittling its innards to twirling wet tatters. Chopped pieces of carcass and entrails flew with the splatter while the tail, caught in the spokes, spun like a thick tearing snake then sailed into the horde—just splattering chunks and necrotic-puss blood. One wheel digging in, one still flinging blood, reining again the chariot leveled and the upended wheel slammed down crushing a cretin, the steel-ring fellies gouging deep ruts as the warrior rolled and fought on.

Within the violence and bedlam of the battleland claws gouged and telsons stabbed as swords sculpted with razors of flame. Dark Ones went down. Warriors went down. Casualties everywhere. More shrill banshee screams. Blood soaked the sand.

* * *

In the growing darkness…

…The corridor remained in the sky, glowing as it continued to diminish in size, the battle arena taking on the shades of dwindling twilight as stalwart warriors and wicked lion-faced scorpions soared.

* * *

Teeming and tangled…

…White-hornet birds and black flying rats. Black and white glided in snarls of aerial combat —circling, weaving and careening, spirals, dives and loops— fast-moving golems and warriors winging throughout a rabid canvas of gray.

The rider didn't see it coming, its telson spiking in one side, then out the other of his head. Thrown from his mount as the broadsword slipped from his hand, the Mystic tumbled toward the ground thousands of feet below. Floating, he was falling, and bounding he was smaller, one more tumble, then gone.

Another—

Whistling wind, then the buzzing getting louder, a Dark One spiraling before it banked with a side roll and dove. Without warning the Mystic's blade swept with a razor-bright light of —shattering — *crackling*— flame— flashing through its mid-line axis. The demon separating with the wind as horse and rider galloped between them;

and somewhere back there both tumbling halfshells disappeared in the confusion below.

Another rider killed a deviant —momentarily coasting before beginning to fall— then others quickly snatched it, cannibals gobbling it up. The Mystic didn't see the next attack until —*stab*— through the armor and ribs injecting venom. Involuntarily jerking, reining and pulling up short caused the gentle giant to stumble then roll falling through a cloud as the warrior slid from its back lost in washover mists of overcast gray.

Pure opportunists, vulture-villains circling and watching from above, they spiraled and descended targeting the falling Percheron's vulnerable underside. Catching then latching onto it as it plummeted they took the animal, stabbing repeatedly, claws savagely locked in its belly and flanks. Crying a pain-stricken neigh the horse's eyes glazed as death flushed its veins and the majestic creature succumbed. Still descending; rolling over one final time before they all disappeared in a cloud falling toward the plain.

Over there—

Attacking from behind a man-beast seized a rider by his shoulders clawing at his armor —*no good*— unable to get through. Wielding the broadsword the Mystic swung over his head, then behind, but the cretin evaded the blade. Both struggling, they cascaded piggyback through the strata until the scorpion's tail arched, segments locked tight, and stabbed down through the helmet. When its stinger snatched back the Mystic's arms went limp and he slumped forward onto the withers. Savoring the kill, licking its festered lips —a sudden razor-sword of flame, unexpected, from the side— severed the ghoul's thickset neck. Claws-locked-dead —an ugly blink of surprise— as a second Mystic flew by and the golem's mutated head slid loose then coasted away.

Bursting through a cloud—

Lunacy in a dive, wings lying low, the Dark One coming straight for them. Full gallop, refusing to yield, obsidian hooves pounding sky churning whorls of fire. Head on —speed and boiling wind— more momentum. Leaning forward onto the withers, blade flashing fire the warrior struck —colliding— stinger lacerating horseflesh. The scorpion's scaled-armor breast was laid wide by the razor-light as the demon's aculeate telson sank in the Percheron's chest —then through— out and up, into the Mystic. A battered tangle of torsos, wings, legs and blood all died in a gruesome collision that fell from the clouds.

The canopy spun in a whirlwind of confusion and battle: unshod hooves scattering ribbons of fire, buzzing banshee dragonfly wings, singing and heinous screeching jabber-laughter screams, a backdrop of abhorrent savagery. There were thousands —millions— too many to count.

Beneath them, dwarfs on the plain—

Dodging rumbling chariot wheels and massive unshod hooves coming down from above, the warring forces were dark armor and talons gouging holes in the land. Among the upheaval of ravaged ground, flung sand and severed body parts countless dashing P.T. Barnums and Wilsons winged bullet-burn marbles and starfire jacks.

From above the battleland was torn and burned with flashing broadswords and shrill with dying screams, confused with rushing feet, pockmarked by raking claws and overrun with the incessant rattle of dragonfly wings. It was a distorted boil of unending motion and sand-colic froth, the abrasion of an intense and violent battle.

But down here —everything, everywhere— was absorbed in the commotion of crushing destruction and the impenetrable abyss of death and confusion in a world of scattered sand… and the darkness of horrific, crawling-flesh terrified screams.

In the sky—

Soaring and scanning its necrotic face flicked puss in the wind, searching for a victim. Then—there, it spied one, its target below. Dragonfly drone to silence, wings folded flat, the black-hearted heathen swooped in for the kill.

Ponderous hooves throwing flames, the bounding Percheron bolted and rolled —and the broadsword did the rest— the Mystic hooking a heel on the horse's hip, sliding off to the side, swinging and severing the wings from the scorpion-dragonfly's back: an

Apache warrior's trick. Wrecked as a fish out of water the disabled, miscalculating golem nose-dived like a depth-charged submarine rock.

Certain to die, falling straight as a stone it spied another rider a thousand feet below. *Getting closer.* Unreasoning and evil it focused on the helmet, gray wind and speed whistling through its claws. *Almost there...* the unsuspecting rider below, watching something else, broadsword raised *...got him.*

Spl—aat!

Crashing onto the Mystic its telson lanced through a shoulder as the sword stabbed up through the ugly puss-dripping face. Killed instantly, impact hurled the warrior from his mount as both shattered saber-tooth cretin and rider plunged through the clouds.

Saturated with a contrast of black and white momentum the slate canopy swirled as they fought, too many to count, too much chaos to track. The sky was a deluge of galloping horseflesh and dingy scorpion-sting rats as Mystics and human-beasts soared. Thick and violent, the wind howled and the layered clouds churned as the storm intensified... with death skimming all directions like that.

The ghost ship—

Feet squared with his stance Smith rocked up on his toes bunching his buttocks and clenching his teeth. He hated them, despised them all. He dug his toes, the claws, into the deck; then bulging his thighs and tightening his calves distended his muscles splitting the seams of his trousers almost to his pockets. Sole torn open, the left boot was up around his ankle, the other just gone somewhere; and he didn't really care. He muttered an invective, then snarled... getting closer.

Overhead—

Launching lightning bolts the storm sliced fiery holes through the clouds resounding with thunder's deep echoes, highlighting the rain in the wind. Not as brightly now, Legend corridor still glowed ringed by white shimmering fire, the canopy's expanding gloom enclosing the battleland within enigmatic mystery. Encompassing the battleplain the storm's boundary wound like a dark seastorm's swells churning opaque mountainous clouds that circled the three monolithic peaks.

The storm's texture was changing with its heightening darkness and strength.

On the hummock their eyes reflected the coruscating sheet lightning flares while thunder intoned doldrums in their heads; they were warriors standing defiantly against the quintessence of evil in an esoteric coliseum. And there, on that plain, within the eye of that storm the prelude of phenomenal events was unfolding, a confluence of circumstances on an unworldly battlefield with an unexplained riddle, and the pieces of... *the Puzzle.*

Out there, on the plain—

Pistons hammered the mechanical drone of melancholy and death as the 'Queen' pushed tenaciously heaving sand in her wake. Hostaged from the deep, now pained with quicksand-effect she ground on; but her innards groaned.

Mottled scales lining his furrowed brow and misshapen nose, from the bow he scanned with yellow-gray eyes and innate evil; then he bit the stub of cigar and sneered. Rotten seaweed squeezed between his fingers as he tightened his grip on the broken rail and leaned back; then inhaling a deep breath and seething, he roared. Refocusing his attention derisively he licked drool from his lips and pulled a drag from the cigar. Eyes narrowed, blinking intently he sucked another rasping, protracted breath gurgling an unnatural growl; inhuman malevolence evident in those eyes. Focused, he watched *her,* and the man. On the dead ship... getting closer.

Underfoot, undaunted—

The original Barnum and Wilson, and all the rest scrambled like gophers shooting marbles and jacks, their slingshots bullet-burning ragged starburst holes and perfect little circles —unfailingly felling dark scorpion rats.

"Heads up," P.T. shouted, "incoming!" With a rubber band, *whap,* the jack smacked through a demon's face and ripped out its back terminating its dive with a wilted, cratered-sand splash. Tongue in cheek, concentrating and squinting as he aimed again P.T. brought down another, then grinning satisfaction, blinked and wrinkled his nose poking in a pocket for more ammo.

The sand rise—

Three dragonfly-drones dove for the children huddled within the perimeter of armed warriors, the first swooping inches over their heads. Terrified, a child bolted and ran just before the second's talons hit intercepting her scream. A Renoloi spun and jumped for the stolen child —*rrrip-sloosh*— struck from behind when the third jackal raked by, its telson splintering her spine in a spill of sullied entrails and blood. Disemboweled liver and lungs wafting viscid steam, she lay on the ground fingers still reaching, quivering with death.

Sword in hand a Pilgrim swung as a screecher flew by. Miss. He did his best protecting the children, but as he turned after the miss an aculeus ripped through his chest. Gone.

The battlefield—

In the admixture of a million colliding combatants charioteers rolled into the horde, broadswords searing through chitin and talons, mighty animals lathered with heat, nostrils flaring gouts of hot breath, obsidian hooves kicking up sand. Pounding over the battlefield they were visions of fury and gleaming images of light spinning whorls of fire, wheels and hooves rumbling in cadence with their ground-shaking gait. The battleland seemed to tremble as riders and war chariots plowed into the crush of Dark Forces, an endless sea of raking claws, insanity and dragonfly lion-faced fangs, a plain emanating the stick-in-your-throat taste of death and cauterized flesh.

Darkness and force with blood in the wind, it was the chaos of war where Mystics went down and intrepid dwarfs died as Dark Ones were trampled and fell from the sky. Thunder rattled then peeled above a shuddering land where confusion and dying splashed in red-violence spray that saturated the plain... then congealed on the sand.

The hummock—

Lent ducked as he swung opening its gullet, its claws just missing his head. Pussface nose-dived then flopped end-over-end and squirmed momentarily, head stuck in the sand, a twitching dying leech. Then for good measure—just one more *whack!*

Kalo spun and released then was gone. Faster than the bowstring's snap she had leaped and was again taking aim. Sensing targets with an intrinsic gift, one instant she was there, the next she'd vanished. Her speed was uncanny; her aim was flawless —more quickly than a wraith she dissolved and reappeared— an extraordinary warrior, and more.

Less than one second: talons were reaching for her neck, she defiantly standing her ground; still as a statue, solid as stone. It was upon her, claws closing, when with an arrow in her fist she ducked and went for its throat, then leaped —a blur— twisting the arrow from its neck —and disappeared— leaving a sour gush where she just had been. As the ghoul's pincers clamped shut its eyes blinked confused astonishment, before it wavered, buckled and fell. For a few fading beats its wound squirted blood that pooled beneath its head; then with drifting consciousness it expelled a breath of withered lost soul, a shadow that was destined for Hell.

The other side of the hummock—

Knife in hand, Reed waited —a bumblebee buzz— the screecher swooping in. Slashing forcefully, he missed and ducked as it zipped past then circled back and hovered above him. Wings oscillating, its leprous face oozing, Scarface blinked as it glared from beneath festered eyelids. Then from between its legs the aculeate tail came at him.

Dropping to his knees Reed tuck-and-rolled to the side in an explosion of scatter-flung sand as the deadly telson flashed in and missed, and then quickly stabbed missing again. Still moving, in one continuous motion he was clear of the legs and onto his feet and fiercely lunged sinking his blade just below its oscillating wing joint. Screeching, Scarface tried to fly off but Reed's weight dragged the blade down —intestines escaping like startled worms of sloppy tripe— opening a gash in its side. Still trying to break free Scarface struggled frantically, but Reed grabbed a leg, jerked—slammed it back down.

Ten feet away—*whoomph!*

Severed in aerial combat above a scorpion's tail splatted onto the hummock as Scarface again tried to lift off; but determined to finish it, Reed grabbed a handful of guts and yanked stretching its intestines elastic wrap tight drilling it to the ground again. Howling, the ghoul clawed and shoveled carving a circle in the sand, then scraping and digging ignited its wings and shoved off gaining flight. He leaped with the knife but missed and went down then rolled, as thirty feet above the maimed man-cretin set upon him again...

Fiend coming, buzz saw jaws and claws—

...Scrambling to his knees he dove for the severed tail lying nearby —rolled, grabbed it— and heaved, the tail and telson spearing Scarface in the neck injecting a jetstream of venom as he dove out of the way and it splat in its own gut pile.

Reed: eyes wide, adrenaline trembles. Scarface: a popped pimple, flat on its face, lights-out-dead with the dying quivers. Its legs involuntarily contracted in a shriveling fetal curl as the thorax gurgled and bubbled and its mouth filled with vomit. Finally, time for a breath.

Thirty feet from Reed—

Incoming —a flicker of glimmering edge— Ames took the man-dragon straight on through the head. Spiraling, it crashed as he pivoted and stepped back whirling his weapon, bringing it back to his side. Watching it all, nerves tight-tangled twine, anticipating another he scanned the clouds in the churning backdrop of lightning-flash thunderheads that crackled then exploded and rumbled like drums chasing phantoms. Overhead wind-pulse swept in gray wings of mist and shadow, the Dark Forces saturating the sky, while below on the plain they crawled like a plague of vile locusts with leprous dead faces and ungodly lecherous eyes. Still millions of them.

Standing ready on the hummock he twirled the scimitar supply slicing figure-eights creating a shield of shimmering blade before him. Flawlessly honed with tensile he could not comprehend, and tempered with unexplained mettle, its edge was empowered with unrealized prowess. Only a man, and a singular sword.

Another dove at break-neck speed. He stood firm, not even a flinch; then at the last possible instant he sidestepped and swung. No more than a grainy image, the scimitar decapitated the man-scorpion in midair, the instantaneous burst of bloody wind and splattering drops hurling the dead-missile carcass into the ground beyond him while the head spun askew knocking a Wilson or Barnum down. But they all looked the same so you just couldn't tell. Uninjured the floundered dwarf bounced back up and brushed himself off then scurried away rejoining the fracas.

Heavy sounds, approaching hoofbeats—

The cadence of two horses coming from behind caused Ames to turn as the Centurion Mystic rode in ponying a mount. Leading a riderless horse the Centurion reined in, the drawn Percheron halting and snorting. Expectantly the Centurion tossed the reins to Ames who reacted without thinking and reached for them, and remarkably the semitransparent woven satin braids materialized when they touched his hand. Realizing he held the reins; without hesitation he took two steps seizing the mane at the withers and swung upon the mighty animal's back.

Darting glances —Ames, then the sky— Reed looked on dubiously as his friend shifted his weight settling upon the horse's bare back. Ames twirled the scimitar. "Can't be," Reed finally had to say. "That's not possible."

Huddled inside the perimeter of fighters on the sand rise Jade excitedly tugged on Seana's arm pointing at the Centurion, her gaze riveted on the vision and cautiously rising to her knees, with a child's innocence she whispered, "There is my angel."

Holding her newborn and preoccupied with the ongoing battle, Seana answered distractedly, "Yes sweetheart, they are everywhere." Seana didn't understand what the child really meant.

Tracking the sky but still watching his friend, Reed wondered as another Mystic glided down ponying a second horse. "Doc, what do you think you're doing?" Ames cast him a grin as he patted the creature's muscular neck. "Doc... it's gonna go, *poof,* and you're gonna fall flat on your ass."

A smile: "Won't hurt; the sand is soft."

The second rider reined in alongside Reed and offered him the reins. Turning as he looked up at the Mystic, Reed hesitated. "You guys aren't real, you're ghosts." Still tendering the reins, the white warrior did not respond as his mount snorted and pawed, anxious to rejoin the legion. Appreciating the man's reluctance, the Mystic looked at the Centurion...

...And without speaking, in a garbled, disguised voice the Centurion said, *"Reality is possessed of many dimensions. Reed, can you believe?"*

His gaze passed from the rider to the Centurion, and finally to his friend. Encouraging, Ames nodded; and accordingly Reed nodded. Then back to the Centurion, "Yes, I suppose..." and circumspect he reached out to the magnificent horse.

Within the visored helmet green eyes smiled, and in the garbled, disguised voice the Centurion assured, *"Then Reed, all you need do is... believe."*

Carefully, gently, Reed's hand caressed the Percheron's strapping shoulder —or where it seemed to be, should have been— but his fingers passed through the vision and his expectation withered to disappointment.

"Reed," Ames reassured, "it *is* real. Touch it."

A second time Reed looked at his friend. He had faith in his friend, believed in his friend... and slowly, intently, trusting him, he reached for the Percheron again: lustrous summer-slick sheen, magnificent long flowing mane. The docile vision-like creature affectionately turned its head and looked at him with expressive eyes of aquamarine. And the hair and hide, the feel of it materialized as his hand delicately stroked the animal's powerful shoulder and tenderly caressed its neck. The gentle giant nickered and nuzzled breathing warmth in his face and onto his chest. And it *was* real.

Gathering the reins, eyes and smile telling wonder he reached under and around the animal's neck flipping one rein over its back, then took hold of the mane at the withers and jumped pulling himself onto the animal's back. Shifting his weight, settling in, the creature felt warm and strong beneath him. It was incredible. Between his thighs the blood and pulse of life flowed through its veins. The man sensed it. He could feel it. But other than faith he could not explain it. And welling from somewhere deep inside, within his soul, Reed knew; finally, he knew. *It's so simple... just Believe.*

Not too far away, the silent Kalo saw, felt the glow as she watched... and never said a word.

Rushing momentum—

Approaching the hummock where the Pilgrims and Renoloi were entrenched, over the rumble of the wheels, in a garbled voice the chariotmaster called, *"Reed—"* tossing a broadsword. Without thinking he caught it in midair as the charioteer rolled on going afield again. Then realizing he held the magnificent weapon Reed hoisted it, beaming, examining it hilt to tip.

From above—

One swooping at him —reflex reaction— the Percheron stepping back as it spun, him avoiding as he swung the broadsword —a shattering —*crackling*— razor of bright light and rattling flame! The blade's fiery splash searing through as it sliced —effortlessly, incredibly, flatlined, toast— both halves of the man-dragon coasting before it crashed. Kill confirmed, Reed's gaze trailed back to the weapon, his grin revealing, *Lord, it—is—real! Oh yeah, I could get used to this.*

Eyes twinkling-ready he leaned forward drawing the reins and with a touch of his heels to its ribs the mighty horse whinnied and reared raking fire, and they charged onto the battlefield, into the fight. Kicking up starbursts of sand Reed and his mount stormed into the horde as Barnums and Wilsons dodged from underfoot — shattering razors of flame— slicing Dark Ones to death, slaughtering them with soaking blood-splash —then an incredible bound— they leaped into the sky!

Following Reed, Ames turned and rode onto the plain, scimitar braced, pounding sand into flames, meting out death, whinnying reparation and rage. The madness and fury of war.

After the two men were gone from the hummock the Centurion looked at the silent Kalo... the girl blinked twice. Both smiled.

The battle—

Screeching banshee jabber-laughter the Dark Forces battered and stabbed, blood-drenched talons slashing their enemies as war swords sliced through the saber-tooth ghouls. Both armies were compressed in a deluge of inordinate force as they fought and fell. And dodging the crush of rumbling chariots and huge trampling hooves, identical P.T. Barnums and Wilsons scrambled everywhere, cat's-eyes sailing and jacks whistling as they twirled punching perfect little holes with impeccable accuracy and dynamic energy downing ebony scorpion rats.

The violent furor of conflict scattered death on the sand in an ongoing clash of virtue and sin.

Snap—

The half-human grabbed a dwarf and stuffed him in its mouth, chewing with teeth intended only for flesh. Voraciously tearing the little man apart, the golem driveled saliva looking about for another until Ames reined and turned then sliced down through its face severing hair, hide, teeth and bone. Gagging pieces and mucus as it spit pink froth the deviant crowed a gurgly-wheezing sound, staggering, tail twitching, claws grabbing sand. Mount whirling, Ames bent low striking a second time, the scimitar's razor of wind whisking through again. With a sputtering insane half-screech, the red-eyed outcast tried to strike out, but the Percheron stomped crushing its back as Ames sliced through its neck —a spurt of fountainhead blood— the monster's head flopping forward as its body gave up. *Take that.*

In the sky—

Leaning over the Percheron's withers Reed ducked aside as the telson flashed past and the man-scorpion banked then circled to return. With a sweep of his arm he wielded the broadsword —*the crackling razor of flame*— sending both halves spiraling like twirling half-dragon twins that quickly vanished below. Then another from behind that he didn't see coming, the horse suddenly veering as it rolled and buck-kicked, its hind legs crashing into the beast's armored chest snapping both wings like twirling maple seeds; but its crushed hull fell like a rock.

Aloft a rider and golem executed loops and dives as they fought until the villain twisted and coiled then struck stabbing the horse in the neck. Killed instantly the Percheron folded and the Dark One chased the plummeting Mystic.

Falling...

Facing upward, being pursued by the half-human freak — plummeting— the warrior warded off its deadly talons, but the demon kept coming, tail circling around like a snake in attack. The warrior reacted —*a crackling razor of flame*— slicing the cretin in two.

Falling...

Wind-blur and speed, the sand plain was coming up fast as another rider turned and rolled then dove and swept beneath the plummeting warrior —still falling— then abruptly landing solidly on the horse's rump behind the other legionnaire. Whinnying and striking fire with a powerful bound the gentle giant galloped upward again bearing both warriors into the clouds and the eye of a gathering storm.

The 'Marine Sulphur Queen'—

The color and texture of death pushed aside then rolled under as the ghost ship crawled closer to the intrepid league making their stand on the rise. Implacable, her enormous screws churned as she growled through the sand beneath an eclipsed sun and blood-red moon highlighting a flickering twilight sky tethered with long blue-black shadows, undulating with eerie premonition.

Narrower now, his eyes drew back sliding wider apart on his abhorrent skull, and with a succeeding blink his pupils changed from round to vertical, corneas metamorphosed, now yellow-gray and intensely hateful. Almost serpentine, Smith surveyed the slaughter with relish and consummate evil. He gurgled a, "Yes-ss," that oozed from his misshapen mouth, now almost a snout that caused him to slur; still not quite a hiss.

Much larger now, the uniform coat and blouse hung from his hulking shoulders in tattered shreds, his trousers split up the seams of the legs, the left boot split apart but still laced, now up above his ankle. His fingers and toes were clawed, his hair long and flaring wildly, and his tongue looked dark and longer. His skin was blotched with scales now, more than tinged, and still changing color… almost iridescent magenta.

On a dead ship, getting closer.

* * *

The Riddle…
…The final piece of the Puzzle

Three Wise Men watch when the flock returns,
Where a vortex myth… and dark fires burn.
When two warriors stand with a cloistered sun,
In a war without end, never lost, never won.

There the hourglass stops with an endless wind,
Where yesterday waits… and tomorrow's been.
And the power of light crosses darkened skies,
Before it enters a bridge infused with sin and lies.

For destiny lies on the sand and plain,
In a place that was… should it be again.
There a turbid sea will flow in red,
Until the final song harvests lost and dead.

In the fabric of time laced within the eye,
Heralds of prophecy… they forever ride.
To save a world that is flawed in a place that is sorrow,
Wielding the winds of eternity on the wings of tomorrow…
…Time Warriors.

* * *

Darkness poured; thunder rolled…

…As gloom twisted within the canopy in contorted tendrils of violence and viscous murk. Crooked green-white lightning leaped

383

cloud to cloud as ball lightning screeched trailing shrill rocket flares. Wind whistled as it spun with chilling cold in its grip, roused like a cacophony of seastorms and gales. While above, enclosing the conflict, wound a vortex of incredible darkness and depth encircling a singular Light... and the 'Hole in the Sky'.

The 'Marine Sulphur Queen'—

A dead-metal hull of rust and despair, the behemoth freighter continued carving a trench through red land churning under corpses and smoldering spent hulls. Still approaching, she creaked and moaned with her burden of sand beneath a dark angry canopy thickened with gloom and torn by vanishing flashes of erratic flickering flames.

On deck—

Smith roared, his bellow reverberating, echoing long, drawn and vile with a tempest of hatred and the bawl-hollow of evil. From the bow of the dead freighter, wrapped in a shroud of dark mist he watched relishing the ongoing conflict and rampant carnage below.

Above him the sky was a swarm of oscillating dragonfly wings, his deranged killers zigzagging and battling shooting stars of gleaming armor and sackcloth white riders. Aerial combat was so vicious and violent that blood drizzled from the clouds like sultry summer rain showering the battleland, soaking it in red. The mysterious arena of the circular storm was alive with disorder and death, and cursed with an incessant, increasingly cold... *Relentless Wind.*

His soulless core was a smear of blackness as wicked as the conspiracy in his mind, his intent exuded with each bland rasping breath; and from the bow glowering through narrow serpentine eyes, Smith saw him. He was there on the sand, scimitar flashing and splattered with blood. Riding hard, then looking up, Ames saw him as the dead freighter continued churning relentlessly toward the struggling band of people defending the hummock. He had no doubt Smith intended to overrun and kill them, each and every one.

White spittle foam crusted at the corners of his lips, drooling venomous saliva Smith glared down with a sneer. Nerves constricting his breath, a whet knot in his chest, Ames knew it was time.

Satan was waiting —the showdown— the final conflict had come.

Swallowing hard and spurring with his bare heels —*hee-aww*— his eyes locked on his demonic adversary, the man reining and rallying the mighty Percheron to a full-gallop charge heading for the 'Marine Sulphur Queen'... and him.

Bolting—mane flowing full, extending its gait, running the plain on hooves wound in fire, Ames leaned forward on the withers, almost onto its neck. Brandishing the scimitar as wind sliced through his hair and blood-rain splattered his face, his eyes and attention were riveted on Smith. Man and horse thundered over the plain pounding the rhythm of time and a cadence of fury, the Percheron's shattering hooves kicking up sparkling flames and blood that dissolved in the backdrop of grays.

Smith glanced up at it and nodded.

Dragonfly wings banking, it circled from the left and the lion-tooth scorpion dove at the man. Focused on Smith, it was just a glimmer —but he saw it— and as it tried to take him Ames staunchly countered reaching over the Percheron's ears with a sidestrike through the hollow of its skull. Continuing on with the pounding rhythm of hoofbeats his focus scarcely flickered as the scarface vanished cartwheeling somewhere behind him lost in the calamity of blood-rain and fray. Running the tempo of hoofbeats his mount didn't slow down, he wouldn't slow down, would not look away. Up ahead, up there, Smith was waiting.

Ames' eyes were riveted and his champion's were wide and pellucid of aquamarine, hammering the cadence of stallion and man. Tossing its head with the measure of its four rushing feet the mighty Percheron's ears lay back trampling the reverberating fury of undeviating hooves, cratering the battleplain with the rhythm of horseflesh and muscle boiling sand into flame.

Drawing the reins more closely to his chest Ames bent his knees and squeezed shifting his weight and balance over the horse's neck, leaning even farther forward, positioned for speed. At full gait they thundered on until with a tremendous bound the mighty horse leaped into the air and they soared —sudden silence, flying on wind— the incredible stallion climbing through layered sky and rivers of fog, bound for the 'Marine Sulphur Queen'.

On deck—

Venting despise with saliva and glowering yellow-gray eyes, Smith watched from the bow as the man and horse continued to ascend approaching the dead ship, until level with the deck, then rising higher and flying above it. His right hand ground the tip of his saber into the lackluster flesh of gray deck shedding sparks. *What a fool*—he was coming. Seething, Smith waited, and glared.

Beneath the rags of shredded uniform his chest and arms no longer looked mottled and bruised, now beautifully scaled and glistening of iridescent magenta. The seat of his trousers seam had ripped and a reptilian tail snaked out, growing long and spiked, whip-like: half man, half demon, a wivern.

Now fully evolved, Smith the paramount demon stood with his reptilian legs spread wide, toenail claws digging into the rusted planks of the deck. Dark and vile his deformed tongue repulsively slithered slurping spittle; then wiping his mouth with a tattered sleeve he watched as blood-tinged mucus seeped from his iguanian-shaped snout.

Coming down—

Highlighted by an unworldly eclipse and spectral flaming corona, majestic as a Pegasus the Percheron circled once then descended for the deck. *Almost here*—they were coming. Menacingly he growled, "My beauties," then sneered as the stallion stared intently with fearless eyes of aquamarine, tossing its head, snorting crimson and rage.

Clattering hooves—

A splash of bright light, horse and rider landed upon the deck of the 'Queen' shattering rusty steel to twirling shards and ribbons of flame. Smith growled as the horse whinnied and reared, its hooves raking fire that lit up the dark.

Around them—

The storm buffeted with gusts of cold keening wind beneath a solemn canopy of flickering sky etched in streak-lightning fire and ball lightning flares. The firmament shook with percussions of thunder that grumbled then exploded and boiled as the battleplain below turned exceedingly dark. A whirling wall of black wind and tornadic cloud, the storm boundary encompassing the battleland was growing and intensifying, as the canopy seemed to descend and close down upon the plain.

It was then that the corona of the eclipsed sun appeared to almost melt, to begin to flow, to ooze into the storm's boundary, bleeding and crawling in the opposite direction of the swirling shroud... and the darkened sun dimmed, dissolved, and went out. Now the flaming corona ominously glowed as an aurora of aberrant flames and long blue-black shadows rotating in opposition to the movement of the storm's boundary wall. It was eerie and unnatural... almost like dark burning fire.

Below, on the plain—

Chaos and savagery, scattered sand, running feet; the battleland was talons and broadswords, stingers stabbing with snakestrikes, the 'Queen's' huge uncompromising propellers still churning and pushing. She plowed over everything crushing it beneath her keel, forging onward, grinding it all to admixture of bloodied ground. Armor and chitin were crammed together pressing from opposing directions, both armies hard-packed with helter-skelter disorder; confusion of battle on a plain emanating the stick-in-your-throat taste of death and cauterized flesh.

On deck—

Cautious, watching him, Ames silently stared. Sizing him up, derisively Smith glowered then snarled. And the hiss.

The time had arrived. The final conflict had come.

Smith charged. Man and horse charged. Ribbons of flame and fireflash whorls, swords clashed with red flames and shattering indigo blue-violet sparks!

Man against Evil, Ames deftly checked as Smith savagely lunged and struck, their weapons clashing—crashing again and again.

And with each metallic impact shedding grenade-bursts of sparks, mysteriously the scimitar began to glimmer, then flicker and shine more brightly until it was luminescent, then iridescent —and finally, divinely it glowed.

The bowels of the dead ship echoed the storm of ponderous hooves and resounding noise of Smith's heavy footfalls. Crashing thunderously Smith-serpent stomped forward and back cracking ancient steel planking, claws gouging the deck each time he put his weight into a blow. Another miss—the horse spinning as it reared, Smith slamming into a bulkhead causing it to buckle.

Trying to outmaneuver them, shifting his bulk and supple tail Smith lunged but Ames countered and ducked, swords spraying ribbons of fire as the horse raked the demon's head with its staggering hooves. Stumbling, Smith went down, rolled, then got back up reeling as he turned and lashed out with the scorpion-hook tail; but again, an onerous hoof battered him back. Flung aside the tail snatched back with a whip-cracking snap. The man was determined; Smith was just evil.

—Shattering red flames—indigo blue-violent sparks!

Repeatedly scimitar and saber slammed, sliding, grating and grinding shedding spark-spray of crackling fire —blade against blade, edge against edge— illuminating the gloom, incredible power and dazzling fireflash light. Life and death, their confrontation was graphic and terrifying—vehement, esoteric. Each metallic collision was intense with brilliant violence detonating the grainy twilight of shadows and mist—vitriolic explosions of fire. Time after time the awesome force of their weapons lit up the timeworn barnacle-incrusted deck of the hostaged dead ship, a gray ghost enshrouded with smoldering blue-black shadows eerily illuminated by the reflective glare of unworldly power and light.

Below, on the plain—

The battlefield was running bedlam of dwarfs, white riders and crawling man-scorpions. Vicious and wild, Dark Ones snapped and stabbed with vice-grip pincers and venomous tails as P.T. Barnums and Wilsons scrambled winging marbles and jacks, while mounted warriors did swordplay with the vile dark army. And center stage, near an insignificant sand hummock, a few hundred valiantly made their stand desperately holding back the unending black villainy of the Devil's taloned horde.

Above, and around them—

The incredible maelstrom of tornadic core charged with wind and water-soaked ribbons of flame swirled as the perfect storm; the most violent of tempests streaking white-crooked-fire and crackling thunderous explosions that peeled as they scattered then slammed. Green-white ball lightning shooting stars slashed the canopy with searing dynamic energy, while around them the storm boundary seemed to rise as it breathed, scintillating as it simmered with an eerie aurora of unnatural flaming winds, almost like... dark burning fire.

And there, on that plain, with the chaos of war... blood ran deep on the sand.

The battleland—

With the metallic-clang pounding of pistons and melancholy moans of pain emanating from her superstructure and bowels of her hold, the 'Marine Sulphur Queen' forged on. Overrunning sand strewn with corpses then rolling them under she chiseled a trench toward the band of fighters on an insignificant rise on the plain. Still coming... getting closer.

Standing in the thick of battle and bloodshed—

Kalo saw them fighting on the foredeck: Ames, the man, and Smith, the man-demon. From behind, a Dark One leaped at her; but more fleet than a glimmer of realization she reached to the quiver, spun and let fly, her arrow punching through the palate into its brain. Astonished —bloodshot-dead eyes— before it even had time to retch blood she had vanished. Illusory speed, she disappeared and reappeared —acrobatics— vaulting, striking and springing within the confusion, an extraordinary warrior, a sprite. As she fought, she began making her way for the 'Marine Sulphur Queen'.

On deck—

Cumbersome feet and unshod hooves pounded the steel planks as blades clashed showering fire and blue-violet sparks. The ring of razor edges heralded with strident concussions as Ames and Smith struggled and fought; blow for blow, man against monster in a duel of destiny and death. Battering, their weapons rang and echoed as they slammed together time and again raining firefall flames cascading supernatural sparks.

Smith's saber slashed at them as the mighty Percheron spun — another blade— the scimitar intercepting and heaving it back in a halo of fire and indigo blue-violent sparks. In half-a-heartbeat Ames moved and struck again, the explosion igniting the dark with pyrotechnic wrath while dying embers still twirled in the air — Smith's strength and the man's determination spraying indignation and fire— splinter-light spinning through gray.

Fury and brilliant detonations illuminated the rusted freighter pushing darkness to the fringe, a split-second later gloom rushing back capturing the fizzling embers while shadow goblins danced on the bulkheads and gunwales. Unmasking the violence of their confrontation daylight and darkness parried back and forth —sporadic light, mist and obscurity— spark-flash swirling with dizzying speed.

Eyes wide, blue and fearless, the horse snorted and pawed as reptilian yellow-gray eyes flashed lecherously back. Smith whirled and lunged then viciously stabbed with the wivern tail —between the horse's neck and Ames' chest— two inches, just missed. The man slammed the tail with the scimitar's hilt, Smith recoiling like a whip then hissing, arching it up and away.

The demon charged and swung, Ames countering over the horse's neck, their blades colliding recklessly with showers of splendid firefall sparks. Metallic rings of fury and steel reverberated with resonant echoes peeling from the bulkheads, fireflash sparks twirling into the dark.

Barbarically he threw his head back —and long and loud, Smith roared.

Sidestepping, watching the man, eyes a testimony of hatred and cunning; with sinister intent Smith-serpent snarled. His very persona exuded malevolence and unabridged contempt that slithered with his revolting black tongue dripping venom-saliva. Moving slowly, muscles tensed, he slurped drool from his disfigured snout filled with flesh-eating, chipped boxer's teeth.

Sudden—

Saber in hand he spun and lurched onto the horse's rump, his hind feet ripping and drawing crimson clawlines of free-flowing blood. Vulnerable —the demon behind him— Ames slipped forward onto his knees as Smith drew back for the blow. Momentum and rhythm in sync with the horse, locking both wrists against the withers he rocked and sprang spinning in midair like a trick rider; onto his feet facing his adversary.

Smith swung—Ames blocked.

Steels slammed between them, grating razor edges screeching —explosive blue-violet sparks and alizarin fire— scraping abrasively sword and scimitar peeling, running edges —a strident, grisly scream— shedding fury and dazzling, sparkling flames!

Momentarily blinded Smith's claws dug more deeply in the Percheron's rump as the horse neighed and reared raking with its hooves, throwing its head —a flash of mane. Mano a mano, chest to chest, not even a blink, Ames looked eye to eye into the core of Satan as blood ran red from white flanks.

Smith roared—Ames heaved.

Off-balanced—still clawing, Smith lost his footing and slid then toppled falling hard on the deck. He rolled sideways banging into a bulkhead denting it as clutter scattered and clanged.

Mane and tail sweeping fluidly —blood streaming down its hindquarters— the white stallion curled and spun like a cresting wave of wind-vision ghost as Ames dropped smoothly again onto its back. Its muscles rippled with each solid step, head bowed with the prowess of a war horse, neck thickset and arched, brawny shoulders and strapping breast, unshod fetlock hooves gleaming obsidian sheen; every inch of it coursing with the symmetry of perfect horseflesh.

Gathering himself and getting up, Smith straightened then crouched preparing to strike again. Stomping steel plate the Percheron threw its head as it neighed and reared raking sparks through the gloom of shadows and mist.

The final showdown.

Twirling the scimitar Ames created a glowing shield of luminous blade, magnificent indigo blue. Man and mount were prepared for battle.

The demon lunged—the horse bolted and charged.

Sudden as a snakebite the tail and poisonous aculeus flashed for the horse's point of shoulder, coming from behind like an attacking anaconda with a dagger for fangs.

Ames swung—but missed.

Smith's wivern tail struck with the malediction of venom as it sank into flesh, the magenta tail and telson slamming home in the Percheron's chest, tearing and burrowing savagely—grisly. Bloodbath and venom expelled yellow-red-soak as the stinger tore through muscles and kept boring deeper splintering thick fearless bones. Veined with the purity of aquamarine and startle of surprise the Percheron's eyes filled almost instantly with the sickness of dying. Whinnying, its nostrils flared snorting pink froth and blood as the stinger ripped through its lungs and venom splashed death through its breast —aculeus still tunneling through its heart and liver— then with an ungodly hole tore out through its side. Scarlet foam and blood-spray exploded from the Percheron's flank just behind Ames' heel when the serpent's tail burst from inside and the animal's head dropped as its front legs folded and it stumbled.

Going down…

Ames dove from its back, landed and rolled on the deck.

Tumbling…

He was back on his feet watching as the great Percheron, still impaled on the demon's tail, collapsed and the black-hearted Smith, growling savagely, snatched the horse from the planks. Villainously he hoisted it over his repulsive head revolving both tail and horse above him, slowly, reprehensibly.

Stunned Ames saw it, couldn't look away. He watched, transfixed, an intimidating effect.

With lecherous inhumanity and cruelty spawned of pure unvarnished evil, Smith glared at the man; his so-called precious, invincible mount was now nothing more than hanging meat. He intended to frighten him, to intimidate him, to steal his self-confidence, to usurp his resolve, and make him cower.

Captured by the ghastly sight Ames' eyes involuntarily followed the spectacle of the dead animal swaying up there. Above him the serpent tail turned as it moved slowly, cold as a snake, the magnificent lifeless creature dangling helplessly, blood draining from its breast and flank then dripping from the serpent's tail. It was a gruesome mental image —piteous, shocking, dreadful— a horrific presentment, almost mesmerizing, almost overpowering… almost …but not quite.

All in an instant—

Across the deck he noticed something: motion. Kalo was behind and beyond Smith, on the rusted superstructure climbing toward the pilothouse. He hadn't seen her before, a diminutive figure in the shadows with her bow strung across her back, scaling the tangle of matted sargasso clinging to the bulkheads. She was climbing toward the pilothouse cabin above —*what is she doing?*

Closer, near him: *something moved,* in the shadows, *something else. Smith moved—focus,* blinking back to his adversary.

Drooling repugnantly Smith glowered and snarled as he stepped forward again. Bellowing hideous laughter he roared and viciously snaked the tail heaving the dead horse through the air. Ames didn't look when it slammed down landing solidly somewhere. This time he didn't take his eyes from him; instead, he brought the scimitar up, working his wrists, doing the rhythm and mystery. Before him the magic of fluid motion, the power of grace and remarkable light; the sword, *whooshing,* mystically forming a shimmering shield of razor edge.

Bare feet softly padding rusted-dead metal, he apprehensively faced the paramount demon —Him— Smith. It was time.

Sticky white crust curdled in the corners of his jaws, Smith licked his wrinkled lips drooling vile spittle; the Percheron's blood still draining streamlets of red down the serpentine tail, swaying up there, the telson glistening the sheen of unconscionable death. Belching gutturally Smith regurgitated the stub of cigar and mouthed it, chewing it with flesh-eating chipped boxer's teeth. Amused, he was full of himself. The chaos of battle below on the sand... and here on deck, with this nasty business at hand. Throwing his head back Smith bellowed vicious laughter, then he howled until he roared. He was the epitome of malevolence, the most ignoble and consummate evil. He was evil for evil's own sake.

At last, this was Smith's moment. Those few hundred were remnant Christians in an arena of time and ethereal design.

> *For destiny lies on the sand and plain,*
> *In a place that was... should it be again.*

While silently, in the blended gloom of gray mist, destiny, and the core of a storm, Kalo climbed over the rail onto the bridge at the pilothouse. Wind howled. Lightning flashed.

The 'Queen'—

On a battleland soaked in blood the 'Marine Sulphur Queen' bore down on the determined band of warriors entrenched near the hummock. Overhead the canopy churned highlighted by lightning etching lines in the sky as thunder exploded then rattled and screeching meteors of ball lightning flared. Then around them the storm boundary strangely seemed to moan, an unworldly moan filled with tempests of omen and whirling cold wind, almost like... flickering dark fire.

On deck—

A lump in his throat, Ames watched Smith, the potentate of evil looming before him. His appearance was intimidating, his presence dreadful.

Half-naked, in the tattered rags of shredded uniform his scaled hide infused with magenta almost shimmered in the semidarkness. His size and form were grotesque: half man—half serpent, his most frightening persona. The wivern. With yellow-gray malevolent eyes and hair flaring wildly, he seethed with loathing then hissed and growled, his hideous misshapen iguanian snout dripping mucus that he fetched with his tongue. Finding his stance his claws dug into the deck; then sidestepping he swaggered and swayed mimicking a viper. Brandishing the saber with claw-like fingers, again he gargled a snarl that churned to a hiss gurgling from deep in his throat.

Feet wide, every muscle braced, Ames swallowed hard. Eye to eye, sizing one another up they stared one another down —then murderously, ruthlessly Smith lunged and blades splashed...

—Shattering fire and indigo light!

...Violent fireworks ignited the grainy twilight with metallic peals of savagery and determination that rang overdeck. Maneuvering, the combatants slammed blade against blade, saber and scimitar colliding violently and intensely time after time. Furor startled dark places as blazing firelight illuminated the gloom with blinding red flame and dazzling blue-violent sparks!

Razor edges of death. As fast and suddenly as Smith struck Ames parried and struck back —check or duck, then attack— then strike again and move countering with equal force. Blades crashing, they fought with fury of intent and firefall pyrotechnics in a netherworld gloom of bloodthirsty vengeance.

The arena—

She heaved carving through hummocks plowing over the plain as the dead ship 'Queen' bore down upon the ragtag band of warriors. Astern her monstrous teardrop screws churned whorls of bloody brown sand sucking up fallen corpses then shredding them; piecemeal ground under. Anything before her was boiled up then tossed in the mix as the gaunt hollow giant crawled relentlessly on, the mechanical drone of her hammering pistons echoing over the battleplain.

On deck—

Again, the foghorn blared—the tail stabbed with a rattlesnake's speed. More instinct than awareness, Ames felt it coming, diving from its strikepath and landing hard on a shoulder before he rolled and slid into a tangle of kelp. Scrambling to his feet again, he stepped back taking a stance. Alert, moving carefully, working the scimitar in figure-eights; then spinning he sidestepped. Ready.

Again Smith lunged then lurched back, his assault deflected in a shower of blue-violet fire. Smeared with rust and seaweed smidgens, and saturated with revolting, his appearance was beyond disgusting; and he was incensed. Swelling his chest with heaves of anger he growled driveling acrimony and saliva; and in his eyes slithered the exudate of hate.

Ames stood his ground shrugging off the glower and returning the threat, continuing to twirl the scimitar with its mystical barrier of glowing power. Then strangely, somewhere inside he thought heard words… soft, caring words …and a beautiful voice whispered, *"Fear not, for I am with you"*.

Smith hissed and growled, but hesitated momentarily. *Was it possible he heard the voice too?* Swaying sinisterly, he menaced rocking from side to side; but he did not attack.

Treading softly, facing off as they circled the deck Ames watched him. Again, *the voice*. Ames thought he heard it, was sure he did, very faintly at first; those words, then a song, as though sung by a choir from somewhere far, far away. Then in the sky, on the plain, all around him, he could hear them. The Mystics were singing —and at last he knew why. Their song was the answer —*that's why the angels always sing.* That was why they rode so fearlessly into battle —because they *were* unafraid— so simple.

Again, the words in his head: *"Fear not, for I am with you."*

Ames realized, fear was Smith's weapon, his strength —Satan's weapon— his *only* weapon. Glancing down at Tian and the others on the plain, still some distance away, "Sing—" he cried out. "Sing like the angels are singing!"

He began to hum causing Smith to gurgle and snarl. He hummed louder and the demon wrinkled its lips then growled. Smith roared then shrieked and screamed, then roared again as the man began to sing brandishing his shield of luminous blade with mounting courage.

Below—

Hazel eyes telling faith Tian hummed, then she sang; and from the blood-soaked plain, unsure of themselves and softly at first, one after another others joined in. Renoloi and Pilgrims continued to fight as they sang imitating the song of the Mystics. And as they sang their faith and voices united and grew until altogether they sang the refrain and the beautiful chorus —all of them— altogether, like a choir —and defiantly they fought on!

Although few in number their strength increased —was enhanced, multiplied— with each new voice that joined in the song —their song— accompanied by the white riders. And as they sang the 'Marine Sulphur Queen' began to slow, the drone of her hammering pistons pounding louder and more sluggishly as though straining harder to push her dead hull through the deepening sand. Her pistons clanged with metallic pain, resounding even more loudly as the vessel furrowed ever more deeply; she was struggling, began heaving. The dead ship seemed to be sinking. Abruptly her prow began to rise as the stern dragged, bloody ground crushing against her keel and hull, pouring into her hold. Laboring and grinding she churned even more slowly through the blood-soaked brown sand.

Mystics all throughout the arena and mortals making their rebellious stand all sang together. They sang that incredible, heavenly, mellifluous song. They sang with all their hearts and souls —and courageously, defiantly they fought on!

Incensed, arms spread wide, reaching out with knotted sledgehammer fists Smith screamed until his clawed fingers cut into his palms. His eyes were monstrous and wild, his guts a kettle of deranged anger boiling inside. Maddened beyond reason, venting and loathing with rage he threw his head back and screamed until he screeched, until he bellowed —and fuming he roared!

In the sky—

With more strength than a hurricane the whirlpool of darkness and storm wound expelling wizard-fingers of flame that slammed percussions of vindictive wrath —then rabid blisters of thunder— lightning sizzling erratic tracelines of fire. Billowing clouds swirled and poured in furious rivers of black that cascaded through one another in thick angry waves following the rim and momentum of the storm. Screeching ball lightning streaked, skipped then exploded with deafening shockwaves that rattled the heavens and pounded the sand. And within the encompassing storm boundary clouds unworldly aurora flames swirled, almost like... dark burning fire.

On deck—

Smith went crazy striking blindly and wild. Infuriated, he swung with his tail and took out Ames' feet, then as the man tried to get up, charged wielding all his wickedness and might with his shoulder and size. He bodyslammed Ames knocking him head-over-heels and solidly to the deck. Stunned, the wind knocked out of him, Ames lost the scimitar when it twirled overhead and struck the deck then bounced and spun into a ravel of soggy kelp.

The man gasped, shaken with pain. He lay dazed and bleeding from a fresh head wound. He was vulnerable, unarmed.

Stepping over him Smith bellowed triumphant laughter, then leaned forward and grabbed him by the throat with one hand, hoisting him over his head. Taking a step, with incredible raw strength he threw him —a limp rag doll— over the deck.

When Ames hit the, *thud*, sounded like pain wrenching his left shoulder, contorting his hand in a fetal curl. Pain shot from his fingers to his neck then chewed its way down his spine burning into both buttocks when he tried to get up. Dazed, desperate, looking around he spied the scimitar hilt protruding from a muddy snarl of seaweed not more than twenty feet away; but unstable and hurt he could barely crawl, couldn't get to it. *Sing,* he told himself; but when he tried, he coughed up blood.

Gloating, glowering, Smith-serpent casually began lumbering toward him chuckling as the man struggled trying to get to his feet. Staggered and disorientated Ames got up on one knee, then with a hand managed to pull his other foot beneath him; but dizziness overcame him and he went down on his injured shoulder. He lay there, blood dripping down his face, as Smith nonchalantly stepped closer relishing the moment; and unseen, eighty feet above at the pilothouse, on the bridge, climbing up onto the deck rail, the silent Kalo watched.

Coming for him, Smith swaggered even closer.

Lightheaded, the man grimaced with pain as frustration and blood burned his eyes and stuck in his throat. Now, more than determined, pressing his left arm against his side and protectively cradling his injured shoulder, rolling onto his stomach he tried to get up again. He put his forehead on the deck, then arching his back forced himself to his knees. Hurt, hunched over with pain, on his knees, Ames faced the demon. He tried to sing but couldn't, coughing up more blood.

Smith stopped, sneered derisively, "Doesss it hurt?" Then he mumbled an invective.

De'ja vu, I know you. We've been here before. But this time the man wasn't afraid, only angry, possessed an inveterate will to prevail. Pushing back the pain he dragged his right leg forward and lifting it with his arm firmly placed his foot on the deck. Doggedly he refused to give up.

Unable to believe it, Smith's jaws slacken and slavered before he bit the cigar and scowled. He muttered gutturally, and snarled. Then more invectives.

Forged with pernicious determination the man rose on his right leg dragging the left up until he could set it on the planks. Wavering but on his feet, his vision clotted with dirt and blood, shoulder stooped, again Ames defiantly stood before Satan.

Incredulously, hatefully, Smith glared. Who was he, this pitiful little man, to challenge the Dark Master with such blatant obstinacy? Stubborn fool. Who was he, this pathetic dolt, to so brazenly refuse to capitulate and submit? Stepping insolently, menacingly Smith approached. Saber in hand, intent. It was time to dispense with this insignificant nuisance, this annoying trivial thorn in his side who had twice before interfered and screwed up his grandiose scheme.

Forty paces between them, Smith the sovereign of evil took another step closer... while steadfast, unflinching, Ames remained.

The ghost ship—

'Queen' trembled and groaned as red sand climbed her stern; still crawling her hull. Rivets popped peeling metal, exposing warped bending beams that creaked in her bowels under the enormous strain of countless tons of weight flowing into her, slowing her down. Then, with the, *skre-ek,* of twisting metal emanating her intense pain there came an eerie, unworldly sound, a whisper almost, like an echo from Hell calling the ghost ship back to the graveyard that spawned it.

Almost breathing the voice muttered her name... *'Marine Sulphur Queen'.*

Sand filling her hold, gutting and clogging her bowels, she inexorably forged ahead; but now half submerged her bow planed and she moaned, slipping and plying lower. Foundering.

In the fabric of time laced within the eye...

Above the freighter, the sky was confusion of battle saturated with eerie corona cascades cloaked in vivid blue-black shadows where Dark Forces and Mystics soared. Their numbers were endless and uncountable, seeming to reach beyond the fringe, sweeping throughout the vaulted dark ceiling of storm. The canopy was a winding vortex arena slashed with sudden-lightning claws that shredded the clouds with an unending barrage of unbridled anger in a deepening rotating sky.

Then—

Incredibly, the entire storm boundary exploded as a ravenous wall of flames catapulting screeching meteors from horizon to horizon —brilliant white to blue, to red, to yellow-orange then green, then umber, then scarlet— then more. Darkness and bright, the flames in the boundary wall fumed insatiably, while overhead the canopy almost breathed the voracious heaving fury of a hurricane's unending howl that blotted out sound. It was the intensity of divine anger, a fury of firestorm encompassing the entire battleplain companioned with a drenching cold, *Relentless Wind.*

Violently burning and melting the storm boundary roared as a firewall of liquid-amorphous wrath... all of it *dark blazing fire.*

Tornadic and awesome the congealing whirlpool churned igniting lightning that streaked as electrified flame tearing holes in the sky, while wind-rush of thunder explosively shattered then rumbled over and over, never drifting away.

Smith, the demon, the serpent —Smith, Satan incarnate— sauntered closer... while unafraid to die, steadfast, unflinching, Ames remained.

Eighty feet above, her destiny unfolding, one step at a time; stroking the fetish she wore solemnly Kalo whispered, "And the power of light crosses darkened skies." She looked down at him. "Now... you go back to Hell," and reaching to the quiver —empty— *I am out of arrows!*

The thought of failure seized her, made her tremble; and searching, her eyes flashed to the sky, then desperately over the plain...

On deck—

Thirty paces between the two near the bow, Kalo's thought heralded as clearly as a cry in the night; but neither Ames nor Smith heard, or looked away. Each was focused on the other: this moment, the matter at hand. Ames glared at Smith, a monster, the epitome of evil from the province of Hell. Surreal as it seemed, he was here swaggering toward him on the trembling timeworn deck that was gaunt and hollow as the core of a raven soul layered in rust and strangled with mud-covered seaweed and matted brown kelp.

Then, involuntarily the man's attention was drawn to the silhouette —to her— his eyes shifting above to the wheelhouse where he saw Kalo standing on the rail at the pilothouse bridge. Holding his eyes, she seemed different somehow; now more than a diminutive Renoloi warrior. Much More.

As Smith loomed, slowly approaching from the shadows, Kalo was strangely backlit, almost esoteric, highlighted by the burning firewall of the circular storm encircling the squalor of battlefield and wasteland. Burning ravenously —eerie— the firewall created a unique, mysterious halo around her, an unworldly corona-afterglow resembling sunset spires intermingled with flames... in this place that was forever shaded by blue-black shadows of sorrow.

And finally, he understood. *The constellations were backward... opposing one another.* He looked at Smith: *Orion, the hunter,* and Kalo: *Sagittarius, the archer.*

At last he knew what it all really meant.

On deck—

Drooling repugnant vindictive spittle Smith stopped and heaved his shoulders back then bellowed vicious laughter, his throaty voice booming haughtily casting echoes from the dark-metal bulkheads of the dead ship. Wicked eyes etched with loathing and pervasive bloody veins, gutturally he growled, "It is time for harvest." Then he howled savagely, and *drew back* his saber...

Listing and rumbling as her bow continued to rise, the stern going under with a boil of sand all around, pouring in and filling her hold, the dead ship 'Marine Sulphur Queen' was sinking. Seeming to struggle, and moaning, the gray metal ghost groaned in the sand-froth that swirled up and began sucking her down.

Below, on the plain—

With Kalo's unspoken plea still hanging in the air, as the great Percheron reared, the Mystic saw her. Spurring, then riding hard the Centurion sheathed the broadsword charging at full speed, answering her call. A fury of fire and shattering sound, the Centurion thundered toward the freighter on the incredible white stallion. Pounding winds of starlight, surrounded by strange flaming darkness, they ran the battlefield and rabid chaos of war.

Lightning flashed—the firmament crackled and peeled. Thunder shattered and rolled—a climax of mercurial disorder. And with unbridled wrath—the encompassing storm boundary roared!

Snorting gouts of crimson and rage the mighty steed cratered great flaming holes tearing fiery red wings from dark bloody sand. Crossing the battleland they rode with the zeal of a lightning bolt and the fury of heaven stampeding through the fray trailing boreal fire at their heels.

At full gate, holding the horse's mane with one hand, the warrior leaned over and grabbed a bow from a pile of dead ghouls near a fallen Renoloi warrior. And back upright. Still galloping —full speed— the Mystic snatched an arrow from the hide of another dead scorpion —then reining— lifted the visor, flinging the helmet aside. Hooves digging in, the mighty horse whinnying as it reared, the Centurion set the arrow to the bow and called out, "None but mortal can overcome evil —*Kalo!*"

As the helmet sailed through the air the voice that was once garbled and disguised abruptly changed to a voice that was wholly familiar. It was pure as sunshine, of one with green eyes and the breath of spring flowers, a voice that Tian knew and recognized instantly.

—Then click,

With the sound of the Centurion Mystic's true voice everything stopped —suspended, stalled— all movement ceased and the wind suddenly stilled. Dead calm swept the battleland with the interruption and suspension of time. Asystole silence.

There the hourglass stops with an endless wind,
Where yesterday waits... and tomorrow's been.

Time stood still as the transcendental conflict continued in a succession of motions mirroring an out of body experience. Frame by frame, snapshot by snapshot, it was a progressing sequence of surreal freeze-frame motion, visages and images flicking by one picture after another. It was a chronology paralleling thumbing through an old photo album... one incredible detail at a time.

—Click,

On the hummock Tian's hazel eyes flashed astonishment. She looked at —instantly recognized— the commander of the Mystic army. Tears flushed her eyes and a lump stuck in her throat. Disbelief constricted her voice and undying love flooded her heart as she marveled and almost choked on the Centurion Mystic's name when she cried out, *"—Kimo!"*

—Click,

Bow pointing up, the stern disappearing, being swallowed by sand as high above them on the bridge of the sinking 'Marine Sulphur Queen', standing on the deck rail intuitively Kalo turned. She was intrinsically drawn to Kimo's[12] voice, searching her out. There, highlighted by the wrath and tempest of the mysterious fiery-dark storm, she saw her below. Blinding wizard-fingers of lightning flashing lines through the sky —dazzling ball lightning flares— and the silent Kalo watched as...

—Click,

...Kimo released the arrow with an unworldly, powerful, *Snap!*

—Airborne,

The arrow instantly transformed from wood to shimmering white light molded with the power of Holiness and the purity of Faith. Sparkling and burning it whistled faithful and true, blazing through the canopy bright as a shooting star, straight as a beam of sunshine, and sharp as the limit of creativity. Arcing gracefully, it soared over the prow of the freighter like a scintillating meteor, passing overhead midway between Ames and the monarch of Evil, the ruler of Hell.

—Click,

On deck, drooling repugnant vindictive spittle Smith stopped and heaved his shoulders back then bellowed vicious laughter, his throaty voice booming haughtily casting echoes from the dark-metal bulkheads of the dead ship. Wicked eyes etched with loathing and pervasive bloody veins, gutturally he growled, "It is time for harvest." Then he howled savagely, and *threw* his saber at Ames...

—Click,

Defiantly Ames stood stock-still, refusing to falter, even to flinch; steadfast he remained. Then he saw the arrow streaking overhead —an incredible shooting star— and it seemed ridiculous even as the thought flashed through his mind: *Make a wish... and Believe!*

—Click,

Bow in hand, Kalo leaped from the deck rail, spiraling and somersaulting as she lithely descended. Twirling and spiraling again she almost seemed to glide through the air —graceful as a seraph, precise as a ballerina— absorbed in circumstance, drawn by destiny. Tumbling in midair she snatched Kimo's shimmering arrow in mid-flight setting it to her bow; and still descending, almost floating, the mystical warrior spiraled and rolled somersaulting again. Then she pulled back... drawing the bow.

Coming down in front of Ames she aimed...

—And an incredible, nonpareil, *Sss-nap!*

...Catapulting the gleaming arrow to flight as she landed lightly between him and the Demon, his antagonist Smith.

Illusion and speed. The fletched messenger hurtled toward Smith with the authority and power of Light as his twirling saber cartwheeled bound for Ames. Closing —targeted on the intended victim— and her in its path. With vanishing velocities Smith's saber and Kalo's arrow flashed opposite directions crossing paths in mid-flight.

Pieces of the Puzzle... from the past and the future.

Then...

—Fit!

...Kalo's arrow punched cleanly through the *bridge* of Smith's nose, dead center between his blood-veined yellow-gray eyes, instantaneously slicing and burrowing through his brain cracking cartilage and bone then spitting out through the back of his scaled, frazzle-hair skull.

—Thud!

His saber struck spine-chillingly vicious and murderously cold, carving through flesh and bone, cutting all the way through until the hilt slammed solidly into her sternum, lodged between her breasts.

Blinded, bellowing hatred and rage and clutching his misshapen face with his monstrous clawed hands, Smith tried to grab the arrow —to pull it out— to get it out. He wailed and screamed; then staggering, spraying spittle and wrath he heaved his chest out and retched as he roared.

The sickening sudden impact slammed Kalo backward to the deck, onto her back in front of Ames, her eyes almost instantly glazing as she gasped for breath, trying to breathe. Flat on her back she writhed with pain but showed no surprise, only expectation, resignation, acceptance... and absolution of Love.

Stunned, Ames saw her self-sacrifice *—Oh God, not again—* as shock overwhelmed him.

First disbelief splashed with its fog-rush, his vision swirling in dark wavy shades; then the realization of her lying there —her pallor— and inside him the nausea of a cold-vomit flush. He could see the varnish look in her eyes, and abhorrence almost gagged him pushing up in his neck. It completely filled him until it ached in his ears, and that quickly his face and cheeks burned; then overwhelming sorrow with her vacant stare, and that sickening awful knot twisting deep in his guts.

For just an instant his vision clouded with disbelieving tears, then an incredible sudden-hatred crashed through him —and its crawling, grinding gristmill— that grating, seething despise that stewed to antagonistic red anger, mounting until it was madness — that exploded as white-boil and rage!

Words got trapped in his head. *Smith*— he could see him. That piece of shit Smith was still screaming and staggering in front of him, trying to get the arrow out, clawing at his freak-ugly face. Hate swirled in his gut. *Smith*— he could see him —and anger heaved him over the edge!

Pain didn't matter. Leaping, he went sideways and dove hitting the deck hard —sliding, reaching for the scimitar— grabbed it. And rising to his knees he reeled facing his adversary, his soul and rage exploding with fury! Weapon in hand he screamed, *"—Nooo!"* as he hurled the scimitar overhand, with both hands, with all his might!

Twirling end-over-end, the weapon became a pinwheel-razor of indigo blue-violent fire, the luminous blade a sheet of lethal whirling razorblade edge and blue-violet flame! Spinning faster than a buzz saw it roared like a blast furnace shattering the thunder of helicopter wind. It was a fiery pinwheel of vicious velocity, a cartwheeling razor edge of whirling fury and flaming, fiery scimitar blade!

His aim was precise, absolutely lethal —perfect— *Crr—thw—ack!*

Dead center the scimitar sliced through Smith's face, down his midline, opening him up and blowing out his chest with an explosion of intestinal spray and blood that spewed vile sheets in the wind…

—As he erupted with Hell's sacrilegious burning fire—and that scream!

…With the force and fury of the blow the scimitar disappeared, dissolving and vanishing as Smith's chest —entire body— began splitting apart. Opening and severing —ripping in half— the demonic man-serpent was tearing in two, shredding down the center expelling juice-spray and fluid-boil from his chest. Fire and froth bubbled, blasted and gushed, spilling out and splashing onto the deck. Smith stood inert —but he still screamed— screamed until he roared!

Standing there, he roared…

—Distorted-motion, each half beginning to fall toward the deck, a ragged, shredding, tearing-open wound severing his persona. Both his arms jerked apart, out wide, fists violently clenched squeezing blood from his palms.

He screamed...

—As both halves kept separating and falling.

He howled...

—And scathed with the most vile and unconscionable wail imaginable, blood and flames splashing everywhere, entrails slinging and twirling through the air.

Still roaring...

—Clenching his fists with death and decay overtaking and overpowering him, ravenous wings of fire exploding and boiling up out from his chest.

He was falling...

—And shredding, coming apart; flames and screams.

Howling...

—The world standing absolutely still, the hourglass sands frozen in time; all of it happening in freeze-frame motion as his gut-wrenching shriek wailed echoing absolute hatred for mankind, ricocheting from everything and all places.

A horrendous god-hating screech...

—Then suddenly the sand boiled up fiercely and frenetic and swept over the bow of the ship. Lightning sizzled and flashed. Thunder shattered and boomed. And the circular storm wailed in the tempest with a Holocaust's Roar!

The Serpent was going limp, falling...

—And tumbling apart, falling backward, blood splashing and entrails flinging fire through the air.

Falling...

—Until finally, *Crash!* Both halves of his severed persona slammed violently onto the deck of the sinking dead ship 'Marine Sulphur Queen'...

—And God commanded, *LET THERE BE LIGHT.* *[in part]*
(Gen. 1:3)

...His clenched fists, his evil hands, finally opening in submission. Smith's vile soul, his deceitful incarnation and empty shell erupted exploding violently, bursting into flaming light that swept everywhere —throughout all places— dissolving his man-scorpions and smog and the layers of clouds as it sent them shriveling like evaporating wisps of smoke in the wind. His clamoring and winging army of Dark Forces withered and vanished. Gray was disappearing, wisps swirling as they rose in updrafts of dissipating gloom, then wafting away. Daylight was coming through.

In an engorging whirlpool of sand the bow of the dead ship was finally taken under by the churning sinkhole; enormous waves of sand rolling and swirling downward into the funnel creating a whirlpool that took the dead freighter under... then shrinking, and settling, the movement of diminutive particles slowed as the sinkhole gradually closed ...and the 'Marine Sulphur Queen' was gone, slipping away to somewhere else. Lost in time.

After that... the sand was still.

Above, the impenetrable canopy continued unraveling as filtering remnants of water and gloom withered and dissolved letting in patches of azure.

A cerulean sky... opening.

Then finally on this place, upon this plain, an aureate yellow globe sun and the Saturn-like rings shone through. Daybreak.

And there was light.

The world of darkness and gray... was no more.

And God saw there was light.

God said, *IT IS GOOD.*

CONCLUSION

Quiet of aftermath, the litter of dead...

...The mood of it, sorrow and loss. Bodies everywhere. To the horizons and beyond the fallen were strewn in a lake of congealing dark blood. Battered, twisted and mangled, or floating with the undulating rhythm of death, warriors and demons drifted gently buoyed on brown-crimson waves. This place was reticent, subdued... until eventually the tide and tarnish of carnage and war receded soaking into the sand.

On the plain, to the limit of vision lay an indescribable tangle of shattered hulls, bloodstained horseflesh, garish wounds and inert weapons of war. Smeared red, countless dwarfs, dark scorpions, stalwart Percherons, and white warriors lay still. Tasseled helmets were scattered among shreds of mangled dragonfly wing and severed legs and claws curled fetal with death; entangled remnants stained with demise in an unending struggle logged somewhere in the pages of time.

As far as the eye could see, and then beyond, was a banquet of the most terrible and senseless waste of life imaginable. There on tainted sand it lay all around them: so much loss, so much unnecessary despoil and forfeiture of life. The battleland was a bloodbath landscape of sacrifice saturated in crimson and the sacrilege of wanton and ruin, all of it sultry with the coppery stench and squander of death.

Gradually the sea of blood was ebbing, seeping away. Here, life with all its promise, hopes, and dreams was gone. But Evil is like that. Always has been... and will be.

Ames rose from his knees in the sand where the 'Marine Sulphur Queen' had deposited him and Kalo when it went under; and as he stood he must have wondered if the strange ghost ship would ever rise again. But the man did not look around at the bloodshed; instead, he gazed sadly upon her, the precious soul who had saved him. Before him Kalo lay silently... her spirit floating somewhere with the wind. Tears slid down his cheeks.

From the far reaches of the battleland—

Identical P.T. Barnums and 'Just Plain' Wilsons came quietly in; solemnly, in deference, with their slingshots and walking sticks. There was no chatter. This was a quiet time.

Silently Pilgrims and Renoloi stood together near the sand hummock... those who survived. All around them was a landscape of carnage and senseless slaughter prophesied a long time ago. And now as before, as always, was the single constant... change.

Kalo—

Approaching slowly then kneeling beside her, for some reason Lent mumbled, "Had to be." Reverently he withdrew the saber from her chest, gathered Kalo in his arms, and lifted her.

Standing behind him, Ames watched as the youth walked with measured steps to Tian and Reed, tears tracing saltwater lines down his dirty face. From beneath a shaggy mane of matted hair, with a heavy heart his pensive dark eyes drifted, focused on no one in particular. And with the precious young Renoloi warrior cradled in his arms he stopped and stood before them; then strangely he murmured, "Thy will be done."

From behind him Ames consoled, "I'm sorry, but... she's gone."

Without looking Lent whispered back, "No, she's just sleeping, resting." Ames didn't understand what the youth really meant. Reed stepped forward offering to take Kalo's body, but Lent refused him and turned away murmuring, "She's not heavy... she is my friend."

The hummock—

Accompanying the dwarfs, slowly, taciturnly, the army of Mystics came in from the battlefield. Treading softly on a plain of bloodied sand, they were gathering around, their magnificent steeds covered in the red banner of war. With the Centurion Kimo leading them, the army of Mystics drew closer encircling the heroes, gently pressing closer until they were all assembled. For a time, it was very quiet, until one of the smaller Mystics finally removed his helmet then nodded cordially and unassumingly to Reed.

Reed's eyes opened wide as he whispered to Ames, "I know him—from my dream." Ames nodded.

An affectionate nod and a blink, "How's she goin', Reed?" Old Sam inquired moderately. Then he twitched.

Wondering, not really knowing what to say, Reed answered with a cautious, "Ok, I guess. And you?" Old Sam's grin exposed green teeth spaced with decay between chapped lips that he licked with his capable tongue. "But you're..." Reed began to say.

"Not really," Old Sam corrected, "but you'll figure it out... when it's time for you, for yours to join us. Someday."

Nervous, rodent-like almost, Reed twitched. "Okay, Sam," he managed.

"Old Sam—if you please." Then the wiry little man with twinkling green eyes offered a wink and a grin, picked his nose retrieving a long juicy string-booger and popped it in his mouth, then wiped his finger on his armor.

Without fanfare—

The Mystic army formed a circle enclosing the small band of survivors, and placidly, unassumingly, one by one they removed their helmets tucking them under an arm: Alex, Evening, David, Goliath, Kale, Tondra and Tarin... big and small, old and young, they all rode together. Corin, Josh, Bernadette, Sally, Rawlin, Donovan, Denen, and so many others... each and every one, garbed in lorica segmentata, belonged to the legions of the Mystic army.

But far back in the ranks four white warriors did *not* remove their helmets. Their identities remained concealed, hidden from those on the sand.

All those precious souls whom Ames believed were gone, all the friends he thought he had lost along the journey, like an unraveling ball of twine... they were all there. The journey had taken and transformed them, but they were all there, now again reunited with the ragtag band of survivors. They rode magnificent Percherons with ponderous unshod hooves that could splash flames through the sky.

And finally, nickering as it moved forward through the ranks was another horse. It stepped softly as it approached. This animal bore two riders, the alabaster warrior whom had been struck from the sky and had fallen toward the plain and was saved by the other Mystic. The equestrian removed her helmet... and Kristina, whom Smith had dumped in the sewers to die, and had been raised by the rebels and planted within Smith's own forces, nodded. One arm loosely around her waist, sitting double behind her Karen took off her helmet as well; and as she did, both mother and daughter smiled lovingly upon John Ames.

He did not speak; he didn't have to, the tear in his eye said it all. Alan moved quietly alongside his wife and daughter, each knowing what love and true happiness is, and will be... in the end.

The Centurion—

Kimo dismounted and approached Ames and the others, Lent standing patiently with Kalo still in his arms. Then, with a voice as gentle as a mother's love and as caressing as her soul, Kimo turned to Tian, Ames and Reed, and said, "Witness a miracle... and believe."

Reverently Kimo turned from them and faced the vast bloodstained battleland, raising her arms, opening wide the fingers of both hands; and as she did the aggregate of the entire Mystic army began to hum their beautiful song. Each Lilliputian dwarf and every mighty Percheron knelt down upon one knee and bowed its head, the music of the Mystics rising to a chorus more beautiful and glorious than any choir, their refrain resonating exuberantly and joyously across this desecrated land.

One by one the three colossal peaks of Legend Range began to shimmer until they glowed, each spilling forth a wellspring of pure watery light that cascaded as glimmering rivers, then over the plain to its center, the heart of this mysterious place. From the first mountain peak ran purest red, more florid than any rose petal. From the second poured cobalt blue of deep water and truth. From the third mountain peak gushed yellow that was vibrant and wild as daffodils in a high mountain meadow.

Each color burbled and swirled as it glided and wound like a perfect sparkling river, a waterflow with oxbow bends meandering and coursing toward the middle of the plain. True as time they flowed, the three primary colors from which all others emanate... the wellsprings of life.

In the center of the plain the three rivers of color and light converged winding together, spiraling and intermingling like the stars and nebulae of the Milky Way. Then in a sudden swirl they splashed upward blending together forming an incredible column of transparent, crystalline light that revolved as a vortex of starlight and scintilla born in the womb of the universe's farthest, unknown regions.

The column was beautiful and awe inspiring, and at its base on the plain, it burned with cool, white sizzling fire. All the while the music continued, the voices of the Mystics and dwarfs multiplying, increasing... it was so beautiful.

For God so loved the world, that he gave his only begotten Son, that whosoever believeth in him should not perish, but have everlasting life. (John 3:16 KJV)

A finger of sparkling light slipped free from the revolving mother column, darting forth as it swept down upon the battlefield like countless firefly fairies flitting on sparkling-diamond wings. Whisking delicately here and there, the zephyrs of motion trailing glimmering sunbeams and twinkling moonbeams swirled and darted gently gathering each fallen dwarf, Mystic, Percheron, Renoloi, and Pilgrim within its holy embrace.

The harvester collected each and every soul, those near to the people assembled on the plain, and those far, to the outermost reaches, far beyond where they could see. Good souls, those blessed and saved by grace, were gathered to the last by the shimmering fingers of light. Not one was forgotten, not one left behind.

Once all were gathered the holy light spiraled and wound momentarily, then arced and ascended darting exquisitely toward the heavens, to the glowing, unfathomable, mysterious realm of far distant celestial nebulae. To the limitless reaches of infinity... and Beyond.

But as for the cowardly, the faithless, the polluted, as for murderers, fornicators, sorcerers, idolaters, and all liars, their lot shall be in the lake that burns with fire and brimstone, which is the second death. (Rev. 21: 8 RSV)

Then sudden and powerfully, from the revolving mother column a hand of divine flame and fiery wrath boiled up and burst forth streaking and reaching out. It swept violently and incinerating across the battlefield dissolving everything it touched. Bellowing a lion's roar in cascading tongues of flame scorpion hulls, legs, wings and trifling pieces were instantly absorbed within the desiccating holocaust inferno, the people cringing as firestorm swept the plain with an incredible choler of flame. And it did not overlook a single malignant, wicked one, even to the smallest shard. But not a single Mystic, mount, Renoloi, dwarf or Pilgrim, by flame, was harmed; not singed, not so much as even touched.

In a breath the all-powerful ethereal fingers of flame rose up then descended onto the plain grinding and roiling with extraordinary righteous force, churning and burrowing into an irascible windstorm of sand. Then ardently, and eternally, they were drawn to the very core of this world. And there, forever, those wretched lost souls would remain.

Swallowed within the fire of wrath the fallen Dark Ones vanished, while all across the battleland the sand transformed to flawless, unblemished, undefiled silica. It was purified, sanctified, light tan and resplendent. It shimmered and glowed emanating warmth... Holy Ground.

At last, when the good souls were resting in heaven and the others were all burning in Hell, Kimo turned once again to the people gathered on the plain. She smiled lovingly. "A promise. The Judgement of God," she whispered. "Now, behold, His true power."

Reverently she turned, and with outstretched arms, with all her might she reached to the heavens, to the revolving column of pellucid, transparent light…

…And slowly, powerfully, majestically, before them the most awesome of visions transpired as the Finger of God touched the world with magnificent brilliance casting limpid shimmering Light upon the battle plain.

Descending from the canopy Legend Light formed absorbing the mother column, and within the heavenly whirlpool of illuminated firmament a gargantuan revolving column of sparkling Light appeared. It was a perfect cylindrical undulating texture and cloud of living eternal essence. Incredible beyond words, it hovered and remained.

The Light was infused with minutiae quasars, pulsars and starburst explosions that whirled within its spirit and presence. Hebrew and Roman writings appeared. Egyptian hieroglyphics, Aramaic texts, symbols and other scripture and writings became visible covering the pellucid surface of Legend Light. It was brilliant, but did not blind them. Intense, but it did not harm them. It Was.

Reaching out, Kimo extended her arms, and Lent, without speaking, surrendered Kalo's body, Kimo taking the young warrior to her breast and kissing her forehead. Kalo's arms and legs hung limply, hair fluttering in the soft breeze, flowing beautifully like gossamer strands of golden spider silk. Silently Kimo turned and walked onto the plain carrying Kalo's body. Hushed with wonder the people watched as the Centurion carried the fallen Renoloi in the direction of the mysterious Holy Light. Purposefully, *take a step, unfaltering, take another.*

At length, "What's she doing?" Reed whispered to Barnum.

Standing beside him P.T. replied, "Following the path." Next to them, Ames was listening.

"You aren't making a whole lot of sense; you know it, short stuff." Barnum did not reply and they continued to watch as Kimo crossed the plain with Kalo in her arms.

Solemn, "Couldn't have done it..." Ames admitted when he finally did speak, "...without her, we wouldn't be here."

"There's more truth in that than you know," Wilson agreed, "but only mortals can overcome evil. It is their choice... each and every one. There are always obstacles and temptation... and free will. Smith was unable to thwart creation, but he could still have corrupted its final outcome. The decisions had to be made of free will."

Reed: "So what you're saying is that we were kinda like the ten deciples?"

"There were twelve of them," Ames corrected mildly.

"Twelve? You sure, Doc?"

"Pretty sure."

"Well, how about that; I always thought there were ten. Confusing them with Snow White and those dwarfs I guess."

Barnum and Wilson just smiled.

A moment of quiet.

"Following the path..." Reed looked at P.T. "What path? What does that mean?"

P.T. blinked and alluded warmly, "'Footprints' an old poem... a difficult journey ...and you needed help this time." Without speaking Wilson nodded agreement.

Ames murmured, "Footprints: tracks in the sand."

"God truly is Love," P.T. told them, "and all of life is a mystery. His riddle: to study, to learn... and hopefully, finally to understand."

"So what does that, that poem, have to do with us?" Reed asked.

P.T. smiled warmly. "Reed, when times were difficult, it was not your weapons that saw you through," the bantam revealed, "it was *she* who carried you."

"All of you," Wilson added cordially.

Ames, Reed, Tian and Seana looked from one to the other, then again at the dwarfs as Wilson explained, "She was given to you, your guardian angel. If you recall, last time He sent His Son"

The multitude of identical twin dwarfs and formations of Mystics stood quietly watching as Kimo carried Kalo toward Legend Light. Mysteriously and awe-inspiring the column of undulating light constantly changed as it revolved and murmured the whispers of a spiritual presence they could sense and feel, but not comprehend. Glowing and scintillating it hovered above the plain, the essence of holiness woven within the fabric of truth. It lived and breathed with the beauty and enigma of minutiae starbursts and the secrets of swirling transient quasars and pulsars. And More.

Unfathomable and warm—

It remained suspended in the firmament, waiting for them. And they approached.

Out on the vast sand plain Kimo entered the limpid esoteric veil of Legend Light's glimmering texture, both she and Kalo enveloped and absolved as they stepped into its dazzling, perfect radiance. With the semitransparent light swirling around them those watching could still see Kimo and Kalo; but this, they could not understand.

Puzzled, Seana asked, "What is she doing?"

"*Shhh* —be patient," P.T. hushed her.

None of them knew what was happening within the shimmering fabric of light as sparkling quasars and spiraling pulsars mysteriously whirled and spun, and a shaft of Light flowed in from above and down upon Kimo and Kalo. Fascinated, transfixed, those on the hummock silently watched.

Bathed in radiance and the solace of faith Kimo reverently lay Kalo on the sand and knelt over her as sparkling lights and miniature starfire explosions flashed and swirled down upon them. The scintilla swept about them, embracing and flowing through them creating an aurora halo around them. Then a venerable tongue of flawless healing light suddenly splashed through them, and luminous with undefiled love Kalo's eyelids fluttered as the Light levitated her. Reverently she raised her arms, reaching toward heaven, and as Kimo watched she was gently born upright and stood on her own.

Together, facing one another, Kalo smiled; and compassionately Kimo smiled.

After that the shimmering living winds of starlight and healing flame diminished, and a moment later, holding hands, both emerged from the radiant field of revolving light. Together again, without speaking they began crossing the plain returning to those gathered near the sand rise. From the hummock they all saw it... not a sound. Only the music... the beautiful music. Kimo and the resurrected Renoloi warrior Kalo had been returned to them.

Without fanfare—

Like those chosen for Noah's Ark, two by two, P.T. Barnums and identical Wilsons began filing into Legend Light. Too many to count, from all across the plain they marched quietly and orderly into the revolving holy spire... and as they did the dwarfs swirled upward and away, vanishing like the passing of shooting stars.

Hand in hand—

Kimo and Kalo approached the people and stopped before them. With tears in her eyes and her child cradled in her arm, Tian stepped forward. She looked lovingly at Kalo, then gently caressed the fetish she wore. Next, Tian turned to Kimo, but could not say it.

The Centurion Mystic already knew, and placing three fingers on her forehead Kimo revealed, "I have always been with you, did you not know?" Both looked at Kalo.

Ames inquired softly, "Who are you? What are you?"

Reed ventured, "Kindred spirits?"

Turning to him, "No," Kimo answered as Kalo smiled sweetly, "more than that."

"More?" Reed asked, almost prodding.

"Twin souls," Kalo told him blinking peacefully, "a dichotomy, two halves of the whole." With her disclosure the Mystic Kimo and the Renoloi Kalo united coalescing to form a single being, one person. More than they could comprehend, no one said a word, until with the breath of pause the twinned spirits, Kimo and Kalo separated... parted again.

"Unbelievable," Reed murmured.

Ames simply stared; then finally, to Kimo, "It was you in my visions and dreams... wasn't it?" he asked.

"In your visions... yes," she said.

"And on the rimrock... the Mystic who came from the sky and saved Kalo and me from the Night Hunters..." Strangely quiet, looking at him Kimo the Mystic did not respond, so he said, "We would have died then and there —but it was you, wasn't it?"

He waited. She seemed to be thinking, considering.

At length she blinked placidly; and when Kimo finally answered her voice was soothing, her words measured, subdued. "In truth, John... no, it was not I who was there. As Kalo told you, she and I are a dichotomy, two halves of the whole." The Centurion and Kalo looked at one another; then Kimo disclosed, "It was *she* who saved you on the rimrock."

Stunned, Ames looked at the girl as she modestly nodded her confession and smiled. She blinked her green eyes twice, and Kimo did the same. "How? That can't be."

"It is true. It can be," Kalo assured. Then she explained, "At that time, on the rimrock, I believed; but I was not certain. That is why I asked the Mystic's identity."

"But we were together, Kalo. To be there yourself, as you, and also to be there as the Mystic..." Ames stopped.

"You would have to already be dead," Reed whispered. "That means you would have to have been dead, the whole time... all this time."

Kalo remained silent.

"That's not possible," Reed murmured.

"How?" Ames asked softly.

Kimo interceded as Kalo looked away, over the plain. "That answer is forbidden." Her gaze followed Kalo's, and changing the subject she serenely observed, "Purified with fire, sanctified with love. This land is sacred, John. This is Holy Ground."

"A garden of sorts," Wilson mused.

"A garden?" Reed needled. "Wilson, it's desert, just sand."

"No," Kimo agreed, this is truly hallowed ground." Then warmly she inquired, "Reed, can you tell me where we are, even now what time this is —when this is— where we are at this moment?"

Pondering, "This is —or at least was Montana— until the world —it all ended with Armageddon— and we traveled to the future."

Kimo smiled knowingly. "Did you… really?" Then she asked again, to Ames, "John, can you tell me?"

"No, not really." Reed knew there must be a catch, and in a quandary, he mumbled until even Kalo smiled.

Kimo explained, "Reed, the battle of which you speak — Armageddon— was not a single event. Each creation has its Armageddon; but it is *Life* that is an unending struggle of good and evil." She proposed, "Tell me, when does the straight line of infinity become a loop?"

Neither answered. Neither could.

Ushering with a lighter note to a simpler concept, P.T. diverted them deciding, "Adam and Eve and one lowly snake *was* kinda' boring —don't you think? This way is much more interesting."

Distracted Reed frowned. "You know you guys have a really peculiar sense of adventure."

The dwarf grinned. "Oh Reed, you love adventure; you thrive on it."

With a glimpse at Seana, "That's the same thing she told me." Then back to Barnum, "What are you guys, voyeurs, some kind of perverted little munchkin-midgets?"

"Not at all," Wilson assured feigning innocence.

"And," Reed prefaced, "I suppose there will be dinosaurs again?"

In unison the dwarfs grinned. "Naturally."

"Cool," Lent beamed; but the smile evaporated when Reed's disapproval shot along with 'the look'.

Turning to P.T., Wilson teased impishly asking, "What kind of dinosaurs shall we do next?"

"What kind? You guys are serious," Reed spit. "You mean there're dinosaurs just because you shrimps like to '*do*' them?"

"Of course; why did you think?" the disarming Wilson replied. "The Boss does the work order and blueprints, but we're allowed considerable latitude with the actual work—you know—the construction. Pretty much, the rest is up to us. Takes time though, because we're little. But we did a good job, don't you think?"

"You do the work, the construction?" Reed repeated.

"Sure," the engaging P.T. replied. "We told you before, we're workers —anything and everything— anything that isn't finished..."

"...And everything that has to be done," Wilson finished; then appended explaining, "actually Reed, it's a throw-back to his carney days, instills fond recollections of his circus adventures, so we sorta placate with the dinosaurs."

Lent: "Makes sense."

"Placate with the dinosaurs—" Reed snorted, "that's just... not right. You're demented."

"Oh, that hurts," P.T. chided.

"Well okay, I didn't exactly mean it like that; but next time could you at least make them a little smaller, and gentler. People been gettin' eaten here —'case you haven't noticed." With that he turned sharply adding, "—And Lent, if it's not too much to ask—just don't help 'em here, okay?"

Deflated, "'Spose you'd prefer herbivores?" P.T. proposed arbitrarily, almost crushed.

"Actually, yes."

"*Re—ed,*" the dwarf carped, "that would take all the flavor out of them."

Shaking his head petulantly, "You're a warped little individual; you know it."

Eyes twinkling, P.T. allowed, "I'd concede to being a bit colorful..."

"—Off-color."

"What-*ever*—" P. T. chaffed, "but I'm certainly not inclined to go so far as warped."

"No, you're warped alright, a shrink-wrapped warped little ragamuffin in bib overalls—sicko little gomer."

"Nevertheless, you just gotta love me."

Irritation withering Reed grinned, admitting, "Yeah, I do."

Ames and Wilson together: "That's scary, Reed. Now *he's* starting to sound like you."

"Yeah, what-*ever*," Reed huffed. "Just proves there's a little bit of me in all of us." Then 'the grin'.

Kimo interceded with a calming effect, "John, Reed, you have done well; this world, this creation will survive and flourish, in part, because of you."

Grinning mischievously as he glanced at them Wilson innocently fielded, "Wonder what He will name it."

"Perhaps one day," Kimo disclosed, "it shall be called Earth."

Each man looked at the other, wondering. Holding their children Tian and Seana quietly moved closer to them; they too had heard of Earth before.

Kimo smiled affectionately. "This world has begun anew and *you* will be born in fifteen billion years. You see, the creation you saved was your own.

Reed asked, "Our creation? But I thought we went..." words trailing off.

"Perhaps you did," Wilson suggested, "but your perception of time is archaic. Don't think of time as a straight line; it's a loop. You begin and go forward; but eventually all things return to their point of origin, to where they began. That is nature's way, the design."

"Cycles," Kalo intimated.

Both listening, Kimo went on explaining, "Perhaps a little differently this time, but another chance for humankind. See what you can make of this opportunity. God's gift." Then changing paths and subjects again, "John, you have much to record."

"To record?" and 'the excuse', "but I don't know what to say."

Fondly, "The words will come," but firmly, "you must set in writing the new creation."

Still mounted, Alex tossed a leather satchel to Reed. He caught it and opened it as Ames fumbled with his words considering what Kimo had just told him. Peeking inside and seeing the satchel's contents Reed grinned when he said, "Two reams of Georgia-Pacific and a ten-pack of Pilot pens. Not too shabby."

"It is better than parchment," Kalo offered.

Ames looked from one to the other of his companions, then hesitantly at Kimo. "You're asking me to write a—the Bible?" Vacillating, "But, I'm only a man. I can't…"

"—No John, *I* am not asking."

He tried again. "But I don't—I won't know what to say."

The corners of her mouth upturned slightly in an elegant, sagacious smile as she proposed almost in passing, "Perhaps, you will be inspired." Then serious again, "Believe, John. The words will come. Others will add to the story, but it must begin with you."

Reed interjected wryly, "Naturally He chose you 'cause we all know I'm a man of action, not words."

"And illiterate," Ames remarked.

"Oh, now that was uncalled for, Doc."

"Touché," P.T. chimed.

Without preamble Reed turned. "Wilson, may I ask you something?"

"Certainly."

"What is the circular storm—exactly?"

"A hole in the sky," Lent told him simply.

Circumspect the little man grinned. "Some might call it that. Some might call it a portal, or doorway."

Reed: "A time warp, a wormhole?"

"Well, perhaps less than that, and more than that."

"You're not making sense again. A portal—to where?" waiting for an answer.

The dwarf responded evasively, "Remember, even now, as always, things change."

Reed frowned. "You're not going to tell me, are you?" Wilson grinned.

"Quantum physics and strange attractions," P.T. said disconnecting their dialogue."

"Yeah, and fractured math," Reed added resigning himself to the fact they were avoiding an answer.

"Time we should be going," Wilson told his twin.

"Indeed, it is," Barnum agreed.

Wilson turned to Ames extending a pudgy right hand. They shook and the dwarf turned curtly offering the same to Reed.

"What, you're not gonna go, *poof*," gesturing, "and just be gone this time?"

"Not this time," Wilson assured politely. They clasped hands firmly but warmly. "Take care, my friend."

P.T. Barnum mimicked his twin, taking a bit longer than necessary with Wilson urging him along, until almost aggravated P.T. asked, "What's the rush, 'Just Plain' Wilson?"

"We've work to do, anything that isn't…"

"—I know, I know. What a pest you can be at times; but you're cognizant of that of course." Wilson tugged at his sleeve and begrudgingly P.T. began to follow —but just had to do it— and he turned back to Reed. "—By the way," he disclosed in his scruffy little voice, "Eve won't eat the apple this time so things may turn out differently."

Remarkably agile for such a stunted-short guy, Wilson spun and smacked him on top of the head so sharply he knocked his blue watch cap off. "Now you've gone and done it, Phineas Taylor Barnum." P.T. scampered after his cap laughing as Wilson groused, "You'll get us both in big trouble one of these days with that incorrigible mouth of yours." Wilson chased after him, cuffing him again, pulling at his shirt as Barnum giggled gathering his cap from the ground; then almost dragging him along, both scurried off in the direction of the revolving spire of Legend Light.

"Au revoir," the rascal P.T. Barnum shouted over his shoulder waving a stubby goodbye as Wilson strong-armed, coaxing him along.

Their hearts warm with affection and emotion, the people waved; and still watching as the dwarfs crossed the sand Ames considered, "P.T. Barnum and 'Just Plain' Wilson."

"Curiouser and curiouser, Doc."

Fondly shaking his head Ames grinned. "Quaint names."

Kimo smiled. "Yes, He does have a sense of humor."

"And they're kick-ass little sling shooters," Reed observed. They all looked at him.

"Sling shooters?" Ames mimicked.

"Well sling-shot-shooters sounds kinda stupid —and well— you know what I mean." Next, he suggested, "Slingers maybe." Ames just shook his head.

"What-*ever*," Lent scoffed, "that's not the only thing that sounds stupid."

A stern glance: "You're gonna look stupid with a knot on your noggin', kid."

Defying him Lent scoffed, "How passe'."

Ignoring them Ames scanned the plain introspectively and inquired, "Kimo, may I ask you something?"

She already knew.

With fleeting zephyrs the wind faded, distraction diminishing as calm slipped closer and everything seemed quieter somehow. Softly, reverently she told him, "John, Legend Light is the Finger of God... the storybook of the Creator. It is all knowledge that ever has been or shall be. Legend Light is perfect knowledge."

Drifting from the holy spiral of revolving light his eyes met hers. He did not speak. Inside his head he heard, *yes.*

Extending her hand, she took his in hers —he blinked— and together they had crossed the plain in less time than the thought. Alone, they stood before the mysterious wind-like shimmering texture of Legend Light. It lived and breathed emanating the perpetuity of eternity before them.

Blessed are the pure in heart, for they shall see God. (Matt. 5:8 RSV)

He heard, *John, you may ask one question.* Kimo let go of his hand and John Ames slowly, very carefully, reverently stepped barefoot into the semitransparent veil, the living texture of Legend Light.

It overwhelmed him.

He could not comprehend it.

It was so beautiful.

Bowing his head, he clasped his hands in prayer, as the most wondrous sensation poured in. Peace completely absorbed him and serenity infused him as unconditional love flowed through him, filled him. All around him was knowledge and wonder. And More. It was there, within him, surrounding and embracing him; so much and so precious, more than his ability even to imagine, to the limitless reaches of infinity. And Beyond. It was all encompassing, everywhere. And Warm.

The breath of eternal peace and life suffused him like gossamer strands knitting fragmented pieces and lacing contentment and a closeness with his Creator that he could not have imagined before. Like the headwaters of small streams joining and forming the river, it all permeated his heart cascading into his soul.

Slowly he turned and saw Kimo, out there.

She smiled warmly, and without speaking she told him: *"All that ever was and will be; infinite possibilities lie before you. Do not be afraid. Things will always change; the variations are limitless. Be patient John as your destiny unfolds. Enjoy life with Tian. Hope and the future are malleable and eternal; make yours what you want it to be. Focus... ask only one question."*

As John Ames stood within Legend Light looking into Kimo's eyes, smudges of mud and bits of blood-caked sand coagulated in his wounds withered and whisked away disappearing from his skin and tattered clothes. His wounds diminished and healed. His beard disappeared... and his hair turned pure white.

John Ames stood there, humbled, a man. For a very long moment he felt God's presence within and near him; and quietly he knelt down, closed his eyes... and aloud, he prayed.

Moments passed... precious moments.

Finally, John Ames opened his eyes —and blinked— and he was beside Kimo. Legend Light revolved awe-inspiring and venerably behind him. He blinked again and he and Kimo were once again reunited with the others near the hummock on the sand plain.

Rimmed by three granitic monoliths—

This was a quiet place. This place was sacred. Holy Ground.

Captured with wonder, quietly he stood looking at Kimo until from behind him the silent Kalo murmured, "We will not be going with you." Ames turned to the girl, who was no longer a girl. She was now a woman, more exquisite than a vision, more vivid than a dream. "We will remain here." She was standing with Lent. Understanding, Ames nodded.

"Sorta' like Adam and Eve," Reed intimated.

"Something like that," Lent answered amiably.

Assembled formations, riding in columns the Mystic army was moving slowly and taciturnly into the spiral corridor of Holy Light.

Calm and silence flowed over the land—

It seemed as though all else was fading and time was waning toward twilight trailing its veil of unexplained mysteries with its hush of serenity. The unique sweetness of darkness was enfolding them, enclosing them, leaving only the remnant band of Renoloi and Pilgrims near the sand rise...

...And Ames, Reed, Tian and Seana, holding their newborns, were illuminated like actors spotlighted on a stage. Around them the theater of light was shrinking, a diminishing field, growing smaller. And withdrawing from the luminous halo, without a sound Kalo and Lent stepped back... then drifted away.

The warmth and peace of this new darkness was still closing in until finally the background and surroundings completely receded. Now only they and the Centurion Mystic Kimo stood alone near the sand hummock. Everything was still... somewhere in the pages of time.

A gentle Loving voice, from far, far away:

"Lo! I tell you a mystery. We shall not all sleep, but we shall all be changed." (I Cor. 15:51 RSV)

Only they and the Centurion Mystic stood together. It was very quiet here... Now. This was their time, their moment; and John and Reed knew it.

Remembering the battle with the Trogs, Reed touched the scar on his forehead; then softly asked, "I died, didn't I? All of us… we're dead, aren't we?" Kimo did not answer, so he turned to his friend with eyes searching for answers. "Doc, you told me when you fought Smith in the Complex sub-level, he ran you through with his saber." Ames nodded and Reed looked next at Tian. "And in the lake, 'Black Water'… you drowned." And finally, sadly he turned to the woman he had come to love so much. "When the trimaran capsized and you were lost, then finally made your way to camp like they said; you weren't just injured… you died too."

Reed realized, "At one point or another, somewhere along the line each of us died." He knew, and whispered what he did not want to say. "We're all dead… even now." He turned to the Mystic.

Softly, unassumingly Kimo inquired, "What do you believe?"

A deep sigh. "All this time, and we didn't even know it." But just to be certain, he asked, "Are we alive… or are we dead?"

Endearingly she replied, "Reed, can you tell me… is it real when we wake, or is it real when we dream? Can you imagine that what you suppose may not be?"

He did not answer, could not answer.

"And more than that, Reed, can you suppose that perhaps death is only your own conception, just another level, another layer of dreams. What if death is no more than a deeper, more profound dimension of dreams?"

Calm and darkness were moving in. Flowing harmoniously they drifted intermingling within the shadow of faith; secretively stealing, wafting quietly, unobtrusively creeping in around them… and all else was slipping away …fading.

The Mystic Kimo whispered, "Life is possessed of many dimensions." She asked, "Reed, which world is reality—which is the dream? And more than that, which is your imagination, and which dream is real? —or so it may seem.

"No more riddles, please," Reed entreated.

Kimo inquired placidly, "Then can you tell me, which world is real; are you here now, or where you have been, or will be? Which world is the dream… or was it all only a dream, and if that is so … which dream is real?"

Finally, she revealed, "Perhaps all that you know, or *believe* you know, is only an illusion. Perhaps all of existence and all that we are, are only imagined. Perhaps it is real only because you *choose to believe* it is real. Is there only one existence, one reality —two— or a limitless number, each guarded by a lion at the portal or a tiger at the doorway?"

Reed murmured, "The black hole; the circular storm."

The spotlight was shrinking... a diminishing circle, growing smaller …fading. Near him, now shrouded within the soothing comfort of soft darkness, Kimo smiled. "There are many mysteries. All of life is a puzzle with no solution and no end. Tell me, where are you now? Is reality where you have been… or where you will be?" Lovingly she gestured raising her arms and opening her hands, "Behold, the mysteries of the Creator's Universe."

From somewhere far, far away, very faint, came a muted buzzing sound. And softly, mesmerizing, Kimo whispered,

"Close your eyes,

Sleep…

Dream…"

EPILOGUE

And as they did...

...Somewhere in the vast and endless reaches of the universe, in a medium-size star system within the Milky Way galaxy, on an insignificant blue-green planet...

...On a cold October morning, in the not too distant future — *bzzzz*: the alarm.

Conscious, and another day, waking. Swept away with waning drowsiness were fleeting images of the night's slumber, as reaching over he snuffed the irritating drone with a hand. Throwing back the comforter and sitting up he pivoted on the edge of the bed planting both feet firmly on the carpeted floor. Cooler room air swept in displacing the snuggly, warm-from-under-the-covers feeling; then sensing the chill in the soles of his feet: "Cold again today." Muttered words. Still groggy, rubbing his eyes and impersonally scratching he mused, *why do women yawn and stretch in the morning —stupid joke;* but he smiled anyway. Lethargically he stumbled out of bed, stubbed his toe on an errant boot, wend a course for the bathroom and hot shower; then two cups, black.

And shortly—

"Why is it, Doc, that every time this subject comes up we invariably seem to assume adversarial roles?" Reed's well-muscled frame was wrapped in a cobalt-blue pea coat, collar turned up to deflect the wind. Having met along the way they walked briskly toward the Science Complex.

"Probably 'cause your attitude is so predictably inflexible." Wide-awake from the cold Ames bowed his head slightly, chin into his coat.

"I really don't think I'm that inflexible. We've pretty much proven the 'Big Bang' theory since the nucleus of the pulsar was deciphered, and the current study on dark matter and dark energy has corroborated a substantial part of the universe proportion concept."

"Reed…"

"Since the Hubble, the Hipparcos satellite, the Microwave Anisotropy Probe, the Youngstown, and the elliptical probe spectrometer —wherever that is by now…"

"—About nine trillion miles into deep space."

Facetiously: "Yeah, figures you'd know."

Ames grinned. "The Hubble gave us a first real view of deep space. Hipparcos and MAP determined with reasonable probability that the universe is about fourteen or fifteen billion years old. The Youngstown…"

"—I know Doc. And even with everyone else still debating the concept, I 'spose you've figured out the 'String Theory'."

"Not yet. Still working on that."

Reed shrugged. All I'm saying is that it's like a puzzle, more and more the pieces have come together."

"Precisely my point," the other came back. "In all the known universe, isn't there a phenomenally exact order?"

"Agreed, there is a definite order; but it could be random chance, one in a billion. It doesn't necessarily mean there's a, God behind it all."

"Nor does it imply there isn't."

Offhand, changing the subject: "Doc, do you ever get the feeling of having done something before? You know… de'ja vu."

"I suppose from time to time everyone does; why?"

"Nothing really," shrugging the thought aside, "just wondering." Reed's question stirred a memory in the back of Ames' mind, something he couldn't quite put his finger on. No more than a glimmer… but it was there, a snippet from the chronicle of time.

Was it long, long ago, just a whisper of memory and the feeling of de'ja vu, or the fleeting warmth of something ever so precious dwelling inside, then mislaid somewhere? A cloistered, sequestered thought… and the name, *Tian*.

Still walking, both were silent a moment…

Dormant grass, meticulously trimmed before winter, lay a brown carpet below naked aspens, evenly spaced native junipers and Douglas fir. The grounds were impeccably maintained for appearances, as was the building. They entered the Complex dwarfed by its enormity.

...And they kept walking, one step at a time.

* * *

While far away, on the other side...

...Where reality and the dream world merge. Another time, in a new and distant place beyond the horizon threshold of the black hole, Kimo murmured, her voice fading, "Open your eyes..."

...And sunrise blossomed over the valley washing a world dotted with thatch huts in warmth, beauty, and peace. And color returned: yellows, golds, reds, orange, greens and blues, all vivid and clean. Everything new. It was a beautiful world, unmarred and pristine. And sound returned. There was laughter and distant voices of people working and playing and learning. And love. And in their ears and through their hair just the gentlest of zephyrs... a stir of the wind.

Scanning the landscape both looked down upon the valley and village as they sat together on the high plateau of Legend Mountain. Here, three granitic monoliths, one at each margin of the horizon surveyed this world, a New World. This was a beautiful creation, a new place. Their World.

In the basin far below Renoloi and Pilgrims were moving about. From this vantage point they all seemed very small, the size of ants in a bustling colony flourishing on a landscape carpeted with deep chlorophyll green and dotted with plots of freshly turned loam as dark as anthracite. Thatch huts freckled the gently rolling vales with splotches the 'color of dead grass', and here and there smoke trails wafted easily from cooking fires until their bluish haze dissolved in the backdrop of sky.

* * *

And unseen...

...In the forest, sequestered in a beautiful haven, hidden in a quiet niche... *there was a private place.* There, from deep underground, a pure, clear spring bubbled to life then trickled as a meandering brook, gradually gathering somewhere farther on as it grew to a river destined for somewhere unknown. And there as well, carefully hidden in that private place, at the bank of the gurgling spring a small, bent, withered tree straightened, budded, and blossomed... and bore twelve kinds of fruit.

* * *

Leaning forward a bit...

..."Doc, who is that over there on that patch of ground?"

Squinting and straining to see more clearly, "Looks like Deet."

Reed nodded. "Yeah, it does; wonder what he's doing?"

"Looks like he's planting something."

Leaning back and settling in, getting comfortable again, "You don't 'spose, it's corn." Reed chuckled as he resumed scrawling circles in the dirt with the stick.

Tian padded up the trail carrying the baby, then Seana with her child and Jade in tow, holding her hand. Focused, eyes traveling the ground, Jade was straining to keep up until she looked up and spied him.

"Uncle Reed!" she chimed gleefully quickly scampering ahead of Seana and Tian, reaching out for him to pick her up.

Laughing, "Come here, punkin'." He playfully hoisted her, and after the hug and she was comfortably settled-in on his knee he resumed drawing circles with the stick.

Trailing now, Tian and Seana approached, and then sat down. Slipping an arm around her, Ames played the index finger of his other hand upon their son's nose as she maternally cradled him to her breast. Things were well.

"Uncle Reed, where have you been? I looked and I looked, but I could not find you."

"Oh, not too far away, sweetheart. Right here actually."

"What's that you have in your hand?" Ames asked Jade.

She offered her small hand and its contents. "Paper that has words I cannot read. I do not know what it means because I am too little." She handed him a crumpled scrap of paper, a fragile page of a book, and very carefully in the palm of his hand she unwrinkled it, opening and smoothing it out so he could see her treasure.

Part of a page from the Bible.

Looking back and forth between the men, with a delicate finger she pointed and asked, "What is that word?"

"Resurrection," Ames told her. The page seemed familiar. "Where did you find this, Sweetie?

"A pretty place, in the woods, under a small tree with lots of beautiful flowers," she told him enthusiastically. Then squirming and looking up again, her little brow furrowed. "Uncle Reed, what does resurrection mean?"

He thought briefly, hugged her, then answered, "It means that today your world *is* better than it used to be." He smiled introspectively as he scrawled a couple more circles in the dirt with the stick.

Ames noticed. "Reed, you're always scribbling circles on the ground. Why do you do that?"

"Circles?" He stopped, "—Oh, those." Twitching his nose and scratching his head, "I used to wonder about that myself, just something inside, like a voice, a distant whisper." Reflecting, almost pouty, he nibbled his lip then answered, "No, Doc, they're not circles, they're cycles… cycles going on and on forever." He smiled.

—Suddenly, above them,

Streaking as brightly as a shooting star, a corsicant light splashed upon them illuminating the plateau, and they all looked up to the high ledge above them. Dazzling and majestic, the Centurion Mystic and white stallion were there.

Thrilled and clinging to him, "Uncle Reed," Jade said, hushed-excited, "there is my angel."

Still sitting, shifting her weight, "Uh huh, sure is," as the others rose to their feet.

"She is very pretty," Jade intimated.

"Yes, she is," the man agreed as Kimo hailed smiling down upon them from within the gleaming visored helmet.

"The time has come to say good-bye," Kimo told them without speaking.

Captivated, Jade watched the shimmering warrior. "Good-bye, angel," she whispered intently.

As they waved and murmured their farewells, tears welled in Tian's eyes. She thought, *I miss you so much.*

Knowing, Kimo nodded with compassion, behind the gleam of helmet visor her green eyes smiling. *"Do not cry. I am well."*

"Will I ever see you again?" Tian asked softly.

"I am always with you... in your dreams." Kimo the Mystic reined her mount as the mighty Percheron impatiently pawed the high ledge striking sparks into ribbons of fire. Quieting the steed, she patted then stroked its powerfully muscled neck soothingly, then raised a hand to say farewell.

Tian tried not to cry, but a tear of love escaped. "I will always remember you."

As the Mystic waved and the magnificent horse reared, they heard, *"We ride the winds of eternity on the wings of tomorrow... to the limitless reaches of infinity. Ours is a glorious kingdom."*

And as the loss in her soul healed... Tian smiled.

Then in a splash of light and brilliant flash of shooting star fire, the mighty Percheron and Kimo streaked upward and away, to somewhere out there. *"Rejoice, we are the guardians of heaven... we are Time Warriors,"* and trailing scintilla of starlight and evaporating embers they vanished from sight.

On Legend plateau it was quiet for some time as each considered so many things, things that had happened, unbelievable things... and so much more.

Reticent, at length Reed wondered, "So what's the answer?"

From somewhere in heaven: *"The answer is that there is no answer. All of life is a riddle, a puzzle with no solution. Since the beginning there shall be no end... only more pieces going on and on forever. Cycles."*

For all they had been through, all that had happened,
Still, only pieces,
The Puzzle... and More.

Eventually—

Eyes drifting from the sky, to one another, then all to the valley below; this was truly a beautiful world... and it was their own.

"Kinda irritating," Reed muttered, "we never will know what it's really all about."

Ames grinned. "Well, you've still got me —and you know what I'm all about."

Looking up: "Don't start on me, okay?"

Seana soothed, "Reed, do not be grouchy."

To her: "Grouchy, you think I'm grouchy?"

Standing beside him, "Oh Reed," she said smiling sweetly delicately stroking the top of his head, near the back, where he couldn't possibly see without two mirrors. Tian grinned.

"Don't be messing up my hair."

"I am not," she assured, "there is no hair in that spot." Tian smiled.

A playful glare as he swatted at her hand, "And don't *e-even* start with that going bald crap."

Lightening the mood, she thumped him. "Reed, you—are—sooo—easy."

"Yeah, easy my ass..."

Ames looked down at the top of his head. "She's right. Shoulda worn a baseball cap...

"—With a button on it," Seana finished.

The pretext of a sigh, Ames mumbled, "Too late now though." Tian joined in, leaning forward and stroking his head tenderly.

Knowing what she was up to, Reed glared. "Okay, go ahead."

"The wrinkle," she said sweetly, "just smoothing it out." He slapped at her hand too, but she was too quick. "Shoulda worn a baseball cap with a button on it," she agreed.

"It ain't funny."

Tian, affecting empathy: "Damned shame actually."

"Doc…"

"Yeah?"

Reed darted her a glance; then back to Ames and asked, "Why do you teach her stuff like that?"

"Would I…?"

Seana jumped in. "—Well, what about Bloody Bones, Reed? You tell me stories about Bloody Bones all the time."

A snap-reaction, both men in unison: *"Bloody Bones is real!"*

"Oh yeah— well real *this!*" Seana waived them off with a flip of her hair and an open 'talk to the hand' gesture. Ames looked at Reed.

Reed, culpable: "I just don't know what I'm gonna do with her."

"Uncle Reed," Jade interrupted tugging on his shirt.

Looking down, "Yes, sweetie?"

"Will you tell me a story?"

"We're kinda in the middle of something right now. How 'bout a little later, ok?"

"Ok; but remember, you promised to tell us about Goldilocks and the Rough Riders."

Reed hugged her and grinned wondering how she could even remember something like that; then shaking his head, said, "Kids, should just bar-b-que 'em and eat 'em while they're little and their bones are still soft." Jade giggled lovingly.

Slipping an arm around Tian, Ames cordially patted Reed, his friend, on the shoulder. "Been a long day; time to go home," and he and Tian leisurely started down the trail to the valley, their village below.

Gathering Jade in his arms Reed got up, tossed the stick away and began following them. She latched onto him with childish enthusiasm and kissed him on the cheek causing him to smile as Seana, with the baby, snuggled alongside them.

"By the way, Doc," he said hurrying to catch up, "what did you ask?"

With a half-turn and a glance back, "What?"

"Your question. What was your question, the one you asked in Legend Light? You never did tell me."

Feigning innocence, "I didn't? I thought I did."

"No—you—didn't. So, what was it?"

With an arm snuggly around Tian, Ames smiled as he stopped to face his friend. He considered a moment, then said, "Imagine, if at your fingertips you had consummate knowledge, complete absolute knowledge, all that ever had been and all that ever would be."

Riveted, "Yeah?"

"What question would you ask?"

"Shit I don't know; what should I ask?"

Ames looked him in the eye expressly, and answered, "Exactly—*that* was my question, Reed. '—What should I ask?'"

"Well… what was the answer?"

Refusing to tell Ames soberly shook his head, then said, "Wait until the moon is full."

"Wait until the —*what?*"

"Come on, let's go home." He and Tian turned and started down the trail again.

Following them, "Aww come on, what was the answer?" Becoming disgusted, "Oh—no—you—don't. Don't pull that. Quit screwing around now. Don't do that to me." Seana grinned. Ahead, Tian and Ames just smiled and kept walking, getting farther away. "Come on now, I gotta know. You know if we weren't such good friends, I'd hafta kick your…" but Ames didn't answer, Reed's voice trailing off as they descended following the path, this time a winding mountain trail.

Going home.

* * *

It seemed very real; but perhaps it was all just a single night, and an incredible, ethereal dream.

Blessed is he who reads aloud the words of the prophecy, and blessed are those who hear, and who keep what is written therein; for the time is near.

I am the Alpha and the Omega says the Lord God, who is and who was and who is to come, the Almighty. *(Rev. 1:3 and 1:8 RSV)*

Watching…
With infinite wisdom and unending love,
From somewhere beyond the limitless reaches of infinity,
…God smiles,

Because
When You Believe… There Are Always Possibilities.

ENDNOTES

1   Renoloi... pronounced RE-NO-loy
2   Nitana... pronounced Ni-ta-na
3   Tian... pronounced TI-an
4   Seana... pronounced Shaw-na
5   Tere... pronounced: Terry
6   Kalo... pronounced KA-lO
7   Temporal residue... bits and pieces of time itself dragged along through portals or windows of time; explaining how the Accumulation went through the Black Hole
8   Griffins... legendary Greek creatures with the body of a lion and head and wings of an eagle; known for guarding treasure and priceless possessions.
9   Sargasso kelp... olive-brown seaweed having bladders on its stalks
10   Time Shear... a fictional phenomenon of transitional flux. Passing through time at such an incredible speed that it manifests the illusion of punching holes through eons, resembling a space capsule's reentry into the atmosphere. A sparkling, burning meteoric fireball dragging a flametrail of spiraling atomic cloud through portals or windows of time.
11   'Big Brother'...ref. George Orwell's novel *1984* written in 1949, depicts life and conditions when citizens are under constant surveillance of an intrusive, out-of-control government.
12   Kimo... pronounced KE-mO, Tian's second who was killed by the Trogs in 'Alpha and Omega'

www.ingramcontent.com/pod-product-compliance
Lightning Source LLC
Chambersburg PA
CBHW050610110726
47899CB00001B/52